RECLAMATION

KRISTEN ZIMMER

Bywater BOOKS

2025

Bywater Books

Copyright © 2025 Kristen Zimmer

Print ISBN: 978-1-61294-329-9

Bywater Books First Edition: December 2025

Printed in the United States of America on acid-free paper.

Cover and interior design by TreeHouse Studio

Bywater Books
PO Box 3671
Ann Arbor MI 48106-3671

www.bywaterbooks.com

*For the United States of America, and everyone who loves her
and sees her potential despite her many flaws.*

Don't lose hope; we fight together.

This government is committed to operating according to the will of its citizenry. So long as the principles of the people remain the same, so too shall the fundamental principles of The Unified American Territories: All citizens of able mind are required to contribute to the betterment of society. Work hard and achieve! The beggarly shall never prosper.

Unified American Territories'
Edict of Establishment
Article I, Section II

FLETCHER HAD BEEN ENJOYING the luxury of her sole day off work, reading *The Scarlet Letter*. Happily. Quietly. Until some unknowable thing, a strange tug in her chest, made her look up. She shut down her antiquated digireader with a tap of the cracked screen and watched from her bedroom window as a sleek silver sedan pulled to a stop at the curb outside of her dilapidated row house. Agents.

She couldn't see them through the car's blacked-out windows, but it was obvious. The simple fact that the vehicle had the shine of something new was enough to give the Agents away. Being from The Vault, or The Northern Territories, as Fletcher's part of the country was known officially, she rarely saw any cars on the road at all; cars in such impeccable condition were all but complete anomalies. Why do they even bother plastering the Department of Reclamation's seal on the doors? she wondered.

That hideous seal. Words failed to capture how much Fletcher both loathed and feared it. The great red and black per bend crest, showcasing a scroll of parchment in one half and a tasseled mortarboard in the other, had always been reviled by citizens of The Vault. It meant that someone hadn't paid their dues, and The Department of Reclamation had come to collect.

The Department of Reclamation employed the Agents who did the strong-arming for The Federal Bureau of Education. While the BOE housed the bookkeepers, The Department of Reclamation's Agents handled the unseemlier work . . . and their work was generally quite unseemly. The Governing Council of The Unified American Territories had long ago authorized Reclamation Agents to use brute force "in the event of necessity."

More often than not, visits from Agents did end in violence—if not on their first visit when a potential Reclaimee received their Notification of Violation, then most definitely on their *second* visit when the Agents returned to take the Reclaimee into custody. Reclaimees seldom initiated said violence, of course; Fletcher had heard that most cried or begged for just a few more moments with their loved ones. They would be flogged once or twice and give up or otherwise be knocked out with narcotics. Occasionally, a Reclaimee would try to escape. Those individuals had it much worse. Fletcher closed her eyes and, although it pained her to do it, allowed herself to envision the brutality Agents inflicted upon braver people: arms twisted so violently that shoulders snapped out of their sockets, fingers bent backward with such force that the metacarpals fractured, skulls cracked against living room floors. She shuddered as if her skin had been kissed by an icy wind.

Reclamation Agents were no strangers to The Vault, considering it was the part of the country reserved for the impoverished, the destitute, and the disillusioned—those who needed "excessive assistance" from The Government. Those like Fletcher. She would need at least ten more fingers to be able to count the number of times she had seen Agents in her neighborhood in the last week alone. Watching these two men march toward her home, she couldn't help but wonder if they had come for her this time.

"Fletcher," her father's voice boomed through the dimness of her room. "Can you come out here, please?"

"I'll be right there."

She peered into the tarnished mirror atop her bedside table. Using the remnants of daylight to aid her vision, she pulled her long blonde hair up into a ponytail. "Alright," she sighed to herself, her sharp jawline clenching and her hazel eyes burning with angst. "If they are here for you, you'll find out soon enough."

"What's the matter, Dad?" Fletcher called as she rounded the corner into the living room. It was almost full dark, and the candles had not yet been lit.

At first, Fletcher was barely able to make out the silhouettes of the two tall figures, haloed by the setting sun. She had to squint so that her pupils could adjust to the murkiness of twilight. Her breath caught in her throat once she focused on the men in black suits and reflector-lensed sunglasses standing just inside the entryway. All day Fletcher had had a gut feeling that the eleventh hour of her grace period was all but spent, but she'd hoped her instincts were wrong.

"These men want to speak with you." Her father motioned for her to come stand beside him. She followed his directive and crept into place.

"Are you Fletcher Daniels?" the taller, snowy-haired man asked as he removed his sunglasses, folded them, and placed them in his breast pocket.

Fletcher swallowed a gob of saliva, knowing that there was a decision to be made: She could either cower in terror at the idea of the torture these men represented—perhaps concaved cheekbones, smashed teeth, a broken, bloody nose—or look them straight in their eyes and let them know that she would not be intimidated. *It's only pain. Pain doesn't last forever.* After a pensive moment, her mind made itself up—she stood her ground. It was not in her nature to cower even in the presence of these reprobates. "Yes, I am," she replied.

"Ms. Daniels, I'm Agent Flynn. This is my associate, Agent Ryder." The man gestured to his cohort and then offered his hand for Fletcher to shake.

Don't touch him! She didn't want to make the job any easier for the bastards. Fletcher had heard stories of Agents coating their hands with chlorthidamyde so their targets would be rendered unconscious on contact. *Clever ogres.* She gawked at Flynn's palm, her hands balling into fists where they rested on her outer thighs. "I can't say it's a pleasure to meet you as that would be dishonest. So why don't we skip the pleasantries and get straight down to it?"

"As you wish," Flynn shrugged.

Fletcher watched uneasily as the second Agent, Ryder, reached into his suit jacket. Had she provoked the Agents by flouting their innocuous pleasantries? Anything she said or did could be taken as a hostile action. She could feel her disdain for the men radiating from her in supersonic waves. They must have been able to sense it.

She braced herself for the worst, stifling an instinctive flinch as Ryder's hand emerged from his pocket with a tiny silver cube in tow. He squeezed the sides of the cube, and it projected an aqua-colored hologram into the air. He fiddled with 3D icons before returning his attention to Fletcher. "Facial Recognition Program initiated." A robotic female voice leached from the HoloPod, followed by a thin blue laser beam. Fletcher froze as the ray of light expanded into a grid that combed, inch by inch, over her face. She knew such software existed but had never encountered it before. The process was painless, though oppressively bright, and over in a blink.

The beam evaporated into nothingness. "Identification confirmed," the robo-voice declared.

Ryder and Flynn exchanged a look.

"The Federal Bureau of Education," Flynn began, "hereby

serves one Ms. Fletcher Daniels with a Notice of Violation for failing to abide by the terms of the National Student Loans Debt Repayment Agreement. You have neglected to meet your loan repayment obligations for three consecutive months, thus falling approximately $2,000 Redback into default."

"I have not neglected my repayment obligations," Fletcher contested. "I contacted the BOE four months ago to renegotiate my terms. I filed a litter of digiforms requesting to have my payments adjusted based on my income. I was told my account would be relegated to 'deliberation' and that my payments would be on hold until a decision was reached."

"Is that a fact?" Flynn sneered. He turned to his partner and nodded.

"Am I to understand that you are gainfully employed by a Government-owned establishment, but are still unable to meet your repayment obligations?" Ryder asked.

Everything is a Government-owned establishment these days, Fletcher thought. Didn't these men know that free enterprise, free thought, free travel, freedom on the whole was a myth in The Vault? Life, liberty, and the pursuit of happiness had died here alongside the United States. "Yes." Fletcher folded her arms across her chest. "That is what I am saying."

"It says here that your occupation is Digital Book Technician of the Northern Territories Public Library, Boston Branch, and that it is a full-time position. Is that correct?"

"That's correct."

"What does your job entail?" Flynn questioned.

Fletcher soughed. "As you've clearly never set foot in a library before, I'm happy to explain it to you. A long time ago, books were printed on bunches of paper and bound together by a spine with a front and back cover. Then they became digitized and available for download on the internet. The government of this country decided the internet was bad, so now all of our books are stored on digicards that are inserted into digireaders, most of which are owned and lent out by the library because who could afford to own one of their own? I'm responsible for the organization, lending, and returning of said cards and readers. The Boston Public Library has approximately 26 million digibooks and twenty-five thousand digireaders in its collection, so you can imagine I'm very busy."

Amused, both Agents laughed. "I didn't know people from The Vault bothered to read," said Ryder.

From the corner of her eye, Fletcher saw her father wince at the Agent's mockery. He knew his daughter would not take kindly to it and placed his hand on her shoulder in a silent plea for her to curb her temper. Fletcher gritted her teeth but knew she would not be able to keep quiet for long. She could only handle these thugs insulting her intelligence in very small doses. Her quota for the day had been met the moment they had walked through the door.

"Oh, I assure you we read," she asserted. "Most of the younger Vaulters have gone to college, but *you* know that." The fact that no one in The Southern Territories wants to hire a college graduate from The Vault is the only reason you mush-minded cretins even have an occupation, she thought. "If you think I earn a pittance because Vaulters are ignorant, you're mistaken. I can't afford to pay my bills because librarians in The Northern Territories aren't paid in Redbacks; hardly anyone is. We're still dealing in Greenbacks up here."

Fletcher knew she was pushing her luck with the tone she was taking, but she carried on in a hurry, unable to keep in check her distaste for these men and everything they stood for. "I don't know if you and your partner are aware of the currency conversion, Agent Ryder, but it takes five Greenbacks to equal one Redback. I can't afford to pay $666 Redback to the BOE every month when I only make $1,000 Greenback a month. Please, allow me to do the math for you: $1,000 Greenback is equal to $200 Redback. See the problem? Asking me for $666

Redback each month is like demanding solar energy from the moon. It's impractical and, frankly, not going to happen."

"Look at that!" Ryder chuckled. "Unparalleled math skills!"

"I learned much more than math at New Harvard, Agent Ryder."

"I'm sure." He pointed to his HoloPod. "I see you majored in US History. That's a useless subject, don't you think, considering over a century has passed since its abolishment?"

Fletcher grumbled, irritated by the Agent's arrogance. "You know what the old scholars say: 'Those who cannot remember the past are condemned to repeat it.'"

Flynn scoffed, having grown tired of petty banter. "Yes, well, I trust that you will remember your past and perhaps learn a little something from it. I regretfully inform you that The Bureau of Education has denied your application for income-based fee adjustment. Further failure to make full monthly payments will result in summary judgment, and you will be consigned to the Knowledge Reclamation Process. If the Bureau does not receive the full amount of $666 Redback for October by the thirty-first of the month, we will be visiting you again."

"Regretfully inform" me, my ass. Fletcher opened her mouth to speak again.

Her father cleared his throat with a cough. "Thank you, Agents."

They exited, and he watched with an anxious eye as the two men strode toward the old stone staircase leading down to the street. Once he was sure the Agents were out of earshot, he turned on his daughter. "That smart mouth of yours is going to get you killed. Agents are not the people to wise off to, especially not Flynn."

"Calm down, Dad," Fletcher groaned. "There is no way they could have ended me on the spot. I'm up for Reclamation, remember? If the Federal Bureau of Education wants to suck all of the schooling out of my brain, they need me alive to do it."

"This isn't funny!" her father yelled. "Agents don't care how bright you are. If anything, the BOE is even more interested in taking back knowledge from a person with your smarts. What happens when they hook you up to their machines or whatever it is they do, and drain too much from you? Do I need to remind you what happened to your mother? She couldn't even feed or dress herself when they brought her home from the Processing Center! Is that what you want, to have the mind of a toddler for the rest of your life? Because it happens you know, more often than The Department of Reclamation cares to admit."

Fletcher stiffened at the mention of her mother, her mind flooding with what little knowledge she had of her parents' life together. She knew that they had married within a year of her mother's graduation from The College of Mathematics. Her mother, Astrid, had a fairly well-paying job at the Hall of Records, where she met Jericho Daniels and fell very quickly in love with him.

For a while, Astrid and Jericho had been able to get by, their combined incomes enough to cover Astrid's debt with scarcely enough left over for other monthly expenses. But all that had changed when Fletcher was born. The added cost of caring for a child put Astrid behind on her loan repayments.

Fletcher was three years old when the Agents came for her mother, and only four when her mother died. Jericho had explained to her that Astrid's brain forgot how to send signals to her lungs, and so one day she stopped breathing. Fletcher was too young when her mother passed away to remember very much about her, but the woman she could recall had loved her very much and always smelled of the sweet aster she often picked from the wild fields on the outskirts of the city.

Even though she knew firsthand that it could happen, Fletcher didn't find the prospect of coming back dumb-as-a-rock nearly as frightening as coming back a Berserker. She did not want to return to her home after undergoing Reclamation the way her best friend Jonah had returned to his: without his sanity, little more than an angry, aggressive shell of his former self. She feared becoming a suicidal robot or potentially psychopathic killing machine more than she feared death itself.

"What am I supposed to do? Tell me!" she shouted. "Sure, you're a Government employee, a big-time janitor at the Hall of Records, but even with both of our incomes pooled we'd never be able to afford what they're asking. Six hundred sixty-six Redbacks a month? It's not like we have tons of them stashed away. I honestly don't see how I can avoid Reclamation." She paused, rubbing at the budding ache in her forehead. She had been able to keep her composure while the Agents invaded her home, if only to give the appearance of strength and defiance, but now, standing alone in the dark with her father, she was incapable of holding her panic at bay. Reclamation was in her imminent future. She would have to resign herself to it, unfair and awful as it was. She breathed in the scent of the ancient hickory floorboards beneath her feet, basking in its smoky familiarity. The wood was hundreds of years old. She mused on how much more pungent it must have been when it was still a living tree, and the thought calmed her.

"Look," she continued, "maybe I'll be one of The Lucky Ones and be *fine* when I get back from the Processing Center— you know, still me, just a little less bookish. Or maybe I'll be a Veg like Mom, or a Berserker like Jonah. There's no way of knowing and no way of escaping it." As she said it, she realized it was an absolute truth, and she could almost feel her heart breaking, though more for her father than for herself. He may not have possessed the education so prized by society, but he was a good man. He worked hard. And not only had he lost his wife to Reclamation, soon he might lose his only child to it, too. If she didn't come back to The Vault with her sensibility intact, her father would be on his own—all by himself in a callous world that doled out more hard times than it did easy ones. She worried for him.

She glanced up at the framed diploma hanging on the living room wall, her name scrawled across it in fancy, bold font above the embossed New Harvard University seal. A hundred thousand Redback for a piece of parchment paper. *Ridiculous!* For the first time in her life, Fletcher found herself wishing that she wasn't smart, that she didn't have an intellect worthy of university fine-tuning. If only she had performed poorly on the HiEd Exam, if she were only average, she would be safe. The Government wouldn't have insisted she go to college. She wouldn't owe anything to anyone, wouldn't have to give up her mind and risk her life in order to square her debt.

"Please, Dad, let's just live for today, okay? All we have and all that really matters is right now, who I am in this moment, not who or what I might become." She scraped together every last bit of resolve she could find, willing herself to feign composure. It was a talent she'd had for as long as she could remember, the uncanny ability to make her eyelids as sturdy as dams, capable of preventing hot torrents of tears from assaulting her cheeks. She watched her father's expression soften and that was all it took to break her. Tiny droplets of salt water rolled down her cheeks; she was powerless against them.

Jericho reached his strong arms out through the space that separated them and drew his daughter to his chest. Enveloping her in the tightest embrace he could without crushing the life out of her, he whispered into her ear, "It'll be okay. We'll figure something out, Little Princess."

Fletcher half-smiled at the nickname her father had given her when she was ten years old and had insisted on reading *A Little Princess* over and over until she'd memorized every last word. It was an ancient book made of paper—yellowed pages that smelled like fallen autumn leaves—that had once belonged to her mother.

"Sure, we'll figure something out," she agreed, despite not

at all believing that they would or could. Disheartened, she wrenched herself from her father's arms, wiped at her sodden face and headed for the front door.

"Where are you going?"

Fletcher reached for her jacket hanging on the wall-mounted coat rack, then turned back to her father. Heaving a sigh, she said, "To see Jonah."

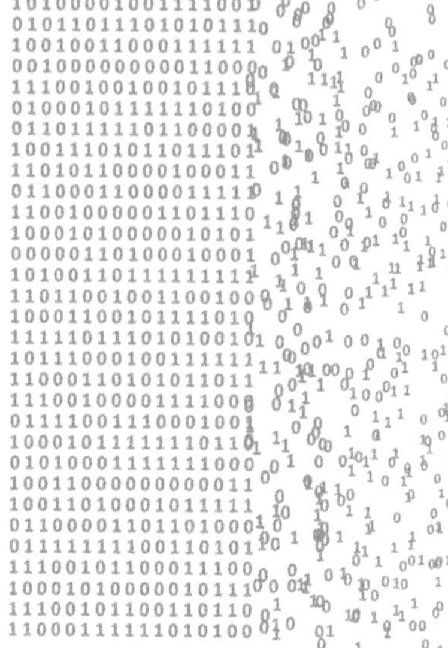

chapter two

FLETCHER APPROACHED THE HEAVY wooden doors of the Alcedonia Institute and, just as she had done a dozen times before, stopped to read the Latin inscription in the colossal stone archway. *Dum vita est, spes est*—Where there is life, there is hope. She mumbled beneath her breath, "Sure . . . unless you're from The Vault." She pulled at the corroded handles and the doors swung open, their rusted hinges spitting out a piercing shriek.

She ventured down the corridor, every now and again glancing up at the peeling paintings hanging on the mildew-coated walls. This hospital was the Government's idea of a sanctuary for the insane? *You're lucky you don't go mad just walking into the place.*

"Can I help you?" A woman in a shabby lab coat called out to Fletcher from behind an oval desk in the center of the lobby.

"Yes, hi," Fletcher started. "I'm here to see Jonah Quinn."

The woman scooted her squeaky rolling chair to the left in order to consult her computer. Fletcher noted it had a keyboard, a physical one made of plastic rather than the kind that projected onto the surface of the workstation, which meant that it was as archaic—though truthfully the word that came to her mind was "shitty"—as everything else in the building.

"State-of-the-art piece of equipment you have there."

"Naturally. The Government keeps its health care facilities here in the North in stellar condition." The woman peeked up from her screen. "It looks like Jonah Quinn has received his full course of neurosedative injections for the day, so he is clear for visitors. I need you to place your right hand on the scanner, please."

Fletcher did as she was directed and watched as the neon blue laser combed over her palm, logging all her personal identification information into the system.

"Thank you, Ms. Daniels," the woman continued after a beat. "You've been successfully registered. I take it you know where his room is?"

Fletcher flicked her eyes at the winding staircase to the right of the desk. "Up the steps to the second floor, eighth door on the right."

Fletcher ascended the staircase, taking each step slowly and deliberately. She hadn't seen Jonah in a while. Though she felt guilty about it, she had to stay away, had to try to distance herself from the harsh reality of what her best friend had been reduced to. It cut her to the bone seeing Jonah lashed to his bed, the dingy leather straps cropping off circulation to his hands and feet.

It had been six months since Mr. and Mrs. Quinn had sent Jonah to Alcedonia. They waited a full month after his return from the Processing Center to do it, until it became clear that he had lost too many pieces of himself to Reclamation to ever be the same again. When he first came home, Jonah had been in a near-comatose state, unresponsive to everyone and everything around him. Then one day, for no reason at all, he started screaming at the top of his lungs. It was as if someone had toggled a switch inside his head, pushed the button marked RAGE in his mind.

As she continued up the stairs, Fletcher thought back to the day Jonah was admitted to Alcedonia. She'd heard his shouts through the thin dividers separating her father's apartment from Mr. and Mrs. Quinn's. She hurried next door and arrived to find Jonah pinned to the floor, Mr. Quinn's elbows and knees jammed into his back. Fletcher looked on in dismay as Jonah thrashed against the dull carpet, deep-crimson blood streaming down his face from a jagged gash in his forehead. She was ashamed to say that she stood there, paralyzed, watching Mr. Quinn's tears splash down onto his son's smooth-shaven head. Jonah used to have such beautiful, golden curls, she'd thought. *Those monsters took everything away from him.*

"Run and get a Bluecoat!" Mr. Quinn yelled when he noticed Fletcher shuffling in the doorway. "Hurry now!"

Startled into action, she had scampered down to the street and flagged the first police officer she could find.

Ever since that day, Jonah had been at Alcedonia—more of a prisoner than a patient really. Fletcher knew the chances of him ever being released were slim. The sweet, bright boy she had known all her life was dead and gone. She mourned the loss of him every single hour of every single day.

Fletcher arrived at Jonah's room and slid open the mucky Plexiglas door. Upon first glance of his face, she saw that his eyes were open and locked on her. She jumped backward, surprised, unable to remember the last time she'd seen his dazzling green irises. Usually when she visited him, his eyes were closed. Rarely, if ever, was he aware of her presence.

"Hi, Jonah."

Jonah did not return the greeting, only followed her with his gaze as she walked across the room to the threadbare high-backed chair beside his bed. An expression of familiarity flashed across his face, and for the briefest moment Fletcher thought he may have recognized her. But then she realized he was pumped full of too many drugs for that to be possible and figured his expression for a fleeting neurological glitch or subconscious wishful thinking on her part. "I'm sorry I haven't been around much lately. I'm up to fifty-five hours a week at the Library. I still can't pay my damn bills, though," she told him.

Jonah blinked.

She knew then that it would be a one-sided conversation, as always. Still, she wasn't sure if his eyes being open would make it harder or easier on her. "Agents came to my house today. It looks like the BOE is going to reclaim my education at the beginning of next month." And then, without warning, her resentment came roaring out of her like an avalanche. If there was anyone in the world who could understand her frustration, it was Jonah—or it would have been Jonah, back when he could still comprehend such things. The thought was crushing, but not enough to stop her tirade. "Those years at New Harvard, gone in an instant. All that work, the hours and hours of studying! Being clever is a curse if you're from The Vault, you know that?"

She felt the heat of her anger like flames in her chest, in her cheeks—so hot she could combust and set the hospital room ablaze at any moment. She let the fire intensify. "The Government hooks us up to their stupid machines, tests our IQs, and if our scores are high enough, we're coerced into universities, saddled with huge amounts of debt, for what? They're only going to clean our slates or turn us into Vegs or bloodthirsty monstrosities! They know we can't afford to pay for school, yet they make the brightest of us go. They set us up for their brainwashing. I hate it. The whole damn system. The Agents, the BOE, the Knowledge Reclamation Process, everything!"

She saw that her agitation excited Jonah and stopped speaking as he began to struggle against the fastenings around his wrists. He whipped his arms inward toward his body, grunting in pain as his biceps flexed.

"Okay, okay." She calmed her voice. She leaned forward in her chair and rubbed her knuckles against his cheek. "I'm sorry. It's alright. *Shhh.*"

Jonah gradually returned to a tranquil state. For a while he remained motionless. Then, breathless and without warning, he burbled, "No hate."

Fletcher gasped in astonishment once her mind had processed that it was Jonah who'd muttered those words. It was the first thing he had said to her in the better part of a year. She hadn't even been sure he was still capable of speaking. "Jonah! What . . . what did you just say?"

Jonah's tongue labored against the sedatives and his own saliva to speak again. "No hate talk. Agents hurt you dead."

"Hurt me dead?" Confused, she narrowed her eyes at him. "You mean they'll kill me if I say I hate them?"

He relaxed his hands. His eyelids fluttered. "Mmhmm. Keep it inside."

"Keep my hatred inside? Okay. I won't say it out loud. I'll just think it in here." She brought her finger to her temple and tapped it twice. She knew he was right. Perhaps that was part of it—the why and the how Reclamation affected different people so differently. *You didn't keep your hate inside, and you ended up here, like this.*

He struggled against a ripple of muscle spasms, but managed to part his pinky from the rest of his fingers. "Swear."

"Pinky swear." She wrapped her little finger around his. Water welled up in her eyes as their skin made contact. She blinked it away. *He remembers me. We used to pinky swear.* It was a revelation she was thankful for.

"Run." Jonah croaked and swallowed a hard mouthful of air. "Agents come, you run. Be brave. Not like me."

"Oh, you silly boy." She groaned. "You are brave. You always were so much braver than me."

"You still climb trees?"

"Sometimes," Fletcher said.

"Better than me."

She flashed a wounded smirk at him and then rested her head against the cold metal handrail of his hospital bed. "I've missed you so much," she whispered.

"Mmm," he murmured and shut his eyes. "I'm tired now. Go away."

Fletcher chuckled. Jonah was in there somewhere, in all his beautiful, pushy glory. She remained on the edge of the chair and stroked his arm until the heavy unevenness of sleep-breathing began.

"I'll see you soon," she mouthed once she was certain he had fallen into a deep slumber. Afterward, she quietly made for the door and slid it closed behind her.

She took off down the stairs, an invigorated spring to her step. As she reached the lobby, she smiled at the woman behind the oval desk.

"This is his third good day in a row," the woman announced as Fletcher pressed her hand to the scanner to sign out. "He's making progress."

"It would seem so." For the first time in months, Fletcher allowed herself to dream of a world where her best friend had returned to her. As she left, the mildewed walls appeared less grubby and the dull hues of the paintings hanging on them were somehow more vibrant.

Fletcher slipped her hands into the pockets of her faded-black leather jacket and shivered as the wind whipped against her body. The bitter chill of fall in what used to be New England had long since set in, which made walking the streets at night unpleasant.

Autumn in The Vault had grown more and more unforgiving in recent years. Come late September, Fletcher made a point of rarely leaving her home once the sun had set. She'd had to do it that day, though. A staggering urge to see Jonah had taken hold of her once the Agents served her with the Notification of Violation. Jonah was a constant reminder of what could happen to a person if they were unable to repay their student loans.

She thought back to the afternoon Jonah received his Notification. He'd graduated from university with a degree in Architecture that prior spring. Even with that, the best job he could find was at a scrap heap, working for two Redbacks an hour. By The Vault's standards, that wage was enough to make him a wealthy man, but it was not enough to make any significant dent in his debt. He'd tried to cheat the system by making a payment every other month, and his strategy worked for a bit, but the BOE eventually caught on.

Jonah had just completed a twelve-hour shift at the junkyard, his hands and navy jumpsuit covered in slick, dirty grease and oxidized steel shavings. He met Fletcher at New Harvard Square after her classes had finished for the day. They walked home together and talked for a while about what she'd learned that afternoon in her Second American Revolutionary War seminar.

The conversation ended when their row house came into view. Jonah's cool green eyes burned with alarm when he realized the Agents were waiting outside his front door.

"Looks like my time is up." He grimaced at Fletcher.

She frowned, then took a step forward. "Let's go find out."

He flung out a stiff hand, grabbed her elbow and pulled her back to his side. "This is my problem. I'll handle it myself." Before she could protest, he broke into a jog toward the building. "I'll talk to you later," he yelled back to her over his shoulder.

A terrible tremble ran up her spine and she folded her arms around herself. She had stood on the sidewalk, immobilized by concern as Jonah and the Agents disappeared into the Quinns' apartment.

A wintry breeze raged through the trees lining her street, bringing her back to the present. She thought she heard footsteps behind her, so she spun around. The whistling wind and rustle of leaves continued as she peered down the road. There was no one else around. "One visit from the Agents and you become a paranoid mess," she whispered to herself before continuing on her way.

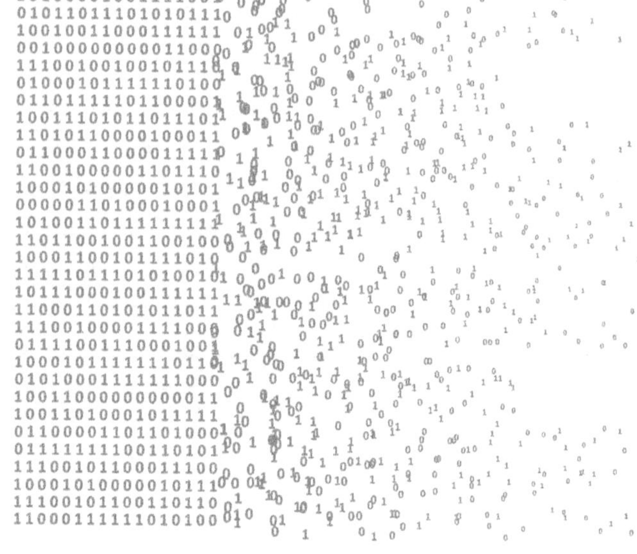

FLETCHER WAS ALWAYS CAUTIOUS when she went out after sundown. Though she had many friends around the neighborhood, she understood Boston proper was not the safest place to live. It was the second-largest city in The Vault—bested only by Indianapolis, the capital city of the Illiana Territory (and that came only after Chicago had been burned to the ground and the Manhattan Atolls, once called New York City, were converted into the country's largest landfill)—and had the highest crime rate of any city in the Northern Territories. The criminal underbelly of Boston mostly involved illegal drugs, or an illegal drug—the only one that really existed anymore: Quell. In Fletcher's city, the fuchsia-colored liquid injections were in such high demand that there were QuellSells on every other street corner. Fletcher herself had never been interested in partaking of the drug, though she could appreciate its appeal. It was a cheap knock-off neurosedative that offered the same calming effect as the genuine medicine, minus the requisite Government mind-meddling and subsequent unpleasant institutionalization. Quell numbed people, helped them get by without feeling like they were drowning, which was why The Government wanted it off the market and why Fletcher was not entirely morally opposed to it.

Fletcher knew that some QuellSells were dangerous, not to be trifled with in any regard, though she also counted a few of them among her neighborhood friends. In general, it seemed many of the drug dealers were just poor kids—some as young as ten or eleven—trying their hardest to get by or help their parents pay the bills. Still, there were others . . .

At that point in her two-mile trek, Fletcher was only a few yards away from her building. She began to let her guard down. And that was when she heard it: the echo of a gunning engine bouncing off stone-faced buildings and the screech of spinning tires. She crooked her head to the left, and from her peripheral vision saw a black cargo van hurtling down the street toward her.

She had no time to rationalize. Something in her gut told her to run, so she ran.

With every footfall, her heart thumped harder against her ribcage. She heard its erratic beating, a drum cadence booming inside her skull. Her breath quickened and passed through her body in time with her pulse. She was not fast enough. Someone reached out through the night and caught her by the hood of her jacket. They tugged her backward savagely, and large hands encircled her torso. Fletcher's sensation of fear blossomed into terror as she began to tussle against her would-be abductor, kicking and flailing her arms.

She tried to scream, but a second pair of hands tied a gag around her mouth before the sound could escape her throat. Her wrists were then bound together with thick brown rope.

The first pair of hands whirled her around, lifting her off the ground. She saw that they belonged to a tall, muscular man who wore dark coveralls. She could not see his face behind a black ski mask.

The giant threw her over his shoulder as though her 120 pounds of flesh and bone were as easy to manage as a bag of raked foliage. Fletcher wriggled her body against him, thrusting her tiny fists into his dorsal muscles as he carried her toward the van. Her efforts were in vain; the man did not flinch even once.

The other person had the slight, curvy frame of a woman about the same size as herself. She moved around the large man and slid open the van's back door. The goon dropped Fletcher onto the floor of the van with a resonating thud. A dull pain rippled up her legs into her spine and she yelped through the gag in her mouth. For an instant she thought her spinal cord might have been damaged until she found that she could, in fact, still move her legs.

The woman climbed up into the van and slammed the door closed behind her. She barked at the driver to take off. Fletcher tried again to scream as the van flew into motion.

"Be quiet and give me your arm, Fletcher!"

Hearing her name sent Fletcher into an even deeper panic. How did these people know her? Did the BOE have Jonah's hospital room bugged? Had they heard him tell her to run, and then ordered their Agents to steal her away under the cover of darkness? At the idea, her fear receded, and anger took its place. She had twenty-nine days left to settle her affairs and say her goodbyes. She would not surrender herself until the very last moment of the very last day.

Fletcher shook her head, motioning an unyielding *no*. The large man grabbed her bound arms, parted them, then took her right wrist into his enormous palm and held it firm. With his other hand, he rolled the sleeve of Fletcher's jacket up to her elbow. He pushed his finger into what Fletcher figured must have been a pressure point. Her forearm was rendered useless. She couldn't wiggle her fingers, much less bend her elbow.

The woman knelt over Fletcher. She pulled a small, white, cylindrical object from her pocket, pushed a button on the side of the gadget, then waved it over the exposed flesh of Fletcher's arm. The thing emitted a high-pitched beep.

"Found it!" The woman pressed the flat bottom of the tube

against Fletcher's skin. "Look at me," she commanded.

Fletcher kept her head down, gaze trained on the floor. She recognized it was a stupid move on her part, understanding that blatant defiance in the face of bodily harm was never a brilliant idea.

The woman placed two fingers beneath Fletcher's chin and lifted her head. Reflex beat Fletcher at her own game and her eyes fluttered upward, meeting the woman's ice-blue irises for the first time.

"Brace yourself. This is going to sting," the woman said as she engaged another button on top of the machine.

Fletcher listened to the apparatus as it whirred. At first, she felt only pressure, then a slight tugging sensation, as though suction had drawn her skin up into the tube. Next, she felt a pain like she'd never felt. Invasive pain that resonated deep within her muscle, akin to stepping barefoot on broken glass, though worse.

Fletcher yearned to cry out, to express the magnitude of agony the little device inflicted, but refused to give her captors the satisfaction.

Then, just as abruptly as the torment had begun, it ended. The only evidence of the trauma was a red mark on Fletcher's arm and the sickening smell of burnt skin in the air.

"The wound is cauterized so you won't bleed out," the woman said as she disengaged the contraption and flipped it over. A blood-soaked metallic ball no bigger than the head of a round pushpin fell into her hand. She held out her open palm so Fletcher could examine the orb, then directed the driver to open his window. She reached to the front of the van, through the open window and tossed the tiny ball out into the cold gloom.

Forgetting her gag, Fletcher tried to speak. The woman, smug, motioned to her own mouth. "That's going to be a problem."

"Promise not to scream? I'll take it out," the large man stammered. His voice was soft and light, and he seemed to stumble over his words like a child who had just learned how to talk.

Fletcher considered his offer. She thought that the van was driving too fast for anyone to hear her cries anyway. She nodded, agreeing to his terms. He untied the gag.

"You people are sick!" she spat. "You can't just pinch me off the street! There must be protocol you have to follow. I'm not due for Reclamation until the first of next month."

The big man gawped at Fletcher, perplexed, then set his sights on his counterpart. "She thinks we're Agents?"

The woman held up her thumb.

The man burst into laughter. "No."

"Really?" she questioned. "If you're not Agents, who the hell are you?" And then she remembered: Word on the street was that kids whose parents had anything worth anything were being kidnapped and held for ransom. She snickered aloud. "You're out of luck if you think you can hold me for ransom. My family can hardly afford a loaf of fresh-baked bread on payday. Obviously I haven't got any money, or I wouldn't be up for Reclamation, would I?"

"Well, you're in luck, because we're not kidnappers," the woman said. "We're with YOR."

"What is that, a riddle?" Fletcher jeered. "Okay, I'll play along. With 'your' who?"

"Youth Opposed to Reclamation," the man declared, as though he had rehearsed reciting the words over and over.

"What are you lunatics yammering about? And what the fuck was that thing you fished out of my arm?"

"You ask too many questions," the woman said. "And you've got a dirty mouth."

"First, the cleanliness of my mouth is none of your goddamn business. Second, I want some answers! I have a right to know who you are and why you've taken me hostage."

The woman bared her teeth. A ferocious growl charged past her lips. "You are not a hostage."

"Tell me what I am then, because this certainly isn't a gathering of friends roaming the streets in search of a good time."

"You really aren't going to shut up, are you?" The woman griped under her breath, "Should've left the gag in."

There she was, mouthing off to a band of kidnappers who, for all she knew, were totally capable of murdering her and leaving her body in a ditch somewhere. That was not how Fletcher wanted to meet her end, but she needed to know who these masked maniacs were and why they had taken her, of all people. "I'll shut up when you start explaining yourself."

"YOR," the woman began diffidently, "is an underground organization made up of kids who are fed up with the system of mandated higher ed, forced student debt, and its inevitable result of Reclamation. Some of us have friends who have been Reclaimed, others have family members. A few of us have even undergone the Process ourselves, like Killian here." She gestured to the man.

Killian, the inarticulate-but-enormous ruffian, rubbed his head. "I used to be smart, but they took too much brain stuff away. Right, Sparrow?"

Sparrow patted Killian's shoulder and smiled at him. "That's right, big guy." She turned to Fletcher and said, irritated, "That's why we picked you up, okay? We were assigned to you."

"Assigned to me? How'd you know I was scheduled for Reclamation?"

"Head Office knows who and where just like the BOE knows. What do you think that thing in your arm was? A government-issued subcutaneous tracker."

"A tracker?" Fletcher sneered. "That's absurd."

"You saw it for yourself. They stuck a beacon in your arm

so they could find you wherever. All they have to do is flip a switch."

"Humoring you for a moment, when was this 'tracker' implanted in me? At birth?"

"You were tested for Renascent Hemorrhagic Fever before you started at university, right?"

"Of course. Everyone was."

"That's what they wanted you to think. But The Government found a cure for that decades ago."

"Yeah, right." Fletcher rolled her eyes in disbelief. "You're telling me there's some kind of radical activist organization running around like knights in shining armor, scooping up damsels in distress, digging trackers out of their arms and whisking them away to safety?"

Sparrow's frustration swelled. "No. Among other things, what we do is try to get to people before the BOE does. You are our latest damsel, and we were told to do whatever it takes to get you out of the city."

"Why? Why were you told to do 'whatever it takes'? What makes me so special?"

"I have no idea. We're just following orders. The assignment came directly from the top." Vexed, Sparrow paused to scrutinize Fletcher. "You must be pretty exceptional. I guess looks really can be deceiving."

"What if I don't want your help? What if I'd rather go home, spend my last days with my father, and take my chances?"

"Then that would make you as stupid as your friend Jonah. He refused us, too. But look on the bright side; you'll probably end up right beside him in the nuthouse. Won't that be sweet?"

Agents come, you run. Jonah's words replayed inside Fletcher's mind. *Be brave.* An upsurge of anger grabbed hold of her. "Don't ever speak that way about Jonah. You may have been 'assigned' to him, you may have read his file or whatever information your Head Office has on him, but you don't know a single thing about him! He isn't stupid and he isn't nuts. He's just broken."

"For a smart girl, you're wrong more often than you're right," Sparrow countered. "We know plenty. Jonah Quinn has an IQ of 148. He received an almost perfect score on his HiEd Exam, and as a result was accepted to Boston Technological University at the age of seventeen. His senior year at BTU, he designed a building that would have run entirely on renewable, eco-friendly solar energy and cost next to nothing to construct since it was crafted solely of recycled materials. One month before his twenty-second birthday, he graduated third in his class—first in the School of Architecture and Structural Design. Jonah Quinn had what was potentially one of the most brilliant engineering minds of our generation, but because he refused our help, he was downgraded to a quivering heap of a rage-fueled time bomb. So yes, he is broken. Do you really want to take the chance of coming back that way? Or coming back so wrecked that you need someone else to tie your shoelaces for you, like I have to do every morning for my brother here?"

She paused, a silent melancholy consuming the air around her. "I know what it's like when someone you love is taken away, alright? That's why Killian and I joined YOR, because we don't want to see that happen to anyone else. We have people who can help you disappear. Without them, The Department of Reclamation will hunt you until the day you die. If they want you, they will find you."

Fletcher exhaled a woeful sigh. With a single speech, this stranger—little more than a talking head obscured by a wool balaclava—had whittled away her resolve. Overwhelmed, Fletcher had little choice but to concede to Sparrow's wisdom. "Where are you taking me?"

"To one of our safe houses. The guy in charge will explain the details of relocation and identification replacement."

Fletcher bit her bottom lip, her prized logic defeated by

the most basic of instincts: survival. "I'll go with you on the condition that I will not be held captive. If I hear this guy out and don't like what he has to say, I expect to be returned to my home unscathed."

"That's p-p-policy," Killian blurted. "You don't like us, we take you home."

Sparrow concurred. "Unlike The Government, we give you a choice."

"Fine." Fletcher's nose upturned. "At least do me the courtesy of taking those ridiculous things off your heads. I like to see the faces of the people I'm speaking to."

"That's fair," Sparrow agreed. She reached across to her brother, pulled off his mask, and then removed her own.

Fletcher's gaze flickered between the duo. "Twins?" She marveled. She had never met a set of twins before. The instances of multiple births resulting from the same pregnancy were rare. Hell, meeting a person with any siblings was uncommon. Most Vaulters could scarcely afford to feed and clothe one child. Fletcher sometimes wondered why anyone bothered to procreate at all. The human propensity for optimism outweighed logic, and on that idiotic whim people kept having babies. Or maybe their biological imperative was too strong to resist. She couldn't say, and it didn't matter to her anyway. That was for the scientists to figure out.

Sparrow confirmed it with a curt nod.

"I can see it," Fletcher said. The resemblance between the pair was striking. For a towering hulk of a man, Killian's nose and lips were oddly delicate. His face was more handsome than the brutish one Fletcher had pictured, despite the serrated scar running from his left temple all the way to his chin. His light brown hair was cropped. His pale blue eyes were dull and tired, though Fletcher could see the remnants of the deeply pensive person he must have been before he was Reclaimed.

Sparrow's eyes had the same aqua hue as her brother's, but

that was where the similarity between those features ended. Neither dull nor tired, Sparrow's eyes glowed with a fiery alertness, an almost savage thirst for life.

Fletcher had expected the wild existence of a rebel fighter to be physically reflected on Sparrow. She wanted her to be a haggard mess of a woman, but was surprised to find that she was quite the opposite. Sparrow's face was symmetrical, with cheekbones and a jawline so refined as to be the product of an artisan's hands. Her chestnut hair fell loose and long down her shoulders.

Fletcher allowed her stare to linger on Sparrow's face a nanosecond longer than she should have. Sparrow caught the gaze, and her lips contorted into a shrewd sideways grin. Before Fletcher could avert her eyes, the van made a sharp turn. The turbulence heaved her into the air and her knees slammed onto the metal floor. She continued to skid forward. To her horror, she realized that if she could not stop herself from sliding, she would crash face-first into the frame of the passenger door and the force could kill her. *That's just wonderful.* She was sure that that thought would be her last.

Unfazed, Sparrow flung her arms up and snagged Fletcher by her biceps. In turn, Fletcher's hands, still bound together, landed on Sparrow's sternum. The double contact steadied Fletcher, yet at the same time made her feel unbalanced.

"Are you hurt?"

"No." Fletcher shifted out of Sparrow's grasp. "I'm fine." She darted her eyes toward the window. She wondered at its matte blackness. It was enough to take her mind off the awkward, unnameable feeling in the pit of her stomach. "Is that spray paint on the windows?"

"Uh huh," Killian grunted.

"Why would you do that?"

"Safe house is a secret," he replied like the question had an obvious answer. He batted his eyes at her then, as if to say "even a Veg like me knows that."

"We've reached out to many people in your situation," Sparrow began. "We blacked out the windows in case anyone refused us and then got the idea of trading our location for leniency when Agents came calling. We're public enemies, you know. There's a bounty on all of our heads."

"All of your heads . . . how many of you are there?"

Sparrow grinned. "Enough."

chapter four

THE VAN PULLED TO an unexpected stop. How long had they been driving? Thirty minutes? An hour? And in which direction? For all Fletcher knew, they could have left the Massachusetts Territory and traveled to Vermontshire.

The sliding door rolled open from the outside. The driver, another man who also wore a ski mask, was standing with a .270 Winchester rifle trained on Fletcher's head. Her breath hitched in her throat at the sight of it. No quick movements, she thought, attempting to suppress her budding anxiety before it got the better of her. This was the first time in her life she'd had the misfortune of peering down the barrel of a gun. She hoped it would be the last, though not as a result of being shot to death.

"Damon!" Sparrow curled her lip at the man. "She's not a damn deer. Get that gun out of her face right now."

Damon lowered the rifle, muttered an apology and evaporated into the darkness.

"Sorry about him," Sparrow mumbled. "This is his first assignment. He's a bit jumpy."

This woman may have just saved her from a bloody death, but the fright of having a masked man hold the business end of a rifle to her head far outweighed Fletcher's ability to convey her gratitude. "Jumpy? Fantastic! He had a gun aimed at my head, and *he's* jumpy? You people really know how to treat your guests, don't you?"

Sparrow huffed. "If you quit with the sarcasm, I'll untie your legs so you can walk with us. Keep talking and I'll let Killian toss you over his shoulder like a duffel bag again."

Killian winked at Fletcher. "I carry you, no problem."

Fletcher bit her tongue. Given the choice between loosing another smart remark or having the hogties cut, she was going to choose the latter. "Okay."

"Good," Killian said as he exited the van, leaving his sister and Fletcher to each other's company.

Sparrow patted her knees and hitched her chin toward Fletcher. Fletcher did not move. "Listen, Ivy League, you might not know this, but that was the universal signal for 'come here.'"

"You just told Damon I wasn't a damn deer. I am not a damn dog, either."

Sparrow let out an annoyed grumble as she pawed at the cuffs of Fletcher's beige cargo pants. She lifted Fletcher's legs off the floor and deposited them into her own lap. After a few frustrated moments of fumbling with too-tight knots, she fished a folded hunter's knife from her pocket. A quick flick of her wrist revealed a menacing, five-inch-long blade. Its smooth edge glistened wickedly in the moonlight.

She examined the rope binding Fletcher's legs. "Don't move. I don't want to cut you." The sincerity in her voice came as a shock to Fletcher. In spite of herself, Fletcher remained perfectly motionless as Sparrow sawed through the rope, though not because she was afraid of being inadvertently stabbed. For some inscrutable reason, she trusted this woman who had snatched her up in the dead of night and whisked her away to who-the-hell-knew where. She knew that no harm would come to her at Sparrow's hands. The woman was alert, quick yet meticulous, and had caught Fletcher when she needed catching. That earned her a modicum of good faith.

A few swipes of the blade and her legs were freed. Instead of removing her legs from Sparrow's lap, Fletcher bent over and folded up her pant legs. Her hands remained bound together as she rubbed at the pink friction burns around her ankles. She hoped that Sparrow would take the hint she wanted her hands untied.

"I'm sorry. I didn't realize how tight I'd tied the rope." Sparrow frowned. "Here, give me your wrists."

Fletcher moved her legs and offered up her hands. Again, she remained stationary as the rope was cut. "Thanks," she said, happy to be free of the restraints.

"You're welcome."

Sparrow hopped out of the van and Fletcher followed, her sneakers hitting the uneven gravel with a loud crunch. She stood stock-still, feeling that something was amiss. It was darker here—wherever here was—than any place she had ever been before. There were no street lamps, nor the familiar glimmer of the QuellSells' trash barrel fire pits, only the light of a million stars and the brilliant full moon. She listened for the sound of something typical: people talking, dogs barking, pedestrian traffic—any sign that civilization was within reach. She heard nothing save for the soft swishing of branches. *Trees.* She breathed in the fragrance of authentic pine and marveled at the freshness of it, at the lack of that bitter chemical undertone she knew so well thanks to the pine-scented cleaning solution her janitor father always smelled of. An antiquated word she had rarely had the opportunity to use came to her mind: *forest.*

The firefights of the Second Revolution had wiped out much of The United States' woodlands. Fletcher didn't think any proper forests had endured; yet here she was, standing in one. All she had ever known was Boston, the sprawling city with its smoggy air, gray skyscrapers, and boulevards. She found herself truly in awe of something for the very first time—nature unencumbered, unblemished by human hands. It was the most miraculous thing she had ever experienced.

A tiny *click* brought her back to her senses, and she was blinded by the artificial brightness of a flashlight. Sparrow focused the beam of light on herself so that Fletcher could see her, then pointed it at the backs of Damon and Killian. "Follow the boys," she instructed.

The women walked together, Sparrow shining the flashlight on the downward-sloping trail. Fletcher's attention darted from the trees to the heavens often, and she tripped twice for lack of minding the path.

"Beautiful, isn't it?" Sparrow asked.

"I've never seen anything like it."

Sparrow smirked at the wonderment in Fletcher's voice. "No, you wouldn't have. Most of the forests in the Northern Territories were seriously damaged during the Revolution. But a handful of very passionate conservationists gave up their lives to defend a small number of acres here. It used to be called Russell Forest Preserve."

"Russell Forest Preserve—347 acres of land located in the former state of New Hampshire—became protected in the early 1990s," Fletcher blurted out. She had read about the place in an old paper flier she had found in the library's basement archives—a cache of old items left over from the time before The UAT came to be. "I can't believe it's still here after 140 years."

"I see you know your history. On the downside, now you know where our hideout is, so I'm afraid I'll have to kill you."

"Seems like a waste." Fletcher played along. "You going through all that trouble to get me here, only to bump me off. Seriously though, I won't tell anyone about your secret lair. Not because I care about protecting your little criminal organization, mind you. It would just be a disgrace to let anyone ruin this place."

"That's as good a reason as any."

They continued down the track in silence for a while until Killian shuffled up to them in a fluster. "We're lost, I think."

"No, we aren't. It's up ahead." Sparrow threw her hand up to ruffle her brother's hair. "Keep going, big guy. Just follow the trail."

"Okay." He scurried back to Damon.

Fletcher smiled. Something about how the brother and sister spoke to each other—in this very sweet, lovely way—touched a soft spot in her heart that she'd forgotten existed. "You take care of him, don't you?"

Sparrow shrugged. "I try to. It's difficult sometimes."

An awkward thought sprang to Fletcher's mind. She wasn't sure if she would be overstepping her boundaries by voicing it. She also wasn't sure how willing Sparrow would be to discuss it with someone she had just met, but in the end her curiosity won out. "Did you and Killian both go to college?"

"Yes."

"Then why was he Reclaimed and you weren't?" She paused. Something in the atmosphere had changed the moment the question left her lips. She couldn't see the tension in Sparrow's posture through the dense shadows of the woodlands, but she could feel it as though the other woman's muscles were her own. "Never mind, it's none of my business. I'm sorry. I shouldn't have asked."

"No, it's okay. It's not something I talk about much. I'll tell you if you really want to know."

"I do," Fletcher confirmed. If there was any hope of evading her fate without having to disappear forever, she needed to know about it. Besides, she liked to know the history of things, and that applied to people as well. After all, a person's history shaped who they became.

"Killian and I both took the HiEd Exam, like everyone else. His brain waves went off the charts when tested in Biology and Chemistry. Mine were highest when tested in Language Arts.

You know how it goes from there: The Government freed us from their monitors and gave us each a list of schools to choose from. All of Killian's schools had obscenely high tuition rates. Mine were what used to be called state colleges, so they were less expensive. He chose to attend New Harvard and majored in Biochemistry. I chose the College of Communications and majored in Linguistics.

"He was one of the lucky few who got a job in The Southern Territories after graduation. He worked for The Ministry of Health in Atlanta. My Bachelor of Arts degree was useless. I couldn't even find a job bagging groceries in The South, and the best I could find in The Vault was an apprenticeship.

"A year went by and I still didn't have a job that paid a living wage. Every day I waited for Agents to come knocking on the door. They never came. Then one day Killian went missing. My parents and I didn't hear a word from him for a month. We thought he'd just gotten busy in the lab, until the Agents dropped him off on our doorstep." Sparrow ran her little finger down her face as she said, "He had this crudely stitched incision running from his chin to his hairline, and he was as dull as a drawer of spoons.

"After I sent at least one hundred digiposts to about as many government agencies, we were finally able to find out what happened to him. He had been repaying his loans and mine. Toward the end of the repayment cycle, the monthly amount of my loan went up. He couldn't afford both his debt and mine anymore, so he stopped making payments on his own loans to focus on mine," she said brusquely. "That's why my brother was Reclaimed and I wasn't. He sacrificed himself to protect me. And that's why it's so hard for me to take care of him. He wouldn't be in this position if it weren't for me."

Fletcher tried to speak. She wanted to apologize, or express her sympathy with some other words, but she was unable to find the right ones. She understood how much it hurt to watch someone you care for adjust to life after Reclamation. She understood how much it hurt to remember who that person was before and how difficult it was to know that they would never be the same again. It was never just the Reclaimee whose life was changed by the Process; everyone who had ever known them was forever altered for the worse. What Fletcher had never experienced, and could not fathom in her wildest nightmares, was the amount of guilt Sparrow carried in her heart. She blamed herself for how heinously The Government had repaid her brother's kindheartedness.

"His scar," Fletcher said. "Jonah doesn't have a scar like that. He has a small, round mark on his left temple, but it looks like a burn from an electrode, not like someone took a scalpel to his face." As soon as she uttered the sentence, she winced at how insensitive it sounded. She was not, and never had been, very good at subtlety. "Shit! I mean—"

"It's alright. They did take a scalpel to his face. Something went wrong during his Reclamation. They tried to fix him with old-fashioned brain surgery. He doesn't really remember what went down at the Processing Center, so we never did get any straightforward answers about it."

As long as they were being honest with one another, Fletcher figured she might as well say everything that was on her mind. "If you've read my file or whatever it is you have on me, I'm sure you know my mother was Reclaimed. My dad told me she couldn't even feed herself after she came home. Killian's cognition and speech may have been affected, but his motor skills seem intact. How is it possible that one Veg can be worse off than another?"

"How is it possible that some people come back unchanged, minus a few years of higher education?" Sparrow speculated. "It's Neuroscience. I don't understand it any better than you do."

"Don't you find it suspect? I would love to get my hands on the numbers, do the math, find out the ratio of people who come back 'normal' versus the ratio of people who come back different, and to what degree the severity of the change may be."

"Yes, I find it suspect. But those statistics are out of reach for YOR. They're so restricted I don't think those reports ever leave the Processing Centers. Head Office has never come across any of that information in the sealed files it obtains. We'll probably never know what really goes on inside Processing Center walls. No one who comes out can ever recall many details about it."

"The truth will come out eventually. It can't stay buried forever, no matter how hard the BOE tries to hide it." If only The Government hadn't blacked out public access to the internet, Fletcher thought. What a glorious tool that must have been.

"Who would leak that kind of information, though? The Government is good to its high-level employees, and they're the only people who would have access to whatever records the Processing Centers keep. They know Reclamation is wrong, but the problem is they're too well paid and therefore too loyal to care."

"What about the people in The Southern Territories? Do they have any idea how bad it is up here, how many of us are destroyed by government-sanctioned deprogramming? Southerners have enough money, enough clout. If they put enough pressure on The Government, it would have to stop screwing with our brains," Fletcher insisted.

"I'm sure they've heard stories, but I doubt they understand how widespread the problem is. They don't live among us. They don't have to care for the broken or send their broken to institutions to do the caring for them. Do you think some rich Southern businessman would really give a shit about rumor? So what if a few vagabonds from The Vault go crazy or lame-brained during Reclamation?

"But let's say there are a handful of Southerners who are aware of and opposed to the true barbarity of Reclamation. It would never become any kind of cause célèbre unless there was hard proof that it was happening on a large scale. Even then, there's no guarantee anyone would do anything about it because that would mean they'd have to stand toe to toe with The Government. Who in their right mind would put themselves in that position, knowing that The Government could take away everything in a blink? Would you jeopardize a comfortable living to do the right thing?"

Fletcher contemplated the question. She wanted to be one of those people who possessed enough righteous indignation and fortitude to say, "Yes, I would sacrifice everything to take a stand." The fact of the matter was she didn't have much of anything to sacrifice. She had never had a "comfortable living," but if she had, would she have volunteered to give any of it up, no matter how honorable the cause? What would a comfortable living look like? The rent paid on time every month. A FloaterBus pass so she wouldn't have to walk everywhere. The refrigerator stocked full of meats and cheeses and fresh fruits and vegetables. The cupboard fit to bursting with baking supplies. She very much liked to bake. She'd discovered that when she took a Culinary Arts class to fill an elective requirement sophomore year. She was good at making cookies and cupcakes, things that required expensive ingredients like eggs and sugar. If she could afford those luxuries . . . "No, I don't think I would," she said with a groan, hating herself for coming to that conclusion.

It angered her to think of how selfish the human race was, of how people could be so unconcerned with the well-being of their fellow man. It wasn't the first time she had found herself disgusted with mankind's self-absorbed nature, but it was the first time said disgust had rocked her to her core. She felt it so deeply, so tangibly, as if it were a throbbing tumor in the middle of her chest. It sparked something in her, an awareness of something greater than herself and her own suffering.

Perhaps, she thought, it was fated that she should meet this seedy group of rebels who tried in their own discreet way to bring hope to those who had none. Suddenly, YOR was no longer a tool she could utilize to save herself from Reclamation; it was something she wanted to be a part of. "I get it now." She grabbed Sparrow's arm, stopping them both in their tracks. "I understand why you do what you do. We have to help ourselves because nobody else will."

"Yes," Sparrow confirmed. "Exactly."

AFTER WHAT FELT LIKE miles of hard trekking, the small group approached a wide clearing. In the center of the clearing sat a sizable structure made of moss-grown rotting logs, large stones, and sheets of plate glass. Dim light trickled out through a bay window in the front of the building. As Fletcher ascended the staircase leading up to the veranda, she noticed a strange mechanical purring streaming from somewhere. "What's that noise?"

"Solar panels," Killian said. Without any further explanation, he scraped his muddy boots on a rubber mat and stepped through the threshold into the building.

"We're way off the grid out here," Sparrow elaborated. "That's partly why this spot was chosen. Zero consumption from The Government-controlled power pool means we can't be traced. Solar panel inverters kind of . . . *hum*. I don't know why."

"Hmm." A weather-battered cornerstone displaying the year of the edifice's construction caught Fletcher's attention. She crouched down into a squat position and ran her fingers over the faded numbers. "What is this place?"

"A Visitor's Center and Ranger's Outpost that never opened. The same conservationists who preserved the forest raised money to build a place where hikers could go for trail information and emergency medical attention. A few months after its completion the Second Revolutionary War broke out."

"I guess people were too busy fighting and dying or fleeing and hiding to take a nice stroll through the woods."

"Good guess," Sparrow said, then waved Fletcher away from the cornerstone and over to the door. "Wipe your shoes on the mat."

"Yes, ma'am." Fletcher followed the directive and trailed Sparrow into the building.

The first room Fletcher noticed was to the immediate left of the front entrance, through a wide oak archway. She wandered in, beyond the spot where an antique grandfather clock stood, and saw that it was strewn with cots and bedrolls. She counted at least a dozen of the military-style folding beds, separated into two rows. It reminded her of a scene from a digibook she'd once read about a group of orphan pickpockets surviving on the streets of nineteenth-century London. The one major difference, however, were the guns.

Each cot had an improvised metal rack mounted on its left underside. Some of the racks held rifles like Damon's Winchester while others held shotguns of either the single- or double-barrel variety—some sawed off, some long. The cache was not made up of shiny, well-kept munitions, but of time-tattered, overworked ones. Most of the ordnance had seen better days. Nevertheless, the arsenal frightened Fletcher.

She wondered how YOR had come by all the armaments. While at university, she had learned of the hefty artillery bans The Government had enacted in the early days of The Unified American Territories. More than two centuries ago the nation's founders—survivors from The United States of America's

Congress, along with corporate CEOs—had made it illegal for civilians to own guns. She couldn't blame them for that. They had survived a four-year war, fought mostly by rough-and-ready Revolutionist militias with lawfully purchased weapons. She thought it was supposed to be difficult to obtain firearms these days, unlike in the past. She looked at Sparrow with troubled eyes. "Where did you find all these guns?"

"You don't need to know that," a gruff voice answered from the opposite end of the room. Both women turned toward its source. Near the base of the stairwell leading to the second floor stood a tall, lanky man. His face was cloaked by the lappets of an oversized black hood.

"Amazing. You managed to recruit the Grim Reaper," Fletcher whispered.

Sparrow suppressed a snicker by clearing her throat. "Søren, this is Fletcher Daniels. Fletcher, this is our fearless leader, Søren."

Søren ignored the acerbic introduction and trudged through the archway. He stood silent before them for a moment, then slipped his hood down, exposing spiked hair as dark as tar and skin as pale as the winter sky. Fletcher reckoned that he was at least half a decade older than Sparrow—who, by her estimation, must have been about twenty-five—which put him into his thirties. Søren folded his arms across his chest and allowed his angry, wild eyes to study every inch of Fletcher before settling on Sparrow. "Why aren't you wearing your ski mask?"

"She asked me to take it off."

"Oh, did she? And if she asked you to shoot yourself in the foot, would you?"

"No, I wouldn't."

Fletcher's brow rose at the bitterness permeating the air between the two. By their postures—both standing straight and rigid, cautious of the other—there was something odd between them, something greater than the occasional tension that was natural between a superior and a subordinate. Her nosiness was piqued as Søren stepped closer to Sparrow.

"I hope not." He nodded, and barely audibly continued. "Remember what happened the last time you got attached to one of your assignments."

"It's not about that," Sparrow snarled. "I wouldn't shoot myself in the foot if *you* asked me to, either."

"I would never ask you to."

"Alright," Fletcher interjected. "I don't know what's going on here, but it looks personal. I can step out if you'd like to talk privately."

"There's nothing to talk about," said Sparrow. "How about we give you the grand tour? That's why you're here, right? So you can see the facility and everything we have to offer."

"Yes. I . . . er . . . I've forgotten my manners," Søren spluttered. "I'm sure you can imagine that happens often around Sparrow."

"I can see how that's possible," Fletcher agreed, the hint of snark causing Sparrow to shoot a look of disbelief in her direction. "I mean, you did tie me up and heave me into a van."

"I apologized for it."

"You did not."

Søren muttered something incomprehensible as he turned his back to them. "Follow me, this way."

Søren shepherded the way up a poorly lit, winding staircase. Every stride he took was followed by the muffled creaking of old lumber. The noise made Fletcher uneasy. She worried that a wrong footfall might cause the planks beneath her feet to give way. She pictured herself dangling defenselessly, clawing at splintered wood. The idea caused her to cling to the banister. "Could use some renovations."

Sparrow let out a chuckle. "Were you expecting one of those old-time Bed and Breakfasts?"

"I'm not sure what I was expecting," Fletcher said, but her perception of the relic Visitor's Center changed once Søren reached the second floor. She watched as he groped along the wall until he was able to locate a small knob protruding from it. He twisted the knob, and bright fluorescent bulbs flickered on overhead.

"This is our identification replacement chamber."

Fletcher's jaw went slack at the sight of the contents housed in this room. It was poles apart from the rest of the building, so high-tech that it juxtaposed everything else she'd seen so far. She was surrounded by machines unlike any she had ever come across before. She recognized parts of the whole—monitors and a fingerprint scanner—but there were two unfamiliar devices in the far crook of the room. The first reminded her of a small, boxy thing called an inkjet printer, a popular household commodity in prewar America that she'd read about in a magazine from the library's archives. The second was an upright silver tube that stood upward of seven feet tall and appeared just wide enough to fit a single person inside. It had a frosted-glass revolving door at its center. Next to the door was a console of colored controls and a hologram projector lens. "What in the hell is that?" She pointed.

"That is a third-generation InvigorStyler Booth," Sparrow answered. "It cuts and dyes your hair, does your makeup. It even has an option to change your ethnic attributes, eye color and shape, skin tone, everything. It's wicked popular in The South. There are salons full of these things down there."

There is no such thing, no way, Fletcher thought. "You're seriously telling me this machine allows you to change your innate racial traits on a whim? You've actually been to The South and seen these salons?"

"I've been there once, to visit Killian in Atlanta. They were on every other street."

"Now I've seen all the marvels mankind has to offer." Fletcher had a burning desire to ask how a ragtag group of poor kids from The Vault could have afforded all of this cutting-edge

Southern technology, but assumed that was something Søren would not appreciate. "And what's the other thing there?" She gestured to the boxy gadget.

"It's kind of like a fingerprint scanner, only it does the opposite," said Sparrow. "We use the lasers over there to wipe your prints, and this etches new patterns into your skin after the sequencer is embedded with your new name, age, and background information."

Her eyes went wide. "Does it hurt?"

"Yes." Søren's gaze found Fletcher's. "The laser wipes your prints by melting the top few layers of skin on your hands. The etching lasers then burn fresh contours in their place."

Sparrow, aware of the alarm written on Fletcher's face, added, "We have a topical numbing agent that lessens the pain, but doesn't dull it completely."

"How does it work, though? How can you conjure a person into existence, identifying marks and all?"

"Is it necessary for you to know every single detail?" Søren asked.

"Calm down. She's curious, just like I was, like we all were," Sparrow fizzed. "We're asking her to trust us with her life so I think that entitles her to ask questions."

That was the absolute wrong thing to say. Søren seized Sparrow by the arm and dragged her into the hall, slamming the door closed behind them. Fletcher remained alone in the room, listening as Søren proceeded to howl. "The person who took off her mask during a retrieval mission is telling me to calm down? You just met this girl! How do you know *we* can trust *her*?"

For someone trying to handle the discussion discreetly, Fletcher thought he was doing a terrible job of it.

"I just know," Sparrow countered. "She understands we're trying to help even if she chooses not to accept the help we offer."

"You're pushing it here. I don't care if she's a 'kindred spirit' or whatever; she isn't one of us."

As she listened to them argue, Fletcher's mind raced with thoughts of her mother, of Jonah, of the countless other Reclaimees she'd never met, some Vegs, some Berserkers, some who had survived with their brains reasonably undamaged, but were nonetheless traumatized, weary and left wanting. All the people, *her* people, who had had their educations stripped away from them without any consideration of the harm it would do.

Enough.

Fletcher cracked the door open just wide enough to poke her head through. When she was not received with livid words, she chanced stepping into the hall. "You're right, I'm not one of you. But I want to be. I think I need to be. It's noble, what you do— helping people escape Reclamation, making sure everything they've worked so hard to achieve remains intact. Reclamation isn't just wrong, it's depraved. The whole system is screwed up.

"Our ancestors never would have stood for this. Long before this country became The UAT, long before our parents' time and their parents' time, when The United States of America still existed, there were rich people, poor people, and people in between, but none of that really mattered. Everyone had the chance to attain greatness if they were driven enough. That was called 'The American Dream.' No one was forced to get a college education, even if they had a genius-level IQ. And if you weren't a genius or you were dirt poor, you had options, scholarships, grants, student loans that had reasonable repayment terms. It wasn't easy, but there was no such thing as Reclamation back then. No one could take your education, much less your life, away from you. No one! I believe in that, in having the freedom to decide what to do with your own life, no one telling you that you're too dumb to do it or too smart not to. It seems to me like YOR is the closest thing we have to an organized revolt against a sick, sadistic government. I want in."

Søren huffed, unable to rebuff her. "Explain it to her," he instructed Sparrow.

"We recycle the IDs," Sparrow began. "Before the war, civilians had their fingerprints on file with certain state agencies. Hundreds of those files were salvaged after the war, and Head Office has access to them. We use the identity of someone who's been dead for centuries. Head Office doctors the necessary verification documents—birth records, education records, employment records, photographs—and files them in the Hall of Records, then destroys any evidence that the identity existed before the war."

"So, what you're saying is you completely erase a person from the annals of history?" Fletcher's features contorted into a horrified expression. An uncomfortable stillness blanketed the room. Stealing a dead person's identity felt wrong to her, as though it were defiling their memory. But given a few moments to ruminate on it, she questioned if it was truly defiling someone's memory if said person's identity could save someone else. If she were dead and the details of her life could help someone else to live, then she would welcome them to take it all—her fingerprints, her background, anything they would need to survive. The best way to honor the dead, she decided, would be to carry their memory with you and be thankful for their life with each breath you take.

"Yes," Søren continued. "It seems like an awful thing to do, but it's the only way. If you've got a problem with that, you'll need to get over it if you plan on becoming a useful asset to YOR."

Fletcher sucked in her bottom lip, considered it. "I'm making peace with it."

"And you'll have to learn how we operate, how to defend yourself and others. Most importantly, you'll have to learn how to safely handle, clean, and fire a gun. While the Agents do try to take every potential Reclaimee alive, they've been known to use deadly force when they believe they can get away with it. You'll need to know how to shoot."

Fletcher was disinclined to the idea of using guns. Still, she acknowledged that the Agents were armed, that they would use their weapons if pushed to do so, and that it was necessary for YOR to be equally equipped and prepared. She stifled her hesitation. "I'll try."

"You'll also need to leave your home, your family, your friends and your job," Sparrow said. "We don't take chances. We lower the risk of getting caught by withdrawing from society at large, but unlike if we were to give you a new identity and ship you off to The Southern Territories, you can contact your loved ones once in a while if you use extreme caution. Are you okay with that?"

Was she okay with leaving her life and all the people she loved? No. But it beat all her other options—having her brain meddled with, possibly dying, never being able to see her father, Jonah, or her other friends again. "Do I have a choice? I'll have to be okay with it."

"Fine," said Søren. "There's less than a month left before the Agents return for you. Sometimes they run surveillance on people up to two weeks in advance to familiarize themselves with their routines; you must be out of Boston before then. We'll take you home tomorrow so you can spend your last few days with your family and friends. You can go to work on Monday as usual, keep with your daily schedule. We will pick you up on Friday, one hour after sundown. This is not negotiable."

"Friday, an hour after sundown," Fletcher repeated aloud to make sure it sank in. "Alright."

"This is a trial run. You'll shadow Sparrow until you get the hang of things; then you'll take the shooting test. If you pass, we'll take a vote to see if you're in. This is also non-negotiable. Do you understand?"

"I do."

"Good." He focused on Sparrow. "You're her Handler now, which means you are responsible for everything she does, everything that happens to her, and everything she needs to learn. Are you able to do that?"

"Yes, I am," Sparrow asserted.

"Show her to the bathroom so she can get cleaned up, then come down to the kitchen for dinner. Charlie is making a pot roast," he said, then headed down the stairs.

Once they were alone, Sparrow grinned at Fletcher. "He's so used to intimidating people into compliance he doesn't know what to do with you. I'm impressed."

"That was him being less intimidating than usual? Gee, how could you tell? He didn't snarl as much as he typically does?"

"Something like that. Come on, let's finish up the tour and introduce you to the rest of the crew."

The long timber table was set for a dinner party if a gang of young vagrants could have dinner parties. A slew of people appeared out of nowhere, conjured from the woodwork like apparitions at a séance. Everyone took to their seats so surely that Fletcher realized this was a nightly event—a family meal of sorts.

Sparrow pulled a chair out for herself and one for Fletcher. Fletcher gawked at the chair, at Sparrow, and back at the chair. Vaulters didn't do that for each other—pull out chairs, hold open doors. They hardly even spoke to one another unnecessarily, not to offer "good morning" or "how are you" as had been common in the time before. It took everything they had to go on earning, slaving away despite the inevitable fruitlessness of their effort. Chivalry in The Vault had been another causality of the war. And yet . . .

"Are you going to sit down or not?" Sparrow questioned.

"Yes. Thanks." Fletcher, feeling self-conscious, took a seat.

In minutes, Fletcher had been introduced to half a dozen people; there were so many new names to learn and so many faces to go with those names. First, she'd met Charlie, a young woman of Asian ancestry who presented herself as YOR's resident house manager, followed by a brooding pink-haired girl named Zoe who communicated in grunts instead of words, a heavily tattooed young man named Philip who was YOR's professed technology expert, and Peter, the group's medic, who would have been described as Black back when America was still a place on the world map.

As she spooned helpings of food onto her plate, Fletcher wondered if all the faces she was looking at were originals, or if they had been chosen from the InvigorStyler's cache. It was such a strange concept to her, having to question whether a person's eye color and skin tone were the ones they were born with. It was also strange to think about Identification Replacement, to realize that some of these people were probably using names other than the ones their parents had given them and the biographies of people who had gone to their graves centuries ago. How exactly did ID Replacement work for these sneaky insurrectionists? Did YOR require its members to change their identities? *Will I have to?* "So," she said once the excitement of the rapid-fire meet-and-greet died down and everyone dug into their meal. "Do YOR members have their identities replaced, too?"

Sparrow refrained from speaking until she swallowed the piece of meat she had been chewing. "Recyclable IDs aren't the easiest things to come by. We keep a small cache of them with the original person's photograph intact so we can program a match into the InvigorStyler when the need arises, but typically IDs are scrubbed and reserved for people like you. Not to mention, it's dangerous for our contacts inside the Hall of Records to tamper with the system too much. The more often they hack in, the more likely they'll be caught. Most of us have had our fingerprints wiped so we're impossible to trace in that regard, but we don't have them replaced." She raised her palm so Fletcher could see the distinct lack of looping ridges on the pads of her fingers.

"May I?" Fletcher asked, reaching out to touch the other woman's digits.

"Sure."

Fletcher's fingers combed over Sparrow's smooth flesh. "That explains why you didn't bother to wear gloves when you abducted me."

"Observant." Sparrow smirked. "But we didn't abduct you; we liberated you."

"Call it what you like." Fletcher dropped her hand. "You have this ability to change a person's appearance and fingerprints. Are the changes permanent?"

"As far as fingerprints go I can't say. We've never wiped anyone's prints more than once. It's possible the skin on the hands could become too degraded for assigning new prints after a second wiping. You could change your appearance permanently, but you'd have to restyle every day. After twenty-four hours the styling wears off. You can change back to your original appearance any time, though. The InvigorStyler keeps a record of each person's original appearance, coding and imprinting it on the bottom of the person's foot so the next time they step into the booth they're prompted to either revert back to their original appearance, re-up the style, or choose a new one."

"That's incredible. Do all YOR members have to change the way they look?"

"The InvigorStyler takes a lot of juice to run. It tends to overheat our solar panels so we save it for when we have to go to highly populated areas for hard to find essential supplies, medicines and such. We can't really walk around a major city in broad daylight wearing ski masks, can we? Although whether or not you have to change your appearance depends on how hot you are."

"How 'hot' you are?"

"How hot you are, as in how much The Government wants you. Some people, like my brother, have already been Reclaimed. The Government's "property"—the education received on borrowed funds—has been returned, and the Agents want nothing to do with those people anymore. If you were never up for Reclamation, then you were never a priority on the BOE's list. Some of us didn't perform well enough on the HiEd Exam to be forced to go to university while others excelled in areas that are considered 'negligible aptitudes.' Those people go unregistered, like Charlie, whose household management skills are essential to making this place a comfortable home. Anyone who's never gotten a student loan from The Government can manage to fly under the radar without having to change their physical attributes."

"I suppose you can't fly under their radar."

"Nope. I disappeared before they could serve me with my Notification of Violation, but the system would've caught up with me by now. Killian and I have been with YOR for over two years. It's a safe bet I've been on their list for a while. I alter my appearance when I have to, but I hate doing it."

"Why? I think I'd like becoming a new person, if only to say that I'd had the experience."

"Are you kidding?" Sparrow scoffed. She gestured to herself. "Look at me. I'm hot, and it has nothing to do with the BOE wanting to vacu-suck my brain."

"You're modest, too." Fletcher laughed, genuinely, for the first time in the longest time. "Don't forget to tell me all about how modest you are."

"Ah, right. How could I forget that?" Sparrow flashed a smile, the brilliance of which extended into her eyes.

The awkward feeling Fletcher had had in the van returned. Her gut did a sickly somersault. She stirred in her seat before refocusing the conversation on the topic of smuggling potential Reclaimees into The Southern Territories. "Tell me how it works, shipping people off to The South. They must have places to live, jobs to support themselves. How do you arrange all of that?"

"I can't tell you that." Sparrow said before shoving a sliver of potato into her mouth.

"Oh, what, *that's* classified? You can divulge every detail about the lengths people go to to change their identities but not what they do with themselves afterward?"

Sparrow sneered. "I can't tell you because I don't know how it works. Head Office takes care of those arrangements. Once we get our assignment safely past the cordon, our job is done."

"Oh. I guess that's alright then."

Just as Sparrow was set to respond, Søren interrupted with a loud mock-cough. The room fell silent, and everyone focused their attention on him. Fletcher dropped her fork and looked up at him as well, thinking he must've had something important to say.

"Someone pass the potatoes."

Nobody moved an inch, save to blink or breathe.

"Er, uh, I," he faltered, "Someone pass the potatoes, please."

A round of slow applause broke out. Everyone clapped except Fletcher. She was confused. *Oh yes, that was life changing. Completely worthy of applause!*

"Alright, alright," Søren bowed his head, his cheeks reddening with embarrassment. It was the first hint of an emotion other than anger Fletcher had witnessed him exhibit. As if on cue he added a firm, "But I still don't have any potatoes on my plate, do I?" The applause died down and the previous scattered conversations resumed as Killian handed Søren a bowl of baked spuds.

After dinner was over and the dishes had been cleaned and put away, Sparrow and Fletcher joined a few of the others in the

Visitor's Center Common Area, the second room on the first floor opposite YOR's sleeping quarters. Peter, the group's medic, stoked the flames of a brick fireplace as everyone else gathered bowl-shaped chairs around it.

"Will someone explain to me why you all started clapping for Søren at the dinner table?" Fletcher questioned, still unable to figure it out.

"He said 'please,'" Charlie, Damon, Philip, Zoe, Peter, Killian and Sparrow all answered in unison.

"Is that a rarity?"

"Hell yeah, it is," declared Damon. "He's reintroducing 'please' to his vocabulary, along with 'thank you,' 'I'm sorry,' and every other polite phrase in the English language."

Fletcher furrowed her brow. "Reintroducing?"

"It's taken him years to learn how to do anything but scream, bash his head into walls, and randomly attack people. He hasn't quite gotten a handle on old-school etiquette yet," said Philip.

Fletcher looked at him, startled.

"I guess no one told you." Damon frowned, reading the surprise on Fletcher's face. "Søren is a recovering Berserker."

"He's a what?" She leapt from her seat, engulfed by thoughts of Jonah, the boy who had been so close to her heart since the day she was born. She had never heard the words "recovering" and "Berserker" used together in the same sentence. Granted, she had witnessed some improvement in Jonah's condition, but she didn't dare imagine anyone could recuperate as dramatically as Søren had appeared to. She repossessed her senses, refusing to allow the sprout of optimism to blossom, and found her seat again. "People can recover from that? That is, fully recover?"

"Not all people," said Philip. "It depends on how badly their mind was damaged during Reclamation."

"It all circles back to neuroscience," Sparrow added. "Like I said earlier, why some Berserkers are more violent than others and some Vegs are more, well, veggie than others, is a mystery to us. We've got some very intelligent people on our side, and they haven't been able to figure it out."

"Søren—like most Berserkers, I suspect—will never fully recover," Peter, the closest thing YOR had to a licensed doctor, chimed in. "He struggles every day against the anger in his head. I don't think anyone has ever seen him smile, or even grin. He'll be on neurosedatives for the rest of his life. Even with the sedatives, we don't allow him to handle a firearm. He mostly avoids the guns without us having to say so. And should he miss his morning injection, *whew*, you'd best stay far, *far* away from him. Without his morning dose he loses all control of himself."

"It's true. I've seen him off his meds," Zoe spoke actual words to Fletcher for the first time. "He broke a window with his forehead that day, damn near bled to death. It took Killian and three other guys to wrestle him down."

Fletcher was surprised. Søren seemed so . . . ordinary. Cantankerous, to be sure, but steady. "I don't get it. Why is he the person in charge? A Berserker doesn't seem like the best choice to lead."

"He's the last one left from the original group; he has seniority. And he's had to make some hard decisions. Head Office thinks he's up for it," explained Sparrow.

"Right. Who are we to argue?" Fletcher sighed. "I've seen a Berserker have an episode. It's horrifying," she announced as she stared absently at the intense orange fire. She willed its dancing flames to conceal the melancholy that was doubtlessly displayed on her face. Silence befell the group. She peeked up and noticed Sparrow's cool blue eyes fixed on her.

"Jonah?"

Fletcher remained mute, confirming with a feeble nod.

"I'm sorry." Sparrow placed a hand on Fletcher's knee, giving it a gentle squeeze. "There's no way of knowing if he'll ever get to the point where he can function as well as Søren, but there's always hope."

Fletcher blinked away the tears pooling in her eyes and let out a disbelieving snigger. "I wouldn't have pegged you for the hopeful kind."

"Oh, but I am." she removed her hand from Fletcher's knee. "I hope for a lot of things—mostly that the BOE will miraculously self-destruct one day and take The Department of Reclamation down with it. I know it won't happen, but that's why YOR is here—to at least throw a few wrenches in their gears."

Fletcher shook her head. "You're not hopeful as much as vengeful, I think."

Sparrow's gaze found her brother, who sat a few chairs to Fletcher's left and was quietly observing a conversation that had struck up between Peter and Philip. "Maybe I'm a bit of both."

It was past midnight when the group of vigilantes decided to retire for the evening and the fire was doused. Sparrow escorted Fletcher to a vacant bed adjacent to her own, then bent down and plucked the shotgun from its underside mount. "Sorry," she said over her shoulder. "You don't get a shooter until you've had adequate training, which is to say hours and hours of practice, or until you can hit a target from 100 paces away with your eyes closed."

"I should be getting one soon then?" Fletcher kidded as she kicked off her sneakers and let her long, fair hair free from its ponytail. "Honestly though . . ." She sank into the surprisingly well-cushioned cot. "If you only use your guns in dire circumstances, what is their primary purpose—scaring the life out of the people you're assigned to pick up? If that's the case, it's unnecessary. I was terrified by being bound and flung over Killian's shoulder."

Sparrow lifted her weighty onyx sweater up and over her head, indifferent to Fletcher's presence. "No," she replied, eyeing Fletcher, who watched her tug her tank top back down over her abs. "We don't use them for intimidation. Stick around long enough and you'll find out what we use them for.

Or mostly use them for."

"Okay." Fletcher flipped onto her side. *I don't think I want to find out*, she thought as she dozed off.

chapter six

FLETCHER AWOKE WITH A fright to a quick succession of thunderous cracking sounds. She sprang upright. After giving the room a once-over, she realized she was alone. Another sequence of *rat-a-tat-tats* split the air outside the Visitor's Center. She wiped the crusted remainders of sleep from her eyes, then slipped her feet into her sneakers.

She had heard gunfire once before when the Agents discharged their weapons at a man in the row house across from hers who had refused to give up his daughter and attacked them with a fire iron. She hadn't seen the barrage of bullets, but would never be able to forget the noise they made. It echoed through the city streets like a metric ton of Roman candles combusting one after the other. Hearing those same noises now led her to fear the worst. Was the safe house under attack? Had The Department of Reclamation discovered the hideaway? Or worse, had they followed the van—the van that had delivered her straight to YOR's front door—from Boston?

If this was her fault, she could not flee to safety. That was not an option conducive to anything other than a guilty conscience. Instinct told Fletcher to run in the opposite direction from the shots, but she swallowed her panic. Instead of running away, she hurried toward the commotion.

She tiptoed through the kitchen, now and again ducking behind a chair or appliance to listen while staying hidden from view. The volume of the gun blasts increased the closer she crept to the rear courtyard.

She found the sliding patio door thrown wide open. She stood tall before it, the cool morning air rushing against her skin. Still, there was no one else around. Unsatisfied because she was unable to locate the source of the sounds, she ventured warily out into the daylight, far beyond the courtyard to the distant tree line.

The farther Fletcher wandered into the forest the denser it became until all she could make out were luscious hues of yellow, orange, red and brown—an amalgamation of dying leaves and the branches from which they would soon fall.

Another cluster of shots rang out. These were so deafening, so close to her position that she dropped to the ground. Lying still, she realized that the forest floor was vibrating. It was odd, and she questioned if she were losing her mind, but she could feel the pulsations deep inside her torso, which was how she knew she wasn't imagining it. She speculated that the tremors and gun blasts were interconnected, though it quickly became clear to her that something was wrong: the loud popping sounds did not match up to the vibrations. The gun discharges became more sporadic, the shakings of the earth beneath her body more frequent. Then the shooting ceased, only to be replaced by the din of frantic pounding against hard-packed dirt.

Fletcher lifted her head. The shock of what she saw was almost enough to stop her heart. An enormous moose charged at her, galloping at a speed that could challenge a bullet train. Its antlers were the size of a small child, with six deadly points perfect for impaling a petite woman such as herself. The animal would be upon her within seconds. There was no time to pivot out of its path: she was going to be trampled to death, or skewered, or both. She wondered which would hurt less. *What a way to go.* She closed her eyes and took her last breath, hoping that her end would be quick.

Crack!

A bullet exploded through the beast's skull. Fletcher winced as a spray of still-warm blood and pinkish brain matter splattered across her face. The animal, dead, tumbled over itself, slamming to the ground snout-first with a nasty thump. It scraped to a halt inches from Fletcher's body.

Before she had a chance to process what she'd seen, she rolled onto her back, panting in disbelief. She rested there, still as a stone, and contemplated the hideousness of what she had just witnessed. It was one thing to know that every living thing would eventually die, but it was something else entirely to watch a living thing die. The poor, unmoving creature . . . .

She stared up at the sky, preoccupied with apologies for playing a part in the animal's demise, until Sparrow leaned over her, blocking the azure from her vision. Sparrow's face was the first thing Fletcher had been happy to see since she'd woken up.

"Good morning, Ivy League! Nice of you to join us." Sparrow reached out, grabbed hold of Fletcher's hand, and helped her to her feet. "Next time try to avoid nearly being killed by stampeding venison, okay?"

"Okay," Fletcher whispered, still caught in a daze.

"Nice shot!" exclaimed Charlie as she and a few of the other YOR members jogged toward the downed moose. She glanced over at Fletcher's gore-soaked face. "Are you okay?"

"I—" Fletcher wheezed. "I think so."

Sparrow laughed at Fletcher's breathlessness. "Now you know what we use the guns for."

If she had been in her right mind, Fletcher would have replied with a string of obscenities. Instead, she frowned. Then, after a long beat, "That's excellent. I very much appreciate the horrifying introduction to the effects of ballistic trauma on living tissue. When can I go home?"

"Have you changed your mind about joining us because we hunt our own meat?" Peter asked. "We don't go to the markets often. Hunting and planting our own produce are the easiest ways to avoid attention."

"No, I haven't changed my mind. It's just . . . I've never seen anything killed before. It's sad. I know it's a survival of the fittest kind of thing, but that doesn't make me feel any better about it."

Sparrow handed her rifle to Peter, then raised her palms to the sky. "It was you or the moose. Personally, I'd be glad it was the moose."

"I have to be glad it was the moose, don't I?" Even though the shock of the event had yet to dissipate, Fletcher was grateful to still be breathing. She couldn't help considering that Sparrow had saved her life three times in less than twenty-four hours. That she needed to be saved so often made her feel pathetic. She resolved to toughen up, or at the very least, work on becoming less of a damsel in distress.

She plucked a spongy chunk of the dead animal's brain from her loose blonde hair. "Being drenched in blood was not the way I had planned to start my day."

Sparrow slung her arm round Fletcher's shoulders. "Let's leave the boys to deal with the meat and get you cleaned up. Afterward, Charlie and I will take you back to Boston."

Riding in the back of a van with blacked-out windows felt different in the light of day. It seemed less ominous, less intimidating. Yet she was more uneasy than she had been when she thought she had been kidnapped. This time she was going home, but she knew she would not be there for very long. In less than a week, she would become detached from everything and everyone she knew. She found it difficult to imagine and was overcome by sadness when she tried imagining it. She wasn't sure who she'd miss most, her father or Jonah. Her father. She'd wanted space from him lately, as was normal for a young woman. And if she could have, she would have moved into her own apartment. But leaving him like this was so final. Permanent. Irrevocable.

"We should hit the city limits in five," called Charlie from behind the steering wheel.

Sparrow twisted around in her seat and shot a look of understanding at Fletcher. "I know it isn't going to be easy for you to up and vanish, but there's always a chance our circumstances may change. Try to hold on to that; don't think of it as a 'goodbye,' which hurts too much. Think of it as an 'I'll see you again someday.'"

"It's different for me, though."

"How so?"

"When you left home to join YOR, you took your brother with you. Your parents still had each other. I'm all my dad has. And Jonah—it's so hard for his mom and dad to see him the way he is that they don't visit him often. I'm worried about my dad and Jonah being on their own, no one around to take care of them."

"Jonah has an entire hospital staff to take care of him. I know that isn't the same as family, but he's at Alcedonia in the first place because his family wasn't able to provide him with the level of help he needs."

"But my father. His whole life has revolved around taking care of me," Fletcher admitted. "I don't think he'll know what to do with himself if I'm not around."

"He'll figure it out, just like he would've had to figure it out if you were lost to Reclamation. But with us you won't be lost; you'll just be someplace else."

"Hmm. That was profound."

Sparrow was caught off guard by Fletcher's earnestness and blushed.

"We're here," Charlie interrupted. She brought the van to a stop at the far end of Fletcher's block and engaged the parking brake.

"This is your stop," said Sparrow. "Remember, follow your normal routine, try not to act suspicious and tell *no one* that you're leaving. We'll meet you Friday at five o'clock. You'll have ten minutes to get here before we assume you've changed your mind and hightail it back to the safe house without you. Clear?"

"Crystal," Fletcher confirmed.

"Okay then. We'll see you Friday."

Fletcher threw open the door, stepped out onto the broken pavement, then slid the door closed again. She watched the van drive off until it was nothing more than a sable speck on the gray horizon.

"Dad, I'm home," Fletcher hollered as she entered the apartment. He wasn't in his usual Sunday afternoon spot on the old blue couch in front of the window, where he'd sit reading his antique books by the light of the sun. She wandered through the house, stopping to peer into her father's room. "Dad?" She tried again, but he was nowhere to be found. *Where could he be?*

She rushed through the narrow hallway to the kitchen. On the old glass table, she found her father's government employee-issued HoloPod projecting a note into the air.

Fletcher,

Had some business to tend to. Don't even
think about leaving this house again until
we've had a chance to discuss the stunt you
pulled. You may be twenty-two, but you still
live in my house, which means you still have
to clear it with me if you're going to stay
out all night. Before you ask, NO, I will NOT
accept "but I'm up for Reclamation and want

to raise all the hell I can before it's too late"
as an excuse for anything. Park your behind
on the couch and keep it there till I get home.
Shouldn't be but a little while.

Love,
Dad

Fletcher heaved a sigh. There were plenty of things she was going to miss about her father, but HoloNotes detailing how much trouble she was in were not among said things. She stumbled over to the couch, folded her hands in her lap, and waited for Jericho to arrive home.

"I'm sorry," she said the instant her father strolled through the door. She did not even wait for him to acknowledge that she was there, sitting on the couch as she was told to. For a moment she assumed he was angry. She prepared herself for him to be. Instead, he stood, jaw slack, staring at her. It was as though he had expected to never see her again, as if she was an impossible specter returned from the grave.

Jericho threaded his fingers through his straw-colored beard. "Have you got a hug for an old man?"

"Don't I always?" Fletcher hopped off the couch and fell into his arms.

Jericho squeezed her. "You'll never be too grown up for me to worry about you."

"I know." Fletcher closed her eyes, relishing the security of her father's embrace.

chapter seven

THE BUILDING THAT HOUSED the Boston branch of the Northern Territories Public Library was a testament to a civilization long dead, a monument that had managed to withstand two and a half centuries' worth of pummeling at the hands of Mother Nature and the bloodiest war in American history. Its white brick façade, auburn-shingled roof, coffered arch ceilings, and marble interior surfaces were out of place among the rest of the city's structures—especially those on Boylston Street, which were assembled of gray slabs of decaying concrete, crumbling bricks, sheets of broken, begrimed glass, and the mud-colored mortar that held it all together.

Fletcher used to love the old library. She had fallen in love with it at first sight, on a class trip in primary school. For years before working there she spent as much time in the building as she could. Sometimes in the spring or summer, when the library was devoid of patrons, she would sneak out into its enclosed rear courtyard, where she'd sit and stare at the daffodils and daisies sprouting along the edges of the green patches of grass, or lose herself in the trickling fountain. When she was young and had first discovered the piazza, she didn't understand why The Government bothered to keep it so manicured, so full of beauty and color. But as she grew older, she came to realize that all public parks were kept in immaculate condition, blooming with life, for a singular purpose. As the inscription above the doors of the Alcedonia Institute proclaimed: *Where there is life, there is hope.* Hope was all her people had—hope that perhaps one day things would get better somehow. Hope was the only thing standing between Vaulters and the sensible alternative of death by suicide.

The day Fletcher had grasped the true function of the building and its scenic square, the purpose of the absolute awe it inspired with its fine-detailed loveliness, was the day a black shadow was cast over her heart. Of course it would be beautiful. Something had to be. She was sure that no other building in the world was quite as resplendent because no place on Earth could possibly be as bleak as The Vault.

She hated the library now. More often than not, she felt trapped by it. Still, she drank in the normalcy of work over her first few days back, bathed in the familiarity of menial tasks. But by late afternoon on Thursday the immediacy of her withdrawal from society had crept up on her. She knew she only had to survive one last day in this world that was so oblivious to anything grander than its accepted misery. She still had so much left to do before YOR returned to save her from the nightmare of Reclamation. She had spent the last few nights with her friends from school and the library. That night she planned to see Jonah.

At a quarter of seven, Fletcher and the rest of the staff prepared to shutter the library for the night. She began with her usual rounds through the stacks, clearing out the straggling patrons who remained and turning off the emeralite lamps atop the reading room tables.

She was alone in the upper tier, returning digibook cards to their proper shelves, when she heard the familiar whoosh of the main doors flying open. She had gotten so used to hearing the automated sliding doors open and close as people left the building that the sound scarcely registered in her mind. She peered across the sweeping walkway, fixed her eyes on the vintage analog clock fastened to the far wall; its face read twenty minutes past. The last patron had cleared out fifteen minutes earlier. She leaned over the balcony and glanced down at the front desk, knowing that if someone had entered the library, they would have to pass by it. No one did.

The atmosphere shifted, the same way the air always thickened a split second before lightning struck the earth. She remained motionless for a few more seconds, trying to shake the feeling that something awful was about to happen. The sound of footsteps hammering against the atrium's marble floor interrupted the stillness.

"Hello? Grier? Remy? Brian? Will somebody please answer me?" She pitched farther over the balcony and waited for a response.

A pretty, raven-haired young woman of about Fletcher's age stepped out from between two towering shelves to the right of the lobby. She pushed her bangs out of her face and squinted up at Fletcher. "Sorry, did you call me?"

Fletcher's angst deflated to relief. "Grier, what took you so long to—"

And then Fletcher heard the brisk clacking of hard-soled shoes striking tile before she caught sight of two men in suits rushing toward Grier.

Stunned in place, she watched as fear bloomed in her friend's eyes. As far away as Fletcher was, she'd swear she was able to see Grier's pupils dilate. The taller man, with silver hair seized fistfuls of Grier's curls, and something clicked inside Fletcher's head. She knew, as surely as she knew that the sun set in the west, that this was it—the only fight-or-flight moment of her life of any real consequence. She could stand by as yet another of her good, honest, hard-working friends fell into the clutches of The Government. Grier would likely be lost indefinitely—her mind broken, her intelligence stripped away—but no one could or would blame Fletcher for that. Nonetheless, Fletcher knew that if she did nothing or, worse, fled in fear, she would forever hate herself for her cowardice.

Fletcher had once read an article about a notion of courage unique to those who had witnessed acts of terror. Written over a century ago, the article depicted the aftermath of a gruesome attack on an annual event called The Boston Marathon. The people of her city had responded to that experience with resilience, their constitutions banding them together in a time of unspeakable horror. "With the deepest affection for our city and our country, we stand united for liberty and justice," the article read. "We are Americans. We are Patriots. And above all, we are strong." What Fletcher needed right at that moment as she watched her friend struggle for her life was that type of strength—the kind of courage a person could only discover by reaching deep inside where, against all odds, they would find the nerve to stand up for what they believed in.

Be that kind of strong.

"Grier!" As the name tore from her throat, she sprang into action, racing down the staircase, her fists at the ready to swing.

The Agents had Grier in a vise grip, one with his arms wrapped around her torso and the other with his arms wrapped around her legs. They hoisted her off the ground and moved in tandem toward the exit.

"Leave her alone, you bastards!" Fletcher screamed. She hurled her body at the Agent holding Grier's feet, knocking him into a glass bookshelf and sending both crashing to the ground. The bookshelf shattered, pieces of it tinkling down around the Agent. He wailed in agony as his shoulder crunched against the marble and shards of glass tore open his palms as they met the floor.

Fury and hatred seethed through her veins, having been left to simmer long beyond their boiling points. Her animosity had bubbled up to the surface and was impossible to contain.

She leapt atop the wounded Agent in a fit of unbridled anger, poured all of her stockpiled rage down on him like the wrath of a vengeful god. "You son of a bitch!" she roared as she pounded on the Agent's body. Over and over again, her knuckles made contact with his ribs, his sternum, his face.

The Agent attempted to push himself to his feet. Every time he moved, Fletcher struck him down, bludgeoning him with blow after vicious blow. She felt his muscles rippling beneath his flesh. And finally, she felt the bridge of his nose snap.

Fletcher glanced down at her hands and saw that they were soaked with the Agent's warm, red blood. Though her nature dictated that she should have felt some semblance of regret for inflicting such damage on a person, the only sensation that came to her was elation. She smiled to herself at the thought of continuing to strike the man until he was nothing but a bloody, bloated sack of meat.

"Get her off of me, Flynn!" the downed Agent howled to his partner between Fletcher's thwacks.

Flynn. It would be him. Fletcher abandoned her assault on Flynn's partner and scuttled upright. From the corner of her vision, she saw Flynn release his hold on Grier. Grier began to dash toward Fletcher even before her feet had hit the floor. Fletcher thrust her arms out to her friend, and that was when she remembered the tiny, metallic ball Sparrow had removed from the soft, antecubital space opposite her right elbow: the tracker. *Oh, dammit!* If Grier had one, she didn't have a prayer of escaping. Fletcher took Grier's right arm into her hand and pressed her thumb against the flesh of Grier's inner elbow. *There!* She felt a hard, round object beneath her skin where nothing hard or round should be. *We all have them.* In that moment, everything she had learned about YOR was confirmed, as was her determination.

Not dwelling too much on the harm it could cause Grier—

trauma, infection—Fletcher bent down and grabbed the smoothest, sturdiest sliver of glass she could find. She snapped upright and touched the edge of the glass to Grier's skin.

"What are you—" Grier began.

"Trust me. It's the only chance you have," Fletcher interrupted. She made a clean, straight slice across her friend's forearm. "I am so sorry," she said as she dropped the shard and plunged the tips of her thumb and forefinger into the open wound. Grier cried out in pain as Fletcher plucked the tracker from her arm. She threw the little ball on the floor and crushed it beneath the sole of her shoe. "Now get the hell out of here! Don't go home. You won't be safe there."

Though blood dribbled from the slit in her arm, Grier did not hesitate. She turned heel and bolted for the sliding doors.

In the time it took to find and remove the tracker in Grier's arm, Flynn had helped his flailing partner—who had slipped repeatedly on slick, bloody glass—to his feet, and handed him a handkerchief. "Clean yourself up, you utter disgrace, and go after the girl." He watched Grier as she fled. "I'll deal with this one."

Once his partner had limped through the exit, Flynn fixed his fierce gray eyes on Fletcher.

Fletcher saw the anger in him—or, more accurately, she felt it. Externally, he was cool and collected, but inside he was fuming. *What the hell am I doing?* she asked herself. I just thrashed a Reclamation Agent. This cannot end well. Swallowing her trepidation, Fletcher squared her shoulders and bent her knees, bracing herself.

To her surprise, Flynn did not attack. Instead, he seemed content to look her over head to toe. His forehead crinkled as his lips peeled back to reveal a grand, toothy grin.

Fletcher thought there was something unnatural about Flynn's smirk, something heinous and foul. He looked like a predator about to pounce on cornered prey.

"Well, well, aren't *you* the dark horse?" he said.

A mixture of ire and dread quaked through Fletcher's bones. She shivered at the vileness of the man's voice, but presented a front of tenacity. "You'd be surprised what a person is capable of when they hate someone as much as I hate you."

"Flynn, come in. Over." The tinny audio of a soundwave ended the moment's unease.

"Go for Flynn," the Agent spoke into the air as though the ether itself were his transmitter.

"Subject apprehended. Over."

"Copy that. Over and out." Flynn's grin widened, his eyes gleaming with pleasure. "All that effort for nothing, eh, dark horse? Pity you couldn't help your friend. Don't worry, though. I'll be back for you in a few weeks."

The anger drained out of Fletcher, replaced by a resounding gloom. She would not give Flynn the gratification of seeing her spirit break, however. "I'll be waiting for you with bated breath."

"Hurry home now, little girl," Flynn declared as he retreated.

Fletcher looked daggers at his back until he disappeared from her sight. Her mind snapped back to the day in the forest when Sparrow had killed the moose—the surprise and the sorrow she had felt in that moment, watching the life hemorrhage out of the creature. She had never wished to inflict that kind of pain on any living thing until this very second. Flynn was the Agent who had come for Jonah. Fletcher's father had told her that he was also the Agent who had come for her mother all those years ago. He would love nothing more than to be the one to take her away, too.

It would be a privilege to watch that man die.

She resolved right then to murder Flynn someday, and knew, at least in that moment, that she was capable of doing it. His death would not be quick. She would cut his face from temple to chin in honor of Killian's scar, burn his flesh to mirror the marks on Jonah.

Jonah! Her battering of an Agent had likely put Jonah in

grave danger. A thousand Agents could be descending on his hospital room at that very moment! Or . . . what if they chose to target her father instead? *He's strong, but he can't fend off an army.*

Dread made itself at home in her mind. She had to warn her father, tell him about what she'd done. She also had to check on Jonah. The problem was she couldn't be in two places at once. She paused to breathe and analyze the situation. The Alcedonia Institute had private security guards, all Vaulters, some of them armed in case any Berserkers became too dangerous to handle. Being Government employees, they would obey whatever orders were issued to them. At the same time, targeting an Institute the size of Alcedonia would be a nightmare for the BOE. Agents couldn't storm into a fully staffed hospital and haul away a defenseless, drugged-up boy without cause: that would be too harsh, even for them. And people would hear about it. She decided that if she oversaw Government actions, she would make sure revenge was enacted discreetly to avoid the prospect of the locals acting up.

Flynn's departing words: "Hurry home now, little girl."

Shit. Dad . . . She broke into a frenzied sprint.

The front door of her apartment had been knocked off its hinges. The candles were lit, and their glow streamed unobstructed through the doorframe.

She hurried through the short foyer, tripping over the splintered remains of what used to be a door and scattered pages from her father's torn-up books and other personal belongings that had been destroyed.

"Dad!" She searched for Jericho in every room. He had disappeared without a trace, not a HoloNote left behind.

"No! Dad, no! Please!" she yelled, frustrated and frightened, until her lungs tingled from hollowness. She collapsed backward into the kitchen wall and slithered down to the floor. Not knowing what else to do, she pulled her knees to her chest. *I killed my father.* The thought played on a loop in her mind. Her willpower vanquished, and a flood of tears assailed her cheeks, her lips, her chin.

I killed my father.

Long skinny fingers wrapped around Fletcher's shoulders. The hands they belonged to shook her hard. Someone was kneeling in front of her, speaking words she could not understand. She strained to concentrate on the sounds, on whoever was making them, but the whole universe was out of focus—skewed and hazy, like a dozen flash bangs and smoke grenades had detonated inside her skull.

"Your hands. Fletcher, what happened to your hands? There's blood—"

Fletcher recognized Mrs. Quinn as the woman took hold of her blood-caked hands. The balmy sensation of flesh-on-flesh was the catalyst that caused the blurred edges of the world to sharpen into something identifiable.

"I killed my father," Fletcher whimpered. It was the only phrase she could muster, and it was the most nauseating thing she had ever said. Her gut quivered. She lurched away from Jonah's mother on all fours and upchucked onto the kitchen floor.

Mrs. Quinn rubbed Fletcher's back until she was through being sick. "No, sweetheart, you didn't kill your father."

Fletcher sat down again, cross-legged with her back against the wall. "Yes, I did." An account of the evening rushed out of her in a single breath, an automated response to the trauma of it all. "Reclamation Agents came to the library. They tried to take my friend. I attacked one of them. I beat him till he bled. So they came here and took my father. If he isn't dead already, he will be soon."

Mrs. Quinn's eyes widened with shock, and then, as only a mother could, she softened her gaze. Her voice was tender as she spoke: "No, Fletcher, the Agents would be responsible for that. Honey, you did a very brave thing by trying to help your friend. Wherever your father is, he would be proud of you."

"He can't be proud of me if he's dead!"

"You don't know that he is." Mrs. Quinn smoothed Fletcher's messy blonde locks away from her eyes. "I don't think they'll kill him. It's more likely they'll keep him for trade. If you were brave enough to engage them in a fight when it wasn't self-defense, they probably think you'd be brave enough to try to skip out on Reclamation. I reckon they'll hold him until they come back for you, and when they find you here, they'll leave him be."

"Trade? My father for me. His life for mine." *My dad is their hostage*, she thought. *Now I can't leave.*

Mrs. Quinn's face soured into a pained grimace. She nodded lightly, as though even hinting at the word *yes* would hurt her beyond quantification.

Fletcher wiped the tears from her cheeks with the back of her palm. "That is a thousand times more vicious than any beating I could have doled out."

Mrs. Quinn exhaled a steady breath. "Fletcher, to be honest I'm not sure your father was here when the Agents showed up. We heard the ruckus from next door. The Agents knocked and knocked but got no response. After a while I guess they ran out of patience because we heard them break down the door. We couldn't make out their conversations, but they didn't sound happy."

"I'm sorry?" A million emotions wreaked havoc on Fletcher's senses upon hearing Mrs. Quinn admit that neither she nor her husband had tried to help Jericho in any way. Among said emotions were outrage, sorrow, and disbelief, but the one that

most hit home was the crushing sense of betrayal. Her father had been the Quinns' neighbor and friend longer than Fletcher had been alive . . . So, what was their excuse? What was anyone's excuse for such spinelessness? "You mean to tell me you heard the whole thing and you did nothing about it?"

"Oh, sweetheart. You're so young. In so many ways that makes you immune to fear. I don't expect you to understand." Fletcher could see the pity in Mrs. Quinn's eyes. It had nothing to do with being remorseful for not lifting a finger to help Jericho. No, she pitied Fletcher because she thought her incapable of grasping the concept of "doing whatever it takes" to stay alive. That only served to flare Fletcher's resentment even more.

"Yes, I do understand! I understand that every person in this country values their own life above anyone else's. I understand that our humanity is on the brink of extinction! I understand we've forgotten that we're all connected. If a single innocent person is dragged out of their home and tortured or killed because The Government knows it can get away with it, we're all at risk. Don't you see? If it happened to my father, what makes you think it couldn't happen to you? When will everyone realize that we've turned the other cheek so many times we've run out of cheeks to turn?"

"Courage—true courage, the kind a person is born with— is uncommon. I'm sorry to say I don't possess it," Mrs. Quinn murmured. "But you do, Fletcher. You have a boldness about you most people don't. I wish I had a quarter of the grit you have in your heart."

"There isn't any grit in my heart, Mrs. Quinn. I'm just sick of the way we're treated—like we don't count, like we're subhuman." Fletcher pushed herself to her feet. "If you're right that my father wasn't here when the Agents showed up, that means he could still be out there somewhere. If you'll please excuse me, I'm going to clean this place up and wait to see if he comes home."

"I hope he does show up." Mrs. Quinn gave Fletcher's hands a gentle touch before making her way toward the exit.

After Mrs. Quinn had gone and Fletcher's wits had returned to her, she scrutinized her palms in the candlelight. She scowled in disgust at the sight of the Agent's dried blood, both because it had once run through the veins of a vile human being capable of doing despicable things to people whose only crime was being poor, but more so because she had been the one to draw it from him. Didn't that, by equation, make her just as wicked as him? Causing pain and suffering was not exclusive to the BOE and their Reclamation Agents; she was capable of it, too. All people were, given the right circumstances. Fletcher never wanted to—never dreamed she would be able to—beat a person half to death, yet she had. For Grier, she told herself. Somehow, that wasn't enough. She could easily abhor the Agents, loathe them in every corner of her consciousness, because their work and their beliefs were loathsome, but being able to defend herself and others against them without feeling guilty afterward was something she was going to have to learn to do. Becoming a member of YOR meant she had to be ready and willing to fight.

Some of this blood belongs to Grier. She remembered removing her friend's tracker and felt an overpowering need to rid her skin of the gore. She hurried across the kitchen to the sink, twisted on the tap. Cool water ran over her hands as she scrubbed them clean—every crevice, every fold, beneath her fingernails and around her cuticles. She watched the rose-colored water spiral down the drain. With all traces of the sanguine fluid gone, she could see that her knuckles were swollen and beginning to bruise. Come morning, varying shades of violet would replace their natural pallor. "Sometimes you have to draw blood. They make you," Fletcher said aloud. Carrying the frustration of knowing who she would have to become, of the things she would have to be prepared to do, she set to work tidying the disaster the Agents had left for her.

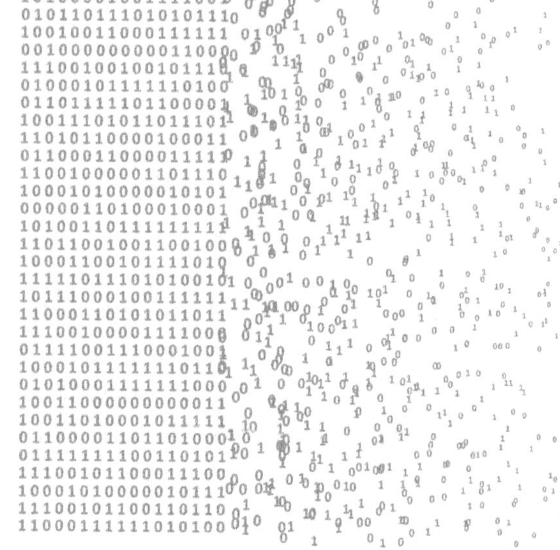

chapter eight

HER ANIMOSITY FOR THE Agents grew exponentially with every piece of fractured wood, every tattered sliver of yellowed paper she swept into the dustpan. Fletcher was sure that if Mrs. Quinn had been around to watch her wield the broom, she would have seen that she was not fueled by courage, that there wasn't any "grit" in her heart. Rather, she would have recognized that Fletcher ran on equal parts petulance and virulence. And why shouldn't she? Reclamation Agents were a scourge to her people, an ever-present thorn in the side of every Vaulter. They exemplified a tyrannical Government that ruled its peasant caste with diabolical terror tactics and forced debt.

Fletcher was reminded of the fact that she had nothing, owned nothing, as she searched the apartment for something that could serve as a suitable makeshift door. The best she was able to find was a moth-eaten blanket, which she tacked to the top of the doorframe.

It was midnight by the time she had managed to get the house back into order. There had been no sign of her father. By then, her hope that he was safe somewhere had all but evaporated. She had no idea where he could be, or what she should do next. Exhausted from being sick with worry, she crawled onto the couch, curled into a fetal position and fell into a restless slumber.

Fletcher woke as dawn approached, the sun beginning to crest above the horizon. The living room remained engulfed in darkness, and she could hardly make out the tops of her feet, much less see to the far side of the room. Even so, she knew she was not alone in the apartment. The carpet near the end of the hallway rustled, the way carpet sometimes did when a person tiptoed across it.

It wasn't her father advancing toward her, that much Fletcher was sure of. This person was much lighter on their feet than her father could ever be. Despite realizing that there was an intruder in her home, she was not frightened. If it had been an Agent, she would have felt it right away. The malevolence they exuded was unmistakable, like a pheromone only they possessed. Fletcher had a strange sort of sixth sense for it and could always tell when one of them was close.

She leapt up and jerked the hood of her overused gray sweatshirt off her head. "I know you're there," she called out through the shadows to the intruder. "You're not as stealthy as you think you are."

"I'm sorry. You don't have a door to knock on."

It wasn't so much the voice she recognized as it was the attitude. "Sparrow?"

Sparrow strode into the burgeoning sunlight and removed the cowl of her paltry leather jacket from her head so Fletcher could look upon her face. "Get your things. We have to go."

"I can't go anywhere. I have to find out what happened to my father. If the Agents have him—"

"They don't," Sparrow said.

"How could you know that?"

"No time for a Q and A." She reached out through the last bits of dark, took Fletcher's hand, and threaded their fingers together. Fletcher balked at the contact, but did not break it. Sparrow's skin was icy to the touch. She must have spent the night outside. Why would she do that? *Unless . . . was she guarding me?*

"You saw what happened here last night, didn't you?"

Sparrow did not confirm it with words. Instead, her face flushed and her palms were clammy. She stared into Fletcher's eyes, fixing her in a trance. Fletcher could sense, in that moment, that Sparrow contemplated spilling every little secret she had, but the inkling was ephemeral. Rather than give Fletcher the answers she sought, Sparrow said, "Listen to me, dammit. I have to get you out of here."

"No." Fletcher ripped her hand from Sparrow's grasp and turned her back to her. "Maybe the Agents didn't catch my father last night, but who's to say they won't come back for him?"

"You don't even know what kind of trouble you're in," Sparrow barked. She grabbed Fletcher by the forearm and spun her around so that they were standing face to face again. "Your father isn't in danger, okay? It's you they want. They're pissed, and they'll be coming for you soon." Sparrow halted to take a breath, and with it her annoyance withered, giving way to desperation. "Please, Fletcher, I swear I'll explain everything to you." Her voice quivered. "Just come with me."

Fletcher saw the glimmer of desperation in Sparrow's eyes. She was astonished to witness her demeanor change so abruptly. But what she found even more astonishing was the realization that Sparrow no longer considered her an assignment. She did not want to be Fletcher's Handler, either. Rather, she appeared to want to be her sentinel, the person who protected her from the evils of the world—from the Agents and the government that sought to destroy her. All Fletcher had to do was acquiesce to it. "Fine," she submitted. "Give me a minute to pack."

Sparrow nodded. "I'll give you two."

After stuffing a scruffy khaki messenger bag to the brim with clothing, Fletcher shouldered the pack and the women headed out. Sparrow operated on paranoiac high alert, her feral instincts in overdrive. She kept a vigilant watch on their surroundings as they walked side by side, block after block. To Fletcher, it looked like an ordinary weekday. The streets teemed with ashen-faced peons heading to their thankless jobs: factories, work yards, whatever sweatshop may have offered them a nominal paycheck. There was not a single Agent or suspect vehicle in sight. She thought it was as good a time as any to tell Sparrow they had to make a stop before they fled the city. "There's something I need to do before we leave town."

"Uh huh, and what is that?"

"I have to say goodbye to Jonah. I didn't get the chance to say it to my dad, and I don't want the same thing to happen with him."

"Absolutely not," Sparrow stressed. "I'm sorry. That isn't a possibility. You are way too hot right now. I'm not taking any chances."

"I'm not asking you to take any chances. I'm asking you to wait at the van with the others while I go see my best friend for what might be the last time ever."

"I'm on my own. And I don't have the van," Sparrow confessed. "We're walking to the city limits. There's an abandoned mill on the river where I stashed a motorbike. I couldn't ride it into the city because it's not street legal, but it's fast. Fast was the best option."

"You came here alone?" Fletcher stopped walking to frown at Sparrow. "Are you out of your mind? What if you needed backup or whatever? What if you encountered—"

"It was too much to ask of anyone else, to stick their neck out for you," Sparrow murmured. "*I'm* your Handler. *I* made the promise to keep you safe. It was a calculated risk coming for you."

"Isn't every move YOR makes a calculated risk?"

"Yes, but this mission was particularly risky."

"Why?" Fletcher eyed her. There was something Sparrow wasn't telling her. She deduced it was something substantial from Sparrow's hesitation to answer. "You swore you'd explain everything to me. Explain why this 'mission' was so perilous."

"Yesterday," Sparrow said, unable to look Fletcher in the eye, "we found out the Agents were going to seize Grier at the library. We knew you would be there. I was afraid that if you had to watch it happen, you'd do something bordering on insane."

They knew about Grier yet did nothing to help her. It took Fletcher's brain longer than it should have to process that piece of information, but when it did sink in, she felt the urge to shriek at the top of her voice. "What?" she howled, unconcerned that her volume might garner unwanted attention. "You people are supposed to be The Vault's last, best hope! But for all the rhetoric you spew, you sure don't hesitate to sit on your hands when it matters most!" Resentment seized hold of her then. She felt disgusted with YOR and with herself for believing in something that was so obviously too good to be true. Without another word, she tightened the strap of the messenger bag across her chest and bolted for the closest side street. She had no idea where she was heading. She only knew the impulse to take off was too strong to combat.

Not to Fletcher's surprise, Sparrow chased after her. She heard the pitter-patter of Sparrow's boots smacking concrete as she gained ground. Fletcher was determined to outrun her. She accepted the challenge and pushed herself harder and harder still. All she wanted was to get beyond Sparrow's reach, to leave the woman in her dust. She thought it might work out that way, too, but before long Sparrow had overcome her.

Fletcher struggled to take in oxygen as the other woman slipped into a backward sprint and ogled her from a few feet ahead.

"I can do this all day," Sparrow articulated easily. "Can you?"

What were the odds that she could keep up with her, prepared for long distance running as any fugitive was likely to be? Her panting and the weight of her hefty knapsack told Fletcher it was impossible, yet she was ready to die trying. "A lot of use you gutless wonders are," she puffed.

Sparrow hit a standstill and threw her arms into the air. Fletcher assumed she would try to block her path. Instead, she allowed Fletcher to thunder past her. "I got to your father before the Agents did!" she hollered at Fletcher's back. "That's how I know they didn't catch him."

Fletcher slowed to a halt, doubling over, breathless.

Sparrow sauntered up beside her, reached around her hunched frame and palmed her shoulders. She pawed at the strap of the messenger bag, but Fletcher was hesitant to let her relieve its burden. "Yes, I've been keeping tabs on you. I watched through one of the library windows as you attacked that Agent, and I thought the same thing you did—that they would go after your father." Sparrow lifted her sleeve and revealed a flat, white wristband to Fletcher. "We call this a CommBand. Philip invented it. It transmits text messages back to the safe house over a secure frequency. We're only supposed to use them in emergency situations. There's nothing in our policy that covers what to do when one of our assignments flies into a fit of rage and beats the hell out of an Agent. It's never happened before, but I figured it qualified as an emergency, so I contacted the Visitor's Center. Søren gave the go-ahead, and we set up an extraction point where they could pick up your father; then I hauled over to your place and told him everything. He packed

some things and left a few minutes before the Agents arrived . . .
Now, give me the damn bag," Sparrow fizzed through clenched
teeth. Fletcher handed the obnoxious thing over. "Stand up and
put your hands on your head," Sparrow continued. "It'll be easier
for you to catch your breath that way."

"Where is he?" Fletcher muttered once she could breathe
again.

"They took him to a secondary safe house. I don't know where
for security reasons, but he's being given the royal treatment—a
new ID, set-up in The South. He'll be on a train out of The Vault
by nightfall."

"He's safe? You're sure."

"I wouldn't say it if I was less than sure." Sparrow took hold
of Fletcher's shoulders, looked deep into her hazel eyes and said,
"I promise you he will be fine."

Fletcher searched the brunette for any signs of uncertainty
or deceit. Seeing none, a wave of relief washed over her, and with
it came gratitude. Although she had no idea where her father
was or where he would end up, she knew he would be all right.
Sparrow had protected him from the Agents' wrath with blatant
disregard for her own welfare. She'd acted boldly, selflessly, and
Fletcher could not help but be amazed by that. "Thank you,"
she said, then kicked herself for how insufficient those two
words were. She thought she should embrace Sparrow. It made
sense. Throwing her arms around the woman felt like a much
more sincere way of conveying her gratefulness, but it was an
impulse she could not submit to. There was still too much to
say, too many details left to unearth, and so she let the notion
pass. "From now on, I want to know everything you know. Start
by telling me the truth about why YOR chose to save me above
Grier, or anyone else."

Sparrow took a glance around. Satisfied that she and
Fletcher had the alleyway to themselves, she began. "We can't
save everyone," she said, sounding doleful. "It just isn't possible.

There are tens of thousands of potential Reclaimees to every one member of YOR, and that's only in the old New England region. The Vault makes up half the country—imagine how many hundreds of thousands more there are in other areas . . . There aren't enough places to hide everyone, enough false identities, enough jobs in The South. I wish we could help every Reclaimee; they're all exceptional in their own ways. You, however, are extraordinary."

"I'm *not*, though. I'm—"

Sparrow cut Fletcher's thought off at its legs. "If you want to know what I know, please be quiet and let me speak."

Fletcher squinted, cross at her tone. "Go on."

"The HiEd Exam doesn't just measure a Vaulter's IQ, or even in which area of study they'll excel. It measures how likely a Vaulter is to oppose the status quo. These Vaulters are predisposed to rebellion. It's something inside them, something about the way their brains work, that sets them apart from the rest of us. The BOE categorizes these people as STs, 'Significant Threats,' and notes it in their charts. STs are rare, maybe one in ten thousand, and as far as The Government is concerned they "must" be removed from society at any cost.

Do you understand? The Knowledge Reclamation Process isn't only a punishment for defaulting on student loans. It's a convenient method of culling the population, of weeding out the truly unique. We can't afford to let that happen. STs are more important to our cause, to Head Office's long game—whatever that may be, because I honestly do not know—than anyone else. Getting them away from The Government's reach is priority one for YOR. And your test results were—" Sparrow inhaled as her ice-blue eyes met the bright hazel of Fletcher's. "Fletcher, you're the highest-scoring ST the BOE has ever encountered."

"What?" Fletcher asked, feeling suddenly panicked. Again, she lost her breath, but this time it was as though someone had reached into her body, taken her lungs into their hands, and clamped their fists around them. *I'm a Significant Threat? Little nobody me, with my useless degree in US History? I've spent my entire life with my nose buried in digibooks! I work in a library, for crying out loud! When was the last time anyone found a librarian threatening?* Her muscles went tense with fright. Her toes curled in her ratty sneakers and her hands trembled uncontrollably. It was too much. Her shoulders weren't strong enough to carry so heavy a burden. "Someone must have gotten it wrong."

Sparrow sighed. "No one got it wrong. We have a copy of your chart at the Visitor's Center. I'll ask Philip to pull up the hologram if you need to see it for yourself to believe it."

Fletcher ached to disagree. "But I'm just a girl. All I'm armed with is a sizable vocabulary and poor impulse control. I don't even have enough good sense to know when I should be petrified, thus explaining my outrageous attack on an Agent, hello!"

"I can't pretend to know what makes you who you are, what sets you apart from the rest of us, but the BOE sure as hell is afraid of you, and I think they have every reason to be." Sparrow touched Fletcher's bicep, rubbed her thumb over the material of her sweatshirt. "I'm sorry I didn't tell you all of this sooner. The apprehension you're feeling now? I really didn't want to be the cause of that."

Fletcher, soothed by Sparrow's touch, exhaled. Now was not the time or the place to fall to pieces. Her emotions had been running too high since the events of the prior night. She knew that she had to rein them in, or else she would go on making foolish decisions.

She bit her lip, stealing a few silent seconds to collect herself. As rationality returned to her, her mind combed over the details of Sparrow's story. "You said that the BOE records all this information in our charts. Did Jonah meet your sacred ST criteria?"

Sparrow removed her hand from Fletcher's arm before

answering the question. "No, he didn't."

"Why was YOR interested in helping him in the first place?"

"The same reason we're helping your father, to earn your trust. Head Office figured if we could help Jonah, you'd be more apt to trust us. They never anticipated that you'd want to join us—not so early on in the fight, without a solid plan detailing your usefulness to the cause. I had a feeling you'd want to stick around, though, after we failed to relocate him, after the Department of Reclamation took him and screwed him up. I knew you wouldn't let them get away with what they did to him, given the opportunity for payback."

"Bullshit." Fletcher rolled her eyes. "Was that written in my exam results somewhere, too?"

Sparrow hesitated, then thought better of it. "We've been watching you for a while. We know your habits, your strengths and weaknesses. Jonah is one of your weaknesses. It was obvious—to me, anyway—that you really loved him, maybe more than you realized." She broke off and shuffled in place. "What wouldn't we do for the people we love?"

Fletcher was taken aback. That was the first time anyone had ever called her out on it—the fact that her feelings for Jonah may have been different than she had led everyone to believe. In truth, she had considered the possibility of it herself. For a while, when they were younger, she thought she could grow to love him the way a girl was supposed to love a boy, but she refused to nurture the seed. Perhaps she was unwilling to taint their friendship with silly girlish swooning. Whatever the reason, it never did pan out. Fletcher had always believed romance a fickle thing, anyway—more fleeting than it was everlasting—and so she gave it little consideration. The illustrious "butterflies in the stomach" phenomenon so often referenced in love stories had never been something she imagined useful. Being in love had never saved anyone from Reclamation or helped them make impossibly short ends meet. Her father and mother had loved each other profoundly and look at them now: alone on the run and dead, respectively. "It isn't like that with him," said Fletcher. "Besides, living in *this* world, I fail to see any value in romance."

"Well, you're free from *this* world—if you still want to be."

"Like I have a choice. If what you're saying is true, then staying here isn't a viable option for me anymore, is it?"

Sparrow shook her head. "Not if you want to prolong your life expectancy, and definitely not if you want to help other Vaulters prolong theirs."

So, these were her options: stay in Boston and wait for death to come calling or escape to relative freedom and try to bring positive change, however small it might be, to The Vault. As worried as Fletcher was for her father and Jonah, she knew she would not be any use to either of them if she were dead. On the other hand, were she to die, she would no longer be a danger to them. The Government would have what it wanted and in turn leave them in peace. *What's so great about life, anyway?* she mused. What's the point of it, to suffer and then depart? The point is to leave a trace, an indelible mark. *I haven't made mine yet.* Even though it would be safer for everyone she cared for if she were to humbly expire, Fletcher did not want to lie down and die. She wanted to go out fighting, maybe making the world, or at least her world, a better place. "Let's go, then."

Fletcher had walked along the Charles River many times, but had never happened upon the watermill Sparrow led her to. It was well hidden behind a patch of overgrown shrubs, and was as outmoded as it was ugly, with an oxidized water wheel attached to the side of a ramshackle wood-shingled building. The sliding barn doors staggered off their hinges as Sparrow pushed them open, revealing her motorbike.

Fletcher had never seen a motorbike up close before. She

did not like the look of it. It had mammoth tires connected to its frame by huge spring coils. The body of the thing was black and burnished but looked flimsy and incapable of supporting the weight of one person, never mind two. She ambled over to the instrument of their escape and ran her hand across it, pushing down now and again to test its sturdiness. Dismayed, she noticed that parts of the machine were not even forged of metal. "This thing is made of plastic," she said.

Sparrow finished securing Fletcher's pack to the rearmost part of the seat with a cargo net, then raised her head. "That thing is called a fender, Ivy League. And so what?"

"So I am not getting on this bike."

Sparrow wandered closer to the center of the bike and pitched her right leg over the cushioned seat. Straddling the beastly contraption like a professional, she smirked at Fletcher. "You won't be sitting on the fender."

Fletcher looked at her straight-faced. "No, but the rest of the bike is attached to the fender. I am not getting on anything that has plastic parts and reaches speeds of who-knows-how-many miles per hour."

"Come on, I know you've got the guts." Again, Sparrow smirked, this time while offering Fletcher her hand.

There was something about Sparrow's earnestness—or something about the way her blue eyes shimmered so strikingly, as if daring Fletcher to live up to her potential—that made Fletcher capitulate to her, however tentatively. She took Sparrow's hand and used it to steady herself as she mounted the bike. "I had better live to regret this, so help me."

"You'll be fine, I guarantee it. Here, put this on." She swiveled back to Fletcher and handed her a nicked-up silver helmet. Fletcher donned it, wobbling her head from side to side. Her long blonde hair, difficult to manage when it wasn't pulled up in a ponytail, spilled out the bottom of the helmet, draping around her shoulders. She needed a moment to adjust to the weight of the headgear and the heaviness of her too-long locks against her neck.

"Where's your helmet?" She flipped the helmet's thick photochromatic visor up and questioned Sparrow.

"On your head. I only have one."

"But—"

Sparrow ran her hands through her long brown ringlets, rolling them into a close-fitting knot at the back of her head and securing it in place with a black elastic band she'd had around her wrist. "I don't want to hear about it. You're wearing the helmet, end of story."

Fletcher huffed and flipped the visor down again. She was frightened by the fact that she had sat on the bike; she was unable to muster the gall to argue. Instead, she watched Sparrow press a small lever on the left side of the steering handles and then force her foot down on another lever near the bike's motor. The engine roared to life. The vibrating chassis shot a tingle up Fletcher's thighs, straight through to her tailbone and up her spine. Out of reflex she clasped Sparrow's shoulders.

"Put your arms around my waist," Sparrow hollered over the deafening sound of the motor.

Fletcher faltered, feeling unsteady both in mind and body. "What? Why?"

Sparrow laughed. She bent her elbows up to take hold of Fletcher's hands. She had to pry the material of her jacket out of her charge's clenched fists. "Fletcher, you have to hold on properly or you're going to fall off."

Falling off the monstrous vehicle did not seem like a pleasant way to die. Fletcher gave in, wrapped her arms around Sparrow's hips, and gripped firmly.

Sparrow rocked forward in the seat, testing the strength of Fletcher's hold. "That's good. Now, listen to me, this is important. I need you to help me steer. When we hit curves in the road or make turns, you have to lean into the curve."

All the blood in Fletcher's circulatory system rushed to her head at once. If she weren't able to lean into the curves, she would be the reason they both went tumbling to early graves. "I . . . I don't think I can do that."

"Yes, you can," Sparrow assured her. "It's not hard. Use my body as a guide. When you feel me move, move with me. We're a team. We'll do it together. Okay?"

Fletcher pressed her chest so tight to Sparrow's back that she could feel the brunette's ribcage rise and fall with every breath she took. Sparrow was even and sturdy, packed full of confidence. It was reassuring, and Fletcher was thankful for it. "Okay."

"Are you ready?"

Not in the slightest. "As ready as I'll ever be."

They rolled down the hidden drive leading toward the road. Once they reached the highway they picked up speed. A back-biting wind battered Fletcher and she shivered, her flimsy hoodie not thick enough to keep her warm. But it was more than just the cold in the air, or the swiftness with which they were traveling that made her quake; it was the knowledge that her life had been forever altered.

As the cityscape in all its drab, broken-down glory blurred past her, she marveled at how the fractured windows of The John Hancock Tower caught the sunlight and twinkled like stars out of place in the daytime sky. Boston was beautiful even in its decay, and while she might never live there again, it would always be her home.

chapter nine

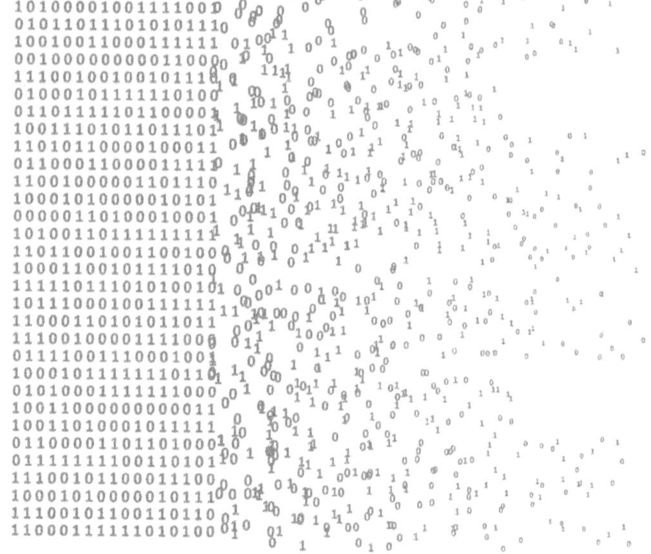

"DID YOU KNOW THAT the United States was three times the size of The UAT?" Fletcher asked absentmindedly as she and Sparrow ventured away from the shack where they had parked the motorbike and toward the place that was to be her new home—the ancient Visitor's Center. "Nothing west of Illinois was salvageable after The Great Plains Catastrophe."

"Of course I knew that. They say everything out west is still so radioactive that it'll be another quarter century before any healthy plants begin to grow."

"I've heard that, too," Fletcher exhaled her vexation. "But did you know the whole thing was an accident? An *accident* killed off half of the US population."

"Come again?" Sparrow's features contorted.

"Our history digibooks teach us that US Revolutionist Forces launched an attack on eight nuclear power plants between Nebraska and California, but that isn't what happened. I suppose someone thought it would be a good idea, since The Great Plains states had the most active Revolutionist forces, to take out their electricity—the one thing that ensured they could communicate with each other. No electrical grid meant no computers, tablets, mobile phones, nothing hi-tech. Fossil fuels had all but gone the way of the dinosaurs once The Government restricted their distribution, solar power was in its infancy and impractical for everyday usage, and they hadn't discovered cold fusion. Ultracapacitors didn't exist yet. Everything ran on low-yield batteries back then so after a while all their tech needed to be plugged in and recharged."

"That's luxurious compared to what most of us up North live with today," Sparrow interjected.

Fletcher nodded. "As I was saying, the US Government bombed the power grids in Region Four of the Nuclear Regulatory Commission Zones, which inadvertently caused major damage to the nuclear reactors. They didn't think it was possible for the reactors to melt down. They were designed to prevent the release of radioactive material, but somebody somewhere screwed up the build, and eight of the twenty reactors from the Heartland to San Diego experienced cataclysmic failure."

Sparrow looked at her, horrified. "How do you—"

"A team of journalists did an investigation before the free press was shut down. They wrote a series of articles about it, laying out all the facts they uncovered. I found copies of the articles in archives buried in the basement of the library."

"You're telling me the United States government exterminated its own people?" Sparrow bent down to pick up a fallen branch from the forest floor. She swung it once, splitting the air with a whoosh. "Sounds about right. Our government has been the bad guy from the beginning. I guess it followed in the footsteps of its predecessor."

"No," Fletcher shook her head. "It was far from perfect, but The US government was by and for the people from its inception. It didn't become the enemy until it suspended the Constitution in an effort to protect itself from its citizens' right of rebellion. We know things became volatile before then, of course, which is why the Second Revolution even began: the growing division between rich and poor, radically dissimilar political principles between the two central parties, plus differences of opinion as to whether The Government was disregarding its own Bill of Rights by imposing the beliefs of one specific religion and limiting free speech and free travel, and the killing blow—a prolonged and deadly pandemic. The last president enacted restrictions, constraining protests and both immigration and expatriation." A snigger left Fletcher's mouth. "It's ironic. In the end it wasn't foreign terrorists or the Revolutionists that destroyed America; America destroyed itself. It expected its military to fight its own civilians to regain order. Much of the military did that, but there were factions that sided with the Revolutionists. Many of the country's police forces did as well."

Sparrow reached a sudden standstill. She squinted at Fletcher, but Fletcher continued. When she realized she was walking alone, she stopped and turned to find Sparrow. Their eyes met, but neither spoke. Fletcher wondered what was running through the woman's mind.

"Your chart was right. You really are too smart for your own good," said Sparrow with an impishness to her voice. She dropped the stick she had been amusing herself with and took a step toward Fletcher, closing the gap between them. "It's captivating," she continued in a near-whisper, "but dangerous."

"If that was your idea of a compliment, you should try harder. I don't want to be 'dangerous' any more than I want to be endangered," Fletcher whispered back, then started for the Visitor's Center again.

"Nice talking to you," Sparrow called at Fletcher's retreating figure, and hurried to catch up before she vanished over a peak in the trail. "By the way, your dad told me to tell you something."

"What?"

"That he loves you. And to mind your Handler."

Fletcher shook her head. "He did not say that last part."

"Oh, but he did. He said, 'I know my daughter. She's a handful. Tell her to mind her Handler.'"

Fletcher smiled to herself. "Okay, maybe he did say it."

"Do you remember which bed is yours?" Sparrow asked, tailing Fletcher into the safe house's bunkroom.

"It's the one with the empty gun rack, right?"

"Huh," Sparrow clucked. "That's right."

Fletcher sought out the cot with the firearm missing from its mount and dropped her bag onto it. She stretched out her arms, then folded them across her chest and turned to face the other woman. "I guess this is home sweet home now."

"Looks like it." Sparrow shot Fletcher a slight sort-of smile. "You can unpack your things if you'd like. There's a cubby in there for you." She motioned to a doorframe at the far end of the bunkroom.

"Alright." Fletcher nodded, picking up her bag once more. She followed Sparrow through the threshold into a small, quiet antechamber. The chamber—illuminated only by the sunlight flowing through a rectangular window in the far wall—smelled of hoary wood. The long, thin hollows carved into both of the room's sidewalls were separated from each other by six-inch-wide timber slats. Most of the cubbies contained clothes hanging on metal hooks and assortments of trinkets sitting atop mantel shelves.

Fletcher paused to consider it all. "You don't get much privacy around here, do you?"

"Not really. You get used to it, though," Sparrow replied. "This one's mine. You can take the empty one next to it, or that one down there." She pointed to a free compartment a few feet away on the opposite wall. It was farther removed from the cubby next to it than any of the others, offering, if nothing else, the illusion of personal space.

Fletcher walked to that one and plopped her duffel on the floor. She unzipped it, then began to unload her belongings: three pairs of worn denim jeans, a pair of sweatpants, two pairs of shorts, some faded T-shirts, the second of the two hooded sweatshirts she owned, and her shabby leather jacket. Aware of Sparrow's eyes on her back, she blushed as she removed a handful of undergarments and shoved them as far back on the shelf as they could go. Finally, she pulled her favorite thing out of the bag. She held it in her hands, examining it with the reverence it deserved.

"Oh my days," Sparrow gasped, and Fletcher looked up to find the other woman standing beside her. "Is that a book? A *paper* book?"

Fletcher traced the embossed cover with her index finger. *A Little Princess.* "Yes."

"I've never seen one before." Sparrow regarded it with wide-eyed wonder.

"Not many people have. It's what they called a hardcover."

"As opposed to what?"

Fletcher couldn't help but grin as she slipped the cover open and caressed the timeworn pages. "Paperbacks."

"Paperbacks," Sparrow repeated the word as if to savor the sound it made, the feel of it as it fell from her lips. "It's beautiful."

"Yes, it is. It's the only book in my house the Agents didn't destroy. I'm glad I kept it well hidden."

Sparrow reached out to touch the book. Fletcher flinched ever so slightly at the movement. Still, Sparrow noticed, and stopped herself before her fingers made contact with it. She dropped her hand, self-conscious, and grinned at Fletcher. Fletcher read her posture with ease: *I shouldn't be so presumptuous, to touch it without permission. I'm sorry.*

"My hands are too rough," Sparrow started. "I wouldn't trust myself to hold it, but maybe you could read it to me sometime?"

Fletcher's breath hitched. She had never met anyone besides

her mother who had read this story and wanted it to remain that way. She liked the feeling of having something that they shared, something that was just theirs; so few things were. "Maybe," she said, doubting that she ever would.

"Okay." Sparrow shook her head. "I'll let you finish up here. You should try to get some rest. You're going to need it over the next few weeks as training is going to run you down. I'll wake you for dinner."

"Thanks." Fletcher turned back to her cubby and placed her mother's book on the high mantel.

KILLIAN LUNGED AT FLETCHER with a fleetness that surprised her. Logic dictated that a man of his stature—a man with dulled faculties, no less—should not be quick on his feet, and yet he was. Fletcher managed to anticipate that his punch was coming. She juked to the right, dodging the blow by millimeters. Instinctively, she leapt into the air, bent her left arm and plunged her bony elbow downward into his ribcage. She followed through with her right hand and landed a backhanded strike to his face. The sound it made, a sharp *clap*, was louder than she had expected.

Killian halted his advance. "Ow!" He lifted his fingers to his cheek and rubbed the spot where Fletcher had hit him.

"Oh, I'm sorry!" Fletcher frowned.

"S'okay. You did good." He reached for her wrist, gently took her hand into his own and folded her fingers into a fist. "But fists are better." He drove her knuckles into his palm three times. "See?"

"I do. It's more forceful, more effective." Fletcher smiled at him.

He nodded. "But you're fast. Good, uh, good re . . . ree—"

"Reflexes?"

"That!" Killian snapped his fingers and beamed, happy that she had understood him. And Fletcher did understand him, more and more each day. He had been teaching her fighting techniques, sparring with her every morning in the forest clearing beyond the safe house's rear patio. Fletcher had had her choice of sparring partners—even Søren had been willing to show her how to throw down, but that was an absolute nonstarter for her—and since she knew she would not be able to bring herself to hit Sparrow, she had chosen Killian. She had taken quite a liking to him once she'd realized what a gentle giant he was.

It was refreshing to spend time with Killian. He was calmer than the rest of YOR, and more soft-spoken. He didn't talk strategy for procuring much-needed supplies, argue about the best way to go about missions, mull over endless plans for the salvaging trips and sneaky government sabotages. He was quiet unless he felt he had something important to contribute to the conversation, but in general he seemed to simply enjoy listening to the others speak.

What Fletcher appreciated most about Killian was that he handled her with kid gloves. He understood that the life of a rebel, the necessity of constant readiness, the training and all the sore, swollen muscles and bruised flesh it entailed, was very new to her. She never felt pressured to suck up the pain and get back to the grind; he let her work through it at her own pace. She never felt pressured to get everything right the first time. She trusted him to walk her through her mistakes with patience, with compassion, and he never failed to do that.

"Can we give it another go?" she asked, despite the aching in her triceps.

He shook his head. "Don't wanna get punched in the face."

Fletcher grimaced. "Killian, I'm—"

"No, no! Joking." He threw his hands up. "Don't be sad."

She exhaled relief. "Must be your sister's influence."

Killian chuckled. "Okay, c'mon. We start again." He took

a step back, bounced on his tiptoes and shook out his hands, preparing himself to fight.

Fletcher shifted her body so that her left side faced Killian.

"Fists," he said. "Wanna see 'em, always."

Her knuckles cracked as her fingers balled.

"Put 'em in front of your face, like this." He demonstrated.

Fletcher held her fists up higher.

"Good." He nodded. "Come at me."

"What? No, I can't." This was different. She had never been the one to attack him before. She'd never attacked anyone before, save for the Agent in the library—and even that was a panicked attempt to defend her petrified friend. She had threatened to murder Flynn in the moment, but that was a postulated crime of passion that would never come to fruition. She could not see herself as the aggressor without solid provocation. She could be considered mentally tough, a side effect of an existence where the looming threat of Reclamation forced her to realize how precious and fragile her mind and her life were. But was she physically tough? *Hell no.*

"Don't be weak, come at me!" Killian shouted.

Fletcher, shocked by the uncharacteristic change in his tone, the intensity in his expression, was startled into action. She let out a guttural roar—what she imagined a battle cry should sound like—and ran at him.

Pitching all her weight behind her left fist, she let it tear through the air. The punch crashed into Killian's gut, but did not throw him off for longer than an instant. She followed up with a second, right-handed punch, which made full contact with his chin. His head snapped to the side, and he momentarily lost his footing.

"More!" He made a quick recovery and stutter-stepped toward Fletcher. He swiped at her with gigantic knuckles as he closed in. Fletcher ducked the blow, responding with a southpaw uppercut. She connected with his chin. This time Killian truly felt it. His head bucked back, and his arms drooped to his sides. It took more than a beat for him to regain his bearings, but when he did, Fletcher saw that his lower lip was split. Blood dribbled down his chin, saturating the collar of his shirt—a blotch of burgundy contrasting with the eggshell-colored fabric.

She faltered in her attack, relaxed her stance, and approached him with concern. "Killian, I didn't mean—"

Killian wiped the blood from his jaw with his rolled-up sleeve. Squinting at Fletcher, he shouted, "No backing down ever!" He thrust out his right arm, and his open palm smashed into her upper sternum. The force of the blow was so intense it knocked Fletcher backward a full foot. She landed on the cold, hard-packed soil, the air gone from her lungs.

As she lay there struggling to breathe, she heard Killian stomping toward her. He materialized above her, intensity drained from his features, and pawed at her calves. "Kick my legs. Make me fall," he said, crashing her shins into his knees.

"Can't . . . breathe."

"Agents don't care." He dropped her legs, then formed a mock pistol with his fingers. He aimed at Fletcher's forehead. "You're theirs now."

He was right. If this were a real brawl, if an actual Agent had overpowered her, she would be seconds away from capture, or—if, thanks to the InvigorStyler, she was unrecognizable as a wanted potential Reclaimee—seconds away from death. She asked herself if that was how she'd want it to end, sprawled out on the floor and wheezing? An easy conquest, too beaten down to keep fighting? Snuffed out in irrelevancy, no help to anybody?

No.

A tide of anger swelled inside her. She gathered her remaining strength, concentrating it into her lower torso. Rolling to her left, she lifted her hips. With a dynamic rotation, she launched a windmill kick at Killian. Her shins made contact, one after the other, with the soft muscle behind his knees. She felt his hinge-joints buckle. He went down hard. As his shoulders slammed into the dirt, Fletcher scrambled to her feet. She hovered over him, ready to strike even though she still gasped for air. There was something empowering about putting a man twice her size on his back. She felt triumphant.

The applause from the patio took her by surprise. She glanced over to find an audience amassed there: Peter, Damon, Charlie, Zoe, Philip, Søren and Sparrow. Her cheeks reddened as she stared at them. "Have you all been there this whole time?"

"Pretty much," said Charlie.

Fletcher waved them off, then turned back to Killian, who had pushed himself up into a seated position, elbows resting atop his bent knees.

"Are you okay?" She extended her arm and braced herself to take his weight.

A chortle leaked from his mouth. "You kicked my butt." He accepted her hand, but his bulk nearly dragged her to the ground beside him.

Fletcher sniggered at herself, at the absurd mental image she conjured of a little girl trying to lift a fallen ogre to his feet. She dug her heels into the ground. "Up you go," she said, and this time up he went.

He brushed the dust and broken bits of dead leaves from his arms. Fletcher went round to his backside and did the same for the hard-to-reach spots.

"Thanks," he mumbled after Fletcher had finished and come around to face him again.

She patted his bicep. "No problem."

"Getting him up was harder than putting him down, huh, Ivy League?" Sparrow asked as she approached, remnants of laughter ringing through her words.

"Now you come over? Asshole."

"What she said." Killian motioned a thumb at Fletcher.

"Come here, you mess." Sparrow pulled a crumpled cloth

napkin from her pocket and pressed it to her brother's still-bleeding lip. "Hold it there."

"Convenient napkin you just happened to have in your pocket."

Sparrow shifted her attention to Fletcher. "I expected to need it for you," she retorted, a hint of playfulness to her tone. "And if you think I'm an asshole now, just wait. It's time for your last set of Hell Week runs."

Fletcher moaned, already exhausted.

"S'okay, you got this," Killian mumbled through the napkin.

Sparrow pitched a thumb at her brother. "What he said."

"Fletcher, you're faster than this. Let's go, pick up the pace," Sparrow yelled. It was nothing new. She'd been doing it for seven days, loping alongside Fletcher on the improvised running track near the woodshed and encouraging her to do better, push herself harder. Fletcher was close to the end of her final run of Hell Week, YOR's appropriately named crash course in speed and strength training.

The agony that was Hell Week included being startled awake every few hours to alert the rest of the team to danger, gathering the weapons and essential supplies and hurrying to the vehicles, followed by two continuous hours of weightlifting, then sparring sessions with Killian, and finally, to the dismay of Fletcher's fatigued muscles, running.

The track portion of her training began with a set of suicide sprints, followed by five 100-meter dashes, and concluded with endurance drills: 800-meter, 1,500-meter, and mile runs—all of which had almost killed Fletcher at one point or another. Every race flowed mercilessly into the next. Fletcher's scrawny body was in such shock that she contemplated suicide at least five times over the course of the first few days, but she had started to adjust.

The long, excruciating mile behind her, Fletcher staggered across the finish line and found Killian with a capped carafe of water at the ready. Some of the others were with him as well, all looking impressed.

"Good job!" Killian handed her the water and patted her sweat-soaked back. She nodded at him, uncapped the water, and took a long swig before bending double.

"Your time on that mile was great," said Peter. He showed Fletcher his stopwatch, the numbers 8.27 flashing on its screen. "You shaved almost twelve seconds off your time from the first day."

"Congratulations!" Philip chimed in. "You've survived the worst week of your life."

"Please tell me . . . it gets easier . . . from here," Fletcher panted, still bent over, one hand on her thigh and the other clutching the carafe. She offered it to her running partner.

Sparrow took the carafe from Fletcher but did not drink. "It does get easier; you'll see once you've been brought into the fold. We do an hour of weight training each morning, a couple sets of sprints, a few of the 100s. Our group run is a mile at your own pace. I'm sure you can handle it."

Fletcher stood upright. Sparrow passed the carafe back to her, and she sipped the cool liquid. "It'll be a dream compared to this week."

"The real fun begins tomorrow," Sparrow said. "We start weapons training."

"*She* starts weapons training tomorrow," said Søren, his presence catching everyone off guard. He had an eerie way of slinking up behind you, as Fletcher had learned. He pointed to the young woman who, even after Fletcher had been on the compound eight full days, still hadn't said more than a few words to her. "Zoe will be training Fletcher on the Remington."

"Excuse me? That's not happening," Sparrow protested.

"Fletcher's left-handed. The Mossberg 500 will be easier for her to maneuver. And I'm her Handler. I am going to teach her how to shoot."

"She can use the Mossberg, but Zoe is going to teach her or she's not going to be taught at all," Søren snapped.

"This is ridiculous. You don't trust me with a shooter now? You're one to decide who can handle a gun."

Søren scowled. He snatched Sparrow's wrist and dragged her toward the shed. To Fletcher's surprise, Sparrow did not put up much of a fight. They stopped a hundred yards away from the rest of the group.

Fletcher was unable to hear the words being exchanged, but she could see Sparrow's agitation as she waved her hands through the air.

Everyone watched the interchange in silence, though Fletcher had the feeling she was the only one dumbfounded by the scene. "What's his issue?" she queried the group. "Sparrow seems like a good shot. With a single bullet, she took down the beast that almost trampled me."

Philip was the one to answer. Everyone else looked down at their feet or pretended not to notice she had said anything at all. "Sparrow is a fantastic shot, better than any of us."

"Then I fail to see the problem with her being the one to train me."

"You should ask her," Charlie said. "If there's something you need to know, Sparrow oughta be the one to tell you. She's your Handler, and we don't want to get in the way of that."

"Anyway, we don't talk behind each other's backs. It's a trust thing," Zoe added.

The argument between Sparrow and Søren came to an abrupt end. He turned and started for the safe house. Sparrow scuttled back toward the group, kicking up dirt and small stones along the way. She rejoined the haphazard circle, remaining silent for a moment before exhaling. "Fletcher, will you take a walk with me?"

Peter and Charlie stared at Sparrow with mouths agape. Zoe rubbed at her right temple. Killian and Philip said, "huh" and "mmm." Fletcher, too, found it troubling that she had been asked in such an even tone to take a walk. She was beginning to understand that when Sparrow was angry, she didn't ask anyone to do anything; she commanded it.

"Sure." Fletcher waved a feeble goodbye to everyone and followed Sparrow into the woods.

The women walked until they reached a crescent of tree stumps that had been smoothed by decades of wind and rain; Sparrow found two that were situated close enough together to accommodate a quiet conversation and sat down on one of them. She tapped the flat top of the second stump.

Fletcher sat facing Sparrow. It was such a tight fit that their knees rested against one another's. Fletcher was hyper-aware of the contact yet did not move. She wanted to be able to look into Sparrow's eyes as she spoke. If that meant forfeiting her personal space, so be it.

"You're going to start your weapons training with Zoe."

Fletcher's eyebrows climbed her skull. "Why?"

"Because that's what Søren wants." Sparrow puffed a noisy breath.

"But I want to learn from the best, and I hear that's you."

"Is that what you've heard?" She allowed a puckish smirk to flicker but covered it. "It's true. Zoe is very competent with a rifle, though. She has excellent aim. She'll be a good teacher."

"You still haven't told me why I can't train with you."

Sparrow rubbed her palms against her sweatpants, stalling, searching for the right words. "A little more than a year ago we had an assignment who was with us longer than she was supposed to be—complications with her resettlement in The South," Sparrow began, no longer looking at Fletcher as she spoke. "She was an artist, a painter. Her work was becoming

106

pretty popular in The South actually, but that's unimportant. She had a bit of Greenback saved up and wanted to get paints and brushes so she could work while we waited for Head Office to come through with her job placement. One day she asked if I could take her into Temple—a town close to here, but far enough from home to be safe. We go there sometimes for basics we aren't able to find in our deserted property raids. I didn't think twice about taking her; it's a quiet village. I'd never seen Agents nearby. But that afternoon there were Agents in town, probably serving some local kids their Notifications of Violation. We ran into them on our way out of one of the shops, and they recognized my assignment as a fugitive."

Sparrow froze, grimacing. "The real problem, in hindsight, is that I didn't make her get into the InvigorStyler before we went to town. It was supposed to be a quick trip. She didn't see the point of going through the trouble of changing her appearance, of wasting the power to run the machine. She said it was wasteful enough that I'd have to use it, supposed that if she was seen with someone whose face no one knew, that would be innocuous enough. I should've insisted. She was too hot to be out in public undisguised. That's one rule that should never be broken."

She took a moment to steady herself, her jaw clenching as she swallowed her remorse. "I tried like hell to fight off the Agents, but I was unarmed, you know, to keep from drawing attention. One of them—a big, mean bastard—knocked me unconscious. When I woke up it was dark, and my assignment was nowhere to be found. They took her. We never saw her again. I don't know why they left me behind, likely couldn't be bothered with an unregistered backwater nobody like me. Sometimes I wish they'd taken me, too . . . You see, my fondness for her clouded my judgment. I couldn't do my job. I failed. Søren is suspicious of my ability to make smart decisions. He isn't confident that I won't get you captured, or worse." She motioned a finger between herself and Fletcher, then set her hand to rest on Fletcher's knee. "He wants us to keep our distance from one another as much as possible."

Fletcher gazed at Sparrow with wide eyes as she digested the story. She wears her guilt like a badge, she thought. *A scarlet G over her heart.* "Were you planning to tell me this at any point?"

Sparrow gave her a subtle headshake. "I was hoping I wouldn't have to. I know I messed up. I promised myself from that day on I would do everything I could to keep my friends—my family—safe, that I'd make myself worthy of their trust." She locked eyes with Fletcher and held them there. "Now, I'm making the same promise to you. I will keep you safe, and I hope to earn your trust."

How could Fletcher respond to that, the most earnest thing anyone had ever said to her? "I made a commitment to YOR, which means I'm determined to train until I'm capable of taking care of myself and the group." She said it with a voice devoid of emotion, but her body betrayed her. She glided her hand along her knee until her fingertips met Sparrow's. She waited a minute for Sparrow's reaction, but when none came, she carried on, draping her hand over the brunette's. "And I do trust you."

Sparrow's head whipped up. Her eyes focused on Fletcher. "You do?"

Fletcher affirmed with a nod. "You've been honest with me up to now, even if it did take a bit of coaxing from time to time. You've saved my life more than once, but beyond that, you saved my father's life. After all that, how could I not trust you?" She inhaled, feeling oddly exposed, and withdrew her hand from its resting place atop Sparrow's. "I'm sure you've guessed by now that I don't trust people easily. I certainly don't know Zoe well enough to give her my trust, especially since she'll be teaching me how to handle a dodgy old weapon. The idea of it makes me uncomfortable. I'd rather train with you, but Søren doesn't seem the type to be swayed once he's made up his mind."

"He isn't." Sparrow sucked her bottom lip into her mouth. Fletcher could see her mind at work, hatching a plan to circumvent the rules without flouting them entirely. "Officially, you have to train with Zoe."

"There's a 'but' in there somewhere."

"But I don't see how there would be anything wrong with me tagging along during your training sessions, giving some extra pointers, enriching your learning experience. Two teachers are better than one."

"Yes, in theory," Fletcher agreed. "How is Zoe going to feel about it, though? I suspect she isn't interested in bending the rules to any extent."

"Zoe and I have an understanding, or, well, a silent agreement to stomach each other. She usually keeps quiet about her dislike for me because I taught her to shoot."

"Did you? I thought Peter was her Handler."

"She was Peter's recruit. He's a gifted medic, but marksmanship is kind of my thing," Sparrow replied, her confidence unabashed. "How else do you think Zoe came to be second best?"

"YOU KEEP FORGETTING TO mention the recoil," Sparrow called out. She'd been sitting atop the mossy rock wall, watching Fletcher's introductory gun lesson. Every now and again, Fletcher sneaked a peek in Sparrow's direction, and every time she caught her biting her bottom lip, trying to abate the urge to take over Zoe's position as tutor.

"There it is!" Zoe, who hadn't yet let Fletcher touch the gun, shoved the weapon into Fletcher's arms.

"Wait," Fletcher said as she watched Zoe throw her hands into the air.

Zoe ignored her. "You've been itching to say something all day," she said to Sparrow. "I've seen it on your face. Why don't you come over here and show her how it's done since you want to so badly?"

"Alright, I will." Sparrow jumped down from the retaining wall and sidled toward the makeshift firing range.

Zoe met her halfway, shrugged, then continued to the rock wall.

Fletcher, the very picture of angst as she stood with the muzzle of the shotgun pointed at the forest floor littered with dead leaves, squinched at Sparrow. She raised the Mossberg by its stock. "So, this thing . . . can you get it away from me, please?"

"No. You've got to get used to holding it. It's yours now." Sparrow examined her.

"Not that I want it, but fine."

"Right. First things first, your stance." Sparrow stepped behind Fletcher, seized her by the hips and slipped her left leg between her thighs. "Your legs need to be spread farther apart, a little wider than shoulder-breadth," she spoke into Fletcher's ear and nudged her knee against her right leg.

Fletcher adjusted her posture. "Like this?"

"Yes, but your toes should be pointed outward at around thirty degrees." Sparrow used the outsole of her sneaker to reposition Fletcher's feet. "Bend your front knee a little and use it to brace yourself. You are the base of the gun; you have to be stable. If you're not, the recoil could knock you on your ass, which is not as fun as it may sound."

For the first time since leaving home Fletcher laughed. A week ago she would have fought against it, but things had changed. In spite of the persistent pangs of worry she felt for her father and Jonah, in spite of the fact that she was now likely one of the most wanted fugitives in The Unified American Territories, she felt at peace with it all. For reasons she couldn't quite put into words, she felt for the first time in her life like she was free.

"Okay, let's refocus. Square off with the target." Sparrow pointed to a brown burlap sack in the distance. "When the gun fires, your instinct is going to be to lean back, but you have to stand your ground. Otherwise, the muzzle will swing out and you'll end up shooting something or someone you weren't aiming at."

"That's great! Thanks for the warning," Fletcher replied as she brought both of her shoulders forward while trying to maintain the proper distance between her feet.

"No problem at all. Now that you've found the perfect stance, on to Step Two, how to hold a gun in firing position.

Rest the butt of the gun in the cradle of your left shoulder. Keep your dominant hand near the trigger, never on the trigger until you're ready to shoot, and your other hand wrapped around the center of the fore-end." She reached her arms around Fletcher's shoulders and guided her unsteady hands to the correct locations on the body of the gun. "Wow, Ivy League, you're shaking so hard," she observed with a hint of amusement.

"No shit, I'm holding a deadly weapon," Fletcher sassed. The shotgun's power was palpable and absolute. She didn't like the feeling of holding an instrument built solely for causing destruction. She thought she would've conquered the discomfort of being around YOR's stockpiled weaponry by now, but it hadn't happened yet. Secretly, she was glad the gun mount below her bed had remained empty.

Sparrow took the attitude for what she knew it to be: angst. She moved one hand to the small of Fletcher's back. "It's okay, just take a breath. It isn't loaded."

"Sooner or later, it will be loaded."

Sparrow let go of the fore-end and gestured to a small switch an inch above the gun's trigger. "This is called a safety. When the safety is on, the gun can't fire. That little green dot means the safety is on." She flicked the button toward the gun barrel, revealing a bright red dot. "The red dot means the safety is off and the gun is ready to shoot. Red dot means danger, got it?"

"Got it."

She flipped the safety on again. "As long as you see the green dot, you have nothing to worry about. Feel better now?"

"You do realize I could use this thing to murder every last person around me, right?" Fletcher said. She sensed that Sparrow's lips had spread into a smile.

"You could, but you won't. Take the safety off."

"No."

"No?"

"I'll rephrase—absolutely not," Fletcher grumbled as she

dropped the gun from firing position.

Sparrow moved to stand vis-à-vis with Fletcher. She took the shotgun from her hand. "Yesterday you told me that you trusted me. Did you mean it?"

Sparrow needed the answer to be "yes," that much was obvious. "Yes," Fletcher affirmed. And it was true.

"So, you believed me when I promised to keep you safe?" She regarded Fletcher with such eagerness that it made Fletcher flinch.

I want to. I'm trying to. "Yes."

"Then please turn the safety off." Sparrow handed Fletcher the gun and stepped out of her line of sight, prompting the blonde to shoulder the stock of the weapon once more.

Fletcher scrutinized the barrel of the Mossberg. "By the way, no one ever explained to me where all these guns came from," she said, time-wasting.

Sparrow groaned and relieved Fletcher of the weapon again. Without warning, she trudged off the firing range toward the line of trees surrounding it.

Fletcher stood staring at her backside.

"Where are you going?" Zoe yelled from her place on the rock wall.

"Let's go, both of you." Sparrow threw the retort over her shoulder and kept marching.

Fletcher and Zoe trudged silently after Sparrow until bewilderment got the better of Fletcher. "Is she okay?"

"You're doing a hell of a number on her," Zoe responded under her breath.

"What is that supposed to mean?"

"Nothing."

"Whatever." Fletcher waved her off. At that moment, she decided that she liked the Pink-Haired Girl much better before they had exchanged any words.

"Get in." Sparrow motioned the unloaded Mossberg at the black van, then pulled a set of keys from the pocket of her stained blue jeans.

"Not if you're driving," Zoe wisecracked.

"Get in the damn van."

Zoe's demeanor changed instantly. "If you're taking her to town, she needs to—"

"You had better stop right there," Sparrow replied through gritted teeth.

"I'm just trying to look out for you."

"Thanks. I've got it."

"Okay." Zoe slid open the door and situated herself in the van's back seat. "You coming?" she asked Fletcher.

"Fletcher is riding up front with me." Sparrow drilled Zoe with a glare that dared her to argue.

Zoe slid the door closed.

Sparrow lifted the handle on the passenger side door, which squeaked as she opened it for Fletcher.

Fletcher scooted into the seat, nodded a thank you to Sparrow before she closed the door with a slam. She watched through the windshield as Sparrow walked around to the driver's side. "Will you please tell me where we're going?" she asked once Sparrow had placed the shotgun in the space between the driver's seat and center console, then made herself comfortable behind the steering wheel.

Sparrow jammed a key into the ignition and turned over the engine. "You'll see when we get there. Think of it as a trust exercise."

The only measurable experience Fletcher had in an automobile were the few times she'd traveled between Russell Forest Preserve and Boston. By comparison, this drive was short—six or seven minutes. They couldn't have gone more than a couple of miles from the Visitor's Center, and they were still well within the boundaries of what Fletcher imagined was once called North of Nowhere, USA.

The texture of the ground beneath their feet changed suddenly from packed dirt and small stones to shrubbery. "I can never remember where it is. The landscape is all the same, just hills covered with green stuff everywhere," said Zoe, trailing Sparrow up a bluff.

"I know where it is."

"Where what is?" Fletcher wheezed. She had struggled most of the way through the brush, occasionally needing to use her hands for scaling too-steep embankments of boulders and loam.

"Keep climbing. We're almost there."

They clambered up one last hill before reaching their destination. The knoll was thick with bushy tendrils, much like every other overhang they had come upon on their hike. At first glimpse, it seemed unremarkable to Fletcher, until Sparrow swept aside the unruly vines. Camouflaged behind those emerald coils was a gigantic square hatch made of rusted steel.

"It's a bunker!" Fletcher exclaimed.

"You're wicked quick on the uptake," said Zoe.

"Leave her alone and help me with this." Sparrow wrapped both hands around the hatch's long pull handle. Zoe followed Sparrow's lead, and together, spines bent and muscles bulging, they threw open the access.

The high noon sunlight revealed the first few steps of an

old concrete stairwell leading down into the pit of the Earth, but died away without warning, obscuring the true depth of the passageway. Fletcher peered past the visible stairs and into the blackness beyond. "You first," she motioned to Sparrow. This may have been a trust exercise, but she was not naïve enough to dive headfirst into an enormous hole in the ground, the access to which may or may not have been lockable from the outside, upon the invitation of anyone in the world.

"Naturally," replied Sparrow, and began her descent sans hesitancy.

"Your turn," Zoe said.

Fletcher considered her. "Please, I insist, after you," she feigned politeness, but the Pink-Haired Girl was wise to her game.

"Smart." She winked at Fletcher.

"That's what they tell me."

Zoe ducked into the bunker, leaving Fletcher alone beneath the bright blue sky. She closed her eyes and inhaled the crisp fall air as if every breath that entered her lungs from that moment on would be stale and littered with centuries-old dust. "Alright." She braced herself and ventured into the shadowy unknown.

Descending into the bunker, Fletcher felt very much like she was being swallowed whole by some gigantic otherworldly monster, its mouth constricting around her deliberately, savoring her flavor. At first, it wasn't the dark that made her uneasy, it was the stench. The musky scent of stagnant air had assaulted her nostrils the instant she'd left the flora and fauna behind. As her pupils dilated in accordance with the growing dimness and her feet faltered more and more in their search for solid ground, the darkness had begun to take its toll on her.

Sparrow met her on the fourth step, flat micro-flashlight in hand. "Three more stairs," she said, guiding Fletcher's way with a narrow beam of bright light.

"Just happened to have that handy, did you?"

"I always keep it in my pocket. It's good to have, just in case."

"Useful," remarked Fletcher. "I'd like one myself."

"I'll work on that."

"Where's the stupid switch?" Zoe wondered from somewhere deeper inside the cavernous chamber.

Once Fletcher had reached the landing, Sparrow led the way farther into the compartment. "It's here," she said, thumbing a cord that dangled from a hook in the right-most wall.

Fletcher heard a snap, and a series of freestanding panel lamps sputtered on. "You're pretty familiar with this place," she observed, scrutinizing her Handler.

"I come here when I need time to myself. It's quiet, but close to home."

"I can understand the need for—what the hell?" Fletcher blurted out. Her eyes darted in every direction. The cement walls of the archaic shelter were lined with racks upon racks of large-caliber long guns. "You brought me to an underground cage full of guns! Not the best way to inspire me to feel safe around you. This is a death trap."

"You wanted to know where we got all of our weapons." Sparrow swept a hand around the room. "Here's your answer. None of them are loaded."

"Safeties on?"

Fletcher noticed a semblance of pleasant surprise dawn on Sparrow's face. "Of course." She pointed to a wide double-doored aluminum storage locker at the far end of the room. "Ammunition is kept separate."

"Ammunition," Fletcher repeated the word. "What happens when your cache is depleted? You can't really find bullets on the open market, can you?"

"That's a long way off, but we have a plan to recycle our spent shells. There's a way to reload and reuse the casings. That's not my area of expertise, but Peter and Philip know enough about chemistry, technology, and mechanics to work it out."

"Solid plan," Fletcher said as she began to wander around the place. Her disquiet had been bested by inquisitiveness and awe of the bunker's sheer magnitude and its stowed artillery.

In the farthest corner of the garrison, she found a handful of furled sleeping bags alongside a shelving unit stocked with long-expired cans of food. Dangling from the side of the shelves was a flag. Everything about it was different from the banner of The Unified American Territories. There were no black and red bends symbolizing the divide between North and South, no gilded "UAT" charge at its center. Fletcher scooped the well-worn fabric into her hands, caressing it with utter veneration. She counted the red stripes first, followed by the white ones: seven and six. The fifty five-pointed white stars contrasted with the royal blue canton. The beauty of the American flag was pure, the embodiment of a bygone era of optimism and reverie.

Of course, Fletcher knew America was not a paragon of perfection. It had been conquered through the genocide of Indigenous people and built on the backs of African slaves. Insofar as making up for its history, the nation still had been working towards becoming a more perfect union, but the country it had been growing into, the country it was when it died—the freedom it offered to go wherever you wanted whenever you wanted, to be whoever you wanted to be, to not have to constantly watch what you said for fear of who might be listening—had more promise in its death throes than The UAT did from its founding moment. The UAT was birthed from the loins of fascism whereas America had been born out of contempt for tyranny.

Fletcher returned the flag to its hanging position before turning to find Sparrow's eyes. "This was a rebel stronghold during the Second Revolution, wasn't it?" She struggled to keep her voice from breaking, overcome by the evidence of what the Revolutionists were prepared to do: kill or be killed in defense of their principles, in defense of the country they so loved. They never could have fathomed what would come on the back of their loss—the rise of oppression where their beloved liberty used to be.

"Yes," Sparrow affirmed. "YOR's founders discovered it years ago."

A strange gleam in the lamplight caught Fletcher's attention, forcing her to look beyond Sparrow. She saw Zoe standing across the bunker, holding the source of the gleam in her hands.

"Where did you find—"

Zoe pointed at a section of the bunker that was just outside of Fletcher's view. Fletcher moved toward the Pink-Haired Girl. A sensation of warm familiarity blossomed throughout her being as the recessed nook of weapons came into her line of sight. She had read countless digibooks about knights and ninjas over the course of her childhood. The stealth and strength with which they wielded their steel blades had always mesmerized her. She had forced Jonah to indulge her sword obsession almost daily, initiating play-fights with sturdy tree branches. She'd even had a favorite stick—perfectly straight, broad at one end and tapering to a blunt point at the other.

Her ideal sword was not a katana, though it resembled one, its hilt without a cross guard, but with a straight, double-edged blade. Fletcher had thought such a thing did not exist, yet there she stood in front of a multitude of swords of every conceivable build.

She reached into the nook, pulled a scabbarded smallsword from its wall-mounted brackets. It had a round, black leather pommel and matching leather-bound grip, but most incredibly no cross guard. Fletcher wrapped her left hand around its hilt and unsheathed the sword. Its two-sided blade, shimmering under the harsh lamplight, reflected in her hazel eyes. Holding the sword felt natural to her. It seemed to belong in her hands, as though it had been collecting dust in its resting place for more than a century, just waiting for its rightful owner to come and claim it.

"We don't use those," Sparrow said as she joined Fletcher in front of the swords. "They're not practical, particularly for hunting."

"I don't think I'm going to be good at hunting, anyway. And if I have to defend myself or anyone else, this feels much more my style."

"Do you know how useless a sword would be in a shoot-out with the Agents?"

"Futile," responded Fletcher, still clutching the sword in one hand and its scabbard in the other. She slipped the steel back into its sheath and continued. "But Agents rarely use their guns. If they used them often, I imagine there would be fewer Reclaimees. Their jobs are to serve us with notification, and in due course to apprehend and deliver us in one piece to the Reclamation Processing Centers. If ever there were justification to discharge their weapons, don't you think it would have been while I was kicking the shit out of one of them? Still—"

"They didn't," Zoe finished the sentence.

"Exactly. In any case, I don't believe that killing someone should be as easy as pulling a trigger. If I were forced to kill, I couldn't do it that way. I'd have to give them a chance to defend themselves. Everyone has a right to fight for their life, even if said life belongs to a detestable piece of human garbage."

"How can I argue with that?" Sparrow shrugged.

"You can't, because she's right," Zoe said, then turned to Fletcher. "Søren will never allow it. You have to show him that you can handle yourself in a firefight, or you'll get sidelined. No missions, no purpose. No contribution to the group at all, just another person to feed and clothe."

"Enough," Sparrow barked. "She has to learn how to use a gun, but that doesn't mean her primary weapon has to be a gun. We all had to learn how to use one, but really, how many of us have ever fired one, outside of on the practice range or a hunt? I never have. You never have. Søren never has."

Zoe rolled her eyes. "Do you have a personal vendetta against YOR's policies, or is it just that pretty girls make you lose your damn mind?"

Sparrow, incensed, charged at Zoe, stopping inches from the pink-haired woman's face. "Shut your mouth right now or I'll shut it for you."

Fletcher managed to keep the flash of heat in her chest from rising to color her cheeks. "Calm down, both of you. God, I didn't think there could be so much testosterone in a room full of women." She pushed herself between the two, obliging them to separate before the situation escalated. "Let's settle this, alright? I'll learn how to use the Mossberg. If Søren insists that I need to know how to use a gun, fine, but I'm taking this." She lifted the smallsword. "Marksmanship might be your thing, Sparrow, but I know swordsmanship is going to be mine."

"You're on your own with that," Zoe spat. "None of us know the first thing about . . . what is it called?"

"Fencing," Fletcher grumbled. "Don't worry about it. Like you said, I'm a smart girl. I'll figure it out. Now . . ." She clasped Sparrow's hand, drawing her away from Zoe and toward the cement stairs. "Take me back to the firing range and show me how to shoot a gun."

chapter twelve

FLETCHER DREW HER SWORD from its back-harnessed leather sheath. The weapon was designed to be wielded single-handed, but after three weeks of practice, she had just become acclimated to its lightness. She swung the sword, blade splitting the air with a swish, and slashed strips of brown bark away from a dead tree. She hacked and thrust at the thick trunk as she bent and twisted her body, envisaging the harmless elm as an imposing adversary. Zoe had been right: No one among the skillful band of outlaws knew the first thing about swordplay. Fletcher had to improvise her training, reducing what was supposed to be an elegant waltz to a vigorous solo dance. Still, she enjoyed the uniqueness of her weapon and the solitude it afforded her while she learned how to brandish it. Regardless of how pointless it seemed to the others, and despite the spat she had gotten into with Søren about it, Fletcher was determined to hone her proficiency in the long-dead art of swordsmanship. As far as she could tell, she was already the country's foremost living expert on the subject.

"Ladies and Gentlemen," she said aloud as she flitted about the small clearing, "presenting The UAT Champion Fencer of 2138, Fletcher Daniels." She concluded her ballet with a pirouette and a stab of the sword so convincing that its fine point lodged deep into the hardwood stump.

"Why not aim higher and go for World Champion Fencer?"

Fletcher released her hold on her sword and spun around in haste. She found herself gawping at Sparrow. Self-conscious, she sneered at her own childishness. "I doubt I'm the best in the world. Who knows what people do in other countries?"

Sparrow strolled over to the dead elm tree, placed both hands around the sword's grip and liberated it from its wooden prison. "I don't know, you're pretty good with this thing," she said, ogling the sharp edges. "You move pretty gracefully, too."

Fletcher's lips crept into a timid smile.

"Let me just—" Sparrow began, then paused and mimed placing the blade into its scabbard.

"Sure."

Sparrow quick-stepped around to Fletcher's rear. "Your hair," she said, and swept Fletcher's long, fair ponytail aside before securing the holster and slipping the sword into it.

Fletcher looked over her shoulder, murmured, "Thank you."

Sparrow did not move away. She opened her mouth to speak, then closed it.

Fletcher caught Sparrow's expression in her periphery. She could not put a name to it but was certain she had never seen it on the woman's face before. It made her anxious. Eager to put some distance between them, she took a step away from Sparrow before turning toward her. "Did you need something?"

"It's your Initiation Day."

"Today?"

"You've been with us over five weeks, trained hard, proven to Søren and the rest that you're strong enough and fast enough to hold your own. The only thing left to do is—"

"Hit a target from a hundred paces. Right."

"Fifty paces to start, followed by a hundred. You've got one clip to nail the target at least twice from each distance, and you know the Mossberg is a six-shot."

"Four of six. That's sixty-seven percent accuracy—not much room for error." Fletcher sighed. She had been dreading the shooting test ever since recognizing its inevitability. Søren had conceded that she could carry the sword as her primary weapon, still insisting that the test was non-negotiable. After that, Fletcher and Sparrow worked every day—under Zoe's scrutiny—on the Mossberg. She had gotten not-quite-comfortable but much less skittish in her maneuvering of the shotgun, though she never failed to miss the mark every other time she fired it. She'd go six for twelve, twelve for twenty-four, always fifty percent accuracy, no matter what. The elms and birches behind the burlap bullseye were riddled with errant bullets thanks to her. "What will Søren do if I fail? My aptitude for marksmanship is mediocre at best."

"Those are Head Office's requirements, not Søren's. Should you fail, the original deal would apply—ID replacement and resettlement in The South."

"Terrific. Then I'd really be alone."

"Look, I don't know where your father is, but if you were to fail, I'd try my best to make sure you end up close to him."

"You can do that?"

"I said I'd try. But yeah, odds are I could." Sparrow frowned. "Are you going to fail on purpose?"

The notion hadn't crossed Fletcher's mind. In the time she had been living in the woodland hideaway with the pack of plucky miscreants—some of whom had become her friends—her father had never been far from her thoughts. Every day she wondered where he was, how he was, and occasionally whether he was proud of her as Jonah's mother had insisted he would be the night he disappeared. *He wouldn't be proud of me if I purposely failed.* She heard his voice inside her head. "You made a commitment, young lady. You have to follow through. Remember, we're only as good as our word."

"I hate the idea of failure. I could never do it willingly."

"That's good because the only way you could fail is if you wanted to."

"You think?"

"I do. I've never met a person with more determination, and that's in spite of yourself. You have all this insecurity, yet such a strong will. I . . . I don't understand how that's possible."

"That's me, a walking, talking oxymoron."

Sparrow grinned. "'Enigma' is the word I'd use."

Fletcher's stomach jumped again, the way it had that night in the van when she had collided with Sparrow, and then later when Sparrow had pulled a seat out for her at the dinner table. It hit her then, harder than her knees had hit the floor of the van that first night—and of all the things she had realized were wrong or out of place in her lifetime, this was by far the most jarring: her stomach had never jumped for anyone before. Since meeting Sparrow, it had taken to fluttering at will, quivering with an unnameable emotion. It had happened—she'd met someone whose sheer, undeniable magnetism destabilized her barricades. Somehow, Sparrow had managed to burrow her way through her defenses. No, not somehow. She hadn't sneaked in via a weak spot or launched a nighttime ambush. *I let her in. I want her here.*

If ever there was a time to fortify her blockades, it was now. Only a few weeks had passed since her father had very narrowly escaped indescribable horrors at the hands of the enemy. She had barely begun to acknowledge the fact that she would likely never see him or poor, sweet Jonah again. She decided that she would not—could not, despite her longing to—let this breach stand.

She kicked at a pile of fallen leaves, avoiding Sparrow's arctic-blue eyes. "You're here to escort me to the practice range. I suppose Søren sent you to fetch me?"

"Fetch you," Sparrow scoffed. "You're not a damn dog,

remember? And Søren didn't send me. I came because I wanted to, I don't know, give you some words of encouragement. I suppose I didn't do the best job."

"You did fine." *Better than fine.*

"Good. Then let's get this thing over with, okay?"

"Yes, let's," Fletcher agreed, and gestured for Sparrow to lead the way.

Philip drew a line in the dirt with his foot. "Toe the line," he told Fletcher. The nervous blonde stepped up to the marker at the end of the narrow shooting lane.

"Perfect," he said. "Don't move, okay?" He flipped a switch on the small machine in his hand—a tool Fletcher had never seen before—and a green laser combed the forest floor. The device beeped, projecting a flashing "125-ft" indicator onto the ground in the distance. "We're good," he called.

Søren jumped down from his seat on the low rock wall to the right of the firing range where all of YOR had gathered to watch the apparent spectacle that was the shooting test. He lifted the burlap target from its resting place and walked it over to the indicator. After positioning it on the spot, he flipped a terse thumbs up at Philip, then made his way back to his fellow spectators.

"Good luck," said Philip as he turned off his measuring device. Fletcher forced a smirk at him. He pocketed his gadget and backed away from the lane.

As if on cue, Sparrow stepped up to the line beside Fletcher. She clasped the Mossberg around its barrel. "Hey," she began coolly, "it's normal to be feeling stressed right now. I was a ball of nerves during my test. You're going to tell yourself that you can't do it, that the margin for error is too narrow, but you *can* do it." Smiling, she handed the shotgun to Fletcher. "I believe in you."

Fletcher mouthed "thanks," then watched as Sparrow headed for the rock wall.

"Here we go," she said to herself, raising the Mossberg. She checked that the safety was on, then clicked open the chamber. Inside she found a metal slug ready for firing. Sparrow had done her the courtesy of handing her a loaded weapon, which did make the task easier. She snapped the chamber closed.

Repositioning her hand on the forestock, Fletcher brought the wooden butt of the weapon up to rest in the crook of her left shoulder before tapping the safety off. She stared down the shotgun's long black barrel, first with both eyes, then with only her left "Master Eye" open and aligned the front sight just below the center of the faraway target.

She sucked in a great lungful of oxygen, let it out slowly, repeated the process twice. She held in her fourth breath and pulled the trigger.

Fletcher exhaled as the bullet cracked through the ether. While she knew its velocity was in the range of 500 feet-per-second, it seemed to travel in slow motion to spite her. Soon, however, she realized that the result of her effort had been disastrous: The bullet exploded into the trunk of an elm tree to the left of the target, sending splintered bits of timber flying.

"Damn," she muttered. Figuring that she had to allow herself at least three shots to hit the target at 100 paces, she now had only two bolts left to nail the target twice at fifty paces. Her margin for error had decreased to zero.

She pumped the gun's fore-end. An empty bullet casing ejected from the chamber with a *ting* and a fresh shell popped into place. Again, she set her sights on the target. She took two deep breaths. "Come on." She puffed out her second lungful, gulped her third, and pressed the trigger.

The shell charged from the barrel with a furious *whoosh*. *Pop*. A nanosecond later, it blasted into the heart of the target.

"Whoo!" called Charlie.

"Bull's-eye!" Sparrow shouted from the sidelines.

Fletcher smiled, though only for a tick. She obliged herself to recover quickly, not wanting to squander whatever momentum she may have built up. She pumped a new shell into the chamber, squared off with the target and squeezed the trigger once more.

Just as the previous round had struck its intended mark, so too did this one. It pierced the center of the burlap-sack-turned-target.

"Two in a row!" Sparrow leapt from her seated position, throwing a triumphant fist into the air. Her enthusiasm was unequivocal, infectious; still, Fletcher did not allow herself to succumb to it. She had yet to pass the test.

She lowered the gun as Philip approached the line for a second time. He drew the distance meter from his pocket and reconfigured it. The thin green laser again raked the forest floor, beeped and flashed "250-ft" atop the leaves scattered in the distance. Søren, repeating his role as Official Target Mover, carried it the additional length down the slender trail.

Fletcher was aghast. The distance between herself and the target's new location was impossibly great. The entire forest seemed to contract and elongate in her mind's eye, and she had to fight against the vertigo it caused. *Someone please help me.* She sought out Sparrow among the crowd of observers, drilled her with a look of apprehension. "Now comes the hard part," she called to her.

Sparrow shook her head. "Now comes the part where you learn to believe in yourself."

Is that all it takes, believing in myself? she wondered. Not so easy when the world had conditioned everyone for constant disappointment. She raised her head toward the sky, swallowed a gob of saliva. "Okay." She trained her sights on the target's innermost concentric circle and took aim.

The vibrant yellow bull's-eye taunted her, daring her to *just try* to nail it from the incredible distance of 100 paces. "Okay," she said again, and squeezed the trigger.

The shell did not hit gold. Rather, it made contact with one of the target's blue outer rings. The result was not what Fletcher had wanted but it would do. Hitting the target was hitting the target—perfection was not a requirement.

"Alright! One more," hollered Sparrow.

Fletcher glanced toward the rock wall, locked eyes with her mentor, and gave her a slight nod. Maybe she could do this. *Maybe . . .*

"One more." She let out a long, measured breath as she refocused on the faraway bull's-eye. She pumped the shotgun, took aim, and let loose another round.

The bullet clipped the very edge of the target, leaving a small indent in the top left corner where a chunk of paper used to be. It looked as though a tiny, invisible creature had mounted the target and taken a bite out of the outermost ring. Technically, the bolt had hit the board, but Fletcher's muscles went stiff with worry. She dropped her weapon from firing position, faced the rock wall and searched for Søren in the crowd. "Does it count?"

His lips twitched into an understated frown, and for the briefest moment Fletcher could read the sympathy on his face. "No," he said.

Shit. This was it. She was down to her final shell, her last chance to prove herself worthy of taking up arms for the cause, for The Vault.

She straightened herself in the firing lane, met the burlap sack one last time. Instead of taking aim, she flipped the safety on, leaned over and placed the gun on the ground. She rolled her shoulders and her neck a handful of times, willing her muscles to relax, coaxing her body to bend to her command. If she hoped to have control of her weapon, she first had to have full control of her own frame—that was what Sparrow had drilled into her from day one.

Confident that she was loose enough, she picked up the

shotgun again and flicked the safety off. She closed her eyes, visualized the bull's-eye in her mind. When she opened them again, she concentrated on the center of the target. *I can do this.*

Sure, you can, dark horse. A voice that was not her own derided her from inside her skull.

Of all the people she had ever met who had the power to hijack her thoughts, Agent Flynn was the one to do so now. The target transformed from inanimate burlap sack to a mirage of living flesh and blood in the form of the tall, pewter-haired Agent who had stolen everyone Fletcher had ever cared for.

It isn't real. He isn't here. He's a figment of my imagination. She blinked hard, but it was fruitless. She still saw him there at the end of the lane, infirm and wispy as if a phantom, with lips pursed in a priggish sneer, disgust twinkling in his spectral eyes. He was goading her, begging to be shot, departed in full.

Could she murder him, become a killer? Justifiable Homicide, it would have been called in the time before. Self Defense. *He is the target. Shoot the target.* And in that instant, everything changed. The directive took on a life of its own as the anger she harbored for him and his ilk frothed between her synapses. Muscle memory did its job, and her breath left her body in a rush, on pace with the bullet she released from her gun.

It missed the hallucinated Agent, blasting instead into the trunk of a hardwood. Flynn grinned, then vanished, leaving only the plain makeshift target in his wake.

A round of dissatisfied groans came from the gallery. Fletcher had failed. Not all STs were meant to be warriors.

Defeated, Fletcher dropped the empty rifle. It hit the dirt with a dull thud, dragging her spirt down with it. Her shoulders hunched, head bowed in shame, she padded toward the rock wall, her disappointment in herself tangible to anyone who cared to look. *So, this is how it feels to fall short.*

Sparrow held Fletcher's sheathed sword in her hand and

met her protégé halfway.

Fletcher, unable to meet her eyes, uttered a meek, "I'm sorry."

"Don't be. You tried," replied Sparrow, placing her free hand on Fletcher's bicep and giving it a tender squeeze.

"Please, don't patronize me." Fletcher avoided Sparrow's touch.

"If that's what you think I'm doing, you don't know me at all. I wanted you to succeed as much as you did."

"Well, I didn't succeed." She thought about telling Sparrow what had occurred, of the wraithlike Flynn that had replaced the target, but she didn't want the woman to think her a lunatic as well as a letdown. "What happens now?"

"We go back to the house. You'll have half an hour alone to clean up and compose yourself. The test itself was draining, but beyond that you're understandably upset."

"You don't understand, none of you do. You're all in, you all passed."

"You're right, I don't understand," Sparrow agreed. After a somber beat, she continued, "Søren will call a family meeting, your last." Her sadness lingered on her final word. Fletcher comprehended its meaning, the unspoken root of it: *Soon you'll be out of my life, and I'll miss you more than I should, more than you'll know, because I can't say it.* And there was that for her as well, Fletcher realized, beneath the sting of incompetence, beneath the guilt of failing YOR, her father, Jonah, and the rest of her fellow Vaulters. She would miss Sparrow in a dangerous way, a haunting way—the way the desert misses rain, something it never had to begin with, but always needed, could always use. This, then, was the bud of affection left to wither for want of water. Just as well she wouldn't have to fight it; it would die by circumstance.

Yet again she felt the overwhelming urge to embrace Sparrow. This time she decided to indulge it. *What does it matter, now? In a day or two, I'll be gone.* She threw her arms around

Sparrow's neck and felt her body freeze.

Sparrow's hesitance lasted no longer than an instant. Fletcher's sword fell from her grasp as she pulled the younger woman tight to her chest, encircling her torso with strong limbs.

They took a wordless moment to breathe each other in. Then Fletcher whispered into Sparrow's ear, her voice breaking with the weight of an unexpected truth. All she had ever wanted was to get out of The Vault, an escape she fancied unattainable. Now, faced with that improbability becoming reality, she found herself, for multiple reasons, wishing it had remained a dream. "I don't want to go."

Sparrow slackened her grip on Fletcher, put enough space between them to look into her hazel eyes, but did not relinquish her hold on her. "I could fight it, argue with Søren until I'm hoarse. It won't change things, but I'll do it." She didn't say "for you," although Fletcher knew the words were there, resting at the top of Sparrow's throat.

"What's the point?" Fletcher backed out of the embrace.

"The point is you've worked as hard as any of us, you deserve to be part of this family, to go on missions. You're not the best shooter, but so what? You're smart, resolved." She bent down, scooped up Fletcher's sword from the forest floor. "And you aren't defenseless. You're better with this than the rest of us could ever be."

Fletcher sighed. "I have no use for it anymore. I think you should hang onto it, though. Consider it a token to remember me by."

"I won't need it."

Fletcher recognized the faraway look in Sparrow's eyes— longing, capped with a hint of regret. She'd never expected anyone to regard her in such a way, and certainly never wanted anyone to, but now that it had happened, she realized the significance of it, the ache of stifled possibility, the sting of What If.

Lost for words, she averted her gaze and noticed that the

crowd of spectators had dispersed. She watched as their figures retreated up a small hill toward the Visitor's Center. Glad for the diversion, she nodded in their direction and said, "We should go back to the safe house."

"Okay."

They walked the winding path side by side in silence, hands close to, but not quite, touching. It was too hard to be so close. Fletcher wanted more than proximity. Needed more. She craved contact, to feel the warmth of Sparrow's skin, palm on palm, fingers entwined. *To hell with it.* She took Sparrow's hand into her own and laced their fingers together.

Sparrow looked down at their clasped hands, then up again to find Fletcher's eyes on her. "Is this okay?" Fletcher asked.

"Yes," Sparrow said and held on a little tighter.

chapter thirteen

BREAKING DOWN UNDER SCRUTINY was not something Fletcher was willing to do. She had become accustomed to always being in the company of someone, whether on group runs, during strength and weapons training, at meals, in the community sleeping room, even in the combined locker-restroom, with its toilets in stalls and barely secluded showers. Now, alone on the top floor of the Visitor's Center, in the small shower that was once part of a Park Ranger's private quarters, in a room that remained unused save for occasions like this one, she allowed the heaviness of the day to hit her. Fate had found her unfit to assist in YOR's understated insurrection.

Her tears mingled with the liquid that poured from the showerhead, and she reveled in the freedom of it, in the feeling of searing water rushing over her hair and body, in the foamy soap that lapped away the dirt and sweat. She wanted to stand under the spout forever, frozen in time, drenched for eternity, but knew that her half hour of privacy was coming to a close.

She twisted the faucet off, stood there until the water trickled to a stop, and afterward watched the remnants dribble down the grated drain. When nothing but small droplets remained, she swished open the khaki-green plastic shower curtain and stepped out onto the beige tiled floor. She unfolded the clean towel she'd set on a wooden stool in the corner and wrapped it around her body. It was stiff and coarse, the way towels hung to air-dry were. She basked in the familiarity of crisp cotton against her skin, tried not to think about where the towel had been pilfered from. It had been found on a salvaging trip through a deserted neighborhood left over from the time before the Second Revolution—houses that had been abandoned in search of safer ground, discarded along with the inhabitants' American citizenry in favor of refugee status in Canada, or Europe, before international air travel was banned. How smart of those people to flee and how extraordinarily selfish, their brothers and sisters united in battle while they chose to run. They were probably families, some with young children, who feared for their lives and futures, Fletcher rationalized. If only they had known how ugly the future would be.

A knock at the bedroom door startled her out of her thoughts. She walked through to the adjacent room and opened the door, clutching the towel to her chest.

"Oh. Um. Hi!" Killian gave a slight wave, then diverted his eyes to the old floorboards beneath his feet. "Sorry."

Fletcher ran a hand through her damp hair, unable to stop herself from grinning at his bashfulness. "No need for an apology," she said. "Is my 'alone time' up already?"

"Five minutes," he replied, gaze still trained on the floor. "Come to the common room."

"Okay, I will. Thank you."

He nodded, then scurried away down the hall the way a child who had been scolded would. Fletcher closed the door behind him, then turned to the metal-framed bed where she had laid out a pair of jeans, a T-shirt that had once been black but had faded to gray, and her undergarments.

She dressed slowly, intent on using every last second of the aforementioned five minutes. She was stalling the inevitable, she knew, but did not care.

Fletcher heard the arguing before she reached the main floor. Loud voices streamed up the winding staircase, battering her eardrums with an almost physical force. She remained still, out of sight to anyone present in the common room, eavesdropping. It was Søren's voice, deep and booming, and a touch beneath it, Sparrow's, feminine yet enraged. He yelled about rules, spouting phrases like "this is the way we do things" and "there are no exceptions." She yelled about him being so blinded by regulations that he couldn't see Fletcher's value. "You can't deny that she's an asset to us!"

Fletcher could no longer abide the shouting. YOR was a family, a unit that must remain cohesive in order to be effective. Her presence had been disrupting that cohesion right from the very beginning. It was time to end it. She was the only one who could.

"Stop!" she barked, storming into the room. "Just stop it, both of you! Do you even realize you're talking about me as if I'm not a person?"

Her words, like a salve, cooled the intolerable hotness in the room. Søren and Sparrow both gawped at her, self-conscious at their blatant discomposure.

Fletcher, emboldened by the silence, pointed at Søren. "Whatever assets I may or may not possess, whatever talents you do or do not believe I bring to the table, whatever it is that makes me so special, real or perceived, I don't care. The fact, which seems to have escaped you, is that I'm a human being. But since everyone sees me as a prize to be won, that means I *am* an exception to your rules. I'm standing in front of you, willing and able to be part of your team. Tell me how often that happens, Søren? How many Significant Threats to The Government have you shipped South, hidden away for a later date until Head Office reveals their grand scheme for us? And of them, how many have volunteered to stay with you and fight, undertake your minor sabotages until then? Make no mistake, they are minor sabotages. All I've seen in the time I've been with you is a group of kids—smart, capable kids—sitting around in the woods, playing at being heroes like they're on a camping trip. So, since I cannot go home, you have two options: stop coddling me, stop doubting me and give me something to do, dammit, or put me on a train to The South—in which case, hurry up and get on with it because I'm tired of this bullshit!"

"Getting you on a train to The South is not an option." Søren clasped his hands behind his back and began pacing the floor.

"*What*?" Sparrow beat Fletcher to the question. The two met each other's eyes until Sparrow's fluttered toward YOR's leader. "You've had her new ID ready for weeks in anticipation of her failure," she said, irritation mounting in her tone.

"The ID is not the problem. There's been a hiccup in Head Office."

"A hiccup?" asked Fletcher. "My life is in your mysterious overlords' hands, and they've had a hiccup? You'd better start explaining that to me, sparing not a single detail."

"We were able to obtain your new ID," Søren began. "We can replace your fingerprints here, but for practical reasons the ID couldn't go live until the day of transit. The day of transit is here, but the ID can't go live. There's been a break in the chain of communication. Our asset inside The Hall of Records has gone dark."

"How can you be so calm about this?" asked Fletcher. "Suppose it's more than a communication breakdown. Suppose your contact has gone missing. Wouldn't that pose a risk to all of us? The BOE could have found them out, could be interrogating them at this very moment!"

"As a precaution of their own design, no one in Head Office knows the location of this, or any, of our reserve safe houses. My predecessor chose them. She's dead now," Søren said. "The only people who know where to find us are here in this room."

"A small comfort," said Fletcher, "but not enough to put my mind at ease. Maybe it's a temporary setback, or maybe I'm trapped here, useless as a glass hammer because I failed your test, and your entire operation is tanked. Without the ability to assign new IDs, YOR is impotent."

"We have other operations in the works."

Peter stood up then, interjecting, "And a more pressing issue to deal with."

Sparrow folded her arms. "Really, a more pressing issue than Fletcher's future? She trusted us, and now we're screwing her over."

Peter gestured at Søren with an open palm. "He has five days left."

Sparrow nailed Søren with a look. "Has it been a year already? Oh, how time flies when you're stuck in the forest with a recovering Berserker."

"I'm not asking you to go. Zoe and Peter will handle it this time."

"Five days left until what?" Fletcher asked. She was ignored.

"I should go," Sparrow objected. "I know the streets better than Zoe does. She's a terrible driver anyway."

"Go to hell," Zoe murmured.

"No," Søren declared. "I need you to go to the cordon."

"Five days left until what?" Fletcher asked again, louder this time.

"Søren will run out of neurosedative injections in five days," answered Peter.

"And when that happens, he'll revert back to being a pissed-off human wrecking ball." Sparrow side-eyed Fletcher. "We have to go into the city to get him more medicine."

"Does he have a government-issued medical card?"

"Of course he doesn't." Sparrow almost laughed. "We can't have documentation leading back to any of us."

"A forged one then?"

"We don't have the capability to forge those," Philip chimed in. "We don't have anyone on the inside at The Ministry of Health."

"You don't have anyone on the inside anywhere," Fletcher huffed. "How do you get the meds then? Neurosedatives are a controlled substance."

Peter looked to Søren for permission to explain.

Fletcher caught the subtle exchange and deadpanned Søren. "I know you think I'm undependable. You expected me to be better than I am, but you've trusted me with all of this so far. I swear on my life, no matter what happens to me I will never betray YOR." She glanced first at Killian, then Sparrow. "If for no other reason than to protect the friends I've made here."

Søren examined Fletcher for a long moment, gauging her fidelity. "That, I believe." He nodded the go-ahead to Peter.

"I have a friend at a pharmacy that manufactures the drugs. We went to medical school together. He has access to the meds Søren needs, and he doesn't ask questions."

Fletcher squinted at him. "That's a suspiciously good friend."

"We were very close once, before I came here," Peter admitted.

"I see." She understood that he'd meant to say they had been lovers. "He knows what you're involved in?"

"He knows I had to leave him for reasons greater than I could explain. He's sympathetic to our cause."

Fletcher absorbed this new information. "Alright. And the plan is?"

"It's need-to-know. If we tell you, that implies you're going to be included, which you are not," Søren said, rebuffing her.

"She might be able to help Sparrow at Cordon Station,

though," Philip called from his seat near the blazing fireplace. "We have transit passes for two females ready to go. They were both going down there for Fletcher's relocation anyway. The only differences now are that we have to run the InvigorStyler twice and Sparrow won't be coming back alone."

"I'm in." Fletcher nodded.

"You don't even know what you're getting yourself into," said Søren.

"I really don't care." She fixed him with a glare. "I refuse to wait around doing nothing until this case of severe incompetence clears itself up."

"I can't allow—" he started.

"How do you think you're going to stop me? You offered me safe harbor until other arrangements could be made, and now you're obligated to honor that offer. But if I'm not a full-fledged member of YOR, then your rules don't apply to me and I am going to do whatever the fuck I want."

Sparrow used the tips of her fingers to conceal a grin as Søren went slack-jawed at Fletcher's irrefutable logic.

"Fine. Do what you want; just don't expect us to protect you."

"I don't need your protection, Søren. I needed training, which I received. And for that I'm grateful. Thank you." Without giving Søren a chance to respond, she turned her attention to Philip. "What's the mission?"

"Follow me." Philip headed out of the common room toward the stairs, and Sparrow joined him. "That was incredible, by the way," he called to Fletcher over his shoulder. "I've never seen anyone put Søren in his place like that."

Fletcher skimmed Sparrow's profile. "I'm sure someone has done it a time or two."

Philip led the women to the door of a room that Fletcher had never been inside. It had been forbidden to her until now. "This is what I like to call the war room," he said, palming the knob.

As he pushed the door open, Fletcher's eyes swept across a wall of greenish-blue holograms: a few looked like blueprints for various mechanisms, others were cityscapes—one of Boston, and three others she could not name—all with bright red dots scattered across their sprawling aqua 3-D representations, and some were documents with official-looking UAT seals preceding their texts.

Philip pulled a rolling office chair from its spot tucked beneath a large polished-metal desk and plopped into it. He rolled up his sleeves, revealing his tattoos, and motioned to the tools and CPU minitowers adorning the desk. "Welcome to the command center," he said. "You'll travel into the city with Peter and Zoe. They'll drop you off near South Station. From there, your mission is to board a bullet train headed to the cordon at Washington, DC. You will retrieve items that have been left for you in a secure location inside the cordon station. Sparrow, you've done this before so you know the rendezvous point."

"Are you going to tell us what said items are?" Fletcher cut in.

"It's classified, strictly need-to-know. It's better if you don't know."

"Plausible deniability. Got it."

Philip handed a small rectangular holopermit to each woman and continued. "Your transit docs have been preprogrammed. I'm selecting some IDs for you out of the cache right now." He turned to the projected keyboard on his desk, typed some words, then transferred the information to the holopermits with a swipe of his finger. "There. All you need to do is upload those photos to the InvigorStyler, get made over, and you'll be good to go."

Fletcher scanned through the forms on her designated screen. "Hello, Grace Yoon."

"Really, Philip? Jane O'Neil again?" Sparrow looked up from her holopermit. "Why do I always draw the redhead? Changing my hair color is hardly even a disguise."

"Look at that picture. Her face is much fuller, and her complexion is at least three shades paler than yours."

"Shut up," she hissed. To Fletcher she said, "Come on."

"It's fine that I'm altering my appearance to match a facial scan of Grace Yoon, but what if someone wants to check my fingerprints? Those are still Fletcher Daniels originals." Fletcher wiggled her phalanges as Sparrow set up the InvigorStyler booth. "And you don't have any prints at all."

"They won't do any kind of scan. At best, they'll skim our IDs. Two-factor security measures are only in place for people who want to cross the border into The South. They don't give a damn about the safety of The Vault. We're getting off at Cordon Station, retrieving the package, then jumping on the next train back to Boston." She pressed one final button, and the InvigorStyler's access panel slid open with a *whoosh*. Fletcher peered inside the tube. An ultraviolet light cast her face in a purple glow.

"You're sure this thing won't cause disfiguration? This much direct exposure to UVs cannot be healthy."

"You've never heard of a tanning booth, Ms. American History Buff?"

"I have, actually. They gave people skin cancer," Fletcher sassed.

"You'll be alright. Take off your clothes."

"Excuse me?"

Sparrow snickered. "Sorry, that came out wrong. What I meant to say is strip down to your underwear. The machine needs as much flesh exposed as possible to ensure an even skin tone."

"You're serious?"

"If it would make you more comfortable, I'll turn around

while you undress."

"No. I mean, I don't care." Fletcher kicked off her sneakers, removed her socks. She peeled her T-shirt from her torso and dropped it to the ground, then unbuttoned her jeans and shimmied out of them. She stood there mostly naked, feeling insecure.

Sparrow bit her bottom lip and glanced away. "Get in and close your eyes."

"Okay, but if this goes horribly awry, I'll stab you with my sword."

"Deal." Sparrow smiled.

Fletcher shuffled into the tube. Anxiety bubbled inside her chest as the hatch glided closed behind her. She felt as though the walls were caving in on her, and her breath became ragged. She could see even through her closed eyes that the purple lights were growing brighter and brighter until they engulfed her.

A low hum sounded, deepening to a tenor that sent vibrations through her whole body. Her face tingled in an odd, itchy way, as it did whenever she got too close to the stray cats that meandered around her neighborhood.

Her loose hair lifted from her neck as a vortex of vaporous air saturated it from root to tip. She felt a pain—brief yet penetrating, like a line of pins pricking into her skin—in the arch of her right foot. Then, somewhere inside the appliance a buzzer wailed, and all the lights and pulsations fell away. She waited, the soles of her bare feet cold against the smooth steel floor. *Is that it? The timer chimed and the cooking's done?* Her breathing returned to normal.

The cylinder's access opened. Sparrow stood outside of it, a curious expression on her face. "Are you okay? You seem . . . traumatized."

Fletcher exited the Styler. "That was intense. And strange. Strangely intense? Intensely strange?"

"Yeah, that was a lot for your first time." Sparrow handed

Fletcher her T-shirt. "You look great. Come see in the mirror."

Fletcher tugged her shirt over her head, flattened out the wrinkles against her stomach, then stepped into her jeans. She moved around to the opposite side of the InvigorStyler where a floor-length mirror was embedded. The image in the looking glass was not of Fletcher. This person was a stranger with onyx hair and dark eyes lidded with an epicanthic fold; her lips were fuller, the bridge of her nose flatter. Her skin felt different, too—softer.

Fletcher tilted her head to the left, then to the right. She pressed her hand to the mirror. The reflection echoed her every movement. *It is me.* "I think I'd like to stay this way," she said. "I'm beautiful."

Sparrow's reflection appeared behind her in the glass. "Yes, but the *real* you is beautiful, too. You know that, right?"

The compliment took Fletcher by surprise. She found that her new skin blushed as easily as her old skin. "Your turn," she blurted, at a loss for a more appropriate response. "I can't wait to see you as a redhead."

Sparrow released a tiny *pfft* before moving to set up the InvigorStyler for her own transformation.

KILLIAN JOINED FLETCHER AND Sparrow as they waited in the common room for Peter and Zoe to finish their turns in the InvigorStyler. Fletcher shoved her hands into the pockets of her leather jacket, edginess mounting. "All those weapons drills and we're not going out armed."

"Bulky trench coats are our go-to concealed-carry clothes, but they aren't really in fashion this season, so we'd definitely call attention to ourselves by wearing them."

"Cute. That hair, not so much," Fletcher teased.

Sparrow scoffed.

"I know we're meant to be a couple of travelers instead of gun-toting menaces to the Patriarchy, but . . ."

"It feels reckless, going out into the world defenseless." Sparrow completed Fletcher's sentence. "You've prepared your mind and body to anticipate the worst possible situation at all times."

"Right. It's counterintuitive." Fletcher nodded. "Exactly what I was thinking."

"Don't worry, fists are with you always," Killian reminded her. "You know how to use 'em."

Their conversation was interrupted by the sound of Zoe and

Peter plodding down the stairs. They moved to the hallway to meet them at the landing. While Sparrow and Killian seemed unaffected, Fletcher was stunned to see how drastically they had each changed themselves, Zoe opting to pose as a Latina and Peter as a blond-haired, blue-eyed Caucasian. "How is your friend going to recognize you?" she asked Peter. "I don't mean to sound insensitive, but you literally went from black to white."

"He's seen me in this skin before; it's my default disguise. I didn't draw this ID by chance. I chose it myself. The US may no longer exist, but in The Vault white men are still less likely to be hassled by Bluecoats than dark-skinned men."

"I don't think I ever realized that." Disgust distorted Fletcher's artificial features. She was repulsed by the idea of racial bias, but also at her own ignorance of its continued existence. The Vault had always seemed deplorable for everyone, regardless of skin tone. "Racism is something I wish would have faded into oblivion alongside America."

"Racism, classism—oppression begets oppression. Fight one, fight them all," said Peter.

Fletcher ruminated on the words for a moment. Inspired, she responded, "Let's go fight then, shall we?"

The group nodded in unison, then each said their goodbyes to Killian. "Come back safe," he told Sparrow.

"I will." She hugged him.

And the foursome ventured out.

Zoe had insisted on driving, which irked Sparrow. They squabbled over it for a few minutes. Zoe called Sparrow a control freak. Sparrow countered with, "I'm not a control freak. When you're driving, I fear for my life more than I do when I see a pair of Reclamation Agents." Fletcher did not know how to drive, but volunteered to try her hand at it anyway in the hopes that the suggestion would quash the argument. In the end, it had produced the desired effect.

The van with matte black windows dropped Sparrow and Fletcher three city blocks away from South Station.

"You know where to meet us when you get back?" Peter asked as the women climbed out of the car.

"The scrap heap in Mission Hill," Sparrow replied and closed the door.

The mention of the junkyard set Fletcher's synapses alight, conjuring up an image of a smiling Jonah in his cruddy coveralls. The memory was as vivid as a rainbow after a spring storm, and as relentless as the crash of rolling thunder. She could lose herself in it, she was sure, but her attention was needed elsewhere. She shook herself free of the recollection, aided by the sound of the van's engine backfiring as it pulled away.

"Where did you go just now?" Sparrow wondered as she and Fletcher walked the smoky pavement. "Your mind was elsewhere."

"Jonah worked in that junkyard. He called it The Motorcar Graveyard because that's where all of Boston's expensive, obsolete vehicles went to die, postwar. Abject poverty has done wonders for the traffic situation in The Vault. It's a brilliant strategy on The Government's part. If unsavory poor folk want to travel long distances, we're dependent on the high-speed railways they control."

"Huh. Yeah."

As they approached the heart of Dewey Square, South Station came into view. Fletcher looked up in awe at its tall granite arches, Grecian columns, and the giant clock—whose corroded hands had been stuck on the same Roman numerals, 3:21, for an eternity—that topped the behemoth building. She'd never had a reason to pass the station as it was more than a mile outside of her usual route from her father's house to the library, but she had seen a few old snapshots of it. There used to be a statue of an eagle adorning the building's apex until the newly formed UAT Government tore it down. Eagles symbolized freedom and courage, and that was not a message the leaders of The Unified American Territories wanted to send to their Northern citizens.

Sparrow moved to open the door but stopped. "We're going to see more Bluecoats in here than you're used to," she whispered. "Probably a few Agents, too. Act natural and remember you're unrecognizable."

My nerves must be showing. "Okay."

Fletcher noticed the increased police presence the instant she set foot in the station. She was glad to have been forewarned; else it would have affected her demeanor. The second thing she noticed was the bizarre stillness of the place. She imagined that in days past throngs of tourists and commuters would have stuffed such a major transportation hub to the brim. But there were no tourists anymore, apart from the occasional flock of Southerners who came to experience how shitty life was on the wrong side of the wall. It was an adventure for them, something scary and exotic—a day at the zoo, at the end of which they could return to their comfortable lives and tell their comfortable friends all about it. There were hardly any commuters anymore, either. *Who can afford transit passes?* They didn't come cheap, and there were more essential things to spend a day's wages on.

She followed Sparrow into the Station. They came to a standstill in front of a huge digital kiosk displaying the call numbers, track numbers, and departure times of trains headed for various destinations. Fletcher had never fathomed that there would be so many options, so many places to go.

"Can I help you ladies find your way?" a white-haired, dark-skinned Bluecoat in a reflective lime-colored vest asked Fletcher.

"I, uh," she stumbled.

"Yes, please," Sparrow answered for her. "We need train 139. Can you point us to track seven?"

His eyes narrowed. "Headed to the cordon? May I see your holopermits, please?"

Fletcher, uncomfortable, removed the thin screen from her pocket, flicked it on and accessed her transit document for the officer. He scrutinized it before moving on to Sparrow's.

"What is your reason for traveling today?"

Thinking on her feet, Fletcher reached for Sparrow's hand. She intertwined their digits and beamed at her. Twice in one day she'd had Sparrow's hand in her own. *If I'm not careful, I'll get used to it.* "My wife promised to take me to the border wall. I've never seen it before, and I hear it's a modern architectural marvel! It's not much in the way of a honeymoon, but it's what we had the funds for."

The Bluecoat's posture relaxed. He flashed the women a small smile. "Congratulations on your marriage. I hope the wall meets your expectations." He gestured to a set of glass doors to his right. "Head through those doors. Your platform is the one on the far left."

"Thank you so much."

"Let's go, sweetheart." Sparrow tugged Fletcher's arm. "We don't want to miss our train."

Sparrow had been right about not having to clear a security check. The conductor barely examined their documents before waving them onto the train. They found seats in the second car, Sparrow on the aisle, and Fletcher at the window.

"That was genius, the honeymoon thing," said Sparrow.

"I thought he'd be sympathetic to a newlywed couple. He was wearing a wedding ring."

"Oh? I hadn't noticed that."

Fletcher shrugged her shoulders and turned to the window. "I'm observant. My dad says it's one of my best traits."

"Your dad is right."

The train's horn blew three times, and then it chugged away from the platform. As the engine picked up speed, Fletcher felt the rumble of steel wheels meeting steel track. Before she knew it, the landscape outside her window was reduced to a grayish blur. The rumbling dissipated, giving way to a smooth forward motion. "It feels like we're floating."

"We've got a few hours of floating ahead of us." Sparrow sank into the blue cushioned seat. "Get comfortable."

"I need to ask you something." Fletcher broke the long stretch of easy silence she and Sparrow had settled into.

"Go ahead."

She swept her gaze around the train car. It wasn't crowded, but two older gentlemen were seated a few rows ahead, and a mixed party of five was at the front—Southerners, she could tell by their too-brightly colored, too-well-kempt attire. "Put your arm around me," she instructed.

Sparrow was perplexed but stretched her arm around Fletcher's shoulders.

Fletcher cuddled into the nape of Sparrow's neck, her simulated red curls tickling her nose. "The package we're picking up . . . is it from another faction of YOR?"

"No," Sparrow whispered. "There is no other faction of YOR; we're it. There may be other resistance groups in other cities, but we have no way of contacting them. The package was smuggled across the border from The South."

"So you do have Southern allies?"

"How else do you suppose we could've acquired the tech we work with? Most of it is illegal in the Northern Territories. Killian and I had to make a dozen trips down here for all the InvigorStyler pieces. It took us months to secure them all."

"Who are they?"

"I've never had the pleasure of meeting them."

"We're on a mission to retrieve contraband technology from

some unknown benefactors." Fletcher stirred, half anxious, half eager. "I can't believe this is my life. My father would kill me where I stand."

"No, he wouldn't. He'd be proud of you."

Fletcher was unaware that those were words she needed to hear right in that moment until she'd heard them. Jericho had said them to her so many times for such insignificant accomplishments—the first time she had tied her shoes, the first time she had walked to school on her own. "I'm proud of you, Little Princess." She loved that about him, those small kindnesses he showed her every day, and she missed them.

"Thanks." She settled back into her seat, and when Sparrow tried to slip her arm away, she leaned farther into the crook of her elbow. "Can we sit like this for a little while?" It was dangerous, how comfortable she felt with Sparrow, how much she liked touching her and being touched by her.

"Sure," Sparrow replied. Fletcher caught the grin playing at the corners of her mouth.

chapter fifteen

"LAST STOP, CORDON STATION—Washington, DC," an announcement boomed through speakers hidden somewhere within the railcar's tin-like roof. "Passengers seeking transfer into Washington, DC, must be screened by the police before boarding. Please proceed to a security checkpoint, located at Gates Two, Four and Six, and have your documents ready for scanning."

As the train trundled to a halt at an open-air platform, Fletcher gawped at the massive cordon wall just beyond it. The barrier was constructed of solid alloy, stood at least forty feet tall, by her estimation, and stretched as far as she could see in either direction. It was overkill to her, a looming leviathan separating the haves from the have-nots. She wondered how Southerners felt about it, if to them it was a shining guardian shielding their glistening world from the taint of Northern undesirables. "It's hideous," she said, focusing on The Unified American Territories flag emblazoned above a set of giant rolling gates.

"I know." Sparrow stood to disembark. "Follow my lead," she mouthed. "We'll be quick."

They stepped out of the car onto a cement platform, which they followed until the gray slabs metamorphosed into milky-opalescent tile. At the far edge of the concourse rose a grandiose structure of snowy marble, sloping crystal skylights, and twin gilded archways. It was striking how clean the world was here, as though it had been submerged in a vat of bleach and scrubbed spotless. It made Fletcher uneasy.

The golden arches drew nearer, and Fletcher had to squint to see that there were two men in all-white uniforms posted at each arch. The men had handguns—white to match their outfits—holstered to their belts. *Are they soldiers or policemen?* she speculated, not in the least because she realized that their attire functioned as camouflage, but because Bluecoats in The Vault carried nothing more deadly than collapsible batons.

Feeling vulnerable, she reached back between her shoulder blades where the smooth leather hilt of her sword normally rested. She had become accustomed to it being there after weeks and weeks of wearing it around the Visitor's Center. Killian had poked fun at her about it, asking who she was planning to fight while in the kitchen doing household chores. "I have to get used to how it feels," she'd told him. "I want it to be an extension of me." She found nothing and derided herself for forgetting that she hadn't been allowed to travel with it.

Sparrow grabbed Fletcher's bent elbow and eased her arm back down to her side. "Steady," she cooed. Fletcher bit her lip and gave a curt nod.

They opted to enter the building through the archway on the left, and the uniformed man stationed there heaved open the bulky glass door for them. "Welcome to Cordon Station," he said cordially, though the tight, downturned curves of his maw gave away his contempt for the pair of Vaulters.

The only thing that offended Fletcher's senses more than the ostentatious interior design of the train station was how loud it was in contrast to the one she had departed from. There were hordes of people everywhere, laughing and conversing. Some were video chatting on interconnected HoloPods with folks who were goodness only knows where in The Southern Territories while others were sitting at tables stuffing their faces with oversized meals from vendors Fletcher had never heard of. On either side of the first floor and mezzanine were clothing shops that pumped drum-heavy music and saccharine fragrances into the air, their windows displaying wares in violently bright colors—yellows, greens, oranges, and pinks in a variety of fluorescent pigments. Every store boasted a line of overeager consumers.

Fletcher found the whole scene insufferable while the Southerners reveled in it. "How can they live like this? How dare they live like this when Vaulters are surviving on crumbs!" Her volume increased, and even though she could see that people around her were beginning to take notice, she could not keep herself in check. "We're having our education, our cognizance, ripped away from us because we're poor, and these fucking—"

"Stop." Sparrow stepped round to meet Fletcher's gaze. She cupped her face with both hands. "I know how you're feeling right now, but you have to swallow it, alright? I need you to hold it together. Can you do that for me?"

Fletcher subdued her anger with a series of heavy puffs. "Yes."

"Good." She took Fletcher by the hand and led her farther into the station.

The women shuffled through the crowds of people, past the train gates and waiting areas, beyond the eateries and shops, and took a left down a narrow corridor. At the end of the hallway, nestled in the farthest recess of the building, was a swinging door with a window in its upper center. Affixed below the thick pane was a black plastic sign, its bold white letters reading "STOCKROOM."

Sparrow peered through the window before venturing into the room. Fletcher tiptoed across the threshold behind her but halted when the harsh overhead lights flared on.

"They're motion-sensor activated," Sparrow assured.

Fletcher took her word for it and continued to trace her footsteps through a maze of high metal shelves thick with bundles of clothing and cardboard boxes. Skirting a tight bend, she jumped as three standing figures entered her line of sight. A squeal escaped her throat before she could squelch it, a mere second after it dawned on her that she was staring at glossy, featureless heads atop faux flesh-colored torsos.

Sparrow whirled around.

"Mannequins." Fletcher shook her head at her own jitteriness, and waved Sparrow on.

Near the back of the supplies, they came upon a row of retired sales counters. Sparrow scanned each worktop until she found one with an arrow drawn in the fine coating of dust. She wiped away the symbol with her palm, then hurdled over the flat surface to the opposite side. Fletcher leaned over the countertop to watch as she rummaged through a deep compartment, came up empty, and reached into another.

"Got it." She yanked her limb out of the slot, her hand clutching a corded burlap sack the size of a half-tin of beans.

"I guess big things come in small packages?"

"We wouldn't be here if they didn't."

"Why am I here? You didn't need me for that," Fletcher gestured at the flat bag.

Sparrow stretched across the counter, grabbed Fletcher by the lapel and tucked the baggie into the inner pocket of her jacket. "Satisfied?"

"Not at all."

"Hey, Savannah, is that you in there?" A man's voice reverberated throughout the cavernous stockroom.

Sparrow froze, her eyes wide.

Fletcher peeped over her shoulder. She could not see the man, nor his silhouette. *He hasn't seen us yet, either.*

"Hello? I know someone is in here because the lights are

on," he declared, sounding closer to their position.

Damn motion sensors! Fletcher climbed onto the countertop and scrambled into a seated position, trapping Sparrow between her spread thighs. Frantic, she wrapped her legs around Sparrow's hips, her arms around her shoulders—held her closer than she had ever held anyone—and kissed her. Hard. Her fingers caught in too-tight auburn curls, and she tried to focus on how everything about Sparrow was off. She's wearing a stranger's skin, sporting a stranger's features, she told herself. *You're not kissing her. It isn't real.* She might have been able to convince herself if Sparrow hadn't leaned into it so readily, slipped her hands up Fletcher's thighs, rested them on her hips and squeezed.

"What are you—ah, sorry, I'm—" the man jumbled his words as he caught sight of the trespassers.

Fletcher pushed Sparrow away and twisted toward the man. "Oh god!" She covered her face, feigning embarrassment. Sparrow's features reflected her shock, though Fletcher suspected it had little to do with the man standing before them.

"Um, you two can't be back here." The man stuffed his hands into the pouches of his orange bib apron. "It's a staff only area."

Fletcher hopped off the counter. She offered her hand to Sparrow and helped her climb over it. Avoiding the man's stare, she mumbled, "Sorry. We're leaving," then started for the exit, towing Sparrow behind her.

The man stepped aside, accidentally reversing into a shelf. Fletcher could almost feel his glare boring into them as they passed. "Wait a minute," he called after them.

Fletcher closed her eyes and pursed her lips. She took a second to compose herself before turning around to answer him. "Yes?"

"Did you steal anything?" His tenor sounded more distressed than accusatory. Fletcher swept her first solid look across him. He had shadowy bags under his eyes and a stubbly chin in need of a shave. She noted his washed-out denim pants, the graying threadbare T-shirt beneath his smock.

"No. I swear we didn't. Yell for a Bluecoat if you want to, but you and I come from the same place, so you know all a Vaulter really has in this world is their word."

"Just go." He shook his head. "And don't let them hear you call them Bluecoats. They hate that."

Fletcher gave him a nod of appreciation; then she and Sparrow bolted for the door.

Fletcher stood, arms folded across her chest, shifting her weight from foot to foot. Although the next bullet train to Boston was scheduled to arrive at the platform shortly, the wait had become unbearable. She didn't want to talk about what had happened in the storeroom, didn't want to think about how, despite her best efforts, kissing Sparrow made her feel as if a wild animal had been set loose inside her ribcage. "I'm sorry," she blurted. "I practically assaulted you back there. It was rash and inappropriate. I couldn't think of anything else to do that would make us look less criminal."

"You don't have to apologize. It was quick thinking." Sparrow grinned. "You saved me twice in one day."

"That almost makes us even."

Sparrow cocked her head. "What?"

"Nothing."

A few hundred yards down the track, a train began to decelerate. Sparrow read the bold purple numbers on the front of the locomotive, "2249. That's us."

The second passenger car reached a stop in front of them. Its access slid open, and riders began to deboard: an older couple garbed in fine furs; three teenagers, along with their mother and father, all of whom were preoccupied with HoloPods; and a man and woman dressed in tailored suits and reflector-lensed sunglasses.

The female Reclamation Agent knocked shoulders with Fletcher and faltered in her gait. Fletcher's palms began to sweat. The hair on the nape of her neck stood on end. Her arms were obscured by jacket sleeves, but she knew that her skin had rumpled into gooseflesh. *This will either be a brawl, or nothing.* Her muscles involuntarily prepared themselves for the former.

"Excuse me," said the Agent, fixing a stare on Fletcher's face.

Fletcher waited for the glimmer of recognition to dawn on the Agent's features. When it hadn't shown after a handful of seconds, she replied, "Pardon me."

The Agents continued on their way, though Fletcher was still able to hear the woman comment to her partner, "See, some of them do have manners." Fletcher sneered at their retreating backsides. Sparrow saw the disgusted expression and shoved her onto the train.

"I told you you'd be unrecognizable," she muttered as she collapsed into a seat. "Didn't you believe me?"

"I'm cautious never to underestimate an Agent. I understand now why there are no InvigorStylers in The Vault. Everyone would be able to hide in plain sight."

"*Shhh.*" Sparrow motioned at the conductor who had just entered their car. She queued up her travel documents.

Fletcher searched her jacket pockets, one after the other, to no avail. She reached into her inside pocket but found only the small burlap sack. She shot out of her seat, dug through every pocket in her jeans. She could not find the holopermit.

Panic climbed her spine like a ladder. The conductor was a few rows ahead and approaching fast. *I can't blow the whole mission.* She turned her back to him, opened her jacket and clasped the tiny bag of smuggled commodities. She dropped the sack into Sparrow's lap as discreetly as she could. Sparrow concealed it with her palm.

"Miss," the conductor called out to Fletcher.

"Just a second." She turned to Sparrow. "Sweetie, did I give you my holopermit?"

Sparrow scrunched the sack into her fist, slipping her hands into the pockets of her green peacoat. She felt around, pretending to look for something she knew she did not have. "Nope."

"Miss, I believe this is yours." The conductor handed over her holopermit. "You dropped it on the platform."

The sigh of relief Fletcher breathed could have shaken the cordon wall to pieces. "Oh, thank you, sir! I would lose my brain if it weren't inside my skull."

"Glad to help." He tipped his hat and moved along to the next car.

She fell into her seat. Sparrow gave her an incredulous look.

"It must have fallen out of my jacket when that fucking Agent bumped into me." Fletcher rubbed her forehead. "I just want this day to be over already. My nerves are raw."

"Poor Ivy League." Sparrow coaxed her to lean back into her loose embrace. "It's done now. We're going home."

Fletcher soughed. She rested her temple against Sparrow's shoulder as the train lurched away from the station.

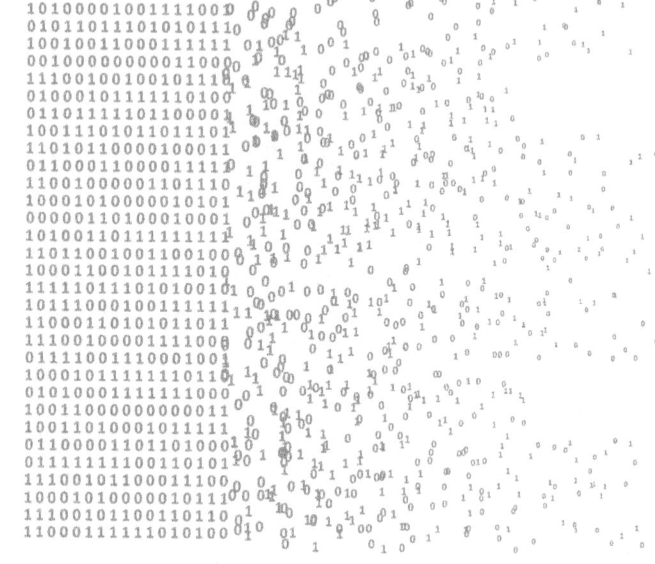

chapter sixteen

BY THE TIME THEY returned to South Station, darkness had swathed the city like a cloak. Fletcher had never been so glad to walk the nighttime streets of Boston. She hadn't made it past the cordon wall into The Southern Territories, but she had still come close enough to dread the prospect of ever having to be relocated there. She'd always known The Southern way of living was different from what she was used to, but hadn't realized Southerners were such gluttonous, covetous creatures until she'd had the chance to be among them. They were surrounded by a cacophony of *stuff*, bombarded by shiny things urging them to open their wallets and buy, buy, buy. They seemed to need high-tech gadgets and swanky fashion and plates upon plates of food to make themselves feel whole. The Vault wasn't high-tech, wasn't fashionable, wasn't swamped with gastronomical delicacies, but it was real, honest. The people here appreciated everything they had even though most of them had next to nothing. To be blinded by junk, to be defined by what you owned . . . that wasn't any kind of life at all. There had to be a middle ground, someplace in the world where people could live contentedly, not deprived, but not in wanton piggishness, either.

"I never thought I'd say this, but I'm happy to be back

in The Vault."

Sparrow laughed. "What, you mean The South isn't your scene?"

"It's so excessive. Those people have more than they could ever need and still want more."

"The world is not enough when you have the whole thing at your disposal."

"I feel gross, like I need to wash that place off my skin."

"Same here. I always do when I've been down there." Sparrow bunched her untamed curls into a bun and moaned, "I cannot wait to be me again."

Fletcher kicked a mound of loose sediment, watching as the tiny pebbles scattered into the road. "Yeah."

They approached a chain-link fence surrounding the Mission Hill Scrapyard. By the light of trash can fires beyond it, Fletcher surveyed the lifeless corpses of flattened cars piled high against the dark sky. She pictured Jonah there, hauling chunks of metal from one end of the yard to the other. Some of the men and women in blue jumpsuits who were working the night shift probably knew him.

"There they are." Sparrow pointed to the cargo van parked near the rear gates of the lot.

As they advanced, they saw Zoe leaning against the driver's side door, waiting for them with crossed arms. Fletcher could tell by her posture that something was amiss.

"How'd it go at the Cordon?" Zoe wondered.

Sparrow patted the outside of her peacoat near the pocket where the burlap sack rested. "All good. You?"

"Not so good."

"Why?"

"Where's Peter? Is he okay?" Fletcher was worried.

"He's okay. He's in the back. Get in. We'll explain on the way home."

For the longest while, the journey to Vermontshire remained silent. Zoe peered into the rearview mirror every few minutes, checking on a browbeaten Peter. Fletcher didn't know him well, he being the quiet type, but even a stranger would have been able to tell his spirit was broken. She was hungry for details, but could not bring herself to press him to divulge them. Whatever had gone down on his and Zoe's mission, it was bad.

"I couldn't get the meds," Peter murmured.

"How come?" Sparrow queried.

He picked at his nail beds. "Mateo wasn't there."

"Alright, but that's not everything, is it? Otherwise, I'd say we could go back again in a few days."

Peter groaned. "I went around to the back entrance of the pharmacy and knocked our established code. I waited, tried again. No one answered. So I thought I'd stroll in through the front door. It was within business hours; it should've been fine. There were three people working behind the security glass. I asked one of the techs I'm friendly with where Mat was." He wiped his eyes with the heel of his hand. "She told me Agents came for him a week ago. He's in a Processing Center being Reclaimed."

Sparrow gasped. "I am so sorry, Peter."

Fletcher knew nothing she could say would offer him any comfort. Instead, she draped her arms around him and pulled him to her chest. He buried his face in her jacket and began to cry.

It was close to ten o'clock by the time the small group returned to their forest hideaway. Charlie met them in the foyer, concern on her crinkled brow. "Everyone alright?"

Zoe walked Peter into the bunkroom, dodging the question.

"We're fine." Fletcher shimmied out of her jacket and hung it on the coat rack. "But Peter got some awful news about his friend."

"Oh dear." Charlie ushered Fletcher and Sparrow into the common room. They were greeted by multiple sets of eager eyes.

"Report," demanded Søren from his chair.

"No injuries. No incidents involving Agents or Police." Sparrow sauntered toward Philip. "I've got a present for you," she said, and tossed him the burlap sack. She sat down in an empty chair and continued with her report. "We were almost discovered by a civilian during retrieval, but Fletcher did some maneuvering to get us out of it." She winked at her.

Fletcher's skin flushed as she settled beside Killian on the cushioned sofa.

"Really?" Søren regarded Fletcher. "So you'd say your mission was successful?" he asked her.

"Ours was."

Sparrow shifted, awkward in her chair. "Zoe and Peter had trouble in Boston."

"Why am I hearing this from you instead of either of them?" There was a hint of anger to his question.

"Because Peter isn't in the best emotional state, and Zoe is consoling him." Fletcher's tone teetered on the edge of antagonism.

Sparrow jumped up. "I'm going to grab Zoe and Peter. We're all going to head upstairs to slip back into our own skins, and when we're done, we'll discuss it calmly as a group." She motioned for Fletcher to follow her.

"Just answer me this: Were they able to get my neurosedatives?" Søren called after them.

Fletcher swiveled around to him. "No."

For the first time since she'd known him she saw fear on

Søren's face. It stirred sympathy within her. She reminded herself that it wasn't his fault he was perpetually one small step away from seething madness. This was what Reclamation had done to him, and it took everything he had to battle against his rage. "We will figure out a way to get you what you need, but not tonight. Tonight we're going to rest, and we're going to comfort Peter as best we can because he found out today that he may have lost someone he loves. Okay?"

Her words sobered him. Softly he uttered, "Okay."

Fletcher was the last one into the InvigorStyler. She found the reversion process less jarring. The machine hadn't needed to be configured this time as it scanned the invisible barcode etched into the sole of her foot. She dressed, then checked the mirror. Her hair seemed blonder, her irises a bit more gold. She stared at herself until she felt at home in her own skin again.

"There you are," Sparrow called to her from the doorway.

"There *you* are." Fletcher moved to her. She reached out and looped a few of Sparrow's soft, brown tresses between her fingers. "Much better."

"I know," she smirked.

Fletcher withdrew her hand. "How's Peter?"

"He's asleep. He was out as soon as he laid down. He just . . . felt too much today. Beyond the shock of losing Mateo, he's disappointed in himself. He thinks he failed Søren."

"Nothing about this is his failure. He did all he could under the circumstances."

"I told him that. Zoe told him that. But he's going to feel how he feels, regardless of what anyone says."

Fletcher sighed. "The only way he's going to feel any different is if we find a solution to Søren's problem. We have to get his medication somehow."

"We really do," Sparrow agreed. "If he goes without, things around here will get ugly."

Fletcher flashed back to the way Jonah was before his parents had admitted him to Alcedonia: flesh bruised and lacerated from constant thrashing, voice hoarse from hours of shrieking. She had wondered then if he would be better off dead, and wondered now if Søren would be as well. "We can't let that happen to him. I don't care how much of an obstinate, unpleasant mule he is. No one deserves that."

"You're right. The trouble is, I don't know what our options are now that Mateo is gone."

Downstairs in the shared sleeping quarters, the grandfather clock chimed midnight. Though Fletcher's mind raced for an answer, her body was enervated. Sparrow's heavy eyelids gave away her exhaustion, too. "We can't come up with a solution when we're both dog-tired. We need to sleep. Tomorrow, we'll revisit this discussion as a group."

"Good idea," said Sparrow. "I'll follow you down."

chapter seventeen

FLETCHER RAN HARD, NOT because she had to—she wasn't an official member of the team, and just as easily could have stayed in bed while everyone else was out brutalizing themselves—but because she wanted to. All the legitimate Youths Opposed to Reclamation had long ago fallen far behind her. Normally during their morning mile run she was smack in the middle of the pack, but today even Sparrow could not keep pace with her. She completed four laps around the improvised running track, then pushed herself into the forest, leaving the rest of YOR to finish their run and do whatever.

She concentrated on the sound of brittle twigs cracking beneath her heavy footfalls, on the wisps of steamy breath, like tiny ghosts, leaching from her mouth into the brisk November air. Her best ideas had always come to her when she was under pressure, and a problem sizable enough to ruin lives and thwart years of hard-fought progress needed solving now. In four short days, when the last of his neurosedative injections wore off, Søren would devolve into a Berserker, and become an imminent danger to himself and everyone around him. Irrespective of her status, teammate or interloper, that was not something Fletcher was going to let happen.

She had beaten through vegetation, over spiny thickets of underbrush, and was circling back to the Visitor's Center patio. In all the time she'd been running, she had not thought up a viable solution. YOR had guns; they could rob a pharmacy or hospital if they were willing to be reckless, but that would take foolishness to a new level. If they were caught, and they likely would be, they would end up in prison, in the hands of Reclamation Agents, or dead—if they were lucky.

Killian was seated on the edge of the wooden patio, brushing up soil with his sneakers. Fletcher slowed to a jog, surprised to see him there.

"Here." He offered her a canteen. She took it and sat down beside him.

The cool water ran down her gullet. Driblets splashed down the front of her shirt. As she wiped them away, she asked, "Have I been gone long?"

"I'm bad at time." He shrugged. "Sparrow said you were gone long. She got worried."

"I didn't mean to make her worry."

"She likes you," he said, narrowing his bright blue eyes at her. "A lot."

Fletcher was uncomfortable under his scrutiny. "I gathered."

"Mmm." He kicked his feet, watched them swing. "You like her, too?"

Caught off guard and unwilling to lie to him, she stammered out the truth, "Yes, I do."

"Scared?"

Of so very many things. "I lose all the people I care about."

"Have people you care about, maybe lose them, better than not having them at all. Lots of bad things happen, make us sad, but . . . always alone is worse."

"You might be right. I don't know."

"S'okay. Sparrow here when you do know." He slapped his

knees. "Come. We all talk about how to keep Søren from . . . going bananas."

"Going bananas," she chortled. "No, we can't have that."

Fletcher stood with her spine flat against the timber-paneled wall, observing the conversation that had begun without her.

"The pharmacy is a no-go," Peter said from the edge of his seat. "I don't know anyone else there well enough to ask them for a year's supply of unauthorized neurosedative injections. I wouldn't ask for a day's worth."

"What about at another pharmacy?" asked Charlie. "Or a hospital? Is there anyone you trust who has access to the meds Søren needs? We're not even talking about a long-term supply, just something to tide him over until we can find a permanent solution."

"You're asking me if I know anyone who would be willing to put their own safety on the line for me. The answer is no. I had one person in my life who loved me that much, and he's gone now." Peter signaled across the room at Charlie.

"I'm sorry, Peter." Charlie frowned. "I had to ask."

"Let's open the question to the group. Anyone? One of us has to know somebody," declared Damon.

"This might be a stretch, but what about our contacts in The South?" Sparrow probed Søren.

"No."

"Why not? They've been more than willing to accommodate our need for other illicit supplies."

"Those supplies aren't illicit in The Southern Territories. Southerners are allowed, encouraged, to formulate and possess new technologies. Access to neurosedatives is tightly controlled everywhere in the country. They can't help me."

"So, what, we look outside the country? Like that's any

less illicit." Zoe's acerbity threw the discussion into upheaval. Everyone began to speak at once. Bickering and side-arguments arose, until all the flustered voices concaved into a sphere of noise.

Illicit. The word bounced around Fletcher's brain like a rubber ball. *Illegal. Criminal. That's it!* "I have an idea." Her voice was stifled by the pandemonium around her. She didn't have time to be polite. She had to announce her thought before it escaped her. "Everyone shut the hell up!"

"Whoa," blurted Killian from his spot on the wall beside her. A stunned silence blanketed the room.

"I know where we can get meds, no questions asked, if we have the Greenbacks."

"We have Redbacks." Søren sprang out of his chair, his face desperate and hopeful. "Where do we get the meds?"

"On any street corner in Mission Hill, from QuellSells."

"Quell!" Zoe cried. "You want him to inject that bootlegged pink trash into his body?"

"It may be bootlegged, but I wouldn't call it trash," Peter interjected. "Mateo did his senior thesis on Quell. He bought injections from a handful of different dealers, analyzed the compounds of each and compared them to a sample of The Government-designed neurosedatives. The chemical similarity was astounding. 'Like compounds have like properties and thus like effects on the body.'"

Zoe was appalled. "But what do *you* know about it? Do you know where or how it's made, who makes it?"

"If I knew how Quell was made, I'd be able to compound it myself. I'm a physician, not a pharmacologist."

"We know two things," Fletcher counted on her digits, "that it's cheap and that it works, or else every other person and their uncle wouldn't be using it. Right?"

"Yeah, okay," Zoe conceded the point.

"There's no way we could buy 730 doses of it at once,"

Damon stated. "I grew up on the streets. I know if we asked for that much, we'd get tagged as Bluecoats and blacklisted. Even if we went to multiple QuellSells, word would get around pretty fast."

"It isn't the best idea to constantly travel into the city for drugs. That's too high-risk. Even when we were getting neurosedatives from a legitimate source, we'd only make one trip a year," Peter said.

"Could we go in one night, a bunch of us, incognito?" Philip wondered.

Sparrow shook her head. "The solar panels will blow if we power-up the InvigorStyler more than a couple of times within a few hours."

"There's a QuellSell who lives across the street from my dad's place," Fletcher said. "We grew up together, used to play all the time when we were kids. I think I could get her to sell me the amount we need, but I'd have to meet up with her looking like me—recognizable, not disguised by the InvigorStyler."

"No! No way. That's a terrible idea," Sparrow protested.

"For once, you and I agree," said Søren. He set his gaze on Fletcher. "All the trouble we went through—*twice*—getting you safely out of the city. Do you really want to go back to the place Agents kicked in a door looking for you? To the home your father had to flee for his own protection?"

"No, I don't want to go back there! There's nothing left for me there. You had me convinced that I'd probably never go home again, and it took a lot for me to get good with that, but I'm willing to do it because you need help and right now it looks like I'm the only one who can help you. We might not be friends, Søren, but you have the right to a sound mind, just like everyone else does. I'll do whatever I can to protect that right. That's the reason I wanted to join YOR in the first place, remember?"

"Do you remember when I told you the one rule that should never be broken: If you're hot, never go out in public undisguised?

I really meant that." Sparrow moved across the room to be closer to Fletcher. She scooped her hands into her own. "The Agents have it in for you. I'd bet they've memorized your face, and you know damn well that that part of town is always crawling with them. I get that you feel like our rules don't apply to you and that you don't want us to tell you what to do, okay? So, I'm asking you, please, *please* don't put yourself in danger by going into the city like this. You will be caught."

Fletcher stared into Sparrow's pleading eyes, slipped her fingers into the spaces between hers. "From where I'm standing, this seems like our only option. If you have a better suggestion, please tell me."

Sparrow dropped her gaze and Fletcher's hands. "I don't."

"I'll turn myself in to Alcedonia," Søren huffed. "If you drop me off outside once my last injection has started to wear off, they'll have to treat me."

"I understand you're trying to be gallant here, but you're a fugitive," Fletcher retorted. "Alcedonia is a government facility. The staff would be obligated to turn you over to the BOE. That would put everyone you know and everything you've worked for in jeopardy."

Søren ran his fingers through his dark spiky hair. "Then I'll become someone else. ID Replacement."

"They won't treat you if your ID doesn't flag as Reclaimed," said Philip. "And you know we can't plant that info right now."

"Besides, you're the only one of us who has contact with Head Office," Sparrow added. "Head Office is the only way to contact our support across the cordon."

"Sounds like you're too important to the cause. YOR can't do without you, so I'm going to do this. For all of us," Fletcher said, motioning to the group.

"You might be doing this for all of us, but if it weren't for me, you wouldn't have to do it at all. I'm going with you."

"You don't go on assignments," Sparrow asserted. "The

aforementioned reasons notwithstanding, you don't trust yourself enough to carry a gun. This would have to be a weapons-hot mission, which would make you a liability."

"I go with her," Killian spoke up. "To keep her safe. Don't have to change my face," he smirked. "Agents don't want me. I'm already messed up."

"Alright. She still needs a driver. Any other volunteers?" Søren swept a glance around the room.

Sparrow waved a hand in his face. "Me."

"Not you. You're too emotionally involved, which is what I suspected would happen. If something were to go wrong—"

"Søren, give it a rest. This has nothing to do with my emotions. Where my brother goes, I go, which has been the deal since the beginning."

"The deal has changed."

"The hell it has!"

"Okay, let's not argue." Fletcher stepped between them. "Since I'm the one who'll be charging into this suicide mission, I want Killian and Sparrow by my side. I can't think of two people I'd rather have backing me up in a dangerous situation." She smiled at the twins and pointed at Sparrow. "But you're going to use the InvigorStyler." She turned to Søren. "Alright?"

"Fine. Give us the room," Søren murmured. He waited a beat, and when no one moved, raised his voice. "Get out now!" Everyone herded toward the exit.

The three remaining YOR members and single outsider regarded one another. Fletcher's forehead wrinkled. "What's—"

"I needed a moment. I'm not used to this."

"To what?"

"Feeling things. Positive things, like gratitude. Is that right?" Søren sought out confirmation from Sparrow. She gave him a nod of encouragement.

"I don't, uh—" he stumbled. "I guess what I'm trying to say is thank you."

"You're welcome."

"Is . . . she one of us now?" Killian inquired.

Søren assented with a head bow. "I'll deal with the backlash from Head Office, if there is any."

"It took you long enough." A sneer tugged at the corners of Sparrow's mouth. "I guess the only thing left to discuss is when this plan should be executed."

"Soon. Preferably before I've had time to process how reckless the whole thing is," said Fletcher. "It has to be at night. Most QuellSells don't operate in the daytime. A lot of them have legitimate jobs."

"Tomorrow night? That gives us plenty of time to do an equipment check and a thorough run-through of the streets and alleyways with Philip on his virtual map."

"Tomorrow night," Fletcher concurred.

"You three go sort it with Philip. I have to share the details of this ill-advised operation with Head Office."

"We'll ignore the shouting," Sparrow called after Søren as he departed the room. He dismissed her with a flick of his wrist. "That went well. Welcome to the family, officially."

"All I had to do to earn it was become his last resort."

"His incredibly heroic last resort." Sparrow knocked her shoulder into Fletcher's. Fletcher responded in kind, but stopped when she noticed Killian had been watching, his lips pinched.

"*Pfft*," he mumbled, then ambled out of the room.

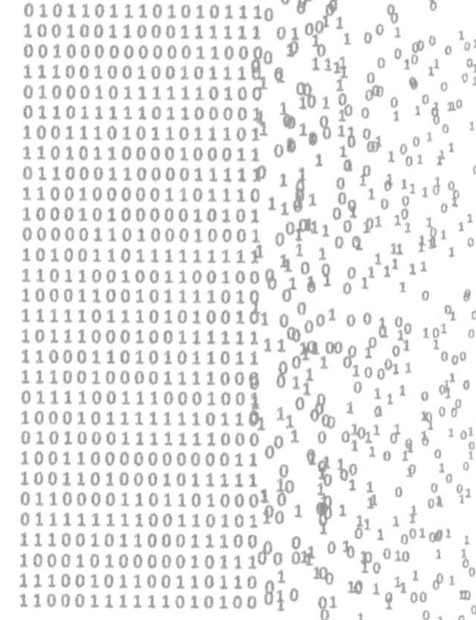

PHILIP STOOD OVER A cumbersome rectangular glass tank in the far corner of his "war room." Fletcher had entered this space only once before, and just yesterday, but was certain that the tank was a new accoutrement. She observed the murky brown liquid inside the container, heard its rolling boil, but had no idea what Philip might be concocting. "What's going on in there?" She wigwagged at the vat.

"I can't say yet. I'll let you know when it's all cooked up."

"Sure." An intricate blueprint of Tremont Street was projected across three holoscreens on the wall. She recognized it as the section that ran between Torpie and Alphonsus Streets, and registered that the red dot on the map represented the terrace house she had grown up in. She squelched her discomfort at seeing it through a sterile technical lens, so glossy in its cerulean holographic representation, so removed from the dirty, derelict reality of its being.

"What corner does your QuellSell friend operate on?"

"Tremont and South Whitney." As she said it, the red dot moved across the diagram to the intersection.

"It's a dead end," Philip observed.

"Always has been," Fletcher gibed.

"I guess we won't be parking on that street," said Sparrow.

"You've been to my neighborhood before. You know the best place to park would be here." Fletcher moved closer to the holoscreen and pointed at the northeast junction of Tremont and Alphonsus. "You've got Tremont right there and Huntington Ave half a mile to the north." She used her finger to glide the map upward. "Both of those intersect with Mass Ave."

"Ah, right. Mass Ave will get us to either old highway 90 or Storrow Drive, and out of the city."

"Mmhmm."

"I should teach you how to drive." Sparrow considered her.

Fletcher stifled a snicker. "Let's take one asinine mission at a time."

They heard a commotion coming from the Ranger's quarters above them. All three of their heads snapped up toward the ceiling as a muted yet irritated voice leaked down through the hoary parquets.

"Should we check—" Philip began.

"I'll go," Fletcher announced. "I already know everything about the neighborhood, and I'm not the one driving." She left them to finalize the getaway plans and proceeded to the end of the long corridor and up the stairs.

The door to the Ranger's quarters was slightly ajar, afternoon sunlight from the windows shimmering through the crack into the corridor. Fletcher peered into the room and saw Søren seated on the bed facing away from the entry. She was about to knock when he began to speak into the open air. "I didn't ask her to do it. I wouldn't have. She volunteered, sir."

"Unsurprising. That's her nature," a tinny voice answered.

Fletcher stiffened. It was the same method of communication the Agents had used the night they came for Grier in the library. But what struck her even more than the titular head of YOR using Reclamation Agents' technology was the fact that she thought she recognized the voice on the other end of it. She barged into the room. Søren twisted toward her. "Fletcher," he spluttered, and touched his finger to his ear. A static charge crackled through the ether, then dissipated. He sprang to his feet.

"Was that an Agent?"

"What? No."

Fletcher's distrust gave way to anger. "You're setting me up, aren't you?"

"I'm not."

"Then what the fuck are you doing with BOE tech?" she spat, inches from his face.

"Head Office gave it to me. It's government surplus. It isn't exclusive to the BOE; all the agencies use it."

She regarded him with incensed eyes. "I put my life, my father's life, in your hands. I don't care how important you are to this organization, if you're lying to me, I swear I will smother you in your sleep."

Eyes bulging and pupils dilated, Søren retreated away from her. "I would never conspire with the Department of Reclamation! I had a home, a family. Now all I have is this . . . this anger they gave me. I hate them!" He rushed at the broad side of the bed, clawed the covers from the mattress. Bunching the top sheet in each fist, he tore it in two. "I hate them!"

"Shit." Fletcher had witnessed a Berserker's fit before. She knew this was only going to escalate. "Help!" She screamed as loudly as she could. "I need help up here! Bring Søren's meds."

She watched as Søren snatched the wooden stool from its place beside the bed and heaved it across the room. It bounced off the floor, slid on its side into the bathroom. "I fucking hate them! Fucking hate—Gahh! Ahh!" He snarled, foam sopping the corners of his mouth. He raised his hands to his head, slapped himself twice. "HATE!" He screamed, spun around, and ran face first into the wall, then staggered rearward.

Blood trickled down his forehead. *A few more bashes and he's dead.* Fletcher had to do something. What though? YOR had trained her for combat. She was confident she could knock him unconscious, tall gangly thing that he was. But what could she do to make him stop without hurting him? She scanned the room, spotted a pillow on the floor near the headboard. She lunged over the bed, snatched up the cushion, then hurled herself at Søren's back. She cinched her legs around his waist, and with both hands on its seams squeezed the pillow to his crown.

"Fuck! Shit!" He smashed his forehead into the wall again and again, Fletcher clutching onto his thin frame as though he were her loyal stallion and they were riding into battle together.

Footsteps pounded in the corridor. Killian, Peter, and Damon rushed into the room.

"Let go of him!" Damon yelled as he and Killian bolted at Søren. Fletcher flung herself backward, landing on the mattress a microsecond before the men were upon him. She released her grasp on the pillow, brushed her disheveled hair from her face and sat up in time to watch them wrestle Søren to the ground.

"Shh, s'okay. You're okay," Killian whispered, ensnaring Søren's throat in his curled bicep. He applied pressure to Søren's windpipe until he stopped struggling. The muscular man sat down. Legs bowed, he cradled Søren's head in his lap. Damon joined them on the floor and rolled up the left sleeve of Søren's black sweatshirt.

Peter approached his limp friend with an auto-injector syringe at the ready. He kneeled above Søren and pressed the syringe into the soft flesh of his inner elbow. When he finished, he capped the needle and pocketed the injector. He stood. "What happened, Fletcher?"

"We were arguing—"

"Søren argues with everyone." Peter cut her off. "What triggered him?"

"I accused him of working for the Department of Reclamation."

"Why would you do that? Why would you even think that?"

"The device he was using to communicate with Head Office is the same one the Agents use to communicate with each other. I've never seen it used by anyone other than Agents. Add to that the fact that he was talking about me; I had every reason to be suspicious."

"You were wrong. We're his family. He'd never betray us."

"He wouldn't acknowledge me as part of the family until this morning! He's treated me like an outsider ever since I arrived, and he only changed his mind because I volunteered to save his ass."

Peter let out an exasperated breath as he lowered himself onto the mattress beside Fletcher. "He's treated you like an outsider because you were one. If you're here and you aren't one of us, you're meant to be protected by us. That's the protocol. You failed the shooting test, but everything changed this morning when you volunteered to save his ass."

"Why?"

He sighed as if to say, *You're so obtuse.* "You're the Most Wanted of us all and even though you knew you'd have to go into the city completely exposed, you were still willing to put yourself in danger for him. Regardless of the rules Head Office has set for us, we've set the cardinal one: Take care of each other, no matter the cost. That's what makes us a family. That's how we survive. You've earned your place."

Fletcher looked down at the unconscious Berserker, guilt weighing heavy on her conscience. "Will he be okay?"

"Eventually."

Eventually? *What the hell have I done?*

"Let's get him on the bed," Damon said to Killian. Fletcher and Peter cleared the mattress as Damon took Søren by the calves and Killian took him by the shoulders. Together, they hoisted him up.

Fletcher seized the blood-soaked pillow from the bed. *This won't do.* She headed for the bathroom, stopping to turn the wooden stool right-side-up and glide it away from the door frame before continuing toward the sink. She twisted on the tap, splashed cold water onto the cushion and rubbed the red stain until all that remained was a pinkish wet spot. Satisfied with her work, she returned to the main room. She flipped the pillow over in her hands and plumped it, then slid it beneath Søren's lolling head. "These things are luxuries around here; otherwise I'd bring him a dry one." She bent down, snatched the old wool blanket from the pile of tousled bedclothes and tucked Søren into it. "How long until he wakes up?"

"Between the adrenaline rush, Killian's chokehold, and the neurosedative, he'll be comatose until morning," Peter told her. "You can all clear out. I'll stay with him for a while."

"Holler if you need anything," said Damon as he exited.

"C'mon." Killian draped his arm around Fletcher and escorted her out of the room.

The door to the war room was closed. Fletcher broke away from Killian and moved to knock on it.

"Not in there," he said, ushering her away from the door. She followed him downstairs to the first floor. At the landing, Killian nodded at the sleeping quarters. "In here."

He turned in the opposite direction toward the common area, but before he could depart Fletcher tapped his elbow. "You okay?"

"Sad for Søren. And for you. For all of us."

"We'll fix it. I'll fix it."

"Can't fix him, only help him hold the broken stuff together."

"Then we'll do that and keep doing it as long as he needs us to."

"Yeah?"

"Yeah."

He smiled.

Sparrow was seated on her cot, legs folded in on themselves. Next to her rested two long guns—a black pump-action shotgun, which Fletcher recognized as Sparrow's personal firearm, and a lean, hardwood-stocked silver .22 rifle, which Fletcher had never seen up close, but knew belonged to Killian. "I'm going to assume Søren is out of commission for the time being."

"You say that so casually."

"I'm not sure how else to say it. This is the third episode he's had this year."

"It's fucking awful. The least you could do is acknowledge that."

Sparrow deadpanned. "You're right, it's fucking awful. His mind is torn up and his default setting is 'confrontational,' but if we try to handle him with diplomacy, he insists he isn't a 'delicate flower.' Nothing gets through to him unless we're argumentative, but we never know what's going to set him off. We're constantly walking a tightrope with him and he knows it. It's something we've learned to live with, okay? It's just our reality. I can't cry about it even if I wanted to."

"Do you want to?"

"Don't you?"

Fletcher flopped onto her cot. "A little bit, yes."

"We've got to focus on the mission, now. You've seen what can happen despite Søren being on a regular course of neurosedatives, so imagine what he'd be like if he were off them." She clasped the barrel of the rimfire rifle between her thighs and inserted a long, bristle-tipped rod into it.

"Give that to me," Fletcher put her hand out, "I'll clean it. You take care of your gun."

"Are you sure?"

"I need to do something. It's not like I have to clean my sword for it to work properly."

"Good point." She passed the .22 across to Fletcher.

Fletcher went to work. Resting the gun across her lap, she secured it by the stock. She slipped the rod deep into the barrel, then removed it, careful not to clip its crown. She repeated the procedure four times. "Am I doing it wrong?" she asked without shifting her attention away from the task.

"You're doing it perfectly."

"Then why are you watching me?"

"I'm not."

She looked up at Sparrow. "You've been staring at me this whole time."

"You clean guns like you're petting a baby animal. You make fighting look like dancing. Everything you do is methodical, yet graceful—even things that shouldn't be."

She felt the familiar burn of her cheeks flushing. "Sparrow."

"Please, Fletcher, just listen. A lot could go wrong tomorrow night. There's something I have to say now in case I don't get another chance."

"Nothing is going to go wrong." Except that absolutely everything could go wrong in an instant. She'd understood that from the outset. Her stomach trilled. There were a thousand-and-one ways the night could go to shit. "Whatever you have to tell me, don't. Save it. Like you said, we have to focus on the mission. Let's not get distracted."

"No." Sparrow placed her gun down on the cot. She reached across to Fletcher and did the same with the .22. "I need you to hear this."

"Alright. What is it?"

"Promise that you'll take care of Killian if anything happens to me. I know the others will always be there for him, but sometimes he needs more than they can give."

Fletcher thought about what the world would be like if, for one reason or another, Sparrow weren't in it. *Darker. Colder. Lacking.* The notion was too much for her to stomach. "Of course I will. I promise."

"Thank you."

Fletcher gave her a somber head nod rather than a spoken "you're welcome," and went about finishing the job she had started.

chapter nineteen

SØREN REMAINED INCAPACITATED WELL into the next day. Fletcher passed the morning keeping vigil at his bedside, all the while remembering the hours she had spent doing the same thing in another location for another man. She had never been the catalyst of any of Jonah's episodes, though. She was guiltless where his loss of control was concerned. Søren's latest relapse, however, was all her fault. She had goaded him—pushed too hard or too loudly. Søren wouldn't be in league with the men and women who had stripped him of his sound mind. What person, after fighting so arduously for so long to recover governance over their own body, would be? She must have been wrong.

At half past one o'clock, Søren stirred, groggy and with a lethargy unbecoming of him. He winced as he lifted his stiff body up into a seated position.

"Good morning, er, afternoon," Fletcher murmured.

"Fletcher," he exhaled as though startled by her presence. He cracked his neck and licked his lips clean of the dried spittle caked on them. "What happened?"

"You had an episode."

"Oh. What set me off this time?"

Fletcher gulped. "You don't remember?"

"No."

"I . . . we . . . had an argument."

"I'm . . . sorry."

"I should be the one apologizing. I said things I shouldn't have said, made some baseless accusations."

He put his hand up. "I don't need all the details."

"Right. Anyway, I'm sorry."

"It's best that you forget about it." And then he smirked. "I already have."

It was Fletcher's turn to be startled. "Did you just make a joke?"

"I do that occasionally." He nodded, stopped, and palmed his forehead. "My head is throbbing."

"Well, you almost cracked it open on the wall, so . . ." She reached for the glass of water and bottle of painkillers she'd had sitting at the ready by her feet. She uncapped the bottle, slid two pills into her hand, and handed them and the water to Søren.

"Thanks." He swallowed the pills and the whole glass of water.

"Do you need anything else? Are you hungry?"

"No. I'm just going to rest a while longer. Will you let everyone know that I'm back?"

"I'm back." What a peculiar choice of words, she thought, like he'd been missing, lost in the woods somewhere. "Sure."

Fletcher watched YOR's leader, looking frailer than he ever had, swaddle himself in the woolen blanket and wiggle into the fetal position. She had never worried for him before yesterday, but knew that she would worry for him again in the future.

If I have a future beyond tonight.

Fletcher found the whole crew around the long kitchen table waiting for Charlie to serve the garden salad she'd put together for lunch. YOR passed around a platter of the last remnants of the nearly murderous moose meat, and Fletcher felt a sort of perverse relief at that. She still carried the remorse of watching the animal die but was glad she had survived. Some things had to die in order for others to live, and she understood that now. The world had always had these rules, and no matter how hard she wanted to play outside of them, she couldn't. Not anymore.

"Søren is awake." She found her place between Killian and Sparrow. "I mean, he was, but I think he's sleeping now rather than being unconscious. He asked me to tell you all that 'he's back.'"

"You had a conversation with him?" Zoe asked.

"Yes. A short one, but yes. He seemed alright—good, even. He made a joke, which I found strange, but is something he does now and again?"

The exhalation of their collective concern was audible.

"There's always a worry that he won't come back . . . right." Charlie placed the bowl of greens on the table and took her seat at its head.

"Relapse. It happens," added Peter. "Sometimes Berserkers will have a particularly traumatic episode and lose some of the progress they've made. In the worst cases, they lose all of their progress."

Fletcher's face dropped. "That's appalling. I can't imagine working so hard to recover, only to backslide."

"Recovery is tentative. It's like having a broken bone that's always on the mend."

Fletcher remembered it, despite her young age at the time. Her mother had remained the same from the moment she arrived home from the Reclamation Processing Center to the moment she died. There was never any improvement in her, only glassy, emotionless eyes. *Dad always said I have her eyes.* "What about Vegs?" Fletcher's attention settled on Killian. She couldn't believe she'd never wondered about it before. "They don't recover at all, do they?"

Peter shook his head. "I've never heard of it happening."

"I didn't think so." Fletcher folded her hands in her lap and focused on them. "How many of you have survivors in your family, or in your circle of friends from your life before YOR?"

"My brother is a Veg," Damon responded. "He's been in the Gelida Institute on life support for two years."

Philip nodded in understanding. "My best friend from back home in Montpelier is a Veg—high-functioning, like Killian, but Reclamation decimated her."

"I don't know how Mateo will be when he returns," Peter murmured. "I can only hope for the best."

"It can happen," Zoe told him. "I have a friend in Bangor who's one of The Lucky Ones. She came back from the Processing Center pretty much the same as she went in, except she can't remember anything beyond high school. They wiped four years of her life from her memory."

"My Mom is a Berserker," Charlie blurted, choking down her emotions. "Agents came for her when she was three months pregnant with me. She got a Stay of Reclamation until she was recovered from giving birth, but being a new mom meant nothing to the BOE. Last I saw her she was in a holding pattern—about as stable as Søren, maybe a little more so—and living with my dad. She spent the first seven years of my life at Alcedonia. My dad was afraid to have her around me when I was little."

"Shit," Sparrow and Fletcher gasped in unison.

"You've never said anything," Sparrow said.

"Until today, Søren was the only person here who knew. He's the only one who's read my file. I asked him to seal it after he recruited me. It hurts too much to talk about."

"This . . . this is why we're all here." Peter tapped the tabletop. "Because Reclamation has a ripple effect. It tears families apart, takes parents from their children, children from their parents. Siblings, friends—it touches everyone."

"I can't help feeling like we should be doing more to put a stop to it," said Fletcher. "Hiding here in the middle of nowhere, sequestering only the few who are deemed worthy of saving because they pose some vague threat to the status quo . . . it's an inadequate solution."

"It's a waiting game," Philip told her. "Plans come together, but the timing has to be right. All the components must be organized before anything can be set in motion."

Sparrow rubbed Fletcher's shoulder. "All we can do is channel our outrage into tackling one problem at a time, no matter how minuscule it may seem in the moment. It might feel like we're not accomplishing much, but we have saved lives. That has to count for something."

"I know. It does."

"Enough talking. Eat up." Charlie pointed at Fletcher, "You'll need the protein for tonight's mission."

Fletcher heard the clock in the hallway chime two. Three and a half hours until twilight, four to full darkness and six until she, along with Sparrow and Killian, set off into the unknown.

chapter twenty

FLETCHER STRAPPED HER LEATHER scabbard to her back, then slipped into the black trench coat Charlie had provided for her. It was two sizes too large for her small physique, despite the modest muscle mass she had built up over the weeks, and did little to hide the hilt of her sword, which lay almost flush against her neck. She hadn't expected her weapon to be fully concealed by the coat, which was perfectly designed to hide a long gun holstered at the hip, thigh or side of the ribcage, but was not ideal for a medieval metal plank lashed between the shoulder blades.

"Here." Killian reached his long arms around her neck, popped her collar up over the sword's pommel. "Better." He grinned.

"Maybe if she were aiming to look like a common street thug," Sparrow teased, the thinner-than-normal lips of her InvigorStyler-generated physique slipping into a smirk.

"Aren't I?"

"Yes. You all are." Søren appeared at the foot of the staircase, his back leaning up against the broad, square newel post. "Blend in as best you can."

Sparrow scrutinized him. "You look like a steaming pile of dog crap."

Fletcher shot her hand out and slapped Sparrow's bicep. "She meant to say you shouldn't be on your feet."

"She said exactly what she meant, per usual." The suggestion of a smile tugged at his lips. "I couldn't let you leave without wishing you luck. You're doing this for me."

"Okay, you wished us luck. Thanks. Go lie down." Sparrow hitched her chin toward the room full of cots.

He gave her a nod. "Stay safe."

"We'll try," Fletcher answered. It was all she could promise him.

Sparrow checked her shotgun one last time. Fletcher knew how she liked it: magazine tube loaded, chamber empty, slide unlocked, and safety on. Satisfied, she slipped the weapon into its hip holster. "I'm good to go. You?"

Killian already had his .22 tucked away under his knee-length coat. "Good to go."

Fletcher's tenseness grew as Sparrow parked the van on the corner of Tremont and Alphonsus. The brunette-turned-redhead killed the headlights and the engine, but left the keys in the ignition. Fletcher slipped over the center console, settled into the passenger seat, and peered into the night. The street beyond the windshield was lit by trash can fires. Her old neighborhood was deserted, save for the bodies huddled around the fire at the top of South Whitney.

"Put this on." Sparrow handed her a CommBand. "Killian will be with you, and I should be able to keep you in my line of sight, but in case you have to run, say the word *Adjutus* into the band. That will transmit your coordinates to me, and I'll come for you."

"Okay."

"You have the money?"

188

Fletcher plunged her hand into the right hip pocket of her jeans, brushed her fingers against the bulging stack of folded synthetic polymer notes. $10,000 Redback, a fortune in The Vault. She didn't know where the money had come from—hadn't asked when Charlie gave it to her, though she hazarded a guess it had been provided by the same Southern sources who provided YOR with every other hard-to-come-by thing they possessed. "Yes."

"Alright. Head out." To her brother, Sparrow said, "Be careful."

Killian flipped a thumbs up, slid open the door, and stepped out onto the cement.

Fletcher closed her eyes, inhaled. These are your streets, she said to herself. You can do this quick and clean. "See you in a while," she murmured as she exited the van.

Fletcher recognized two of the three people standing around the fire on South Whitney. The middle-aged man in the thick brown jacket who was blowing on his cupped hands was called Lance. He lived in the apartment complex across the street from Fletcher and had always been friendly to her whenever they had crossed paths. She wanted to avoid him tonight, though. The fewer people who were aware of her presence, the better. She waited until he had conducted his business and gone on his way.

The second person, a blonde woman a few years Fletcher's senior, was adorned in a dark, puffy coat and wool skullcap. Flether recognized her friend Breanna—the QuellSell she had come to the city to find. Fletcher's gladness at discovering Breanna in her usual spot was short-lived when she caught the third person's profile. She knew his face well, had seen it every day, even looked upon his eyes leaking tears, cheeks smeared with blood from his son's self-inflicted wounds.

Jonah Quinn Sr. exchanged a crumpled Greenback for two hot pink injection-ready syringes of Quell.

No, not him. Fletcher's heart sank to the depths of her

stomach. She halted her advance, pushed her spine against an antiquated aluminum-paneled triplex to her left and tugged Killian onto the wall beside her.

"What?" He raised his eyebrows.

"Hold on."

She watched her best friend's father pocket one of the syringes. He tugged down the high collar of his coat and injected the other into his neck. The pink liquid set his jugular alight with an eerie red-orange glow, as though someone had struck a match beneath his skin. She winced. The light extinguished. It was a chemical reaction she had witnessed before, though never involving Mr. Quinn. She had been unaware of his transformation from doting father to grieving junkie. Even though she wished she could have remained ignorant to it, she understood his choice. It was too great a burden for him to bear, his son very much alive but still gone.

"You know that guy, huh?"

"I used to." *Another version of him.*

The pair remained pressed against the building, surveying the scene and their surroundings from the cover its brick porch afforded them.

Mr. Quinn, swaying on his feet, began an unbalanced retreat from the fire. Once he had made it halfway across Tremont Street toward the row house he called home, Fletcher gave Killian the okay to proceed. She observed the colossus as he walked along the sidewalk beside her and flashed back to the night he had yanked her off the pavement and lobbed her over his brawny shoulder. She had never been more terrified of anyone in her life, including the Reclamation Agents. His stature was intimidating.

"I'm going to need you to hang back a little."

"Sparrow said to stay with you. I stay with you."

"You're a big guy." She mimed his height and flexed her biceps. "My friend doesn't know that you're a nice person, so she might be scared of you. We don't want to scare her, do we? We need her help."

"But Sparrow said—"

"I know, buddy." She patted his arm. "You see this tree right here?"

He nodded.

"If you stand next to it and face that direction, you'll be able to keep an eye on me. I'll only be five feet away. You're a great runner, so I know you can reach me super-fast if I need help. Plus, you have your gun."

"My sister will be so mad at me." He grimaced.

"If she gets mad, I'll tell her it was my idea, and that way she'll be mad at me and not you."

He mulled it over. Watching the process made Fletcher smile. "Okay, but yell real loud if you need me."

Fletcher saw the glint of protectiveness in his bright blue eyes despite the darkness. *This must be what it feels like to have a brother.* She wrapped her arms around his abdomen. He squeezed her.

"Go on," he said, releasing her.

She walked the rest of the way alone.

The frosty wind blustered, whipping Fletcher's ponytail into her face. She smoothed it back, then jammed her hands into her coat pockets. "Hi, Brea," she said, edging up to the trash can fire.

"Fletch?" Breanna strained to see. "Shit, Fletcher, it is you!" She dragged her into a side hug.

"Shhh. Not so loud."

"Right. Sorry. Damn girl, the whole neighborhood thought you were dead or something. Everyone heard about how you fucked up that Agent in the library."

"That wasn't the smartest thing I've ever done."

"Maybe not, but it made you a legend around here."

Fletcher scoffed. "Correct me if I'm wrong, but legends don't have to live in hiding for fear of reprisals, do they?"

"I guess not. Where the hell have you been all this time?"

"Here and there. It's safer not to stay in one place for too long."

"Makes sense. Agents have been casing your apartment hard since you disappeared. They asked around about you and your dad a couple times."

My dad . . . *so, they think we're on the run together? Good.* "I'm sure they have."

"A bunch of us pitched in and got you a new front door. It's shoddy as shit, but it'll keep the scavengers out, human or otherwise. Mrs. Quinn is holding onto the keys for you if you need to grab some stuff."

"That's very thoughtful. I appreciate it. I'm not here for any of my things, though. I, um . . . I'm in need of your services."

"No." Breanna's jaw dropped. "You're on the pink?"

"It's not for me. I have a friend who's really hurting right now. We're in a major drought zone, and I don't know how long the dry spell is going to last."

"How much do you need?"

"How much do you have?"

The QuellSell darted her eyes about the empty road. "Come with me." she said, heading down the dead-end street.

Fletcher peered over her shoulder to the tree where Killian stood guard. She showed him an upturned thumb, then motioned for him to stay put.

"I don't carry a lot of product on me." Breanna led Fletcher into a triplex at the very end of South Whitney, up a winding staircase to the second floor. "It's easier to ditch small quantities if Bluecoats come sniffing around."

"Clever."

"Yeah. This is it." She stopped in front of what looked to be a closet for janitorial supplies, slipped a key into a deadbolt and a second key into the doorknob. Pushing the door open, she flipped a switch and entered. Fletcher followed.

The closet was large, lined with steel storage racks on both sides. There were two rusty folding chairs and a matching square table in the center of the compartment. "Welcome to my office. Have a seat."

Fletcher made herself as comfortable as possible, if comfort were at all possible in a drug dealer's stash house. She undid the buttons of her trench coat and crossed her legs.

Breanna leaned forward in her chair. Elbows on her knees, arms hanging limp, she asked again, "How much do you need, Fletch?"

Fletcher retrieved the wad of cash from her jeans and tossed it on the table. "However much $10,000 Redback will get me."

"*Hweehwoo,*" she whistled. "That is a serious stack." The QuellSell ogled Fletcher. "I've never seen that much scratch before."

Fletcher fought through the anxiety fizzing in her esophagus. "Well, now you have, and it could all be yours."

Breanna pushed out of her chair, spun toward the storage rack behind her. She grabbed a corrugated briefcase from the second shelf, placed it on the table and sat down again. She flicked open two silver latches, and the case's padded top sprang up. She slid it around so that Fletcher could see its contents: there were enough clear vials of Quell inside to wash her face in iridescent pink. "There are a thousand doses in here. That's all I'm holding, and it isn't worth ten grand in Redback."

Fletcher smiled. "Then take what it is worth, plus a little extra for a guarantee of services to be rendered in the future."

Breanna chortled. "I must be the first QuellSell in Mission Hill to be put on retainer." She closed the briefcase, counted out $5,000, then handed the rest back to Fletcher. "Pleasure doing business with you."

"Maybe you can take a sabbatical."

"I don't know how to do that."

"Most Vaulters don't." Fletcher took the briefcase by its smooth silver handle.

As the women reached the street, Fletcher asked, "Any word

on how Jonah's doing?"

"The same. Mr. Quinn has become one of my regular clients. It seems both he and Jonah need a little chemical assistance to get through their days."

"It seems many people do." Fletcher gestured to the briefcase.

"That's why I'm still out here night after night. The Government calls me a criminal, but I like to think of myself as a public servant."

"Wrong. I am a public servant." A voice rang out from the blackness ahead of them.

Fletcher knew who it belonged to before the white-haired man moved into the quivering light of the flaming trash can. Her insides knotted, a flood of nausea overcoming her as she looked upon his craggy face, and below it to his perfectly pressed three-piece suit. He was real this time, not a specter summoned by her subconscious mind to sabotage her.

"Agent Flynn." She spat his name as though she were expelling poison from her mouth. "Brea, you should leave."

"Yes, you should. I have no interest in you. My quarrel is with Ms. Daniels."

"Are you—"

"Just go, Breanna."

"Sorry," the QuellSell mumbled, then took off running for Tremont Street.

"How did you know I was here?" Fletcher questioned Flynn as he approached her.

"Not everyone in this neighborhood is bound by their affection for you, dark horse. People can be bought if the reward is large enough. The reward for the Hero of Mission Hill was exceedingly high. In fact, I believe it was your friends the Quinns who informed The Department of your return."

No. Not them. It couldn't be. "Go fuck yourself, Flynn."

"Now, now, there's no need for that kind of language." Flynn's lips spread into a diabolical smirk. "If you come quietly, we might just call off the hunt for your father."

"You'll never find him. So, I repeat, go fuck yourself. Killian!" The name reverberated between the row houses and apartment buildings, off the high stone wall at the dead end of the road and up into the Mission Hill Scrapyard.

Killian came hurtling down the asphalt like a bull incensed by a matador, not pausing to assess the perils of the situation. Before Flynn had the opportunity to turn and see the monolithic man rushing at him, Killian was upon him. Thick, strong arm outstretched, he clotheslined Flynn. The Agent's body launched into the air, defying gravity. *Fa-thump.* He hit the ground hard, sprawled out in the prone position.

Fletcher brought her wrist close to her mouth. "Adjutus!" she shouted into the CommBand.

The familiar black van careened around the corner onto South Whitney. It screeched to a standstill in the faded crosswalk, cutting off vehicular access to the dead-end road. Sparrow stuck her head out the open driver's side window. Her mouth fell open at the sight of the Agent laid out on the blacktop.

"His car must be close. Find it and shoot out the tires so he can't follow us," Fletcher shouted. "He may have a partner waiting for him." She hesitated. "Do what you have to do to incapacitate them."

Sparrow nodded, artificial red curls bouncing, then hopped out of the vehicle.

It wasn't long before an explosion of gunshots shattered the silence of nighttime in Mission Hill. One, two, three, four— in rapid sequence. Fletcher waited for a fifth, but it never materialized. *He came alone. That's not routine.* He was telling the truth about the Quinns.

After a quiet moment Sparrow reappeared at the top of the block. "It's done. Let's get out of here," she said, waving them forward.

Fletcher and Killian had taken only strides toward the van

when *click*—the sound of a handgun cocking came from behind them.

"Hold it right there," Flynn called after them.

They froze in their tracks. *God, if you exist, please, help us.* Fletcher put one hand in the air while the other continued to cling desperately to the case of Quell—Søren's only hope. "Okay, you caught me," Fletcher replied, turning around. "But you don't want them. They're nobodies—street urchins after a few Greenbacks. This one's already been Reclaimed." She gestured to Killian. "We both know they're beneath you. You're no trifling Vaulter Bluecoat."

Flynn considered her words. She saw the blazing anger in his eyes diminish to embers. "Leave now before I change my mind," he cautioned Killian.

Killian caught Fletcher's gaze, signaled *no* with a pithy head shake.

"Take this." She thrust the briefcase into his arms. He wrapped his long limbs around it, glanced down at it, and up at her again. "Go ahead, it's okay. She's waiting for you." Fletcher looked back at Sparrow, fifty-odd yards away. She could just make out her expression through the dimness: horrorstruck. Hopeless. *She'll be alright. She has her brother.*

"No quick movements from anyone," Flynn commanded. Pointedly, he said to Killian's backside, "Don't try to be a hero, boy. Walk away slowly."

Fletcher heard Killian's feet shuffle in the direction of the van.

Flynn grabbed Fletcher by the collar of her coat. He sniggered as he spun her around. "Silly girl, you brought a sword to a gun fight."

"If I have to kill someone, I want to be close enough to watch the life fade from their eyes," she growled.

He held his gun up to her forehead. "And you think I'm the sadistic one."

"There's something I've been wondering about," she said, not stalling—she knew her death was imminent—but this was her last chance to gain knowledge as she had always been inclined to do. "Perhaps you can clear it up for me."

"What makes you think I'd tell you anything?"

"Because I'm the only person who's ever put up a respectable fight. You're going to kill me anyway, so what difference does it make to you whether I know the answer or not?"

Intrigued, he lifted his finger off the trigger. "Go on."

"Vegs, Berserkers, Lucky Ones . . . what's the difference between them? Why isn't the result of Reclamation the same for everyone?"

"What a question," he mused. "The majority of people in this world fit into one of three categories: those with the mind to plan, those with the courage to fight, and those who stand by, content to do neither. Vegs, Berserkers, The Lucky Ones, respectively."

"And people like me? Significant Threats."

He leered at her. "People like us, you mean."

Us. Fletcher's brow crinkled. "No. You were a—?"

"Oh yes, a Vaulter ST before Reclamation saved me from that pitiful, good-for-nothing existence." Flynn's mouth crept into a serpentine grin. "All Agents were STs once. We possess the exceptional trifecta: a mind to plan, the courage to act, and the resoluteness to do both, which is why you are not going to die tonight. You have a higher calling. You're going to experience true Reclamation. Your eyes will be opened, and you'll become one of us—an Agent most fearsome, I'll bet, dark horse."

So, I am dangerous, after all, but to my own people. To Fletcher the only thing worse than losing control of her own mind and body would be using her mind and body to fight on the wrong side. "I would rather die." She hoisted her knee into Flynn's groin. He curled forward, grabbing his upper pelvis. Fletcher took advantage of his weakened state, planted the sole of her shoe into his shoulder. He staggered backward but remained on his feet.

"Fletcher!" She heard Killian scream for her but did not stop her advance on the Agent. She drew her arm back and punched him in the right temple, then switched fists and repeated the violent act, in triplicate, on the left side of his head. The fifth punch she threw was an overhand so savage that it dropped Flynn to his knees.

Neck bent, Flynn's bloody head swayed ever so slightly, as a leaf trembling in the breeze. Somehow, he had managed to keep hold of his gun, though he appeared in no condition to fire it.

"Fight back, you fucking coward!" Fletcher slapped him across his face. "Or did they take your balls from you, too?" She reached for the hilt of her sword, yanked the weapon from its scabbard and brought it forward in a single sinuous motion. She could have murdered Flynn in that instant, yearned to, had more conviction than she should to take his life than she'd ever thought possible. And yet killing him would not save anyone from *her*. As long as she drew breath, she could be caught, Reclaimed, and weaponized.

Never.

She slipped the broad edge of her cool, sharp blade under his chin and lifted his head with it. "You had better use that gun, or I'm going to kill you."

"With . . . pleasure . . ." He raised his shaky hands, wrapped them both around the pistol-grip and cocked the hammer. As his finger hovered over the trigger, Fletcher squeezed her eyes shut. She thought of Jonah and Jericho. Of Sparrow and Killian. Of Søren, Philip, Peter, Charlie and Zoe. Of Grier and Remy, and all her friends from the neighborhood. And of Astrid.

I'll see you soon, Mom.

Killian's voice rang out, closer now, "No!"

And not too far behind him, Sparrow. "Fletcher!"

Bang!

chapter twenty-one

FLETCHER INHALED. The unmistakable scent of gun smoke filled her nostrils. The sound of cold, malicious laughter assaulted her ears. She opened her eyes. She was alive and uninjured.

"Oh, God, no!" Sparrow let out a shriek.

Bewildered, Fletcher scanned the dark road. Flynn was still on his knees before her, cackling like a madman. Behind her, Sparrow also knelt on the ground. Killian lay flat on his back with his head propped up against her thighs. The pool of scarlet encircling them grew larger as the seconds ticked by.

Fletcher turned back to the Agent. She let out a guttural howl and plunged her sword clean through Flynn's throat. Then, with a twist, she ripped the blade free from his flesh.

Flynn pawed at the gaping wound where his larynx used to be, gurgling and gasping. Blood and saliva spurted from his lips and gushed from the fissure, saturating the front of his suit. Fletcher focused on his slate eyes, once vibrant with the spark of life, now dancing on the precipice of oblivion until finally he slumped over dead. She flicked the remnants of his blood from her sword and sheathed it.

"Killian!" She rushed to her friend's side, joining his sister in the puddle of his blood. She saw the shallow rise and fall of his ribcage, heard the labored wheezing. For the moment he was alive. She was damn sure going to keep him that way. "Where is he shot?"

Sparrow trembled, her small hands pressed against Killian's broad chest.

"Sparrow!"

"Sternum."

"Listen to me. We have to get him home to Peter. We have to carry him to the van, okay? Can you help me do that?"

Sparrow shook her head. "A hospital would be closer."

"He has a gunshot wound, which means he was involved in a crime. Perpetrator or victim, it doesn't matter. All any hospital will do is sew him up while they wait for the Bluecoats to arrive." She searched Sparrow's demeanor for some semblance of comprehension, but found only the blankness of shock. "He's losing a lot of blood, Sparrow. He needs more help than he can get here. We've got to pick him up right now!"

"Tell me what to do."

Fletcher moved to his legs. "Let go of the wound and get behind him. Rest his head on your shoulder and push him up into a seated position."

Sparrow followed the instructions.

"Hook your arms under his armpits. Grab his wrists and cross his arms over his chest."

"Okay."

"Now take his weight on your arms but keep hold of his wrists for leverage." Fletcher slipped her hands under his thighs. "Get ready to lift him, on three. One, two, three." In unison, the women hoisted Killian's limp body off the tarmac. Fletcher led the way to the van, walking backward. She found the sliding door already ajar. "Let's get him on the floor. One, two, three."

They set him down, and Fletcher jumped on top of him, kneeling with a leg on each side of his hips. She swished open the flaps of her coat, tore a lengthy strip of cloth from the bottom of her T-shirt and applied it to the bullet hole, pushing down with all the strength she could gather. "Drive!"

Sparrow turned the engine over, threw the transmission into drive, and gunned the van toward the old interstate.

As they sped up the highway on-ramp, the silver briefcase packed with Quell skidded against Fletcher's boot. In the frenzy, she had almost forgotten about it. She marveled at how fast Killian would've had to move to get it safely tucked away in the van, turn around, and rush to her aid, only to be shot down a foot from her position. *Shot down by a bullet that should have been for me.*

"We left a mess back there, didn't we?" Sparrow asked, her tone bemused, as though she were unsure if she had actually witnessed Fletcher commit homicide or if she had imagined it.

"I did." The gravity of her actions came crashing into Fletcher's consciousness. It stole her breath from her. She had slaughtered an Agent in hot blood and left his corpse exposed for all of Boston to see. "The rats will take care of him. He'll be unrecognizable by morning." Her logical mind may have been clouded by pangs of guilt and fear, but it hadn't abandoned her. *Rats devouring the body of a man I murdered.* Her stomach churned. She inched her face away from Killian just in time to prevent him from being soaked in the putrid bile that ejected itself from her gut.

She vomited twice more before the van came to a stop at the base of the safe house's verandah.

Fletcher remained on the floor of the van, still pressing the crude bandage to Killian's bleeding sternum.

"We need help out here!" She caught the echo of Sparrow's voice as she disappeared into the Visitor's Center.

Thirty seconds passed before she heard a stampede of

footsteps pounding the ground outside the van, and the rumbling swish of the door rolling open. She peeled her gaze from Killian's sallow face for the first time since her last bout of retching. Philip, Peter, Søren, and Damon peered down at her gory charge. Their faces were warped with dread.

"Move him to the galley," Peter shouted, then bolted for the porch steps.

Fletcher did not want to dismount Killian's body. Something inside the primitive recesses of her brain told her that she was the only thing keeping his soul in place. She shook her head, dislodging the thought, and scuttled off him.

The men made quick work of carrying Killian into the kitchen. Fletcher, Sparrow and the rest of YOR followed close on their heels. They laid him on the wide wooden table, the chairs squealing as they kicked them away.

"Sparrow." A feeble voice summoned the woman into the room. She hurried to her brother's side, took his hand into her own dirty, blood-caked palm. It was then, observing the twins from the threshold between rooms, that Fletcher grasped the concept of two individuals being parts of a whole, neither complete without the other. "Mad at me?" Killian panted.

Sparrow did not wipe her tears away. "No," she replied softly, then placed a gentle kiss on his forehead. "I love you, little brother."

He fell into unconsciousness again as Peter entered the room, medical cart in tow. The doctor hitched his chin at the crowded doorway. "Charlie, I'll need your help. Find me as many clean towels as you can, then scrub up. Everybody else get out."

The mass exodus occurred instantaneously, everyone save for Sparrow and Fletcher, who dared not desert her.

Sparrow glowered at Peter. "I'm not leaving him."

"Please, I can't—"

"I said I'm not leaving him!"

Peter shot a pleading glance at Fletcher.

Fletcher licked her lips and stepped through the archway into the kitchen, embarking on the most agonizing short walk she had ever taken. "Sparrow . . ." She approached her from behind and rested her hands on the woman's taut shoulders.

Sparrow released her hold on her brother's hand and whirled on Fletcher, knocking her backward into the log wall. "Don't." She held up her index finger.

Fletcher regained her balance and tried again, more forcefully. She snaked one arm around Sparrow's lower back, the other across her shoulders, and tugged her close.

Sparrow writhed against her. "Get off of me!"

"No." Fletcher tightened the embrace. She cupped the nape of Sparrow's neck and guided the woman's head to rest on her breastbone. She whispered into her ear, "Let Peter try to save your brother's life."

Sparrow deflated with a despondent outbreath. She reciprocated the embrace, clawing her fingers up Fletcher's back and squeezing her cheek into her bosom. Her weeping was muffled, her breathing erratic.

The women stood entwined in grief until Sparrow allowed Fletcher to usher her out of the room.

chapter twenty-two

OVER TWO HOURS PASSED without any word as neither Peter nor Charlie had emerged from the kitchen. The entire house was on edge, unable to sit still for more than a few minutes at a time. Fletcher had just taken the weight off her feet on the couch near the lit fireplace in the common room, and had rested her neck against its padded arm when Søren approached her.

"Can I sit with you?"

She regarded him, amazed at his politesse, and pushed upright, folding her legs one over the other. Søren lowered himself onto the cushions with a groan. "I'm still a little stiff," he commented.

"I'm sure you are."

"Where is Sparrow?"

"On the porch. She said she needed some air after her InvigorStyler reversion, but I think she wants some space."

"You're probably right."

Fletcher massaged her aching temples for something to do.

Søren focused on her fingers. "Is that his blood?"

She examined her digits, front and back, and scoffed at the stubborn hemoglobin residue beneath her nails. "His, or Agent Flynn's."

"Flynn?" His forehead wrinkled. "Are you feeling up to giving me your report?"

"I thought it was the Mission Leader's job to report?"

"Sparrow is in no condition for that so you're the mission leader now. I think you were always meant to be."

Fletcher exhaled, then recounted the events of the night as they had unfolded.

"Stop. What about Flynn?"

"What about him? He shot Killian, so I killed him. My anger got the best of me. I know what I did was wrong."

"I don't care that you killed him," he said. "I would have done the same thing had I been in your position. I'm interested in what happened before that. You were prepared to give yourself up, but then you attacked him. What did he say to you?"

"I asked him . . . why there are so many classifications of Reclaimees. He told me they all have different traits that drive their behavior. Vegs excel at making plans, Berserkers have the spirits of warriors, and The Lucky Ones are content to just exist."

His pupils dilated with curiosity. "And then he told you about STs."

"Yes. He told me what would happen to me, what I would become. In The Vault, you'd hear stories of people never returning from Reclamation. You'd assume something went wrong and they had died. YOR assumes Significant Threats are purposely wiped out, but The Government doesn't kill us. It's worse than that. They brainwash us into taking up their cause, conscript us into their brutal squad of Agents. They must station Agents far from their homes, where no one will recognize them. I refuse to be molded into an instrument of fascism and shipped off to torment strangers. I wasn't going to let myself be taken. I attacked Flynn hoping he'd kill me."

"Well, now you know what makes you special. Reclamation was created for you. Of all the ways a Vaulter's mind can be mutilated, that may be the most malicious." He added with a simper, "I'm uniquely qualified to judge."

Fletcher let out a snicker and immediately regretted it. "Your jokes are really poorly timed. You have to work on that."

He gestured at the silver briefcase atop the end table. "Maybe Quell will be better for that than neurosedatives."

"Maybe."

The grandfather clock chimed, informing YOR that it was two in the morning. Everyone had done their best to settle their nerves: changed into their nightclothes, sat or reclined on their cots. Most had managed to fall asleep, exhausted by their anxiety. Fletcher was wide awake, sitting on the sofa next to Sparrow. She hadn't spoken a word in four hours, and Fletcher knew that she wouldn't break her silence for anyone but Peter.

A creaking floorboard alerted the women to the medic's approach. Sparrow leapt to her feet upon seeing Peter round the bend into the common room, his surgery smock sopped with blood. His rubber gloves snapped as he removed them and squished when he tucked them into one another.

Fletcher stood and took Sparrow's hand.

"I managed to stem the internal bleeding. He has extensive tissue trauma. The bullet was a hollow point. It fragmented into eight pieces. But—"

"But?" Sparrow rolled her watery eyes toward the ceiling. "It gets worse?"

"He's dangerously bradycardic—his heart is beating so slow that it isn't supplying his organs with the amount of blood they need to function properly."

"Are you telling me that my brother is going to die?"

"I'm telling you that I did everything within my medical capability to keep him alive." Peter hung his head and sniffled. "All we can do now is wait and see. It's up to his body to heal itself."

Sparrow sponged her tears away with her sleeve. "Can I see him?"

"He's in an induced coma, but you can sit with him if you'd like."

"I want to tell him a story, like I used to at bedtime when we were kids. He always loved stories." She regarded Fletcher.

"I'm sure he'll be able to sense your presence, and it will be a comfort to him." Fletcher attempted to let go of her hand, but Sparrow held firm.

Aqua eyes imploring, she asked, "Will you stay with us for a while?"

"For as long as you want me to." Fletcher shepherded their way to the kitchen, then paused at its entry. "I'll be right back." She broke off in the direction of the bunkroom.

Careful not to wake her weary friends, Fletcher tiptoed through the room into the chamber of cubbyholes beyond. Using bright beams of moonlight to guide her, she reached into her thin storage compartment and shifted her belongings until she found what she had come for.

In the kitchen Fletcher found Sparrow slouching in a high-backed timber chair, chin resting on her folded forearms beside her brother's head. Killian's heart monitor sounded a slow but consistent beep, and the green line on the EKG screen danced to a tune of sharp peaks and plunging valleys. "Read this to him," Fletcher offered her mother's leather-bound copy of *A Little Princess* to Sparrow.

She shot upright. "Fletcher, I can't."

Killian is lying here, fighting for his life because of me; it's the very least I can do. "Please. I think you'll both enjoy it."

Sparrow gently took the book into her hands. and delicately opened it. Fletcher pulled a seat up close to her, and she began. "Chapter One, Sara. Once on a dark winter's day, when the yellow fog hung so thick and heavy in the streets of London that the lamps were lighted and the shop windows blazed with gas as they do at night, an odd-looking little girl sat in a cab with her father and was driven rather slowly through the big thoroughfares . . ."

The sun rose, flooding the kitchen with the soft light of another late autumn morning. Fletcher watched with bloodshot eyes as Sparrow struggled to suppress her drowsiness. She laid the open book on her lap and rubbed her thumb and forefinger over her closed eyelids. "The words are starting to get blurry," she yawned. Fletcher stroked her back.

"You should get some sleep."

"I doubt I could."

"Try. You won't be any use to him if you're too drained to even read."

"I don't want to leave him alone."

"I'll stay with him." Fletcher moved to take the book from Sparrow.

Sparrow grabbed her hand, tangled their fingers together. "I don't want to be alone, either."

"Both of you go up to the Ranger's quarters and rest for a few hours." Søren appeared in the archway. He made his way into the kitchen and dragged a chair up to the opposite side of the table. "I'll keep him company."

Sparrow motioned *no* with her head. "It's fine. I'm—"

"That's an order."

She deigned to hear his command. "I don't have the energy to argue with you right now."

"Then don't. There's a first time for everything."

"Come on." Fletcher took the book into her hand, and helped Sparrow to her feet. "They'll wake us if anything changes."

Fletcher closed the door to the Ranger's quarters behind her. Sparrow removed her boots and collapsed onto the mattress. Once Fletcher had rested her book on the stool, made her way to the window, and drawn the heavy curtains, she joined Sparrow on the bed. The women lay facing one another. Fletcher did not need to be asked; she stretched out her arm. Sparrow placed her head in the crook of her shoulder, draped her forearm across Fletcher's torso.

"This is my fault," said Fletcher, the weight of her conscience becoming too heavy to carry. "I should never have—"

Sparrow stroked Fletcher's cheek. "You did what you thought was right, and so did Killian. How can I blame either of you for the thing I admire most about you?"

There's no defense against this woman, Fletcher thought. She was too earnest, too straightforward. Tough when she had to be but so, so soft underneath. And she needed softness in kind. *I give up. She can have it.* Fletcher squeezed Sparrow closer. She was warm and small and sad. She wished she could transfer some of Sparrow's sadness into herself, make the load lighter. That was the last thought she had before they both drifted into a deep slumber.

chapter twenty-three

"SPARROW!" Zoe flung open the bedroom door.

Both women jolted awake and sprang upright. Fletcher felt dazed, her heart hammering. She didn't know how long she'd been asleep, but her joints felt unbendable, as though her limbs had remained stationary for days.

"What?"

"Hurry."

Sparrow didn't waste a second asking for an explanation. She jumped to her feet and dashed out of the room. Fletcher heeded the cue and followed her. They ran into the hall and down two flights of steps as fleetly as their tired muscles would allow.

They heard a burst of alarm bells, which gave way to an incessant, high-pitched bleep. "Ready!" Charlie's voice rang out.

The women reached the kitchen in time to witness Peter stab a large hypodermic needle into Killian's heart. "Pushing adrenaline," he said, and pressed the plunger.

Killian's upper body bucked, then fell. The green line of the EKG jumped, then went flat. The bleeping recommenced.

Peter pulled the needle from his friend's chest and dropped it on the floor. "Resuming chest compressions." He placed the heels of his palms, one atop the other, on the bottom of Killian's breastbone. Interlocking his fingers, he pressed hard and fast, counting to thirty, then stopping. He pushed Killian's head back, opened his mouth and breathed into it twice. Killian's lungs filled and deflated, filled and deflated. Then nothing. "Dammit!" Peter began the process over again.

Sparrow looked on in desperation as Charlie readied another syringe.

Peter administered a second intracardiac injection of adrenaline and continued through three more cycles of CPR with no change to Killian's condition. To his credit, the man never faltered in his attempts to revive his friend, despite knowing that the odds were against it. After he completed the fifth round, Fletcher knew it was over. Killian was gone. It wouldn't be long before Sparrow realized it, too.

"Stop!" Sparrow howled. "Peter, please, just stop. We lost him." Her voice wavered, thick with lamentation. "We lost him."

Peter straightened his stance and wiped his sweaty brow. He flipped a switch on the heart monitor. The persistent chirping ceased, and the flat green line disappeared. He walked over to Sparrow, head bowed with grief, and stroked her shoulder. "I'm so sorry," he said, and brushed past her into the hallway.

Charlie dabbed a droplet away from Sparrow's face with the pad of her thumb, then tugged her into a hug. "Take as much time as you need." She, too, left the room.

"I . . . I'm going to say goodbye to him," Sparrow murmured in a stupor.

Fletcher let out a heavy breath and nodded. She remained on the doorsill long enough to see Sparrow lean over Killian's limp body and throw her arms around his shoulders, but had to walk away when her soft whimpering began.

The whole of YOR had gathered in the common area. All the

women and most of the men were in tears. Fletcher sank into the wingchair at the far end of the room. She buried her face in her hands and wept for the loss of one of the most honorable souls she'd ever had the pleasure of befriending. Humanity had lost a paragon of decency when Killian drew his last breath. The world was in desperate need of every drop of goodness it could find, and now there was one less beautiful, precious drop to be found.

"What do we do now?" Damon's voice interrupted the symphony of tears. "We have a funeral for him, obviously, but what rituals do we follow? Are there protocols?"

Søren sniffed, licked a drop of salty water from his top lip. "It's been a while since we've had to put one of our own to rest. Many of you have been fortunate enough to never have witnessed it. As soon as I'm composed, I will inform Head Office of our loss. Tonight, whenever Sparrow is able, Charlie will help her select the outfit Killian will be cremated in. Damon, you and Philip will begin to build a funeral pyre in the clearing of the oak tree grove this evening. Tomorrow morning, Sparrow will choose one of us to help her wash Killian's body." He cleared the phlegm from his throat and gestured to Fletcher. "I suspect it will be you, considering the closeness that has developed between the three of you since your arrival. Once his body has been cleaned and dried, the longest-serving male YOR members among us—Peter and myself—will dress him; then Sparrow and Fletcher will join us in shrouding him. Given the late season, there probably won't be any flowers to collect, but Charlie will spearhead the memorial arrangements, and anyone who wishes to take part in that may do so. We'll lay him out here in the common room where everyone will be able to pay their respects. At sundown tomorrow, we'll carry his corpse to the pyre and set it ablaze."

"Bagpipes." Sparrow entered the room. Everyone shot to their feet. "My father has a set of bagpipes, handed down through generations. He used to play for us all the time. Killian loved it. He'd smile this big, goofy smile and tap his foot to the rhythm. Philip, will you search the archives for a recording? I'd like to send him off—"The last of Sparrow's composure vanished. She collapsed to the floor, clutching her chest and sobbing so forcefully that her body quaked. Every labored breath was an expulsion of her sorrow, as though her very synapses discharged agony as they fired.

Fletcher could not stand it. She hurried across to Sparrow, sat herself on the ground beside her, and eased her crumpled frame onto her lap. She cradled her as she cried and pressed her lips to her crown, her own tears splashing down into the woman's long brown hair. Sparrow clung to her as a limpet to a rocky seashore. And if she decided never to relax her grip, Fletcher wordlessly swore to remain there with her until the breeze whisked their ashes away and Mother Nature blanketed their brittle bones with thorny sweetbriar.

<h1>chapter twenty-four</h1>

AT DAYBREAK, AFTER A long, unrestful night spent dozing, waking and crying together, Sparrow and Fletcher began the melancholy task of washing Killian's corpse. Fletcher was thankful that Peter had made the scene presentable beforehand. He'd stripped Killian of his blood-soaked clothes, laid a piece of wispy fabric over his groin, and cleared the kitchen of the linens he had soiled after his body had expired and his muscles loosened.

Tepid soapy water lapped against the sides of the terracotta bowl as Fletcher submerged a porous oval loofah into it. She squeezed the excess liquid from the sponge and brought it down on Killian's cold forehead. Gently tracing the jagged scar from his temple to his chin, she noticed that his cheek and jaw bones seemed unnaturally accentuated by his taut, milky-blue skin. Her gut lurched at the sight of him, lifeless. Decaying. "Dammit, it should be me, Killian, not you," she whispered. A warm teardrop dribbled down her face onto his sunken cadaver.

"Don't say that! He wouldn't want that," Sparrow reprimanded. She let go of her brother's rigid wrist and looked daggers at Fletcher. "No. Please, Fletcher, do not cry right now," she sniffled. "I won't be able to get through this if you cry."

Fletcher rubbed the wetness from her cheek. "I'm sorry."

"Let's just finish this."

In silence, they continued to cleanse Killian's remains: neck, arms, torso, back, legs, and feet, until the only lingering evidence of the grisly damage his body had suffered was the bullet hole in his chest.

Sparrow lobbed her bowl and loofah into the sink. She dried her damp hands on her gray cargo pants. "I have to get some fresh air."

Fletcher had already grabbed a towel and begun to wick the moisture from the left side of Killian's upper body. She shook her head at Sparrow. "We're doing this first."

"I cannot stay in this room another second and keep my shit together. I can't keep looking at him like *this*."

Fletcher snapped upright and stood with her hands on her hips, the damp towel resting against her thigh. "Keep your shit together or don't—it doesn't bother me." Her voice was soft yet resolute. "Go ahead and cry or scream until you're out of air if that's what you have to do, but we are not leaving this kitchen until we've finished this. He's your brother and he needs you now, for the last time. You'll regret it later if you don't do this correctly and completely."

Sparrow squinted, angry at Fletcher, but Fletcher did not back down. Sparrow was the one to drop her gaze. "You're right," she conceded. She chose a towel from the stack on the counter, unfolded it, and began to dab it against Killian's unyielding flesh.

Sparrow had chosen a pair of coal-black slacks and a collarless long-sleeved white button-down for her brother's final ensemble and laid the clothes over a high-backed kitchen chair so that they would not wrinkle. After they had finished toweling Killian, Sparrow slipped out to the patio while Fletcher went to find Peter and Søren.

The men were waiting together in the bunkroom, looking forlorn and uninterested in conversation. Over millennia of human evolution, that behavior had not changed: the male of the species still avoided talking about their feelings.

"Gentlemen."

Søren looked up from his clasped hands at the sound of Fletcher's voice. "You're ready for us?"

"Yes." She led them into the galley and presented them with the garments.

Peter observed the dress shirt. "She chose well. He'll enter the next life looking very dignified."

"I'll tell her you said so." She left the duo to their duty and went to join Sparrow on the deck.

Sparrow dangled her legs over the side of the low patio. "I have to go to Portland to tell my parents their son is dead," she sniffed as Fletcher approached. The wind whipped up, sending a chill through her body. Fletcher sat down, straddling her from behind, and enfolded her in a warming embrace.

"I'll come with you."

Sparrow leaned her head back against Fletcher's shoulder. "You can't go far from the safe house, not so soon after leaving an Agent dead in the road. The BOE will be hypervigilant. And you being one of the few known assailants of any Agent ever? They're arrogant, not stupid. They'll suspect you even if no one in your neighborhood did give you up. Anyway, you still have your own fingerprints. If you were stopped, they could ID you, even if you used the InvigorStyler."

"Then I'll wipe my fingerprints. It makes sense to now, anyhow."

"Are you sure you're ready to lose a part of yourself forever?"

Fletcher did not hesitate. "To do this with you, yes. Two days ago, I was willing to give up my life. Fingerprints are nothing."

Sparrow turned her head to meet Fletcher's eyes. "You were

willing to die to preserve your authentic self rather than become whatever they wanted to make you. That's noble, and this is noble, too. But I just lost my brother. I can't risk losing anyone else."

Fletcher understood there was nothing she could say to change Sparrow's mind. She maintained reason in the face of unimaginable heartache. Her own rationality would forsake her under the same circumstances. So she said nothing. Instead, she kissed her—Sparrow, sporting her own features, wearing her own skin, bravely overcoming her brokenheartedness. This time it was real, and she meant it with everything she had inside of her.

Sparrow sighed into her mouth. Fletcher was unsure if it was a sigh of despair or relief, but either way they both knew the kiss had been a long time coming.

As she withdrew her lips from Sparrow's, Fletcher saw that tears welled in her lower eyelids. She held Sparrow a little tighter and settled her cheek against her temple. "When will you leave for your parents' place?"

"Tomorrow. And I should stay the night with them. I think they're going to need me to."

"Yes, I think so, too."

The glass ranch slider opened behind them. Søren announced his presence with an *ahem*. The women separated. Sparrow rose to her feet and helped Fletcher to hers.

"He's dressed," said Søren. "We can shroud him, or we can wait awhile if you need a few more minutes."

Sparrow sought Fletcher's reassurance. Fletcher took her by the hand. "I'm ready," Sparrow replied.

"Okay."

The men lifted Killian's stiff body from the tabletop. Sparrow and

Fletcher smoothed a soft white sheet onto it. They laid Killian to rest once more atop the sheet, and Sparrow tucked her brother into it, beginning at his feet and working her way up. Once she reached his neck, she hesitated. She kissed his left cheek, then his right, and lastly, his forehead. Fletcher helped Sparrow cover his face and secure the shroud at the back of his skull.

"Charlie and Zoe are waiting for you in the common room," Søren told Sparrow afterward. "They want to go over the vigil arrangements with you before we move Killian."

Charlie and Zoe had rearranged the furniture in the common room. They situated Killian's empty cot in front of the stone hearth, and there his veiled body would lie for last observances. "Philip was able to find some digifiles of bagpipe music. We've brought the wireless speakers down from the war room." Charlie pointed at two tall towers in the back corners of the room.

"Damon and I went out looking for flowers to pick this morning. None survived the first killing frost," Zoe added.

That won't suffice, Fletcher thought. *Killian deserves flowers.* "I ran through a patch of wild aster still in bloom the other day. There were goldenrod sprinkled in with them, too. I remember where it is. I'll go gather some."

"If you tell us where to go, Charlie and I will pick them. You both look drained, no offense."

Fletcher wanted to be the person to provide the flowers Killian deserved, but for once Zoe was right. She and Sparrow were bleary-eyed, only just able to stand and in no shape for a stroll through the woods. "There's a pond two miles west of here. You'll find them on the south bank."

"Okay." Zoe tapped Charlie's shoulder, and they set out on their search.

Sparrow lowered herself onto the sofa. "What do I do now?" she asked, sounding like a child who had lost her bearings.

Fletcher put her arm around her shoulder. "Now you

concentrate on everything you love about your brother, everything that made him who he was, and you celebrate his life with your family."

Bagpipe music streamed through the speakers, filling the common room with a keening dirge. Blossoms of purple aster and stalks of goldenrod blanketed Killian's shrouded form, the open hearth afire behind him. The YOR family spent the afternoon gathered together in the room, sometimes wistful over the loss of their brother, sometimes smiling at recounted stories of his good nature and laughing at memories of his vivacity. "Do you remember the time we were out hunting, and we found that flock of wild turkeys?" Charlie wondered.

The group fell into hysterics.

Fletcher, perplexed, asked, "What?"

Philip replied through bouts of laughter. "We were all spread out in a small patch of forest, hiding in bushes or behind trees, trying to herd these turkeys together so they wouldn't scatter at the sound of our shotguns, when Killian comes bursting through the brush, screaming his head off. He had this puffed-up, pissed-off turkey gunning for him, squawking and pecking at his ass."

"And we're all like, 'Killian, stop running! Stand your ground,'" added Zoe.

Fletcher suppressed a giggle with her palm. "And did he?"

"No! He sped up, which just made the turkey speed up!"

"They ran right through the flock," said Søren, *smiling*, "sent six birds hopping all over the place, fluttering like mad, feathers flying everywhere."

"So what happened?"

Sparrow chortled. "Eventually he was able to gain a bit of distance on it, and I shot the damn thing. We lost the other turkeys in the scramble, but it didn't matter. We still had turkey for dinner every night for a week. That's how big this bird was."

"Oh, man," Fletcher beamed. "From now on, any time I see a wild turkey I will forever think of Killian running through the woods, screaming."

"Me too," Charlie agreed.

Zoe nodded. "Same here."

Sparrow glanced at her brother's swathed body. The water rising in her eyes glistened in the dying daylight. "I don't know how I'm going to do this without him."

"The pain, that feeling of emptiness, will lose its sharpness over time. It's always going to be there, but so will we. We've got your back, Sparrow. All of us." Søren's voice was kinder than Fletcher had ever thought it capable of being. She realized then why he had been chosen to lead YOR. Though his sternness rarely wavered, he was not afraid of vulnerability as so many leaders throughout history had been. He understood it and embraced it.

The sun dipped below the curved horizon, painting the sky a rich vermilion. Damon, Philip, Peter, and Søren carried Killian's heavy body through the forest. Fletcher, Sparrow, Charlie and Zoe trailed solemnly behind them. The group reached the clearing in the oak tree grove where a tall, rectangular funeral pyre had been constructed of wide logs and wiry branches, and the men set Killian to rest upon it, then sprinkled his body with kindling.

Poking out of the ground near the pyre were two long timber staves, ends wrapped in a dry moss ideal for burning. Søren plucked the torches from the dirt, handed one to Sparrow and the other to Fletcher. He pulled a brushed-metal lighter from his pocket, flipped open the lid, and flicked the flint wheel. Shielding the flame from the cool fall breeze, he lit Sparrow's torch, and then Fletcher's.

The women approached the pyre in step, circling it in opposite directions and touching their fiery torches to the brushwood as they passed. Meeting again where their loop had begun, they recited the Words of Passage in unison as Killian was consumed by the blaze. "Killian Fitzpatrick, with love as a guiding light, we send you into the dark night. May the ferryman deliver you to the shores of the next life, and there may you find peace."

They threw their torches onto the pyre whose flames raged up, up, so high that they obscured the distant dusky clouds. Fletcher thought that if there were Gods somewhere up above looking down on the Earth, they'd see the brightness of that funerary inferno and know that a loved man was being cremated there.

Sparrow rested her temple against Fletcher's shoulder, and the pair cried together.

The pyre reduced itself to cinders three hours after the sun had set, revealing Killian's charred bones to all creation. His skin, fat, muscles, and organs had disintegrated into a grayish dust and mingled with the powdery remnants of tinder.

Charlie checked that the ash was cool to the touch, then produced two small, unembellished clay jars from her knapsack. She swept a pile of dust into each container and packed flat, round corks into their rims. She offered them to Sparrow. "One for you and one for your parents."

Sparrow held the jars so tightly to her stomach that Fletcher worried they would leave oval bruises in her skin. "I guess . . . now we bury his bones?"

"Leave that to us," Charlie said, motioning to Søren and Damon, who had already begun to unpack a satchel of long-handled shovels. She handed a small flashlight to Fletcher.

"Take her back to the Visitor's Center. Make her something to eat—heaven knows neither of you have had a bite of food in two days—and put her to bed."

Fletcher nodded. She slung her arm round Sparrow's tense shoulders and ushered her through the forest in the direction of home.

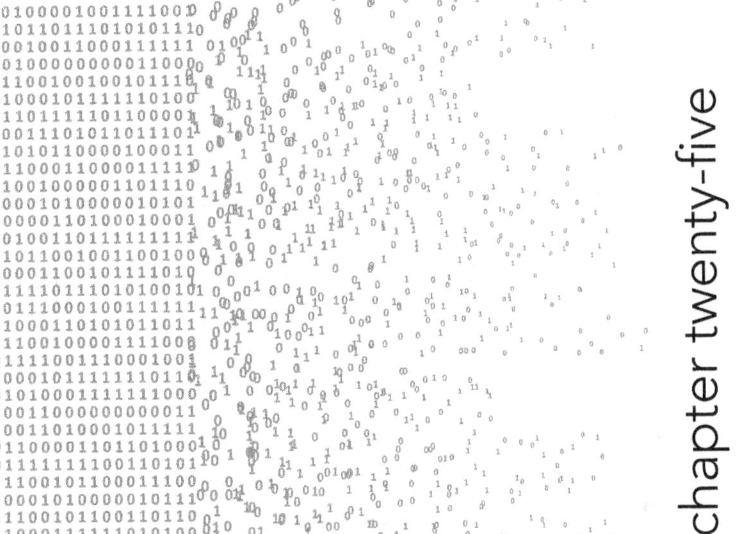

chapter twenty-five

FLETCHER WAS ROUSED BY the serenade of fledgling robins. Her momentary delight at the sweet birdsong withered as memories of the last few days seeped into her consciousness. She opened her eyes to find herself alone in the Ranger's quarters. She had fallen asleep in the early morning hours with Sparrow wrapped in her arms as they lay front to back. Now Sparrow's side of the bed was cold, though the imprint of her slight frame was still in the shabby mattress.

She bounded out of bed and, still in her nightclothes, hurried down to the main floor. She discovered that the kitchen had been thoroughly cleaned. The terra-cotta bowls were scrubbed free of their ruddy wash water and set to dry in the dish rack. The blood-caked loofahs had been disposed of. The smooth, flat tabletop gleamed as though freshly coated with wood stain, and the slatted chairs had been neatly slipped into place beneath it. No traces of Killian's gore remained anywhere.

The common room was also spotless. The aster blooms and goldenrod stalks had been swept away. Every piece of furniture had been moved back to its place. Killian's cot had been folded up and tucked somewhere out of sight, swapped for the low, rustic sofa table that usually sat in front of the hearth.

It's like nothing happened.

Fletcher was furious.

She raced into the bunkroom. Every living member of YOR was wrapped in green woolen blankets, relishing a deep, much needed repose. And then the familiar rumble of a motorbike engine disturbed the stillness outside the safe house.

She ran into the hallway, lobbed open the front door and darted down the verandah's wide staircase. Her shoeless feet pounded the cold dirt of the forest floor until she reached the path leading to the storage shed. She was too late. She stood on the trail looking after the black motorbike, its spinning wheels kicking up dust and detritus as it disappeared into the distance with Sparrow's hunched figure lording over it.

Her resentment diminished and fretfulness sprang up in its place.

Fletcher set a pot to boiling. She pilfered a fistful of dried beechnut from YOR's stores, milled it into a fine powder and made herself a hot brew. *What else can a useless girl do?* She sat arched over the kitchen table, warming her hands on the mug, contemplating what her life would resemble now that yet another person she cared for was no longer in it. *Mom, look after Killian for us, please.*

"She left already?" Søren shuffled into the kitchen, rubbing the grit of sleep from his eyes.

"Yeah."

He pointed a lazy finger around the room. "Did you do this?"

"She did."

"Mmm." He grabbed a mug from the cupboard above the sink, poured himself a cup of brew, and sat across from Fletcher. He swigged the hot drink and scowled. "Too sweet."

"Sorry," Fletcher said, indifferent.

"Want to talk about it?"

"With you?"

"I'm the head of this house, which means I give commands,

but I'm also obligated to address any concerns my subordinates may have. Concern is all over your face."

Fletcher threw her hands up, palms aimed at the ceiling. "I woke up and she was gone. She purged every inch of the house of her brother's remains before sunrise, and then she left without a word."

Søren rested his elbows on the table and folded his hands under his chin. "She's like that sometimes. We all are, I suppose. It's easier to tidy our spaces than our feelings, much easier to try to run from the unpleasant ones than face them head-on."

"She can scour every square inch of the Visitor's Center. She can ride that fucking motorbike to the Canadian border wall and beg Defection Patrol to shoot her, but that won't change the fact that Killian is dead, and I killed him."

"You—"

"Or maybe it's me she's running from. I can't even look myself in the eye. How could she?"

Søren pounded the table. "You did not kill him, Fletcher. Do you hear me? Flynn did. Flynn held the gun. Flynn pulled the trigger."

"And I slaughtered him for it, without a second thought. Rabid dogs are put down more humanely!" Fletcher dropped her head, her mind teeming with self-reproach. "I didn't fire the shot that killed Killian, but I'm no less a murderer."

"You brought justice to a man who would never have known it otherwise."

"Who the hell am I to dispense justice?" She peered up into Søren's obsidian eyes, begging for an answer that would bring solace to her conscience.

"Someone who has witnessed injustice her entire life."

"I'm still just a person."

"We're all just people, doing what it takes to survive. Some of us have to do worse things than others. You did what you had to do."

"Necessity doesn't make every action righteous by default."

"Neither you nor Sparrow would be alive right now if you hadn't dispatched that man. He would never have let you go after—"

"After I attacked him! If I hadn't been so reckless in the first place, Sparrow would be here, and Killian would be here, too." Fletcher's voice trembled.

"But you wouldn't."

Fletcher groaned. "Why aren't you angry with me? Or at the very least, shocked at my belligerence? How can you be so forgiving? You, who's all about control."

"Because I understand. I understand fighting for self-preservation, whatever form that may take. And I understand being overcome with rage that builds and builds until it blinds you. It becomes a brick wall so tall that you can't climb it, so you have to break through it. The difference between you and me is that you can rein it in while I lose myself to it."

"I don't know how different we are in that respect. I'm still angry. I feel it lurking beneath the grief and guilt. I made Flynn pay with his life for what he did to Killian, but that wasn't justice. It was vengeance. He was a symptom of the sickness, not the root of it. I want to tear the system asunder without feeling like a butcher."

Søren's pale skin flushed. His dark eyes brightened with wayward intent. "There may be a way for us to do that, remove one load-bearing stone and topple the entire tower."

Fletcher's interest was piqued. "How?"

"We'll wait for Sparrow to return and I'll call a meeting. We'll hash out the details together as a group. In the meantime, you should have a chat with Philip. I believe you showed some interest in his cooking." He flicked his head toward the ceiling. Fletcher caught his meaning. Whatever Philip had been cultivating in that tank in the war room was ready, and it had an important role to play in Søren's aforementioned plan.

After a workout, a long jog, and a shower, Fletcher met Philip in the war room. She noticed the bubbling gunky liquid inside the glass vat was gone, replaced with a calm, clear fluid. "Do you have something to show me?"

"The fruit of our combined labor." Philip led her to the tank. Using a glass micro-spatula, he fished two small, colorless lenses from the liquid. "These babies are what you retrieved from Cordon Station, in their cured state."

"Contact lenses?" Fletcher was unimpressed. "Every hospital in The Vault has the capability to detect and correct eyesight defects in newborns, but Sparrow and I traveled hundreds of miles and risked our asses for an obsolete method of vision correction?"

"They're not contact lenses. They're audiovisual recorders."

"Cameras?"

"Yes, but that's not all. They're the latest biomechanical tech, designed to be implanted as secondary corneas—completely undetectable by modern body scanning methods because they aren't foreign objects."

Fletcher looked at the things, skeptical. "Then what are they? Anything techy implanted in the body must contain some sort of foreign object, even if it's merely the power source."

Philip beamed. "They don't have a built-in power source. They run on energy converted from body heat. They're made of amniotic membrane, cooked up in a vat of synthetic amniotic fluid—one hundred percent fleshy, organic matter." He placed the lenses back into the tank. "Peter helped me analyze their genetic code, and we were able to modify them to stream data to our hard drives using an AV version of the encrypted interlink in our CommBands."

Fletcher had thought she knew everything she needed to know about the technological resources available to YOR: ID replacement, fingerprint overwriting, the InvigorStyler, CommBands, an extensive cache of old-world weaponry, outmoded gasoline-powered vehicles reconfigured to run on solar power, but this was innovation at its finest, a wonder that challenged the most intricate novelties she had beheld. "I take it back," she marveled. "These can change everything."

chapter twenty-six

THREE DAYS CAME AND went without any sign of Sparrow. By afternoon on the fourth day, Fletcher was beyond worried. She wandered aimlessly around the Visitor's Center, fiddling with her CommBand, teetering between wanting to respect Sparrow's bereavement with her parents and her own need to put her mind at ease. *If she were in danger, she would have contacted us,* she thought. *Unless she couldn't . . .*

Shit.

"Sparrow." She directed her device to target the woman's receiver. "Hey. Are you alright?" Bright blue text scrolled across the CommBand's white display, then vanished into the ether.

Seconds stretched to minutes, minutes to hours. No response.

Her mind wandered to grim places: Agents apprehending Sparrow; tossing her into a cold, dark cell; torturing her body with monstrous apparatuses, her brain with psychotropic pharmaceuticals and other nefarious contrivances.

She laced up her sneakers and went for a run in the waning daylight.

She rushed past dead birch and beech trees, and evergreen white pines, her soles crushing a carpet of rotting brown leaves and green needles, still soggy from the heavy rain the evening before. She skirted the still pond where Charlie and Zoe had picked Killian's flowers—the south bank barren after three consecutive nights of fatal frost. She clambered up grassy hills, over rocky loam, until she happened upon a knoll overgrown with tendrils of hanging ivy. And in the flat clearing to the east, she saw a black dirt bike propped on its kickstand.

She pushed the emerald ivy aside and came face to face with the heavy steel hatch. Any other day, she wouldn't have had the strength to pry the thing open on her own, but today she had enough vexation to harness to tear it off its hinges. With a grunt and muscles flexed to their max, she pitched the hillside trapdoor open and hurtled down the stony stairs beyond without the slightest fear of losing her footing.

Sparrow was bathed in the harsh white of artificial lights, sitting atop a sleeping bag, back pressed against a bare section of wall and knees bent up. *A Little Princess* rested, open to its final pages, on her jeaned thighs. The sight of her sent Fletcher into a tailspin. "What the fuck?"

Sparrow's head snapped up. "I'm sorry." She closed the book. "I had to know how it ended."

"You think I give a shit about the book right now? Sparrow, you've been gone for four days! I couldn't reach you on the CommBand. I thought . . ." Suddenly, all Fletcher felt was relief. She smoothed her blonde ponytail back as if to rub the alleviation into her follicles like a balm. "You didn't even say goodbye." She padded across the bunker and parked herself beside Sparrow.

"I think I'm afraid to say goodbye. Five days ago, I had to say goodbye to my brother and it was forever."

Fletcher thought about her mother, her dad, and Jonah—and, of course, Killian. She covered the back of Sparrow's hand with her palm and rubbed her wrist. "I get it. Having to say goodbye to the people we love makes love feel like a curse."

Sparrow examined Fletcher's fingers as she threaded them

into the spaces between her own. "Love is not a curse. It's a gift; otherwise, it wouldn't matter to us once it's gone. It's one of the few good things in this world, so we have to give it and receive it as often as we can."

Fletcher ruminated on that. "How succinct."

"Succinct." Sparrow shook her head. "But it isn't. It's complicated because people are complicated—intelligent and kind, yet wild and stubborn. When you love someone, you love all of them, their virtues and their flaws." Fletcher watched Sparrow's expression change, saw her eyes brighten with tenderness. "I love you, Fletcher."

Here were two people in love, despite the ugliness of their circumstances—despite half the nation's insurmountable poverty, despite the constant fear of losing oneself and everyone close to them to Reclamation. It was a simple fact, one that had been true for some time. Fletcher knew that. It had happened quickly, faster than she thought possible, and of all the things there were to be afraid of in the world, this frightened her the most. "I—" she squeaked.

"You don't have to say anything," Sparrow added with haste and somberness. "I just needed you to know, in case the perfect time to tell you never shows."

Fletcher took Sparrow's face into her hands, ran her thumbs across her soft honey-hued cheeks, wondering if Sparrow could feel her love in her touch, absorb it through her skin like sunlight. Her amber eyes focused on Sparrow's rosy lips. She glided her fingers beneath Sparrow's long, silky hair, down to the nape of her neck, and tugged her forward into a kiss.

This kiss was different from their last—heavier, hungrier. Needful. Fletcher sensed that Sparrow's mouth was in quest of something more. She indulged her longing, and indeed her own, pressed her lips to Sparrow's a bit more eagerly. Sparrow snaked an arm around Fletcher's waist, her hand resting on the small of her back, pinky stroking a sliver of exposed skin where her shirt had ridden up.

Fletcher felt the soft tip of Sparrow's tongue prance across her lips, pleading to be accepted into the wet-hot sanctuary of her mouth. She granted Sparrow entry, and their tongues began to dance together in a graceful polonaise.

The air surrounding them grew warmer, though a chill shot through Fletcher's body, giving her goosebumps. She pulled away, inhaling sharply as if it were the last breath the universe would ever grant her.

Concern speckled Sparrow's ice blue irises, but Fletcher simply moved *A Little Princess* from its resting place on Sparrow's lap, then, kneeling, straddled Sparrow's hips. She bunched the collar of Sparrow's black sweater into her fist, pulled her close, and kissed her again. Sparrow cupped the supple curves of Fletcher's bottom, moved her kisses from her mouth to her jawline and down farther to her neck. She slithered her hands up the back of Fletcher's shirt and caressed the warm skin covering her spine. She looked at Fletcher with beseeching eyes. "Can I?"

Fletcher nodded her permission. She raised her arms, and Sparrow peeled the gauzy shirt from her body. She unclasped Fletcher's bra and stripped that away, too. She held Fletcher tight, palms settling at the base of her shoulder blades, and brushed her lips, her tongue, against her collarbone, her sternum, her breasts.

Fletcher breathed a low whimper into Sparrow's ear, licked the hot skin of her neckline below it. Sparrow wrapped her strong arms around Fletcher's torso and rolled her onto her back. Fletcher slipped her thumbs under the waistband of her sweatpants, her panties, yearning to be naked with a startling feverishness. But Sparrow, bowing over her, gathered Fletcher's too-eager hands into her own. "I want you to be sure," she said.

Fletcher reached up, draped her forearms around Sparrow's neck, and wrenched her close so that their mouths could meet again. She kissed her hard. "I am," she whispered. She felt

Sparrow's lips creep into a smile as she kissed her once more.

Sparrow gripped the draw-stringed waistband of Fletcher's pants, the stretchy elastic cincture of her underwear beneath them, and inched them down Fletcher's legs. Fletcher lifted her backside off the sleeping bag, aiding in her liberation from the oppressiveness of clothing. Then Sparrow wadded the weighty fabric into a ball and, with a snap of her wrist, chucked it over her shoulder. It hit the concrete floor with a muted thump, and both women burst into laughter, Fletcher covering her face with her hands.

Once their tittering abated and quiet had returned to the bunker, Fletcher uncovered her face to find Sparrow hovering above her, combing her gaze over every last inch of her nude frame. "What?" She realized that no one had ever seen her naked before and blushed, feeling self-conscious despite her bourgeoning ache to be touched. She tried to shield herself from Sparrow's view, but Sparrow nudged her arms away.

"Please don't." She skimmed her pointer finger across a gray-green bruise on Fletcher's left knee. "You're beautiful." She lay down on her stomach, wrapped her hands around Fletcher's calves and spread her legs, positioning them knees bent over her shoulders. She kissed Fletcher's ankles, traced the entire length of her inner thighs with her tongue, and paused to place a delicate peck on her battered knee. Then she dipped her head and took the most sensitive part of Fletcher into her mouth.

Fletcher gasped at the gentle pressure, unlike anything she had ever felt. Her pulse quickened, muscles straining at the earliest hint of divine rhapsody. The throbbing in her core was unrelenting, but in the most ethereal way. She seized Sparrow's head, snatched fistfuls of her velvety brown locks.

Sparrow slowed her rhythm as if to savor Fletcher wholly. And then Fletcher felt a new sensation as Sparrow slid her fingers into her body and began to knead the wet flesh she found there. Fletcher bucked her pelvis against Sparrow, over and over in a zealous cadence. Soon, everything intensified: the sound of her panting in perfect tempo with Sparrow's every lick and stroke, the steady, persistent drumming deep inside of her. She arched her back, bit her lip as her body began to tremble with the force of a star gone supernova. She heralded her climax with Sparrow's name, shouted so loudly that it reverberated off the concrete and steel walls below the shelves lined with weapons.

Sparrow pushed herself up, licked the wetness from her fingers, and collapsed onto the sleeping bag beside Fletcher. Fletcher gave her a moment to catch her breath and swept wisps of damp brown hair from her perspiration-soaked brow. "You," she murmured, in awe of the woman who had introduced her to a piece of herself she never imagined existed. She kissed her deeply, pulled her so close that she could feel the shiver it sent through Sparrow's body.

All of a sudden, she found herself loathing Sparrow's clothes—the scratchy knitted pullover, the thick, dark denim of her jeans. She wanted to feel the heat of Sparrow's skin against her own, unobstructed by man-made material. She glided her hand up Sparrow's sweater, relished the smoothness of her stomach, the litheness of her breasts. "Please," she murmured into Sparrow's ear. Sparrow flashed a coy grin and canted just enough to free the hem of her jumper from being pinned against her by the sleeping bag. Together, the women stripped the sweater from her body before Fletcher pushed her flat onto her back. She explored Sparrow's bare torso with her mouth— nibbled at her clavicle, kissed her breasts, wicked the salty sweat from her midriff with her tongue.

She lay down beside Sparrow, cradled the base of her skull in the crook of her arm and kissed her, parting her lips with a frenzied tongue. She pawed at Sparrow's jeans, unbuttoned and unzipped them, tugged them down just far enough to expose her hipbones. She slipped her hand into Sparrow's panties, her fingers into the wet hotness beyond. Sparrow let out a soft sigh, and Fletcher heard the wonderment in it, resounding as an aria.

Fletcher worked her digits inside Sparrow, massaging her sensitive spot with the pad of her thumb. A series of hushed whimpers fell from Sparrow's lips. Fletcher stopped kissing her for the briefest of seconds and looked into her eyes. "Okay?"

"Mmhmm." Sparrow grabbed the nape of Fletcher's neck and smashed their mouths together again. She rocked against Fletcher's hand, serenading her with a steady influx of contented moans. Fletcher treasured every quiver, every note in her melody of pleasure. If there were anyone on Earth who deserved even a fleeting moment of happiness, it was Sparrow, and she was honored to be able to provide it.

"Oh, God." Sparrow threw her head back, gathered great swaths of sleeping bag into her fists. Her legs quaked, abs tensed. Fletcher was astounded at how she could feel Sparrow peaking, her center spasming uncontrolledly around Fletcher's fingers. That she could be the source of it, such pure, perfect pleasure. *Miraculous.* "Oh, my God!" Sparrow thundered, her orgasm all-consuming. She dissolved into a motionless heap, energy spent.

Fletcher freed her hand from Sparrow's body, marveled at her glistening fingers. Then Sparrow draped herself over Fletcher, arms around her abdomen, legs around her thighs and pressed her face into Fletcher's cleavage. Fletcher heard her sniffle softly as she began to cry. She shifted, seeking Sparrow's face. "Are you alright?"

"Yeah," Sparrow spluttered. "Just . . . thank you for reminding me that I'm still alive."

Fletcher felt a twinge of melancholy in her chest. She swept her lips against Sparrow's shoulder, her cheek, her forehead, and hugged her so close that she could not tell where her body ended and Sparrow's began. Sparrow clung to her as if she were a life raft keeping her afloat on the stormy sea. And together they fell into a sleep haunted by dreams of the people they had lost.

Sparrow jerked awake, panting. The rapid motion startled Fletcher from her slumber. She pushed herself up and discovered Sparrow sitting with her head bent, hands splayed over her brow. "Nightmares?" she asked, rubbing Sparrow's sleep-warm back.

She nodded.

"Is there anything I can do?"

"I don't know," Sparrow grimaced, shrugging. "Hold me?"

Fletcher lay down again and spread her arms wide as Sparrow crashed into them. Fletcher combed her fingers through strands of Sparrow's coffee-colored hair, and the contact seemed to pacify her, if only temporarily.

Fletcher glanced at Sparrow, unexpectedly wondering what her parents were like, if she would ever have the chance to meet them. She thought of how much agony they must be in at the loss of their son and reprimanded herself for not asking about them sooner. "How are your mom and dad?"

"As bad as you'd expect. My mother, she just . . . dropped to her knees, cried and cried. I'd never seen her like that. Dad did his best to be stoic, but he couldn't hide it from me. He was devastated. Killian was the 'good child,'" Sparrow huffed. "We spent the majority of the time sobbing and hugging each other. They're shattered, Fletcher, even worse than I am."

"I'm so sorry," she said, smoothing Sparrow's tousled tresses.

"They didn't want me to return to YOR, but I'm in it for Killian now more than ever. And . . . I couldn't leave you."

Fletcher kissed her forehead. "My sweet little bird."

Her CommBand chirped then. She checked her wrist, and the neon blue text scrolled across its milky silicone surface: No sign of you for twelve hours. Boss man is in a state. Check in ASAP. – Philip

"Shit. We've been here all night. Søren's angry." She scrambled for her clothes.

Sparrow pulled her sweater over her head. "No, he isn't. He's worried. You won't be able to tell the difference from his face, though."

"I don't know, I think we're beginning to understand each other a little bit. I still don't really trust him, but maybe that will come with time." She wiggled into her sweatpants, then rolled up the sleeping bag and put it on a shelf as Sparrow grabbed *A Little Princess* from the concrete floor and tucked it into her knapsack.

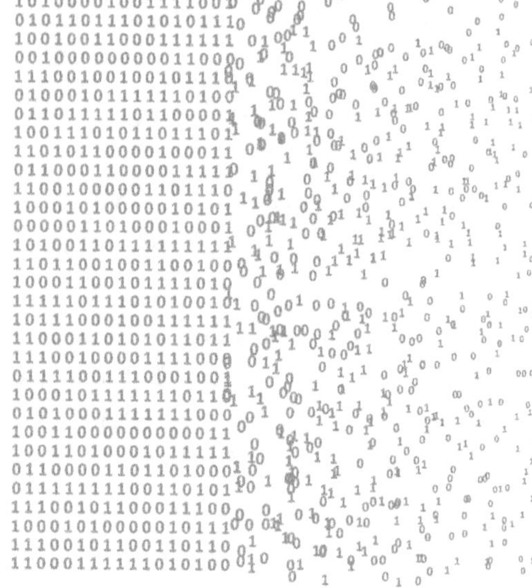

chapter twenty-seven

THEY WALKED INTO THE Visitor's Center holding hands. It was a bolder statement than Fletcher was prepared for, but one she knew Sparrow needed: This was how it was going to be from that point on. Killian had always been Sparrow's anchor against life's tempestuous currents, and while she hated that the vacancy existed, Fletcher was determined to assume the role with allegiance.

YOR crowded around them in the foyer, the relief in their expressions palpable—with the exception of Søren, who scrutinized them with ambivalence.

Charlie hugged each woman. Then she, along with Zoe and Peter, engaged Sparrow in conversation about her spirits and her parents. Søren seized the opportunity of the group's preoccupation, took Fletcher's elbow, and guided her into the alcove between the hall and bunkroom. "You will never, under any circumstances, go off on your own again without telling anyone. Do I make myself clear?" His voice was thick and austere, but Fletcher could see the gleam of fretfulness in his ebony irises.

"Yes."

He rolled a glance between Fletcher and Sparrow. "I'm not

happy about the two of you, but there's nothing I can do to put a stop to it, is there?"

"No."

"It was inevitable, wasn't it?"

Fletcher stole a glimpse of Sparrow, surrounded by people who cared for her. *Inevitable.* "I think so."

"Right," he grumbled. Fletcher bit her lip, knowing that was the closest he would ever come to giving his approval. He shifted his attention to the group. "Charlie, Damon, get breakfast started. There's a new development for us to discuss."

The morning meal consumed and the aftermath tidied, Søren called a meeting to order in the common room.

"What's this all about?" Zoe asked as she dropped onto the cushioned sofa beside Fletcher and Sparrow.

Søren traced the stone mantel above the fireplace, stopping to place a reverent stroke atop the corked clay jar that Sparrow had placed there. "We've all been disheartened these last five days, and that feeling isn't going away any time soon. Some of us have also been restless, though to be honest, that restlessness has existed in this house for a while." He looked at Fletcher. "We've been relatively inactive as a group since losing our man inside the Hall of Records, but a new line of attack has fallen into place—one that has the potential to make a real difference in how we approach our goal of changing the state of affairs in this country. It's time to do something now, in Killian's honor. I'll hand you over to Philip, who will explain in greater detail." He sat in the armchair beside the couch, and Philip took his place in front of the hearth.

Philip set a small oval holoprojector in the center of the coffee table. He then unveiled a pocket-sized translucent box filled with clear liquid and a flat panel-controller with a toggle switch. He laid both objects beside the projector and cleared his throat. "What has been our main obstacle in the fight to abolish Reclamation?"

The room was silent.

"We have info about a growing political movement in The South rallying for reintegration of The Northern and Southern Territories. These Southerners are aware of how heavy-handed The Government is with us. They want the wall taken down, they want a single currency system, and they want to bring income equality to The Vault. Given that we have it on good authority these activists could be open to advocating for the eradication of compulsory higher education, forced student debt and, most importantly, the Reclamation Process, what would we need to persuade them to take up the cause?" He nudged the group. "Anyone?"

"Evidence," said Fletcher. "We need proof that the Reclamation Process is completely dehumanizing, and that it's happening to more people than they realize. It's easy to discount word of mouth, but hard to disbelieve what you see with your own eyes."

"Exactly! We've never had the ability to infiltrate and document anything that happens inside a Processing Center. Søren tried to sneak a recording device in with him when he was Reclaimed years ago, but they were able to ferret out the antiquated hardware with their scanning equipment."

Fletcher peered at Søren, astonished by this new piece of information. The bud of respect she had for him ripened in an instant.

"Uh huh. So what's in the box?" Zoe's pink hair bobbed as she nodded at the table.

Sparrow leaned forward, elbows on her knees, as her curiosity stirred. Fletcher watched the others react in kind.

Philip unlatched the box and flipped open the lid. He submerged his thumb and index finger into the glossy fluid, removed a filmy lens, placed it in the palm of his hand, and repeated the process with the second lens. He presented the contacts to everyone with an even sweep of his hand.

"Mind-blowing." Zoe scrunched her lips to the side.

"Wait for it." Philip snatched the panel controller with his free hand and slid the switch into the ON position.

The holoprojector sputtered to life, casting a 3D image into the air. At first, the holograph looked innocuous, a globular image of a grainy wooden plank. Damon was the first to recognize what the group was seeing. He raised his gaze to the ceiling and did a double take at the projection. "Guys . . ." He reached out to Charlie in the chair beside him, tapped her shoulder, and pointed up. Everyone shifted their vision to the support beam above Philip's head.

"Is that—" Charlie started.

Philip angled his hand just enough to alter the lenses' line of sight, holding up the panel-controller in front of them and waving it around. The holoprojector displayed his figure and movements in high definition.

"That's real-time footage!" Charlie exclaimed.

"Almost. There's a six-second delay due to processing lag. It was impossible to seamlessly integrate this tech with our CPUs, but the hardware is made from the same goo as the human eyeball, so it's bio-compatible, indiscernible from natural tissue. I'm calling them OverSight. Get it? Because they're implanted over the cornea."

Charlie gawped at the devices. "And the images are . . . beamed to us and saved on your computers?"

"Yeah, using The Government's own network as a proxy."

Charlie and Damon shared a glance. "That seems chancy," Damon said. "Even if the things themselves are undetectable, couldn't the signal they give off lead the BOE straight to us?"

"Excellent question." Søren nailed Philip with a cynical expression.

"The images are relayed over the BOE's communication network—like the earpieces the Agents use—and sent to a receiver that looks like it's part of the local government network. Any signal OverSight may emit appears to be coming from and going to an Agent's earpiece. Anyone who happened to be looking for it—and they'd have to be looking very closely to find it in the first place—would just see chatter between Agents. Plus, I've encrypted the data. No one is tracing anything anywhere."

"Did you get any of that?" Sparrow whispered to Fletcher.

"A smidgen."

"Tech-geek name notwithstanding, these are pretty cool," Zoe commented.

Sparrow was troubled. "You said they're implants?" She sought out Peter. "Is the surgery dangerous? Can they be removed?"

"The procedure is minimally invasive, nothing internal. To be safe, I'd say there'd have to be a twenty-four-hour period of the recipient's eyes being closed after implantation. A humid environment is crucial for successful integration with the natural cornea. And yes, it would be more painstaking than implantation, but I believe they can be removed."

"You believe, or you're sure?" Sparrow asked.

Peter stirred in his chair. "Are you questioning my competence as a surgeon?" His voice was accusatory.

"If you're wondering whether I hold you responsible for Killian's death, the answer is absolutely not. I know how hard you tried to save him, Peter. I *saw* it." Her eyes brimmed with tears, but she fought away the torrent. "You were able to set aside the pain of losing Mateo and give my brother everything you had. I'm amazed by that, and I will always be thankful to you."

Peter pursed his lips together and sniffed. He extended his arm to Sparrow, took her hand, and gave it a light squeeze.

"Okay," Sparrow continued. "We understand how the tech works, and how the implantation would go. The only question left is, who receives the implants?"

Philip averted his gaze. He toggled the switch to OFF, then deposited the glassy lenses into their watery case.

Every set of inquiring eyes in the room settled on Søren. He gripped his chair's armrests with pale knuckles. "The lenses should be implanted in someone for whom Reclamation is unavoidable—someone on the verge of summary judgment."

"And who would that be?" Fletcher probed. *This is why I'm here, why I have been all along.* It made sense: Søren never had any intention of helping her escape or letting her stay. If he had told her as much at the very beginning, she might have been receptive to the idea, but her situation then was poles apart from what it had become. She no longer had any inclination for welcoming the notion. She'd started to build a life here, had found someone she loved and wanted to be with. Was she supposed to volunteer to give that all up? *That isn't fair.* She almost laughed at the thought. Life was inherently unfair, and she had always known that. She looked at Sparrow, who caught her gaze and shook her head as if she'd read Fletcher's mind.

"I don't know," Søren answered.

Fletcher examined his expression for any sign of disingenuousness. She found only sincerity. "You don't know?"

"That's what I said." He glowered at her. "I do know that had you, Zoe, Damon, and Sparrow remained in your homes with your families, you all would have been served with summary judgment by now. I also know that I am not willing to sacrifice any more of my people to the Department of Reclamation. Hear me when I tell you this, Fletcher. You are one of my people, regardless of how either of us may feel about it, or each other."

"Then what do you propose we do?"

"We . . . find someone."

"Find someone," Fletcher repeated. "What, we hold tryouts? Put out an open call for volunteers?"

Søren clenched his jaw. "We apprehend someone who

is meant for Reclamation, implant the lenses, keep them comfortable during the healing process, and then return them to wherever it was we found them and let fate unfold."

Just as fast as it had blossomed, Fletcher's esteem for him withered and died. She felt a fizzing resentment mingling with an unexpected disappointment. "YOR doesn't abduct people, we help them!" she snapped, leaping from her seat. "That's in the mission statement, isn't it? We advocate *for* bodily autonomy *against* violent, forceful alterations. You're suggesting we forsake everything we stand for and become the very evil we despise!"

"Fletcher—" Charlie started.

"No!" She whirled on Charlie. "Five days ago I became a killer because I saw no other way out, and my actions are going to plague me until I die. Now he wants to make me an accessory to kidnapping and assault? It's morally bankrupt, and I won't stand for it. My conscience can't take it, I know it can't." She shook her head and collapsed onto the couch. "We find a volunteer, or we scrap the fucking lenses."

Søren inhaled a series of measured breaths, trying to bridle his mounting frustration before it bested him. "Who would volunteer?" he asked through gritted teeth. "Tell me, Fletcher. Who's going to enlist to have their body modified by a group of strangers, and then, after realizing that we could help them evade capture, give themselves up to the Agents anyway? Would you be interested in volunteering for that?"

Fletcher flitted her gaze over Sparrow's profile. "No," she sighed, defeated. "If I can have my life—if that's at all possible—I want it. I want it more than I ever have."

"Because you have something to live for. Everybody thinks they have something to live for, and they do, but not everyone gets the chance. One doomed person has the potential to change that for all of us."

"You want to sacrifice one to save many. I understand the concept, but I don't accept it. There has to be another way."

"You're a student of history," Peter interrupted. "What would have happened two hundred years ago if any of the assassination attempts on Adolf Hitler had gone to plan? Millions of people would have been spared because of one man's death."

"Actually, Hitler's murder would have created a power vacuum, and considering the radical political climate of the times, there's no telling what kind of person may have filled that void," Fletcher schooled him. "We're not talking here about unseating a brutal dictator for the greater good. We're talking about yanking some random, innocent person from their home and their family, holding them against their will, conducting human experimentation on them, and afterward handing them over to Agents, whom we know for a fact will torture them. So, yes, I am a student of history, and I'm telling you that's what the Nazis did, and what the American government did in the years preceding its downfall." She paused to swallow her exasperation. "I don't know about any of you, but I am not interested in villainizing myself, especially to the people we claim to be trying to help."

Sparrow swept a glance around the room, gauging the individual reactions to Fletcher's oration. "We all know she's right."

"You would side with her," Zoe responded. "I'm not saying either of you are wrong, but I don't see what other choice we have. Søren said that even if any of us wanted to, volunteering is off the table. He's not wrong, either. We probably couldn't find anyone in The Vault who'd be willing to do what we need them to."

"This is a conversation of hypotheticals at this point," Søren declared. "Head Office wants to examine OverSight before any steps toward implantation are taken."

"Why?" asked Philip. "It's perfect."

"Since when is Head Office bothered about our daily operations?" Sparrow queried.

"This isn't a mundane mission for machine parts or medicines, or even an ST retrieval. They want to run tests on OverSight using government sweeping equipment unavailable to us here. They want to be sure that everything is as imperceptible as we believe it is. No one wants to risk losing what could end up being our greatest asset."

"There's the problem," Fletcher pointed out. "The higher-ups are concerned about the technology, but no one gives a shit about the person who's going to have the things stitched into their eyeballs."

Søren shook his head. "In the end, it isn't our call. We'll do whatever they tell us to do. Anyone who has a problem with that will be free to leave. But you'll be on your own. We meet with Head Office in two days."

"All of us?" asked Charlie.

"All of us. They're en route to a secondary location as we speak. I'll be given the coordinates of the site when they arrive."

Fletcher murmured to Sparrow, "Have you ever met any of these Head Office people?"

"No. No one besides Søren has."

Strange. "Why do they want to meet with all of us? That's never happened before, has it? It's not really the way they do things—they prefer to hide in the shadows."

"It's not how we do things, either," Peter insisted. "We go out in small teams to avoid the prospect of everyone being captured. That's your rule, Søren."

"I'm aware. I advised Head Office against it, but they were adamant."

"How well do you know these people?" Fletcher questioned.

"Well enough. Over the years I've seen more than a dozen of us come and go—leave, get apprehended, or die—and Head Office has guided me through every defection, every loss. There's no need to fear them, especially you."

Especially me. "That's right, everyone has a plan for me."

Fletcher stood. "My plan for me is to get the hell out of this room, go take a shower, and try to scrub the disgust off my skin." She fixed Søren with a sidelong glare as she left the room.

The swinging door to the communal locker room squeaked open. Fletcher stepped out from under the stream of warm water and wiped her eyes. She tugged at the corner of the opaque curtain and peeked through the crevice. Sparrow crept across the beige tile floor, towel wrapped around her body. She sported a timid grin as she reached for the curtain of the stall beside Fletcher's.

"No." Fletcher stuck her hands through the curtain. She grabbed Sparrow's wrist, pulled her close, removed the towel from her body and slung it on a hook. Sparrow slipped into the shower with her.

They lathered each other's hair and bodies as the hot water flowed over their bare skin. "I don't like the idea of rendezvousing with Head Office," Fletcher said. "It's got me in knots, and I don't know why."

Sparrow squeezed the suds from Fletcher's golden locks. "It's okay to be wary. That instinct will save your life."

"I want to take my sword with me." Fletcher thought about the weapon she had used to slay Flynn nearly a week ago. She'd scrubbed his blood from the blade, but had since abandoned it, stowing it away under the cot she hadn't slept on in so many nights. "Søren won't have it, and there's no way I could hide it from him."

"We'll take guns. Both of us." Fletcher opened her mouth to speak, but Sparrow stopped her. "Killian's .22 is a cinch to handle, much easier than the Mossberg. You'll be fine, I promise."

Fletcher didn't want to use Killian's gun. She didn't want anyone to use it. She thought it should be retired, mounted on a wall for posterity so that anyone who ever caught a glimpse of it would remember the sacrifice Killian had made. And then there was also the desire to protect Sparrow. If Fletcher were going to do something audacious, she had no intention of dragging Sparrow into it with her. She dared not say as much aloud. She knew Sparrow would argue. *She'd follow me to hell.* "It's a terrible idea, bringing weapons. Let's not."

"Your gut is telling you to be ready for the situation to go bad, so that's what we're going to do." Sparrow wrapped her arms around Fletcher's torso and drew her close. "Let's dry off, get dressed, and go out on the range so you can get some practice in on the .22, okay?"

Fletcher laid her head on Sparrow's shoulder, and the tension in her muscles melted away. *I'd follow her to hell, too.* "Okay."

Killian's silver pump-action .22 was much lighter than the Mossberg. Its ammunition was minuscule in comparison to the 12-gauge shotgun shells. Fletcher found it odd, how cool to the touch the slim metal-jacketed bullets, kissed by the November air, were. She loaded the tiny missiles into the slender action— fifteen in all—thinking it was funny how little space the murderous projectiles took up in contrast to how much damage they could do when properly placed. She knew they were capable of shredding a brain because rimfire ammo tended to bounce around inside the skull. She'd seen the destruction this rifle could cause during a hunt she'd been forced to participate in. Killian had used it to shoot a ring-necked pheasant, and the result was gruesome to behold. Irrespective of how small and toylike the .22 seemed, Fletcher was antipathetic to it, though she had to admit that it was less cumbrous than her lengthy katana-esque sword, with its protruding pommel.

Sparrow arranged a stuffed burlap target twenty-five paces down the narrow shooting lane. She scrutinized its footing, nodded at her handiwork, then gave Fletcher a thumbs up. Fletcher angled the dangerous end of the rifle safely at the ground and watched as Sparrow sauntered back toward her, pulling her mane into a high ponytail as she walked.

"Whenever you're ready," Sparrow said. "Remember your stance." She pinched Fletcher's hips, then backed away.

Fletcher adjusted her posture, establishing the equilibrium she'd need to manage the rifle's kickback. She positioned the butt against her shoulder, looked down the sight, and secured the bull's-eye. She yanked the pump back and heard the tinny *clink* of the round entering the chamber. She sucked in a lungful of cold oxygen and pressed the trigger.

The sound of the bullet leaving the muzzle was different from the one the Mossberg made. Instead of the boisterous *boom-crack* she had grown accustomed to, the .22 let out a noise that resembled a forceful hand clap. There was little recoil. The stock of the gun barely lurched from her shoulder at all, and her muscles hardly flinched. She saw tufts of straw fly out of the burlap target as the bullet hit its yellow center. *Lucky shot.* She pumped the gun again. The spent casing expelled itself from the chamber, and another round took its place. She pressed the trigger again. *Pfft!* The second bullet punched through the flaxen bullseye.

Fletcher pumped and pressed, pumped and pressed, without reluctance. It was disconcerting, the excitement that rang through her as she fired each round, how the weapon felt like a natural extension of her body. When she had finished, the bullseye was pocked with fifteen small holes. Broken bits of creamy hay littered the mucky forest floor.

Sparrow ogled the riddled target and Fletcher. "Incredible."

Fletcher held the rifle in both hands, gaping at the deadly thing. "Why was I not trained on a .22?"

Sparrow squeezed her mouth into a thin line. She patted the gun's warm barrel. "This is the only one in our collection and—"

she trailed off.

It was already spoken for. Fletcher completed the sentence in her mind. "Are you sure you're okay with me using it?"

Sparrow stared at the ground. "Killian thought it might be the best fit for you. He wanted to give it to you, but Søren said no. Yes, I'm fine with you using it."

"I'll take good care of it."

"I know." Sparrow smiled at her. "Want to go again?" She removed a box of ammunition from the pouch of her taupe hooded sweatshirt and offered it to Fletcher.

Fletcher took it from her with a simper. "I think I should."

chapter twenty-eight

SØREN HAD MADE A point of sleeping in the Ranger's quarters for two consecutive nights, relegating Sparrow and Fletcher to their respective cots in the bunkroom. Fletcher recognized it for what it was, a power play—an unspoken proclamation that he would in no way permit romantic notions to muddle YOR's objectives or undermine his authority. That was fine with Fletcher as she was not inclined to do the former and had already established a propensity for the latter. As far as she was concerned, nothing had to change regarding either issue although YOR's methodology required considerable refinement in the way of empathy. She could never excuse Søren, or anyone, for blithely suggesting the indiscriminate abduction of a Vaulter, or a bystanding Southerner, for that matter. Most Southerners were superficial, voracious, and bourgeois, to be sure, but they were indifferent, too self-involved to be menacing. If Fletcher had learned anything from Agent Flynn before she killed him, it was that a weak-minded herd would never be a threat. So long as the Southerners were convinced that they needed *things*, most of them would remain innocuous.

Still disgusted with Søren, Fletcher had decided to avoid him, forgoing the early morning group workouts in favor of her own exercise. She'd trudged down to the storage shed, sharpened axe in hand, intent on replenishing the dwindling stockpile of firewood.

She had been whittling away at a downed snag for the better part of the daylight hours, chopping logs into smaller, more manageable kindling, loading them onto the rusty wheelbarrow, hauling it to the shed, and layering the tinder—driest to dampest—into tall heaps, sweating throughout. With every swing of the axe, every tow of the wheelbarrow, she pictured the rest of YOR muddling around the old timber-and-stone building, anxiously awaiting notification of Head Office's arrival at whatever esoteric location they had selected for the conclave. The sun had begun to dip below the tops of the towering white pines before Fletcher laid eyes on another person.

"Ivy League," Sparrow called to her as she advanced.

Fletcher stopped mid-swing, reared upright, jabbed the head of the axe into the dirt, and steadied herself on its long wooden handle. She dabbed away the moisture that had dripped into her eyes with the sleeve of her muted green-and-tan plaid shirt. Soft rays of sun cast an otherworldly glow around Sparrow's entire body, and Fletcher could not keep herself from thinking that the woman resembled all the depictions of angels she had seen or read about in books. Fletcher had never said it aloud before, but she'd always thought Sparrow was stunning, from the very instant she had revealed her face that night in the van two months prior. "Hi." Sparrow leaned in to greet her with a kiss.

"I'm gross," Fletcher warned, but Sparrow was not deterred. As their lips met, it struck Fletcher how normal the scene would've been in days long past—colonial era farmers chopping wood for fireplaces, their partners greeting them with tender kisses as they came to inform them that the workday was done. But it wasn't normal now, hadn't been in centuries, probably would never be again. She chased away the subtle envy of simpler times. "You were sent to fetch me again?"

"Well, you are quite fetching."

Fletcher sniggered. "I don't think I realized you were punny until right this second."

"I rarely have the opportunity to flex that particular muscle these days." Sparrow's expression dropped. "You should have known me and Killian before all this. Puns were our preferred form of communication."

Fletcher recalled her childhood with Jonah. He had the same dry, sarcastic sense of humor she did. They were always laughing about things nobody else understood. She felt the familiar sting of missing him: He wasn't her brother by blood, but he may as well have been. "I would've liked to have a sibling. I think it would've brought a lot of joy into my house growing up."

"Yeah, I was lucky."

"You'll always have those memories. Keep them close." Fletcher reached out to touch Sparrow's cheek, and Sparrow nuzzled into the caress.

"Søren has news for us."

"I figured." Fletcher grabbed the axe, stepped around Sparrow, and wedged its edge into the chopping block. "Let's go find out what he has to say."

Sparrow took her hand and led the way.

Sparrow and Fletcher entered the Visitor's Center through the sliding glass patio door. The rest of YOR had already congregated around the kitchen table for a change of scenery from the common room. Fletcher noticed that Sparrow's posture tensed. She hadn't been able to spend any significant amount of time in this room since Killian . . . It would take longer than a week for that trauma to begin to heal.

"Hey," Peter said, nodding at the women. "Take a seat." He gestured at two empty chairs beside him. Fletcher and Sparrow sat down as Philip set up his presentation. He entered a series of geographic coordinates into his homemade HoloPod: 42° 47' 12.588" N - 71° 3' 35.352" W. The sequence of numbers and letters meant nothing to Fletcher until a broad satellite image was projected into the air above the table. The image was a relic from prewar times. Fletcher could tell by the multitude of colorful cars parked in driveways and lining the surface roads.

"Based on the latitude and longitude Head Office relayed to Søren, the meetup is here." Philip waved his hand over the projection. It zoomed in on a sprawling rectangular building with what looked to be a rounded battlement, replete with crenels and merlons, bulging into the sky.

Fletcher squinted at the visualization to confirm that her mind was not misinterpreting it. "Is that a castle? These Head Office people certainly hold themselves in high esteem, don't they?" She pushed back in her seat and folded her arms.

Peter and Philip each suppressed sniggers, Peter rubbing a hand over his brow, Philip tapping three fingers against his lips. Charlie shot Fletcher a look from across the table that let Fletcher know she was of the same opinion. Zoe could not have cared one way or the other if she tried, and Damon sat wide-eyed, waiting for Søren's reaction, which never materialized beyond a twist of the mouth.

"Yeah," Philip confirmed. "That's Winnekenni Castle in Haverhill, Massachusetts. It's about an hour and a half drive from here, depending on the condition of the back roads we need to take to get there."

"Sorry, back roads?" Charlie asked.

"Head Office requested that we avoid the highways."

"Right, because rush hour traffic is a nightmare," deadpanned Fletcher. Damon cocked his head, and his brown bangs fell into his eyes as he gawked at her. In that moment Fletcher was reminded of how young Damon was—eighteen, a HiEd Exam truant and ignorant of the old world. *Lucky kid.* "Rush hour . . . back in the day when everyone had cars—you know what, never mind," she said, waving him off.

"It's not a joke if no one gets it, Fletcher." He shrugged.

"Point taken." She focused on the hologram. "I suppose we don't have access to more current satellite photos. So, we're assuming the back roads from Nowhere, Vermontshire, to South of Nowhere, Massachusetts, are passable."

"Correct."

"Starting off strong, we are." Fletcher pumped her fist at him.

"That's enough," Søren admonished. He rested his bony elbows on the tabletop and wrung his hands together. "We're taking the back roads in order to remain as covert as possible. The members of Head Office would be a prize for The Government, more so than any of us."

"Mmm, I'm betting Fletcher would be the gold medal," Philip muttered.

"Thanks." Fletcher winked at him.

"Since it was mentioned, I think Fletcher should stay here," Zoe piped up. Everyone regarded her, surprised at the insight. "Because she killed an Agent and all," she spluttered.

"I second that idea," declared Sparrow, raising her hand.

Fletcher gave her a bothered glare, grabbed her hand, and forced it down. "Where you go, I go."

"Then you both stay here," Zoe replied.

Søren shook his head. "No one is staying behind. We're all going." He pushed his chair away from the table and stood up. "Be ready to leave by dusk." The group watched him as he retreated from the kitchen.

Charlie gazed out the glass doors at the darkening horizon. "Looks like it's sandwiches for dinner." She bunched her dark curls into a bun and set to work at the granite counter, slicing a loaf of bread she had baked two days before.

Fletcher acted as a lookout posted in the archway near the

grandfather clock at the bunkroom's entrance as Sparrow stuffed her sawed-off shotgun, Killian's rifle, extra 12-gauge and .22 ammunition, and each gun's leg holster into her faded hunter green duffel bag atop two ankle-length black trench coats. Fletcher had suggested that they not risk their plan of bearing arms being discovered by gearing up in any of the communal areas. Instead, they would dress in the solitude of the Ranger's quarters while everyone else gathered in the kitchen to eat their quick meal. Sparrow zipped the bag, hurried to Fletcher, and they both bounded up the stairs.

They ran into Philip on the second-floor landing. He examined the women and the bag with his dark angular eyes and ran his slender fingers through his short black hair. "Is what I'm guessing is in that bag actually in that bag?"

Fletcher started, "It's—"

"Smart," he said. "I think I'm going to wear my trench coat. It's perfect for the cold." He feigned a shiver. "Søren is still upstairs. If you two need some alone time, you can duck into the war room. Just don't get any *fluids* on my consoles."

Fletcher rolled her eyes at him, but whispered an earnest, "Thank you."

"This is wrong," Fletcher called to Sparrow, then mumbled to herself, "genius-level IQ, but I can't buckle myself into this fucking thing."

Sparrow finished affixing her holster to her thigh, slipped a spare magazine into its ammo pouch, then went down on her haunches in front of Fletcher. "You've got it on right; the straps just need adjusting." She tugged on the bands that laced through the two side-release buckles, and the holster tightened against Fletcher's thigh. She ran her hands up Fletcher's jeans. "How does that feel?"

Fletcher looked down at her. "The holster or your hands?"

Sparrow raised her left eyebrow.

"Awkward and nice, respectively."

"Banter. Cute." Sparrow stood.

"Sorry. I'm nervous."

Sparrow checked to make sure that the .22 was loaded and its safety was on. She secured the gun into Fletcher's sling with the hook and loop fastening. Then Fletcher shimmied into her coat, felt for her weapon beneath its lappets.

"If you need to draw, slip your coat back first so the gun doesn't snag. It'll pull free easily," Sparrow said as she grabbed her shotgun from the long metal desk and slid it into the caddy on her thigh.

Fletcher held open Sparrow's trench coat at waist level. Sparrow slid her hands into the armholes and Fletcher raised the coat up to her shoulders. She swept Sparrow's pin-straight hair free from the collar. When Sparrow turned to face her, she glided her hand around Fletcher's neck and kissed her. Fletcher puckered into it, then pulled away, grinning clumsily. "What was that for?"

"Your nerves. Did it help?"

"I may need another."

The door swung open and they were caught mid-kiss. Their heads snapped toward the intruder.

"*Blech*," Zoe spat, though Fletcher caught the creeping blush in her cheeks. "We're leaving." She turned heel and marched away.

Fletcher's head fell back as a devilish cackle leaked from her mouth. "Let's always kiss when we know she's watching."

"I can do that," Sparrow agreed, and kissed her again.

chapter twenty-nine

THE WHOLE OF YOR huddled together in the back of the black cargo van like a litter of feral kittens, save for Zoe, who helmed the wheel, and Philip, who was her navigator, constantly consulting his satellite projection. The whitish-yellow glow of neon headlights did little to carve through the shadow that swathed the nighttime thoroughfares of rural Massachusetts. Zoe had been forced to slow the van a handful of times in order to navigate around fallen trees and anomalous boulders that had made their way into the street over the ages. Some areas were overgrown with creepers that had stretched beyond the bitumen boundaries, and weeds that had long ago seeped through cracks in the pavement.

Twice they had nearly gone off the road, the first time thanks to a pothole so deep and wide it could have been called a canyon, the second due to a pack of enormous coyotes roving in the middle of the lanes. That was the thing about streets left to corrode for more than a century: nature had not been shy in her repossession of the asphalt man had laid.

Fletcher had her arm slung around Sparrow's shoulders, and Sparrow had nestled into her warmth, head settled against her clavicle. Sitting opposite them, Søren observed the women for the longest time. Fletcher watched as his stare flitted from her to Sparrow and back again countless times, until it unnerved her. "What?" Her question was piercing, a dagger in the dark. She felt the atmosphere charge as everybody turned their attention to Søren.

"The two of you make sense," he said. "Except we got it wrong: you're the brilliant star and she's the dark horse."

"What did you say?" Fletcher's eyes bulged. She thought she had gotten past the paranoid distrust she harbored for Søren, but it had never truly dissipated, only gone dormant. And now it had uncoiled into consciousness like a snake awakening from hibernation. "Stop the car!"

Zoe stomped on the brakes, and every person in the van pitched forward and to the side as the automobile screeched to a stop at an awkward angle. Philip turned around in the passenger seat, his face twisted with fear. "Fletcher?"

Fletcher leaned toward Søren, her amber irises akin to burning embers under the silver moonlight. "You called her dark horse. That's what Flynn called me. It's not a common idiom. Who the hell is 'we'?"

Søren let slip a guise of trepidation, which disintegrated into perplexity. He waved his hand through the air in a circular motion. "Us. Everyone here. And Killian. Killian said it before any of us, remember, Sparrow?" He narrowed his eyes at Sparrow, and Fletcher sought her corroboration.

"Killian said you were 'fierce' that first night we brought you to the Visitor's Center. He said it to all of us. I wasn't even sure he knew what it meant, but I knew he was right."

"You're combustible while Sparrow's more restrained. Or she used to be until you arrived. That's all I meant," Søren clarified.

"I'm not combustible."

"You are. You're intelligent but impetuous, not as calculating as you'd like to be—a planner and a doer, but not always at the same time. You should've come to understand that about yourself by now."

Fletcher folded under Søren's appraisal. She considered her temperament, how it had changed since that moment in the library with Grier and The Agents when she had decided she'd had enough of the life they'd designed for her and everyone she knew. *So I am dangerous, after all.* She thought back to the night she had murdered Flynn, how he wanted her on his side. And she realized that it had always been a part of her—combustibility. She could be explosive if the right catalyst came along to set her ablaze, and that was fine, so long as it could be controlled. "Sometimes logic isn't as important as action. There's no time to weigh the consequences."

"Like screaming at me to stop the van!" Zoe pursed her lips and scrunched her face into an absurd expression. Fletcher dissolved into laughter at the sight of it. The tension in the car evaporated as the rest of YOR joined her in hysterics.

"Screw you all. She could've killed us." Zoe turned back to the steering wheel and started the van down the road again. "If Sparrow had been driving, half of us would be hood ornaments right now."

Their collective laughter boomed.

Two hours into the journey, YOR happened upon a large street sign shaped like an open paper book, its once clean white frontage peeling to reveal the unfinished metal below. Faded letters read "ENTERING HAVERHILL, ESSEX COUNTY EST. 1640." Fletcher leaned forward and gaped at the sign through the windshield, gripped by a peculiar nostalgia for a time she had never known.

"Headlights off. Daytime runners only," Søren told Zoe.

Zoe scowled at him in the rearview mirror but said nothing.

"Are you serious?" Philip probed. "We can hardly see ahead

of us as it is."

Søren pointed at faint ochre illuminations dotting the landscape in the distance. "People live around here. The engine is loud enough that we don't need headlamps calling attention to us, too."

Zoe switched off the headlights, and the gaping jaws of night chomped down on the van. The darkness intensified every noise, the buzz of the vehicle's tires meeting tarmac and the anxious breathing of the seven souls on board.

"How much farther?" Damon wondered.

Philip referred to his satellite picture. "We take the next left, stay on that street for about a mile, and then we should find a service road to the parking lot."

Zoe turned onto a road that Fletcher suspected would not have been busy even prior to the Second American Revolution when there were millions of vehicles on the streets of Massachusetts at any given time. Here the asphalt had dissolved to dust. Tiny pebbles and larger chunks of rock scraped against the van's undercarriage as it moved.

"Pull in here." Philip gestured to an unpaved auxiliary lane on the right-hand side of the street. They drove two hundred yards up the path before encountering an oxidized gate that resembled a sideways V with a washed-out diamond-shaped ROAD CLOSED sign attached to it.

Zoe put the car in park and turned around in her seat. "Well?"

Philip gawked at the projection, then peered through the windscreen. "It's right up there."

"Let me out," said Søren, and six pairs of uneasy eyes settled on him. "I'll open the gate. You pull through and I'll close it again behind you," he instructed Zoe.

"Sure," Zoe replied.

Damon threw open the rolling door, and Søren hopped out into the gloom. He rounded the front of the van, his silhouette observable in the lurid glow of the daytime runners, and winched up the gate. Zoe rolled the van through and waited.

"Go ahead," Søren said upon his return, his body half hanging out of the cargo area. Another two hundred yards and the broad stone façade of Winnekenni Castle came into view.

Zoe parked, and the group exited the van, Søren in the lead. He craned his head up at the waning crescent moon. "Too dark." Sparrow withdrew her flat micro-flashlight from her coat pocket and passed it to him. He nodded his thanks to her and switched the flashlight on to its dimmest setting, illuminating a broken concrete walkway before him.

YOR warily examined their surroundings. There were no other vehicles parked within sight. Fletcher wondered to herself if they had been stood up.

"There's a light on inside, see?" Damon said, signaling to one of the arched windows at the far end of the building. There was a light, saffron and flickering, like the trash can fires that lit the boulevards of Fletcher's neighborhood.

Sparrow approached Fletcher and took her hand. "Alright?"

"Yes, you?"

Fletcher could only just make out Sparrow's half smile.

Søren guided the group up the footpath to a pair of vaulted wooden doors. He yanked on the curved iron handles, and the doors yawned open with a brassy squeal.

The pack crept into a vast atrium, received by grimy tile floors, walls with flaking paint, and a dust-covered mahogany baby grand piano. Ahead to their left through an open archway, the flammeous light beckoned them further into the cold, cavernous citadel.

Søren held the flashlight high as he walked, its beams bouncing across toothy stonework gargoyles who lorded over the manor from recessed nooks in the walls.

"This place is freaking me out," Zoe whispered as the group advanced.

"Me, too," said Peter.

Søren marched down a trio of wide limestone stairs into a grand hall, everyone else trailing behind him. The chamber had once been a ballroom, evident from a worn dance floor at its center, but nothing else remained of the revelries that had taken place there long ago. At the opposite end of the hall, a fireplace half the height of the room was stacked high with crackling cordwood. Its flames irradiated every corner of the gallery, leaving no shadowy niche in which to hide; yet whoever had been stoking the fire was nowhere to be found.

"I don't like this," Fletcher declared, her senses overwhelmed by the presence of an invisible menace.

"Neither do I," Sparrow concurred.

Philip looked to Søren. "What do we do?"

Søren turned off the flashlight and handed it back to Sparrow. "We wait."

YOR had been sitting cross-legged in a silent semicircle on the old square dance floor for a quarter of an hour when the squeaky hinges of the hoary doors alerted them to an outsider's presence. All seven scrambled to their feet at once. They stood in an arc facing the entry to the grand hall, Søren at the center and closer to the steps than the rest.

Fletcher glanced at Sparrow, who was ready to draw her shotgun in an instant. It was as if Sparrow could feel her gaze. She turned to Fletcher, flashed a wavering grimace, and murmured, "Moment of truth."

Fletcher listened. She heard the distinct sound of hard-soled shoes on tile: three dissimilar gaits. Three individuals approached the ballroom. Her heart rate increased, and beads of nervous sweat dampened her brow. Something was wrong. Her instinct for danger should not have been on high alert if the people moving toward her harbored no ill intent.

Atop the dim stairway, three dark forms appeared. As they descended into the light, Fletcher lost her breath. A man with a hood drawn low over his head was flanked on either side by a forty-something dark-skinned man and a pale younger woman, both adorned in bespoke black suits. It came together in Fletcher's mind. She had always been able to intuit their presence before they announced themselves.

"Reclamation Agents!" The frantic words spilled from Charlie's lips, absorbed from Fletcher's thoughts.

Fletcher felt the weightiness of unrestrained dread as it engulfed YOR.

chapter thirty

"YOU MOTHERFUCKER!" Fletcher screamed at Søren as she threw open her trench coat and snatched her rifle from its holster. She trained the weapon on the back of his head, pumped a bullet into the action and flicked off the safety. He flung his hands up in the air, either proclaiming his innocence or pleading for his life—Fletcher was indifferent—then froze. Someone in YOR gasped loudly, but Fletcher didn't care to know who. From the corner of her eye she saw Sparrow, shotgun aimed, locked, and loaded at the female Agent.

"If you move, you die!" Sparrow shouted at her. "You." She concentrated on the man in the suit. "Put your gun on the ground and kick it over to me."

"I . . . I don't have a gun," the Agent stuttered.

Fletcher adjusted the sights of the .22 onto the male Agent. "Bullshit!"

"He doesn't," the younger Agent confirmed with a raspy voice. "Neither do I."

Sparrow's eyes fluttered to Peter. "Search them. The other guy, too."

Peter choked back his hesitation. He nodded at Sparrow, then did as he was told. He patted the male Agent's upper body, his jacket pockets, then lifted its sides, exposing his neat white shirt. He continued down the man's pants to his socks. There was no weapon. He moved to the other Agent and began at the collar of her suit jacket, swishing her auburn braid away from her shoulders. He checked under her arms, her waist, slacks, and socks. Again, he found nothing. Peter moved on to the man standing between the Agents. His shoulders were hunched and head bowed, most of his face obscured from sight beneath his oversized hood, except for tufts of a sandy-blond beard.

"That's enough, son," the man gruffed, and stretched tall. He pulled the dark hood from his head and smoothed his ruffled hair against his skull. "Fletcher."

It took a long moment for Fletcher to recognize the man. His eyes focused sharply on her, and she saw herself reflected in their hazel hue, identical to her own. "Dad?"

The rifle trembled along with her hands. She was confused. Had the Agents captured him, or was he working with them? Either way, she felt her anger rising. Then she remembered the InvigorStyler—all it needed was a photo reference to work its magic. The man standing before her, accompanied by Agents, could very well be an imposter. "If you're really my father, tell me something only Jericho Daniels would know."

"Astrid and I named you after her great-grandfather, Sergeant Fletcher Kehoe of the US Revolutionist Army. According to The Government, he was a traitor, but to us he was a hero."

"Not good enough." Fletcher shook her head. "That information could be on file at the Hall of Records for all I know. You'd only need access to the system to find it."

Jericho smiled at her. "That's my Little Princess, clever as ever."

Little Princess. Tears sprang to Fletcher's eyes before she could stop them. She loosened her grip on the gun, pointed the muzzle at the floor and launched herself into her father's arms. Jericho wrapped her in a warm embrace, his downy beard tickling her forehead as he pressed a kiss against it.

"Wait, what's going on here?" Fletcher forced herself away from her father. "You're supposed to be living a safe new life in The South."

"I founded this organization, Fletcher—five years ago when it became clear to me that you were university bound."

"You?"

Jericho nodded. "The day you took that damned test was one of the worst days of my life. The BOE stole your mother from me. I wasn't going to let the bastards have you, too."

"He used his position at the Hall of Records to help hundreds of STs escape to The South," Søren said, moving toward Fletcher. "That's why we couldn't upload your replacement ID into the system. He had to leave his job and go into hiding after the situation with you and the Agent at the library."

"You've known this whole time, who *he* is, who *I* am? That there are Agents in Head Office?" And suddenly it clicked why she could never quite bring herself to trust Søren. He had been lying to her face from the moment they met. She knew he was hiding something; she just didn't know *what*. "You were talking to my father that day on the earpiece." Her eyes widened at the realization. "I knew I recognized that voice." *If Søren has been lying to me . . .* Her gut did a slow spin. She sought out Sparrow with a pleading stare. Was the whole thing a ruse? Had she given herself entirely to someone who had been deceiving her?

Sparrow had already lowered her weapon. She holstered it and stepped toward Fletcher. "I had no idea." She reached for her arm, but Fletcher backpedaled away. "Please, Fletcher, you have to believe me."

"She's telling the truth," said Jericho. He motioned to his cohorts. "If she saw Donovan and Xavier on the street, she'd think they were average Agents, and I've only met her once before tonight, when she came to tell me about the fight you had with the Agent who came for your librarian friend. As far as she knew, I was your father and had nothing to do with YOR." He frowned at Sparrow. "I was very sorry to hear about the loss of your brother, Sparrow."

"You despise Agents so much, yet you're working with two of them?" Fletcher questioned Jericho, interrupting the heartfelt interchange between her father and her lover.

"Donovan Trevor," the female Agent said and gestured at the man, "my partner, Xavier Bowman."

"Don't speak." Fletcher raised her weapon again and targeted the Agent. "Or I'll show you what happens when someone really detests Agents."

Donovan did not balk at Fletcher's threat. "I'm glad you killed Flynn," she said.

Fletcher's mouth fell agape, but she hardened herself against the shock. "Tell me why," she dared the Agent.

"I was posted with him once, proctoring a HiEd Exam in Cambridge. That day I watched him strangle the life out of a seventeen-year-old boy who tried to ditch the test—made me want to kill him myself. The Vault is safer now that he's dead. There was no Vaulter left in him because he was a true believer."

"And you're not?"

A fiery expression warped the Agent's features. "You're damn right I'm not."

"Put the gun down, Fletcher," Jericho implored. "She's not an Agent. She's an ST like you."

"Like me?" She scoffed at her father and held fast to her rifle, Agent Trevor's head still in her sights. "She may have been a Significant Threat once, but that is where the similarities between us end. She does the job, doesn't she?"

"I do the job because I have to. The cover allows me to do this." Donovan swept a hand around the room.

"Donovan's boots are on the ground for this organization, same as yours," Jericho declared. "She and Xavier are the ones who flag STs for ID replacement and relocation. All I do is forge and upload files into The Government Records System. You all do most of the work, but these Agents ensure that every ST clears the border security check. They escort every ST to their new home and help them acclimate to their new personas."

"YOR has doctors, scientists, teachers, CEOs, celebrities, activists, you name it—we've installed STs into every position imaginable in The South." Donovan showed a glossy smile. "We saw our first ST appointed to a governorship in the Virginias this past week. We're gaining power."

"And how many Agents do we have? STs are one in ten thousand, right?" Fletcher concentrated on Sparrow. "Out of 65 million people? The Department of Reclamation has a small army of them." Fletcher's tone was accusatory, though she allowed Agent Trevor a brief respite from the business end of her weapon.

Donovan's grin vanished. "Only us."

"Two of thousands." She observed Agent Bowman. "That's comforting."

"You don't understand the hell STs go through, the torment of our Reclamation!" Donovan let her resentment slip. "The Department of Reclamation destroys us, physically, psychologically. Do you know what it takes to fight your way back from that? First you have to be rescued from the cult because you have no desire to stray from the doctrine, and then you need to be surrounded by people who love you enough to spend hours on end locked in a room with you, helping you remember who you are. Most of us never get out to begin with."

"How did you?" Fletcher wondered, then thought better of her curiosity. "You know what, I don't give a shit." She fixated on her father as she holstered her rifle. "I never thought I'd say this to you, and it kills me—but I don't feel like I can trust you right now. We're only staying because you have the tech to confirm that OverSight is foolproof for the poor soul who's going to have to wear it. Philip, give the lenses to him."

Philip pulled OverSight from the deep side pocket of his khakis. He moved to hand the lenses to Jericho, but Agent Trevor stepped forward to receive them. Philip faltered, seeking out Fletcher's permission to hand over the asset to an Agent.

That's new. For a second, Fletcher questioned if she wanted to wield the kind of authority that made YOR look to her for consent to act. She hadn't asked for it, wouldn't have sought it, yet it had just been given to her freely. "It's fine. If she tries to damage them or run with them, Sparrow will shoot her." She flicked a look at Sparrow. *What we have is real. She'll have my back.*

Sparrow placed her hand over her holster and squinched at Agent Trevor. "Oh, I'll have no qualms about it."

That's my girl. Fletcher nodded at her.

The Agents went to work on OverSight, cube-shaped silver HoloPods buzzing. Fletcher smiled to herself as she observed Sparrow ogling every minute motion they made. "Since you've been less than forthcoming, I'm going to assume that you have a plan for OverSight," Fletcher said, addressing her father. "Have you found someone willing to infiltrate a Processing Center?" She watched her father calculate the risk of answering her question honestly.

"No, we haven't."

"Then the concept of forced implantation was yours."

"Ours." Jericho signaled between himself and Søren. "He proposed the idea, and I approved it."

It was then that Fletcher recognized a characteristic in her father she had never allowed herself to see before: callous efficiency, an unsentimental determination to disrupt the system. They shared the same goal, but she could not embrace the coldheartedness of his method. "That is unacceptable. So I suppose what happens next is a coup d'état of sorts. We will no longer blindly take orders from you, or anyone." She turned to the group, "We should discuss the establishment of a more democratic approach to our affairs when we get home. Is everyone okay with that?"

In unison, six of the seven forest-dwelling members of YOR voiced their approval. Søren folded his arms across his chest and nodded at Jericho. "Are you going to tell her, or should I?"

"Tell me what?" Fletcher glowered at her father. Jericho shrank under his daughter's searing glare.

"You're not going back to the safe house with them."

"You must have misunderstood. We're not going to let you make the rules anymore."

Jericho let out a grave sigh. "The Department of Reclamation has Jonah."

"Jonah—" What kind of hell were they putting him through? How much pain was he in right now, and in store for still? Fletcher struggled to breathe, her lungs heaving as though all the oxygen on Earth had vanished. Her heart battered against her ribs, a caged bird fighting with every fiber to be freed. The room around her fell out of focus, faded to gray and then to black.

chapter thirty-one

FLETCHER FELT WARM HANDS patting her cheeks. Even with heavy eyelids and through the thick haze in her head, she was able to identify Sparrow's familiar touch, but it was the panic in her voice that lured Fletcher back to consciousness. "Come on, my love, wake up."

Her eyes fluttered open. She saw her father, Peter, and Sparrow huddled over her. "There she is," Jericho said, bare relief in his expression.

Fletcher knew she was lying on the floor, the cold of the tile radiating through her coat, though she couldn't figure out why or how she had gotten there. She reached up to brush her fingers against Sparrow's face. A globule of saliva splashed over her sandpaper tongue as she tried to speak. The only word that would come to her was, "Beautiful."

Sparrow cupped Fletcher's fingers and kissed them one by one. As her senses began to recalibrate, Fletcher realized that her father had looked away, red-faced, as though he'd intruded on a private moment. "What happened?" she asked.

"You fainted," Peter explained.

Sparrow released Fletcher's hand. She tried to push herself up onto her elbows, but the room was spinning. She slipped.

Jericho caught her. "No, no, don't try to move yet. Lie there for a minute. Xavier," he called over his shoulder to the Agent. "I need the canteen."

Agent Bowman left his partner to the task of testing OverSight and hurried out of the Great Hall. Moments later, he reappeared and stooped beside Jericho with a container in hand. Jericho took the container, unscrewed the cap, then lifted Fletcher's head and held the canteen to her lips. The water was icy cold. It cooled Fletcher's insides as she downed it. Jericho swept Fletcher's bangs from her eyes and flashed the singular Concerned Dad Smile Fletcher knew so well. "Do you think you can sit up?"

"Yes."

Jericho supported Fletcher's shoulders as Sparrow hoisted her up by her hands. Her head throbbed. She rubbed the sore spot at the base of her skull and cursed the tiles for being so unforgiving. As she massaged the pain away, her memory returned to her. Reclamation Agents had taken Jonah, nabbed him from the Alcedonia Institute as cavalierly as one would tear a weed from the dirt. She thrust her hands out, grabbed Agent Bowman by his collar, and jerked him toward her so violently that he lost his footing. "Where did they take Jonah?" she growled, droplets of spittle spritzing his maw. Jericho pawed at Fletcher. She did not relinquish her grasp.

"I—"

Fletcher shook him with all the force she could muster. "Where?"

"The Processing Center in Boston!" With Jericho's help Agent Bowman yanked himself free. He stood up and smoothed his jacket. "It's your fault they took him in the first place."

"What?" Fletcher felt for her rifle. She tore the gun from its straps. Her center of gravity was off. She was kept vertical only by the aid of Sparrow's limbs, but she was not dissuaded. She trained the gun on the Agent. "Say it again."

"Fletcher!" Jericho reached for his daughter.

Bowman lowered his gaze to the floor. "Jericho, show her the hologram before she shoots me, man."

Jericho fished his homemade HoloPod—he'd ditched his trackable government-issued one long ago—from the pocket of his jeans. He turned it on and brought up a projection—a full-body 3-D image of Fletcher, the word WANTED flashing above it.

Seeing her picture on a wanted holo sent shockwaves through Fletcher, and she dropped the gun on the ground.

"Fletcher Daniels, for the murder of Owen Flynn, Senior Agent, The Department of Reclamation." Sparrow read the subscript aloud. "Reward for information leading to capture: Complete forgiveness of Student Loan Debt by the BOE and/or release of associated Reclaimees currently in custody." Her skin went pale. "Shit, Fletcher."

"That holo is on public screens all over the place, up Portland way, down to Philadelphia, and South of the cordon, too. They're going after you hard," said Bowman.

"It's bad, honey. They're holding your friend from the library, too."

"Grier?"

Jericho confirmed with a nod.

"She's a Lucky One, was out of the Processing Center and home with her family in a week," Agent Trevor added as she sidled over to the group. "I'm sure she's not thrilled to be back *there* again." She held out the box containing OverSight, and Sparrow snatched it away from her. "They check out, no readings at all."

"You understand why you can't go back with them, sweetheart?"

Sparrow slipped her arm around Fletcher's waist and pulled her close. "We're in the middle of nowhere. It's the safest place for her."

"But it isn't safe for you if I'm there." Fletcher pressed her palm to Sparrow's chest. "If they catch me with you . . . I can't put you in danger. I won't." She pushed away from Sparrow and grimaced at her father. "It isn't safe for anyone anywhere, Dad, is it? I'm not a safe person. And now that I'd be recognizable in The South, I couldn't have my ID replaced even if you were still working at the Hall of Records. Where would you have me go?"

"Canada. I was hoping we could bribe our way onto a cotton trade ship in Eastport."

"With what, Redbacks?" Fletcher almost laughed at the absurdity of it, the idea that pieces of polymer assigned arbitrary value by a despotic government would be enough to buy her freedom. The UAT didn't have the gold to back up the money it printed, so it relied on an international barter system of exports like cotton and soy. Redbacks were useless to the outside world, and her father knew that. He had been the one who explained it to her. "And what would happen to Jonah and Grier if I were to disappear into the Great White North?"

"They—" Jericho swallowed his words.

"Grier will be sent to an agricultural facility to work herself to death. If Jonah can't be controlled and put to work, he'll be put down," said Agent Trevor. "The BOE will have its retribution, one way or another."

"If they catch me, will they kill me?" Fletcher wanted the answer to be yes.

"You're more valuable to them alive. But I wouldn't be surprised if they made sure your Reclamation is more brutal than necessary."

Fletcher bit her lip so hard she broke the skin. She tasted the blood that bubbled up through the tiny tear, alkalescent and hot. She couldn't let Jonah and Grier pay for her transgressions any more than she could go back to the safe house with YOR. Her actions had ruined any chance her father had of living an ordinary life. She'd caused the death of two people. History would call her a monster, and on some level she knew that she was one. Everyone had to pay for his or her sins eventually, and her time for atonement had come. "Peter, do you have the tools you need to implant OverSight, or do you need to go back to the safe house for them?"

"Excuse me?" Peter looked at her, startled. "What are you—"

"You're going to graft OverSight to my corneas, and then the BOE is going to get what it wants—me."

chapter thirty-two

SPARROW AND JERICHO SHARED an expression of mutual dismay.

"Fletcher, no—"

"That is not going to happen." Jericho raised his voice over Sparrow's.

"It has to."

Jericho's face went stony, as only a father's could. "Fletcher, I care about Jonah as much as you do. That boy has been like a son to me. We tried to help him, I'm sure you know that. But I will not sacrifice my own child to save him, or anyone. Everything I have done in the past five years, every single move I've made, has been to save you from this very eventuality!"

"There is no saving me, Dad! Not now, not two months ago. I was never going to run, no matter what you said or did, and you must have known that. You've always said I'm too stubborn and you're right," she sighed.

"You're damn stubborn and I love that about you! I wouldn't change you for the world. But I cannot let you do this. I just can't, Fletcher. Please don't make me let you go. Not my little girl." Jericho's lip quivered.

"I don't want to do this any more than you want me to. But

you don't have a say in this decision. It's mine to make, and it's the only one that works. The Department of Reclamation will set Jonah and Grier free, and you'll get the evidence you need—no abduction necessary." *I hope they smile for the cameras while they're torturing me.*

Fletcher saw her father stifle whatever argument he had planned to make. He knew her well enough to understand that she would not be deterred. The tears welling in his eyes made his hazel irises glimmer in the firelight. He wrapped his arms around Fletcher so tightly that she struggled to breathe. When he finally let her go, she scruffed his beard. Her gaze wandered to Sparrow, and she whispered to him, "Take care of her for me."

Fletcher turned to Sparrow and clutched her hands. *I've only just found you.* "I'm sorry. I so wanted to be the one—"

"Please, Fletcher, I love you. Don't do this," Sparrow begged, her face so panic-stricken that Fletcher's resolution wavered. And then an idea struck her, optimistic and idiotic all at once.

She looked to Trevor. "You can get me back, right? Turn me Double Agent or whatever."

"I can get you out—maybe—but even if I do, the rest isn't up to me. It'll be your battle to fight."

Fletcher took Sparrow's weeping face into her hands. "Listen to me, okay? I am going to come back to you."

"You don't know that." Sparrow's voice trembled under the combined weight of doubt and despair.

"Of course I do. They can do their worst to my brain, but there's nothing in their arsenal, nothing in this whole wretched world, that can erase you from here." She placed her hand over her heart, then thumbed away Sparrow's tears.

"Swear it. No matter how hard we have to fight or for how long, you'll come back to me."

"My sweet little bird . . . I swear on my mother's ashes," Fletcher replied, then kissed her tenderly. When they parted, she looked at Peter. "How do we do this?"

"Not here." He kicked up dust. "This place is disgusting. I can't sterilize it at all. And I need electricity. To answer your earlier question, my instruments are at home."

"Alright, here's the plan. We go back to the safe house. Dad, you go wherever it is you're calling home these days and lay low. Trevor and Bowman, you go back to your, I don't know, your *lairs*. I'll have the surgery done, take the time to heal and test OverSight." Fletcher gestured to Trevor. "Meet me at the old Brooke Courthouse two days from now at 9 a.m. I'll make it nice and easy for you. You'll take me to the Processing Center, and you'll look like the hero who captured the scum of the earth. You'll use that to your advantage by arranging for me to see Jonah and Grier get released and sent safely on their way because if I don't witness it with my own eyes, so help me, I will raise all kinds of hell for you and everyone in that fucking place."

All Agent Donovan Trevor could say was, "Alright."

YOR headed for the van, and the Agents went to fetch their car, leaving Fletcher alone with her father to say their final goodbye. "I wish you weren't so damn brave," Jericho mumbled as he held her to his chest.

"It's in my DNA apparently." She stepped back and peered up at his face, illuminated by the moon and YOR's headlights, until she was sure that every crease and wrinkle had been scorched into the deepest recesses of her brain. "Find a way to get me out or kill me. Please, Dad. I don't want to live as one of them."

Jericho cleared the phlegm from his throat. "Whatever it takes."

Fletcher thought of what Sparrow had told her that day when she'd dropped her off in Boston to put her old life to rest. "Don't think of it as goodbye. I'll see you again someday."

“You will.”

She walked down the path to the van, not daring to look back.

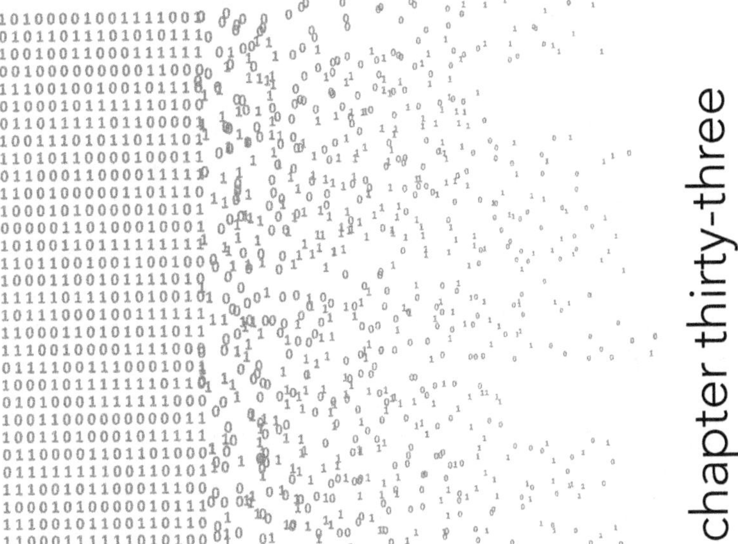

<h1>chapter thirty-three</h1>

EVERYONE WAS SILENT AS they entered the Visitor's Center, an imperceptible veil of solemnness shrouding them. Peter and Philip had agreed on the ride home that the surgery would take place in the war room, as it was the nearest to a "clean room" they could get, and the OverSight technology was too delicate to take chances of electrostatic discharge interfering with the bio-circuitry bonding upon implantation. The men would prepare the war room in the morning, and Fletcher would undergo the procedure soon after.

Fletcher caught Søren's arm as he passed her in the vestibule. "The Ranger's room belongs to me for the next two days. I want every single second I can have with Sparrow, and I want them undisturbed."

He did not meet her gaze or speak, simply nodded.

"Good night," she said to the group and ascended the stairs before anyone felt obliged to try to lighten the mood.

Fletcher flicked on the shaded lamp atop the small dresser and hung her coat on a hook that had been screwed into the back of the Ranger's bedroom door more than a century ago. She leaned her rifle against the wall, undid the straps of the leg holster, and let it fall to the floor. She kicked off her boots without bothering to untie them, then sat on the stool. Never in her life had she felt so defeated. Head heavy, she buried her brow in her palms. Her decision was righteous, of that she was certain, but it gutted her nonetheless.

She was torn away from her mounting self-pity by a knock at the door. She staggered over and opened it. Sparrow said nothing, just stepped through the threshold and draped her arms around Fletcher's neck. When Sparrow kissed her, it was mournful. Fletcher tasted the despair on her lips. She undressed Fletcher slowly, hands lingering too long over every bit of her skin, as if she were committing the contours of her body to muscle memory.

No, not like this, Fletcher thought. Not on the cold concrete floor of a musty old bunker, and not as one last desperate grasp at freedom before capitulation. *We deserve better.* She pulled herself away, admired Sparrow, felt a warmth in her chest that spread throughout her entire being. "I love you," she said, clearly and decisively. "I should've said it sooner. I should've said it to you a dozen times by now." She stripped Sparrow of her shirt, kissed her mouth, her neck, her collarbone, and walked her backward toward the bed. They collapsed onto the mattress together. "I love you," she said again, unfastening Sparrow's pants and removing them. She licked a trail down Sparrow's stomach, rolling her panties down her thighs and off her body. She knelt at the foot of the bed and looked up at Sparrow from between her spread legs. "I love you." Then Fletcher used her mouth to show rather than tell her just how much she meant it.

And as Sparrow finished, she whispered, breathless, "I love you, too."

DAYLIGHT ARRIVED DESPITE THE women's best efforts to stave it off. They hadn't slept, had spent the night making love, wordlessly wrapped up in one another. Now, Fletcher cleaved to Sparrow's torso, petitioning for a few more minutes of togetherness beneath the snug bedclothes before she had to meet the scalpel with twenty-four hours of darkness and the boundless suffering that awaited beyond. Sparrow held her close, now and again kissing her forehead.

"I really hate this."

"*You* hate it?" Fletcher's attempt at humor failed. "I wish there were another way."

"Me, too."

Fletcher shifted. "I need to ask you to do something for me. You aren't going to like it, but I'm asking because I want to keep you safe."

"What is it?"

"Let Charlie take me to Boston alone. She isn't a person of interest to the BOE. She never defaulted on any loans, so the Agents can't touch her, or at least they'd have no justifiable reason to if she isn't actually seen with me."

"No."

"Please. I don't want you anywhere near a Processing Center. Ever. And I don't want the last time you see me—"

"It's not going to be the last time I see you," Sparrow said. "You promised to come back to me and I'm holding you to it. The Agents don't get to take everyone I love away from me."

Fletcher wanted to hold herself to her promise, but the more she thought about it, the less confidence she had that she'd be able to. She pecked Sparrow on the cheek. "They won't."

"I'm going with you and Charlie in case something goes wrong. That's that."

"Fine." Fletcher nuzzled her head into the crook of Sparrow's neck.

They lay together, soundless and still, until the silence was disturbed by rapping at the door. "We're good to go." Philip's muffled voice trickled through the timber.

The women slipped out from the comfort of the warm sheets and dressed.

Before Fletcher entered the war room, Philip handed her a flimsy gown constructed of a shiny aluminum-like material and instructed her to dissipate her body's natural electrostatic charge by touching the metal light switch beside the doorframe.

"Turn around," she told him, then shimmied out of her T-shirt and shorts and into the gown. "Okay." He turned to face her again, and she rubbed her whole hand over the metal plate, making a show of it. "Good enough?"

"Yeah." He opened the door, ushered her inside, and closed it behind her.

The walls were coated with acrylic sheeting, harkening back, for Fletcher, to a series of mystery novels she had read where the murderer fabricated "killing chambers" from plastic wrap to ensure that no DNA evidence would be left behind. It unnerved her. Her body went rigid. In the center of the room was Philip's steel desk, bare of all the hardware it usually held. At each corner of the desk stood a bright white LED tower light, much like the ones in the rebel bunker. The room was cold. Sterile. Alien.

Peter was situated at the head of the desk near a tall metal tray lined with medical utensils. He sported a gown similar to Fletcher's, a makeshift mask and surgery cap of the same material, and contrasting pink rubber gloves. Fletcher was glad for the silly things, though. She chuckled. "Are those dishwashing gloves?"

Peter's face was mostly obscured, but Fletcher heard his surprise when he asked, "There are gloves just for that?"

"There used to be, in the old world."

"Søren found a few sealed pairs on the last scavenging trip. Were people back then spoiled or what?" He looked down at his hands, in awe of the little prewar luxuries, then patted the top of the desk. "Up here, please."

Fletcher suppressed her apprehension, clambered onto the desk, and positioned herself on her back. Peter leaned over her, "I'm going to attach these electrodes to your chest so I can monitor your heart rate throughout the surgery. Okay?"

"Yeah."

He stuck the sensors to the skin above her heart, then turned toward the tray of instruments. When he reappeared in Fletcher's view, he was holding a syringe. "Now I'm going to administer a local anesthetic. You'll feel a slight pinch when the needle goes in, but you'll go numb very soon afterward."

"Wait, I'm going to be awake?"

"Yes. Philip needs you awake so he can remotely calibrate OverSight. I won't lie; it's going to be unpleasant. Once you're anesthetized, you won't be able to move your head. I'm going to use wire speculums to hold your eyelids open and a saline wash to ensure ocular hydration."

"Yep, that sounds unpleasant . . . Let's just get this done."

Peter nodded. "Ready?"

"I guess."

Peter pressed the needle into the soft flesh surrounding Fletcher's left eye. He was right about the pinch, but by the third strategic poke, Fletcher felt nothing. He moved on to her right eye, and the pinching repeated, but again she was numb by the third injection. Almost as soon as he had finished the series of jabs, Fletcher's head got heavy, like a cast-iron kettlebell supported by an anvil. She tried to say as much, but her mouth would not cooperate.

"Wiggle your fingers if you can feel this." Peter tapped her forehead, her checks, the nape of her neck. It was as though the nerves above her throat had been severed as there was no sensation whatsoever. "I'm inserting the speculums now." Fletcher watched him pry her eyelids wide and put the vise-like grips in place. It was horrifying. She was thankful that she could not feel them.

Peter produced a stout syringe and hovered the elongated curved tip a few millimeters from Fletcher's eyeballs. He squirted the salty liquid into her eyes, clouding her vision. She wanted to blink and felt helpless at her inability to.

"I'm going to insert the lenses now." Peter brandished a pair of protracted forceps, a filmy, semi-translucent lens balanced between its oversized pincers. "Left one first, then the right. After I've ensured proper alignment over your corneas, I'll secure them."

Fletcher concentrated on his hands, on his long, sturdy fingers and their steady, precise movements. *Those are hands you can depend on.* The thought comforted her as the lens grew larger and larger the closer it came.

Peter rested the lens over her iris. She was struck by the transparency of it. She had expected it to obstruct her vision somehow or change the way she saw things. She was relieved that wasn't the case, at least initially—it remained to be seen whether that would last.

He repeated the process with her right eye, then moved his face close to Fletcher's. "They look good, but I'm going to do a laser measurement for accuracy." He flipped on the measuring tool and beamed a bright red circle into each of her eyes. "Hmm," he said after assessing the right one, "perfect."

The next thing Fletcher saw was a minuscule tweezer clamped around what looked like a fishing hook with a superfine thread attached to it. She heard the beep of the heart monitor speed up and realized that her breathing had as well. Peter touched her shoulder. "Suturing is archaic, I know, but I'm damn good at it." It was the first time Fletcher had heard him speak so confidently. It soothed her.

He lubricated her eyes again, stabilized the lens with the forceps, and eased the hook through the gelatinous sclera around her left iris. She watched the thread go taut, then slack, taut, then slack, counted every slow, meticulous stitch. If I can survive this terrifying experience, I can survive anything, she thought.

"You're doing great, Fletcher. Moving on to the right eye now." He shifted his position, and the process began anew.

Fletcher had no clue how much time had passed between the beginning and end of the procedure, but she did know that she'd had quite enough of it long before Peter removed the clamps from her eyelids and administered the anesthetic reversal injection. The muscles in her head and neck relaxed, and little by little she regained the ability to move.

She sat up with Peter's help. He brought a cup of water to her lips. "Drink," he said as he slipped off his mask, and she did. Then, without warning, the numbness fell away. Her eyes ached with a viciousness she hadn't anticipated. It was so staggering that all she could do was close them and pray.

Peter forced her eyelids open to examine his handiwork. She winced.

"Pain?"

"Only a lot."

"Narcotics are hard to come by, but I have a stash of pills I can dip into."

She waved him off. "Save them. I can push through it."

"If you say so." His CommBand sounded. He checked it. "Philip has started the calibrations. How's your vision?"

Fletcher glanced around the room, taking in the acrylic sheeting, the forceps, clamps, and other assorted surgical tools resting on their tray. Everything appeared in focus, sharp and vibrant as ever. "Same as it was before."

"Very good." He unraveled a strip of clean cloth. "Your eyes have to stay closed, and the bandage has to stay on until tomorrow."

"Got it, no peeking." She closed her eyes. Peter wound the cloth around her head and secured it in place. At first, the darkness was startling. The tug of claustrophobia began to settle into her mind. Then she felt the heat of Peter's hand on the small of her back.

"What you're doing for your friends is very brave," he said reverently.

"I wish people would stop calling me that. I'm not brave. I'm doing what's necessary."

"No, you're doing what's right despite knowing the stakes. Not everyone has the guts for that."

"It's decency, Peter. That's what people are lacking. Decency."

"I think it's a bit more complicated than that."

She shrugged. "Maybe."

"Alright, let's get you down." Fletcher heard Peter move around the desk. He took her hands and guided her off it. The floor was freezing against her bare feet, and the air felt much colder than when she had entered the room. With every step, she heard the squeak of the floorboards, overstated as if funneled through an amplifier. Perhaps it was her body compensating for her blindness, her other senses being heightened almost preternaturally. The door opened with a whine. Waiting for her on the other side was Sparrow. Fletcher caught her scent, her unique aromatic identifier—oakmoss with a hint of balsam fir—and breathed her in.

"Hey, Ivy League," Sparrow said, slipping her arm around Fletcher's waist. "I've got you."

Fletcher required Sparrow's guidance, not so much her physical support. Still, she leaned into her body and clung to her forearm, letting Sparrow take more of her weight than was necessary. In that moment, she knew Sparrow needed to be needed. "Thank you."

Fletcher slept much of the day, the aftereffects of the anesthetic hitting her hard, coupled with the constant darkness. In her wakeful moments she felt rather like a bear whose hibernation had been interrupted, grumpy and hungry but too unmotivated to move. Sparrow stayed close. Fletcher felt her warmth, smelled her skin, heard her even sleep-breathing, all the little things that signaled a person was alive. She had experienced it all before, but now these little things seemed sacred, seeping into her cognizance, begging to be remembered. She turned on her side and fumbled through the blackness to touch her.

The contact stirred Sparrow. "Are you okay?" she asked with a sleep-thick voice.

"Fine. Sorry. I didn't mean to wake you."

"It's alright. If I'd have slept much longer, I'd be up all night. The sun's already gone down." The mattress contracted under Sparrow's shifting weight. Fletcher sat up as she listened to her cross the room and switch on the lamp. "They're cooking downstairs. Are you hungry?"

"Yes, but also nauseated." She sniffed the air, got a whiff of gamy stew as it wafted up through the rafters. Her stomach gurgled. "Mostly nauseated."

"Maybe just something to drink, then? That warm beechnut *concoction* . . ."

Fletcher smirked at her intonation. "Please?"

"Be right back." Sparrow kissed her forehead, then left the room.

In her absence the space was quiet, too quiet for comfort. Fletcher fretted that that was what her life would become post-Reclamation—perpetual quiet, nothing but human-shaped voids where all the people she loved used to be.

A new scent hit her then, coming from the open doorway—pine tar, smoky like burning kindling. "Hello, Fletcher," Søren said. "Can I come in?"

She wasn't up for conversation, least of all with him. She thought she had made herself clear: two days uninterrupted. *This had better be important.* "Sure."

The legs of the wooden stool screeched against the floor as he lowered himself onto it. "I know I'm—" His tongue clicked against the roof of his mouth. "Everyone's concerned about you. I wanted to see how you were feeling so I could give them an update."

"I'm drowsy, nauseous, sore and stuck in the dark, so . . . not feeling so great, but thanks for asking."

"Are you scared?" he asked, as forthright as he had ever been.

Fletcher wanted to say no, longed to be as courageous as everyone had made her out to be. "Terrified."

"Yeah."

Fletcher gripped the edges of the mattress. "What was it like, Reclamation? Can you remember anything?"

"Nothing of the procedure itself, but sometimes I get flashes." His breath went ragged. Fletcher could picture his face in her mind's eye: pale and petrified. "There was this whirring sound, so loud and near constant. Thin wires, every color you could imagine. The smell of bleach and alcohol, sterile like a hospital, you know?"

Fletcher nodded.

"I'm . . . sorry. About the way things turned out. I didn't want it to go like this. After everything Jericho has done—the only thing he ever asked of me was that I keep you safe, and I failed him."

"I didn't make it easy for you," Fletcher acknowledged. "But you have another chance to do right by my father and me. If I can't fight my way back to being me, Sparrow's going to need someone. So, if it happens, be there for her with everything you have inside of you. Even when you think you haven't got an ounce of kindness left to give, find some. Can you do that?"

He inhaled a sharp breath. "You really love her, don't you?"

Yes. More than I ever thought I could love anybody. "I do."

"That might be the thing that saves you . . . and, yes, I will try to find that sort of kindness."

"Don't try; *do it.*"

"Okay." The floorboards creaked as Søren moved his weight from the stool to his feet and made for the exit.

"There's one more thing."

"What's that?"

Fletcher frowned, knowing that Sparrow would see it as a slight, despite the love behind her intention. The Reclamation Agents had no use for or reasonable suspicions of Søren because they'd already fried his brain. It was safer for him in the city than it would ever be for Sparrow. *And he owes me.* "How's your driving?"

He huffed. "Fair."

"Good. We leave for Boston at first light."

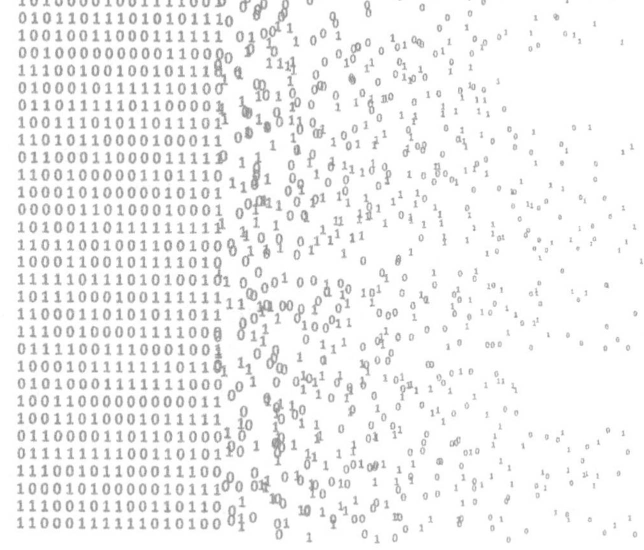

chapter thirty-five

FLETCHER SLUNK OUT OF bed, careful not to wake the woman sleeping soundly beside her. Once on her feet, she unwound the bandage from her brow and, gingerly, opened her eyes. She was still in pain, but that was the only noticeable physical difference: the world was still present, colored in the cool dullness of a late autumn sunrise.

Fletcher used her new eyes, an old ballpoint pen she'd found in the library basement and kept for nostalgia's sake, and the growing daylight to write the inscription on the title page of *A Little Princess*:

> *My Sweet Little Bird,*
>
> *I've guarded myself so fiercely from the idea of trusting or loving anyone, yet you managed to show me the importance of both, and for that I will always be grateful. Take care of this—and yourself—for me until I return.*
>
> *All my love,*
>
> *Ivy League*

She closed the book, laid it on the dresser, and tiptoed to the door. She stopped to look over Sparrow's peaceful face once more. "I'll see you soon," she whispered, and offered a silent prayer to The Powers That Be to deliver her home to her someday.

Søren waited for Fletcher in his innate brooding manner—arms folded, impatient—at the bottom of the staircase. "How do your eyes feel?" he whispered as she descended.

"Fine," she lied. "How will I know when they're recording?"

"As far as I know, they already are, and they always will be."

"Great."

"Sparrow is going to be irate about this," Søren commented as he reached for the front door.

"I know." Fletcher shrugged her leather jacket onto her shoulders, zipped it up, and closed the door behind her.

"I don't…respond well to her when she gets confrontational."

"De-escalate her."

Søren was quiet for a while, leaving Fletcher to concentrate on the sound of gravel crunching underfoot. The van had come into view through the morning fog before he asked, "How do I do that?"

"Let her scream, cry, slap you if she needs to. The Berserker in you will itch to be set free, but you have to keep it in check— preemptively inject an extra dose of Quell, do whatever it takes to stay calm—and let her know that she's not alone."

Søren expelled a hefty sigh as he and Fletcher climbed into the van. He flipped down the driver's-side sun visor and the key fell into his lap. "Strap in. It's been a while since I've driven."

Fletcher clicked her seatbelt into place as Søren turned over the ignition. He put the van into drive, stomped down on the gas pedal, and the rickety beast rocketed forward up the winding dirt drive. Fletcher grabbed the overhead handle, white-knuckling the thing as she swallowed a yelp.

"Reverse into there," Fletcher said, pointing to an indistinct alleyway diagonal to the hideous concrete building that had once been home to the Massachusetts Department of Mental Health and now served as the main Reclamation Processing Center for the former New England region.

This neighborhood, still called Government Center, was bustling with people on their way to work. Most of them were not Fletcher's people—desperate Vaulters grateful for any paycheck they could get—rather, they were Southerners transplanted by The UAT government, willing accomplices to a tyrannical regime. She counted the collaborators, sharply dressed in comparison to the locals, to pass the time: *Thirty-seven, thirty-eight, thirty-nine, forty.*

Then, her new eyes spotted Agent Donovan Trevor, perched on a square concrete bollard in front of the Processing Center, sipping what was no doubt genuine coffee imported from Ecuador, the last of The UAT's Latin American allies.

"Well, it's been enlightening." She said a sardonic goodbye, her paltry attempt at stoicism in the face of paralyzing fear.

"I'm going to stay here until they take you inside."

"You don't have to." She met his gaze, noted the uncharacteristic dolefulness in his eyes.

"Yes, I do."

She gave him a curt nod, then got out of the van.

Fletcher pulled her hood up over her head, making sure to tuck her ponytail into it, and advanced toward Trevor. She stopped a hundred yards from the Agent's position, checked that her surroundings were clear, and let out a loud whistle that sounded like a bird call. Trevor was unresponsive. She whistled again. This time Trevor saw her. Trevor ticked her head to her left.

Fletcher looked to her right at the deep alcove of a condemned building and stepped into its relative shelter. The wait must have been a minute at most, though it felt like an eternity.

"I half expected you not to show," Trevor said, pushing flat against the wall opposite Fletcher.

"You don't know me. When I say I'm going to do something, I do it. What about you? Are you going to get my friends out, or is this going to get ugly fast?"

"*Shh.*" Trevor raised a finger to her lips, then pressed the same finger to her right tragus. "Agent Trevor for command center."

"Go for Trevor," the familiar tinny audio echoed through the alcove.

"I have suspect Fletcher Daniels in custody."

"Say again?" The voice on the receiver was incredulous.

"Repeat that, Agent," another voice chimed in, equally stunned.

"I have Fletcher Daniels in my custody. She has agreed to peacefully accompany me to the Processing Center, provided that Jonah Quinn and the girl will be released in her presence upon our arrival."

"The girl has a name. It's Grier Whiteford," Fletcher said through clenched teeth.

"Are you under the impression that you're in a position to make demands?" The second voice spoke directly to Fletcher.

"I'm in the position to tear the features off your Agent's face. Shouldn't be too difficult to accomplish."

Trevor grinned at that, but the connection was silent for a long moment.

"Come in quietly and we will release Mr. Quinn and Ms. Whiteford in your presence, per your request."

Trevor waited for Fletcher's agreement. She signaled *yes* with a dip of her head. "I'm bringing her in. Our ETA is five. Over." Trevor flicked off her earpiece. "That should give them enough time to secure Jonah and Grier." She folded her arms. "So you came here alone. Where's that pretty girlfriend of yours?"

"Far from this fucking hellhole."

"Smart move."

"Yeah. I'm playing chess here, not checkers."

"I've never played either," Trevor replied, trying to hide her confusion.

"It's an old-world figure of speech. It means I'm smarter than you."

Trevor's brow wrinkled. "I don't know about that. I didn't turn myself in."

"Maybe that means I've got bigger balls *and* a bigger brain than you do."

"Huh. Maybe." Trevor removed her HoloPod from her pocket, pressed a button, and a blue holographic clock projected into the air: 9:15. "Let's go."

Fletcher tugged her hood off, let her blonde hair flow freely for all to see. As she and Trevor walked down the street, everyone they passed—Vaulters and Southerners alike—stared at her. She was famous. Infamous. *That's right, here I am.* Villain. Hero. Murderer.

It wasn't long before they reached the corner of the brutalist building that was the Processing Center. Fletcher watched as four Agents, Jonah, and Grier appeared at the top of the broad cement staircase. Both were paler and skinnier than they had been the last time she'd seen either of them. Regardless, the sight of them was a brief respite from the unbridled dread she had been feeling all morning.

"Something's not right," murmured Trevor.

"What?"

"It doesn't take four Agents for a prisoner release. Two is protocol."

As the small group descended the steps, Trevor's demeanor changed. "The Agents at the rear have their guns drawn." She looked at Fletcher, stone-faced. "Hit me."

"Why?"

"They're going to kill your friends. You'll watch them die, and later they'll implant memories into your brain of some Vaulter doing the deed. That's how they'll turn you and keep you. Hit me hard. Now."

There was no time to process the information she had just received. So, without contemplation Fletcher let out a thunderous scream. *Crack!* Her fist collided with Agent Donovan Trevor's jaw, and the woman's head reeled sideways. In the split second before Trevor bounced back, Fletcher saw the horror that twisted her friends' features. *Thump*! Trevor hit Fletcher in the stomach. She doubled over, clutched her abs. Trevor hit her again, this time in the face. And it occurred to Fletcher that this was not going to be a fight for show, but for blood. Fletcher stood upright, pushing the pain out of her mind. "Come on, bitch!" She balled both her fists, and rushed Trevor, connecting a one-two punch with her abdomen before landing a vicious uppercut. Trevor fell backward onto the sidewalk, flailing a desperate kick at Fletcher's face. Fletcher recoiled, knowing her eyebrow had been torn open before the torrent of blood gushed down into her eyes. She wiped the blood away, twisted back to look at her friends and the gang of Agents. It had worked. The Agents were rushing to aid their downed comrade. From her periphery, she saw Søren running toward her. "Go! That way!" She yelled at Jonah and Grier, pointing to the direction from which Søren approached.

She had seconds at most to watch her friends flee. She drank them in, those two gaunt people escaping unpursued. Whatever happened to her next would be ugly, but for the moment she saw Søren waving them over, the back vent of his long trench coat catching the wind trapped between the tall buildings like the sails of a schooner. She smiled. Just a handful of concrete slabs left to cover, and they would be free.

Thud! Fletcher felt a shooting pain at the base of her skull, so powerful that it brought her to her knees. She heard voices screaming, their words muffled by the ringing in her ears. She raised her eyes, watched with blood-blurred vision as her friends disappeared into the alley. More incoherent screaming, guns waving in her face.

She thought of her father. Of Sparrow. Then the angry voices fell away, and the world was consumed by blackness—

acknowledgments

AS ALWAYS, I HAVE to thank: my family—Al, Debby, Breanna, and Russell—for their ceaseless support (read: constantly telling me to "suck it up" when I complain about my complicated love/hate relationship with writing.) And Liz, who never let me quit on this novel—or my dreams—when I wasn't sure I had anything left in me.

To my literary agent, Mark Falkin, who was as delighted as any lit agent could be about one of their authors switching from writing Contemporary Romance to Speculative Fiction: thanks for taking me seriously and yet again finding my little tome the perfect home.

To Salem West, Christel Cogneau, Marianne K. Martin, Ann McMan and the incredible team at Bywater Books: you embody the bold spirits and scrappy souls of generations of queer freedom fighters who came before you and guide the way for those yet to come. Thank you for everything you've done and continue to do for the sapphic literary community. I am so proud to be a member of this bookish family.

To my editors Anna Burke and Elizabeth Andersen, and my proofreader Nancy Squires: *Reclamation* would be half the book it is and riddled with mistakes were it not for you. I appreciate your hard work and dedication more than words can say.

KRISTEN ZIMMER DOESN'T WRITE quiet stories. She writes queer women who love hard, fight harder, and set fire to every box the world tries to shove them into. Her debut, *The Gravity Between Us*, became a breakout hit, topping Amazon's Lesbian Fiction and Romance charts for twelve weeks and earning praise from *USA Today* and *Reader's Digest*. *When Sparks Fly* kept the fire going, soaring to no. 1. Her third novel, *Forbidden Girl*, is a sapphic mafia romance that bleeds power, passion, and rebellion.

Zimmer lives in Salem, Massachusetts—home of the witch trials and an enduring reminder that punishing powerful women is nothing new. Her books are a loud, proud act of resistance in a time when queer and feminist voices are under attack. She's not writing for permission—she's writing for those who refuse to apologize for who they are.

Follow her—if you dare—on her social media channels.
Instagram: @kristen_zimmer_author
Threads: @kristen_zimmer_author
Facebook: /authorkristenzimmer

**The 2024 Foreword INDIES Publisher of the Year award
was presented to Bywater Books for its twenty years
of ushering in the "coming of age of queer literature."**

"In a year when LGBTQ+ communities faced renewed attacks and the names of DEI efforts were sullied by those in power, Bywater remained firm in its commitment to publishing titles that celebrate queer existence and that embrace diversity. Their world-widening books make us laugh, make us cry, and stand as enduring testaments to the breadth of love and the human experience."

– Foreword Reviews

Bywater Books believes that all people have the right to read or not read what they want—and that we are all entitled to make those choices ourselves. But to ensure these freedoms, books and information must remain accessible. Any effort to eliminate or restrict these rights stands in opposition to freedom of choice.

Please join us by opposing book bans and censorship of the LGBTQ+ and BIPOC communities.

At Bywater Books, we are all stories.

For more information about Bywater Books, our publishing mission, authors, and our titles, please visit our website.

https://bywaterbooks.com

9 781612 943299